Tales from
Arabian and Persian Deserts

Tales from
Arabian and Persian Deserts

JAWAD AL-BAHRANI

PARTRIDGE

Print information available on the last page.

To order additional copies of this book, contact
Toll Free 800 101 2657 (Singapore)
Toll Free 1 800 81 7340 (Malaysia)
orders.singapore@partridgepublishing.com

www.partridgepublishing.com/singapore

CONTENTS

A POEM OF INTRODUCTION

God give me strength and ability to write with justice
So I can write to lead others and never to mislead them
So I can write to teach with a clean language

And my God I ask you, grant me good intentions
So to avoid that which will cause split
That I may write those of faith and history too

So I may write using the sweet language and philosophy
About the people and the tribe whom are alive and dead too
So I can write with good intentions, so I can write with wisdom

So I can write with clean heart and without fear
And never with bad language and never with weakness
But so to write for that reason of good faith and justice

So I can write without hate or favourism
So I can write for a friend but also against a foe
that I should never write of what has not happened but reality

But also I should write of fictions of tales and stories too
That which strike in the mind so others can benefit with
So I can write of the past of what has really happened

Every possible interval I can write of what I can advise
And that will create no problems and may cause hatred
But I can write what others can benefit and bring happiness

So I can write with good aim and with consideration
And allow myself to pass through discipline and fairness
And never with broken language have which leaded to wrong path

So I can write with a brave heart and use my intelligent
To choose my words and not to rush
And use my sense with exactly language

So I can write and understand what my intentions are
Never to be injustice because I choose favourism
Others can blame me that I was not fair to them

So I can write very important, a steady poem
So to increase the sweetness and more they want hear
With the best of the language of wisdom and philosophy

These are my intentions and are my limits
So not cause inner pain to others and think I had intended to
Yet you can not please all, to please all is to please none.

This is the roughly translation of my Swahili introduction poem.

Jawad Ibrahim Ahmed
17-9-2014

ABOUT THE AUTHOR

*M*R. JAWAD IBRAHIM AHMED AL Bahrani was born in Zanzibar island, which is now part of Tanzania. He was born at the area known as Mkunazini in the stone town, in a small house which faces Sunni Madrassa School. He got the school education at the Mnazi Moja Zanzibar Government school, he join school in 1944 to 1948 and then transferred to Mashimoni primary shool to complete his studies, he left school by his own and join the African wharf age at the Zanzibar harbor as a fender making boy, he then was transferred as seaman in the Commander Hall boat who was among in charge of African Wharfage. He then left African Wharfage and joins Port and Marine and also as seaman in a Pilot boat. In 1953 he join a ship M.V.Mombasa seeking adventures as high sea seaman, he was in the same ship when Sir Edward Twining the governor of Tanganyika went to open the Mtwara harbor in 1953. And then he joined one of the local schooners by the name of "Rosy" owned by Messer Fazal Bhanji. In 1961 he joined Zanzibar Electricity board as an engine attendant in the Saateni power station. In 1964 he got married to Miss Saida Allbdalla Ali Al Shaibani and the same year God bless them with their first child and his father named him Naqeeb. In 1968 he opened his photo studio by the name of Studio Tropicana in Zanzibar near Majestic cinema. In 1971 he was arrested and detained for 4 months by the Revolution government. In 1972 he was again arrested with so many others young Arabian and Asian youths when the first Zanzibar President was killed by an Arab army officer. In 1975 he opened a first of its kind, an audio cassettes recording shop, selling musical audio cassettes. In 1975 he left Zanzibar and went Bahrein to his elder brother looking for a better and secure life for his family. In Bahrein he got a job as a time keeper in Swedish company building a pre fabricated houses. In 1976 he left Bahrein and came to Dubai, and got a job in United color film company dealing with photo films processing and printing and then was transferred to a sister company Middle East Film Production Company in Ajman U.A.E. In 1977 he left Ajman and came to Oman and got a job in the Oman Television as a film cameraman as news and documentaries filming. He then became a Documentary films director and produces his own films, and one of his film won the first prize in AGCC Bahrein Film Festival in 2000. The title was "Nature in Oman" and in the same year he was retired and till this day he did not work anywhere but became an Author writing classical story novels.

APPRECIATIONS

*F*OR SOME GENTLE AND WORTH reasons, I take this opportunity to thanks all those who share their time, knowledge, opinion, advices as well as those who gave me a helping hand one way or the other in making this project of completing this ancient classical story book as a success, if for one reason or the other that I have to mentioned names than for sure I have to mention those names of whom without any obligation served me from the beginning of writing this book to the end, many of these people are my own flesh and blood, who never say "NO" when I requested them for any help or services, to me I can say THANK YOU hundreds of times to them, but to mentioned their names in this same book is more worth and deserve than those hundreds THANK YOU if I will pronounce them from my lips, yet I have no other choice but to write it so it should remain forever as history that they too share with me their efforts in helping me complete this book story TALES FROM ARABIAN AND PERSIAN DESERTS. Many thank to you all my dears, without your helping hand I would never be where I am now. I thank my God for giving me strength, knowledge and wisdom in allowing me to put all my efforts on this job and manage to complete it though there are minors spelling and grammar errors here and there, and for that I beg the reader forgiveness and not to criticize me for that but to praise me for the initiative I took to complete this book by myself.

1. Saleh Abbas Al Shaibani   [Advisor]
2. Nadir Jawad Al Bahrani   [Helping hand]
3. Salum Issa Al Bahrani   [Mediator in Zanzibar]
4. Fatma Abdulla Al Sumry   [Errors and spelling corrector]
5. Humud Abdulla Al Sumry   [Computer graphic designer]
6. L'annoud Abdulqadeer   [Helping hand]
7. Naifin Jawad Al Bahrani   [Helping hand & correction]
8. Ali Misifa   [Illustrations sketcher, Zanzibar]
9. Abdulla Humud Al Sumry   [Helping hand] & others in the family.
10. Najuwd Jamal Al Obeidan   [Cover girl]
11. Jamal & Naifin   [For permiting to use Najuwd photo On book cover]

INTRODUCTION OF
TALES FROM ARABIAN &
PERSIAN DESERT

*I*F SOMEONE WOULD ASK ME, what has inspired me to write down story books? In particular, the old style like stories.

There is a fundamental reason behind it.

The first reason, during my school days when I was young, we use to get free of charge story books from the school library. Most of those books were written in Swahili, some were fictions and some were facts. The fictions were stories of A THOUSAND & ONE NIGHT (Alfu laila u Leila), the facts were like THE ADVENTURES OF CHRISTOPHER COLUMBUS, JOHN DEREK and DAVID LIVINGSTON.

The second fundamental reason of my writing inspiration was my father. He used to narrate to me stories of most of the Prophets (PBUT) naming, Moses & Pharos, Noah, Jacob and his son Joseph, Abraham and his sons Isaac and Ismail, David & Solomon and Issa and Muhammad (PBUT).

The third fundamental reason was the fact that I was made aware of my original identity (family root originality,) which is Busra in Iraq. Again this was told to me by my father. Iraq which is also known as the land of A THOUSAND & ONE NIGHT.

I believe in my heart and mind that I have inherited this passion from my forefathers for loving philosophy, composing lyrics and music. Passion of loving nature, and most of all, the passion of envying the past, that oriental past of how our forefathers used to live. These were the fundamental reasons of my inspiration to begin writing of imagination past of where I belong, of where I have come from and where I have lived.

Before writing this book, I have written a story book about a young Zanzibari boy, called ADVENTURES OF BULBUL, this book was written in Swahili and was translated in English. My other book, was titled TALES OF ZANZIBAR NIGHTS, this book is combined with five short stories, mostly imaginative fairy tale stories, very entertaining for the children and worth reading for the elders.

It is my hope that readers of my books will find them worth reading, and praise my writing to encourage me to write more. If for any reason I have crossed any boundary line of misleading and not leading to right path, then here I am saying openly with all my heart, this was not my aim and intentions, but otherwise, Allah be my witness as he knows all my intentions, all the truth about me and why I choose to do these writing, as before my writing I ask and pray to Allah to clean my mind and give me the will of doing the right thing and never otherwise. Please pray for me for my success in my writing doing and so Allah will lead me to that right path I wish to travel to.

Thank you all.

Jawad Ibrahim Al Bahrani
24th February 2014

CHAPTER ONE

(Mr. Fairuz bin Haddaad)

*I*N THE DESERT OF EMPTINESS or also famously known as Empty Quarters (Arrob'o in Arabic) located in the Arabian Gulf countries, there lived one poor man. He lived in a thinly populated and small village. Residents of the village depended on cultivation of palm dates trees and vegetables while a few kept some animals such as camels, sheep, goat and even donkeys.

Apart from these activities, there were also some villagers who had learned various trades in the nearby towns and villages. These included masonry, carpentry, black smothery, carpet weaving and the like.

The poor man's name was Fairuz bin Haddad. He lived with his mother, wife and a son who was known as Saqr (the meaning of this name in Arabic is a Falcon). Saqr had reached the adolescence age; he was already a young adult. His body was big and well built, and he was very handsome. Even at this age, he was taller than his father. He had the opportunity to study both religious and earthly education. In spite of the hard life they led, his father made sure that Saqr would get all the education he needed. So he worked hard day and night to provide for his family and pay for his son's education. So, every morning Saqr would go to the Quran class before going to his other school where he learned language and other subjects on human issues and how best to be a better person.

Every day early in the morning, just after sun rise, Fairuz and his son Saqr would take their breakfast ready to face the day. Their main activity was looking for dried trees, cut them down and chops them into firewood. So, they always left on the back of their two camels, but they would also go with two more camels for carrying the firewood they would find. They had to cross the desert towards where they could find trees. Once they got there they would rest and let their camels rest too. Then they would go into the wilderness searching for dried tree trunks to cut down into firewood. This work would continue till mid-day, just before time for afternoon prayers. That is when they would stop

1

and rest a bit. Then they would load the firewood onto the backs of the two camels before heading back to their village, back to their home.

Since the job of chopping tree trunks into firewood was tough, Saqr, who was becoming stronger and stronger, was the one doing it. He was still he young, energetic and had a heavily built physique. So, he preferred to do the tough part of the job and let his father do some lighter ones. So, he would chop firewood and his father would arrange it in bundles that would be sold to villagers. This too was not a small job. It was always important to ensure that they finish the work by afternoon so that Saqr would have time to attend to his lessons.

Now, let us look back and see what goes on in the home of Mr. Fairuz when he and his son are away in the wilderness. The ladies at the house were always busy occupied by several domestic chores. This is just like in many other households. Women have to attend to a myriad of things. Fairuz's mother was known as Madam Zaitoon, she kept herself busy by caring for some domestic animals such as hens, ducks, goats, sheep, camels and the one horse that was there whom they had named Antar. The wife of Mr Fairuz, whose name was Ramziya, was the one in charge of preparing meals and ensuring that the house was in order.

Therefore, in this order, the family of Mr. Fairuz bin Haddaad was in a great harmony, and this discipline generally helped to ensure existence of a balance in the family. Therefore, this order helped the family run its affairs smoothly because each member knew his or her duties and fulfilled them faithfully. The division of labor made each one to have a contribution in the family. This helped to create respect for each member and their commitment to one another increased. The household of Mr. Fairuz became a model home for many in the village. Mr. Fairuz was well known for his love for discipline and hard work. He was wary towards indiscipline and laziness and the same applied towards exploitative tendencies. He was against them. Now, dear readers this story presents to you The Tales of the Arabian and Persian Deserts. It is about the life that Mr. Fairuz and his family chose to lead.

In certain nearby village within the same Desert of the Empty Quarter there lived a very cruel Sheikh. His main weakness was on young beautiful women. Whenever he saw one, he would want to marry her, that is, in spite of the age differences that existed between them, most of who were of the age of his own grand-daughters. This behavior made many residents of the village unhappy, especially so when they were blessed with a baby girl, fearing that a day would come when their beloved daughter would be forced to marry the cruel Sheikh.

The saddest about this Sheikh's behavior was his tendency of not caring for his many wives. Had he been doing his duties properly, fulfilling the teaching of Prophet Mohammad (s.a.w.) and Allah's command, the villagers would have not found it a problem. Moreover, this Sheikh established very stringent rules in his home to the extent of making his many wives live miserably in the same manner prisoners or slaves would live. He denied them whatever little luxury there was.

In the same village there lived one elderly person who teaches the Qur'aan and other religious teachings. His name was Maalim Mikdad. He was blessed with two daughters. The elder daughter had reached the adolescence age and her name was Fardhada. The younger one was yet to reach puberty, her name as Fadhana. The head of the army under the village Sheikh and his son lived very close to Maalim Mikidad's home. The name of this army commander's son was Muntasir. He was a well bred young man, kind, charming and always wearing a shining face. Above all he was very respectful of all, the old and the young. His father did all he could do to ensure that his son got the best of education. So, apart from attending a common school, he also was privileged to have extra classes by private teacher paid by his father. His father did not want him to fail, so he did all in his power to prevent this eventuality. However, Muntasir was that type of young men who are responsible and he liked his studies very much.

One of the private teachers who taught Muntasir was Maalim Mikdad. Because of being a hard worker and putting all his efforts to learning, especially learning about his religion, Islam, Maalim Mikdad happened to like the young man very much. So, he kept urging him never to do contrary to what the religion taught, and that he should always seek to do only what pleases Allah.

On his side, Muntasir decided that Maalim Mikdad was among teachers he treasured the most and he highly respected him. He was so close to him that even when prayer time came, he would go to his place so that they could walk together to the mosque. Therefore, my dear reader this can clearly show you how Muntasir was close to his teacher, Maalim Mikdad, and not only in a learning and teaching relationship but the latter knew his student deep inside very well. The two became confidants to each other. They shared many inner secrets between them.

CHAPTER TWO

(Sheikh Misbah)

SHEIKH MISBAH (THAT IS THE name of the Sheikh who ruled the neighboring village) was in his study room. He called out to a servant. A servant came rushing. When he had entered he placed his hand on his chest and bent a bit to greet the sheikh respectfully saying: "Here I am oh Saahib-u-summon."

"Quickly, go and summon Naqeeb (Naqeeb in English is Army Captain) Abu Muntasir, tell him I want him here right now," ordered the sheikh even without looking at him.

"Yes my lord, Amrak ya Saahib-u-summuu," responded the servant and quickly left the study room.

It didn't take long before heavy footsteps were heard coming quickly towards the study room. Abu Muntasir opened the door and was allowed to go in. When he was before the sheikh, he saluted and at the same time hitting the ground heavily with his right foot. He announced his arrival by saying, "Here I am my lord".

"Yaa Abu Muntasir?" asked the Sheikh.

"Yes my lord," he responded.

"Tell me; among your duties assigned to you by me, aren't you supposed to inform me about every citizen in this village and their families?"

"Yes my lord," responded the commander.

"It seems you're not doing your job properly, is there something wrong with you?"

"No my lord, I'm very well health wise and in my mind as well, is there something that I've done wrong, Sir?"

"Yes, there is. Let me reason with you without anger, your neighbor, Maalim Mikdad, how many children does he have, and how old are they now, did you forget to inform me about this or maybe you didn't want me to know?"

Naqeeb Abu Muntasir had not expected this question. Truly, he knew that Maalim Mikdad had two daughters. One had already reached the adolescence

4

age and the younger one was yet to reach that age. These were no other but Fardhada and Fardhana. However, because he and Maalim Mikdad lived peacefully, he had not wanted to tell this information to Sheikh Misbah. He wanted to protect Maalim Mikdad and his family from this evil Sheikh. Sheikh Misbah was always harmful to his people – he caused them unspeakable miseries. Naqeeb Abu Muntasir was not always happy with the deeds of the Sheikh. These deeds did not only displease him but all the people in that village.

All in all, a marriage contracted following all legal requirements was a legal contractual agreement. No marriage can take place if one party does not give its consent as well as obtaining the permission of yet another party. However, Sheikh Misbah was a threatening figure and all the villagers feared him because of the heavy penalties that he subjected the people to, the fore, because people were so much afraid of him, he always got away whatever he wanted to do. So, no one could refuse him permission to marry their daughters.

Although religious teachers at the village did not hesitate to tell him about what religion required and allowed, Sheikh Misbah did not pay attention to them. All those who seemed to be saying too much found themselves ending in jail. Sheikh Misbah did not listen to their protests.

Naqeeb Abu Muntasir responded to the allegations being leveled against him saying: "My lord, it is very true indeed that it is my job to inform you about every development in this village, but only when this information reaches me, you did not instruct me to go to each and every house under your jurisdiction and demand to know who resides there and who doesn't. Maalim Mikdad is my neighbor and he is my son's teacher. As far as information on who lives in his house and what and who they are, how do I know? My lord I'll be lying to you, because it is the custom of all your subjects here to keep their own affairs to themselves, moreover, as you are well aware my lord, it is the custom of the people of this land, especially women, to cover their entire bodies and not to expose their faces. It is also strictly forbidden for women to go to places like the market or just wander about here and there.

"My lord there is nothing that I'm hiding from you, but all that take place in the homes of your people and I do not know that information. I'm in no position to force your soldiers to go and demand to be given information of what goes on behind closed doors. So what I do not know I cannot tell it to you. I've always remained loyal to you and will never disobey you my lord, never."

"Mh! Is that so?" responded Sheikh Misbah, adding: "If what you're telling me is true and you've not been hiding things from me, but somehow I was informed that Maalim Mikdad has daughters in his house, I don't know how many and I don't know how old they are. Now I want you to collect this missing information and report to me tomorrow when you come to office, do you understand?"

"Yes, my lord, I do and I will do all in my power to obtain the information and report to you," he responded with his head down.

The Sheikh gave permission to the army commander to leave. Commander Naqeeb Abu Muntasir left the Sheikh's study room being in deep thoughts, his entire self having been put to a great test, his mind rolled wildly. He did not know where to start to save both himself and his neighbor's family from this huge problem.

Since it was still early, Naqeeb Abu Muntasir kept counting minutes and hours before his time at the Sheikh's residence was up so that he would return home and find a way of helping Maalim Mikdad overcome the evil intentions that the Sheikh was harboring against his family. When it was time for him to leave, he left hastily that he would discuss the matter with his son, Muntasir. He was in deep thoughts thinking what he should do to prevent the evil Sheikh from marrying Maalim Mikdad's eldest daughter. He knew that from the moment he received the Sheikh's order he was already in a great danger just like being thrown deep into a desert.

He could not let himself think of what could befall him; so, he preferred to leave everything in the hands of Allah so that only He would make him pass this time safely. Upon getting to his home, he found Muntasir and his mother. They were waiting for him so that they would take lunch together.

He greeted them as was his usual manner. He told them: "Before we take our lunch, there is something very important and very urgent that I would like us to discuss so that we find a solution and make a quick decision on what is to be done. Now, get seated so that I will tell you what happened today at the palace and what might befall us if we are not to do something quickly."

So, he narrated to them what the Sheikh had instructed him to do. "Therefore, when I show up for work tomorrow, I'm supposed to report to him about Maalim Mikdad's family. This is too tough for me that am why I would like to hear your opinion. I know very well what the evil intentions of this Sheikh are, just like you do. You also know too well that if I do not report to him as he demanded, I will not return to this house, I will end up in prison or even losing my life.

"So, what do you think, I'm not prepared to betray our good neighbor even if it means losing my own life; I prefer to fear God rather than this Sheikh. Please tell me what ideas do you have regarding this matter, don't worry, even if it's a tough idea, just speak it," lamented Naqeeb Abu Muntasir.

That was when Muntasir responded to his father saying: "Dear father, this is truly a huge desert into which you have been thrown, it is a great test that you have been put to face, it is very much possible that someone at your work place is working against you, he wants to see you fall, and this person must be extremely dangerous. This situation in which we are now is not good for you and is not good for the entire family. The only time we have is between now and tomorrow, we must find a solution. I truly believe in my heart that your intention of saving Maalim Mikdad and his family is what our religion, Islam, teaches us. And don't you forget father that Allah loves those who sacrifice themselves for others, the one who will never surrender to evil deeds or intentions.

"Sheikh Misbah's insatiable desires have become too much, how come he wants to each girl under his dominion for himself, what about us, whom are we going to marry? Shall we go and marry those whom he has divorced?

"Now, because our time is very short, let us call Maalim Mikdad and inform him what is about to befall his family, he might have a way of helping us all out of this danger, or may be let's decide to leave this village and go to hide wherever we can, and this has to happen between now and tomorrow, the land that Allah created is very big and we will find a place. If you do not want to do any of these, then just wait for tomorrow and report to Sheikh Misbah whatever there is to report about the family of Maalim Mikdad and let whatever may before that family to do so." Muntasir finished saying.

That was when Muntasir's mother also said: "In my opinion, let's follow Muntasir's first idea, let's get out of this village, I know that Sheikh Misbah has his spies everywhere watching us, but it's time we try to free ourselves. Let's call Maalim Mikdad and inform him about all these, he might have a solution to this."

Abu Muntasir was pleased by the advice given to him by his son and his wife. He instructed Muntasir to go and ask Maalim Mikdad to come to his house for an important discussion.

Maalim Mikdad did not delay getting there. When he arrived he was welcomed and made to sit down comfortably. Some coffee was prepared for him. While he was taking coffee, Abu Muntasir explained to him the reason that made him summon him hastily.

Abu Muntasir attacking

"Your family and mine have been living peacefully as neighbors for many years. I've never personally experienced anything bad from you and your entire family; above all you have proved to be a very good religious teacher to my son. I have been witnessing how my son Muntasir has been growing in wisdom and in knowledge of the Quran. He always shares with me some of the verses from this holy book, especially, when I'm down pressed by some issues. The verses he shares with me normally give me the courage to face whatever there is that has been disturbing me. So, I owe you a great deal.

"Our ancestors reasoned that whenever you meet a good student, then there must be very good teachers behind the successes of this good student. I firmly believe that you are a very efficient teacher and that is why my son has shown to be exceptionally good.

"We both know very well the behaviors of Sheikh Misbah, who happen to rule over us. He has the tendency of marrying young girls only later to maltreat and abandon them. He has destroyed lives of several teen of girls in our village. I work for him in his palace. I know him well; however, I have never approved any of his misdeeds. I've never sent him information about any family all the years I've been working for him. All in all, a few times I had to pass on some information brought to me by my junior soldiers, and there are many of these spy soldiers here. I fear God and the punishments that will come on judgment day. It is for this reason that I've not wanted to trade tomorrow's heavenly life for today's temporary happiness here on earth. It's not like me to do so.

"Muntasir is not only a son to me but to you as well; in the same manner I have full responsibilities over your daughters Fardhada and Fardhana as if they are my very own daughters.

"I'm telling you these deep secrets from inside the palace so that you will find a way to help yourself and your family, especially, your daughters. This village seems like to have no place for us any longer. It is for this reason I called you here so as to share with you this information but also to have your opinion at what we can possibly do to rescue ourselves from this danger," Abu Muntasir finished explaining.

For several minutes Maalim Mikdad sat there quietly his head bent down. He collected all his energy and muttered a verse from the Quran saying: "Hasbiya llahu wa nee'ma-l-wakiyl". He then raised his hands upwards, prayed to God and his army of angels for guidance, saying: "Ooh God of justice and Muhammad your prophet, I pray to you and your angels who now witness me, please listen to my prayer and respond to it, I'm nothing before you, you have said in your holy book that 'pray and I will answer you', now please listen to me your servant. Please help us overcome this looming danger. We're not running away because of marriage, but it is what goes before that including giving ones consent to the matter, we cry before you, ooh God please protect us from the evil intentions of this creature. Please protect our children and our own selves."

"Abu Muntasir, I must admit that from what you have told me, I owe you the lives of my family and especially of my daughters," said Maalim Mikdad, wiping away a tear from his left eye.

He then continued: "Thank you very much for having been a very good neighbor of my family. Thank you for giving me this warning. Thank you for your love for us. It is very kind of you to have remembered us during a tough time such as this one. Your decision to leave this village, I fully support it. However, time is no longer on our side. Our ancestors said, 'if you don't time the time, then it will time you', so, let's not give it time to time us. There is no objection to the decision to run away from here, let's use this short time remaining. We need to make careful planning of our escape."

Maalim Mikdad fights Sheikh's spies

Abu Muntasir agreed with him saying: "Maalim Mikdad, it is a must that we must leave this village immediately. However, we face a number of challenges. First, we need to find a reliable means of transport, secondly, we must travel in discreet, and both are not easy matters."

"Don't you worry on the transportation issue," said Maalim Mikdad, "I've a very close friend whose daughter was my student who later was married to the Sheikh and then abandoned by him after having impregnated her. I'm sure this friend will not refuse me my request."

"Alright, however, we need to be as much discreet as possible, from what I know, Sheikh Misbah will place a good number of spies to watch our movements. You should not be surprised to see strangers wandering about in our door steps; they will pretend to be beggars or petty traders. So, I suggest that for the rest of the day today, don't change your life routine and don't show that there is anything disturbing you. When you get home, inform your family of what we are facing and what we intend to do, and please arrange with this friend of yours on transportation issues, I think you now need to go back to your home," said Abu Muntasir.

Then Maalim Mikdad said goodbye to Abu Muntasir's family and went back to his home. Once he got there, he summoned his entire family. He informed them of what he had heard from their neighbors about what was about to befall their family. He discussed with them what has been decided and what each one of them was to do in the coming few hours.

When it was prayer time, Muntasir passed by Maalim Mikdad as was their custom and together they went to the mosque to pray. When the prayers ended, Maalim Mikdad gestured to Muntasir to go straight home instead of waiting for him. He wanted to meet his friend who could give them some horses that they would use to travel.

So, Maalim Mikdad made sure that he met with his friend. Lucky was on his side because his friend understood very well and gave him permission to use taking the horses as per his request.

Maalim Mikdad challenging Sheikh's spies

On his side, Muntasir upon getting back home, he found an old beggar sleeping on the verandah of their house. He was covered from head to toe. He informed his father of what had taken place at the mosque that Maalim Mikdad had stayed behind in order to meet with his friend, the one who would let them use his horses. Moreover, he informed him of the beggar who had established his begging point on the front verandah of their house.

Abu Muntasir was not surprised by this information, somehow, he had anticipated that the Sheikh would send spies to check on his movements along with those of Maalim Mikdad and their families. So, he thought up of a plan to confuse the spy posing as a beggar.

He instructed his son to look for dirty and old clothes from their house. He told him to put them on and ensure that the clothes do cover him from head to toe. He instructed him to get out of the house via the back door and pretend to be another beggar. Once on the streets he should start making begging calls at his loudest.

So, Muntasir did as his father instructed him. He was highly disguised. No one would be able to tell his identity if he were to see him at that moment. Fortunately for him there was no one on the back side of the house. So, he crept out and went into the streets. He moved as if he was crippled, his face was painted with ashes, "Help this poor man, be kind, and help this poor man!"

After a few rounds here and there he headed to the front verandah of their house. He found the spy beggar pretending to be in a deep sleep. He placed himself on the same verandah, not far from the other beggar. He continued chanting: "Help this poor man, be kind help this poor man!"

The other beggar who pretended to be old uncovered his face and said harshly: "You dirty beggar, can't you see that I'm asleep? Why do you cause this entire disturbance to me and the residents of this house? Do you want us to be kicked out of this place? Now keep quiet. Move from here, go and beg elsewhere."

Upon seeing his face, Muntasir became sure that this beggar was not an authentic beggar but a spy. So, he decided to fire back saying: "I'm sorry old man, but this is not your place. How come you want to pretend to be the boss around here? Let me tell you one thing, only the residents of this house are entitled to kicking me out of here, understand? If you think that I'm disturbing you, then move away, go find another place where you will sleep in peace."

Muntasir's words angered the spy-beggar very much. He woke up and sat properly holding his clothes tight so that he would not expose his inner clothes. He said threateningly to Muntasir: "Open your ears you filthy beggar, for your own safety move away from here quickly before I do something bad to you, now get quick!"

"I'm a poor man, help me, be kind to this poor man, give me just a little to eat!" Continued chanting Muntasir loudly.

Suddenly, the front door of the house opened. The owner of the house, who was none other than Abu Muntasir, emerged. He shouted at the two supposedly beggars: "You've come from wherever you were only to disturb us. I didn't build this verandah for beggars to sleep around, now I order you two to move from here now, go and find another place where you can conduct your business, now move, move!"

So, the two beggars had to leave each one blaming the other for their expulsion there. Muntasir made a few rounds and found a back way that lead to their house. His job had been accomplished. He made sure that no one saw him going inside. Once he was inside, his father was very much pleased by his deeds. They had succeeded to send away one of the spies working for the Sheikh.

"So, I think we will have to travel light, that is, if we don't want to be discovered," said Abu Muntasir addressing his wife. "We'll have to leave everything behind, what we urgently need to rescue are just our souls, we'll lock the house. I know that Sheikh Misbah may order them demolished or get confiscated, let's just pray to Allah that things will not get that much complicated. We need to travel light in order to quickly get out of this territory, tomorrow will be a hard day for us, and we should strive to ensure that tomorrow does not find us still on this land that is full of evil."

During the evening prayer time, Maalim Mikdad passed by Muntasir's house and as was their custom together they headed for the mosque. As they walked they were busy scrutinizing people especially those sitting on verandahs to ensure that there we no spies amongst them.

On the way also Maalim Mikdad passed all the plans that he and his family had worked out regarding their escape that night. He told him that the horses would be waiting ready behind Haroon's shop. There would be six horses in total. Moreover, there as an improvement on their original plan, from behind Haroon's shop they would travel by the six horses to the house of the horse owner, from their they would find a chariot to be pulled by horses that they would board. The leaving time from their friend's house would be just before the early hour's prayers.

"Do you understand Muntasir?"

"Yes sir, I do," answered Muntasir.

"There is one more thing that we need to work out," continued explaining Maalim Mikdad, "the country is swarmed up by spies of all sorts, some may become suspicious seeing a group composed of men and women on horses at early hours of the day. Therefore, I and my daughters have decided that these two daughters will dress in men's costumes, and to make this possible, we'll need your assistance, they will have to temporarily borrow your clothes. As for you, you'll have to put on your father's military clothes and so will your father. Therefore, our convoy will consist of two soldiers, three men and only one woman, that is, your mother. The total number will be six. What do you think of this plan?"

"It sounds excellent," responded Muntasir.

"Alright, this is the plan that we came up with at my home, however, go and discuss it with your family, and if there is an area that needs improvement, then we will talk later when we meet for another round of prayers," said Maalim Mikdad.

Inshaallah Maalim, let's ask God to protect us and keep us safe until the time we are completely out of this territory," said Muntasir.

"Insha'Allah!" said Maalim Mikdad.

Upon getting home, Muntasir told his father the plan that Maalim Mikdad and his daughters had come up with regarding their escape. Abu Muntasir smiled and said: "Looking at Maalim Mikdad, it is difficult to imagine him coming up with such an intelligent plan, you will take him as a simple Quran teacher, but his thoughts surpass of many military engineers and war planners. His plan is extremely good, it has all the qualities required for such a trip as the one we're about to make. I especially like the disguising part. It will be very useful in overcoming all the obstacles that will be there. So, go and tell him that I consent to the plan; however, I would like to know from whose house are we going to start the journey early tomorrow morning? It is very important that I know this. And above all I have reservations in using a chariot; I would suggest that apart from the chariot, we also take along a side horse for envy eventuality on the way. We place our journey in the hands of God, only He can make it a successful one."

When the time for evening prayers came, Muntasir and Maalim Mikdad went to pray as was their custom. After the prayers Muntasir relayed to Maalim his father's word on the plans laid down by Maalim earlier.

"I'm glad that your father is pleased with the plan; now let's leave everything in the hands of Allah. Regarding the question of our destination, let's move towards the neighboring village. I've my childhood friend living there. We were friends during those good old days when their village and ours were but one country. I've not informed, because as you are aware, everything must be done discreetly. However, I'm confident that he will not let us down, and from what I know, he is a very kind person, particularly to strangers, that's where we will go." Explained Maalim Mikdad.

"I will take this information to my father. And concerning those clothes, I've already taken them to your house," said Muntasir.

They then went back home, Muntasir to their home and Maalim Mikdad to his home. All preparations were ready. They kept vigil waiting for dawn to arrive so that they would leave.

Early in the morning, Muntasir, his father and mother got ready. Muntasir and his father were in military attires while the mother was covered from head to toe in a galabiya.

Mr. Fairuz and Antar flying

Maalim Mikdad had agreed with Muntasir that he would give them a signal as to when to start the journey and that they should all leave their homes through the window and ensure maximum degree of discreetness. Maalim Mikdad and his two daughters would go ahead while the other family would follow behind.

The two families came to meet behind the village shop as agreed. They mounted on the horses. They went to the house of the person who owned a chariot that they were to take. They found him ready and waiting for them. This part of their journey was uneventful.

Maalim Mikdad, Muntasir's father and mother and the two daughters who were in men's clothes climbed aboard the chariot. Muntasir was to ride on the spare horse as had been agreed.

The convoy started the journey passing by the shrubs here and there that mixed with desert landforms of bear rocks, boulders, rocky hills and sand here and there. They took the road that passes by the lifeless desert. On this route, one is left to totally depend on Allah. If one gets lost in this desert, then it's his end. This convoy had no choice but to face this difficult road. It was hot and from time to time they stopped to drink some water. However, they were cautious because the water they carried was not much because they had to travel light.

After three hours deep into the desert, on one rocky hill they spotted man on a camel. It looked as if it was alone. They slowed down wandering who that one could be. Was it a friend or a foe? It was strange that the camel made no movement.

"Since we're not very experienced with desert movements and paths, won't it be okay if we're to ask this person, he might show us the road," suggested Maalim Mikdad.

"I think that's fine, there is no harm in asking for a way," agreed Abu Muntasir.

However, what was strange was the fact that the person on the back of the camel did not make a move. As they drew closer to him, he kept staring at them. When they were about fifty meters from where he was standing, that was when he disclosed his true nature.

He drew a shining sword from his hip and shouting: "They are escaping! They are escaping". All over the sudden, there materialized about seven other men heavily armed advancing towards the convoy. Maalim Mikdad and his fellows were taken aback. They knew that the evil Sheikh would set up a plan to block them from moving out of the village, however, this was not what they anticipated.

"My brethren, if we're to kill in order to save our souls, that is okay, now each one of us must draw his or her weapon and get ready to face the gang. Just watch that they are on the back of their camels and we are on the bare sand, make sure you hit the front legs of the camels with the blunt sides of your sword, they will fall down, don't pity them, then attack whoever is on the camel, okay?" ordered Abu Muntasir.

"We've understood," the others responded almost in unison.

When the two sides got closer, the Sheikh's soldiers attacked, but Abu Muntasir's side kept a good distance just waiting for the right moment to strike back. Suddenly, Abu Muntasir moved quickly, hitting the front legs of one camel with the blunt side of his sword, this caused the camel to land down in pain. He attacked the soldier who was on the back of the camel, chopping off his head with his sharp sword. The soldier made a howling terrifying sound.

In no time, Fardhada and Fardhana made very quick moves and no sooner the soldiers realized it already two more soldiers were on the ground dying in immense pains. The remaining soldiers realizing this, they took flight, but Maalim Mikdad and Muntasir gave them a chase, hitting the camels from the back and throwing them and the soldiers down. Three more soldiers went down dead.

Only one soldier survived and Abu Muntasir took him prisoner in order to extract some information from him.

"Now, you thug, tell us who sent you to attack us? Who are you?" Abu Muntasir asked still in anger. He was pointing his sword on the neck of the soldier. But the soldier did not want to talk.

"So, you won't talk, isn't that the case? Good, now you will know who I am." Said Abu Muntasir threatening.

He lifted his sword high and pinned it on the thigh of the soldier, the soldier made a howling sound due to pain.

"I'll tell you, ju…ju…just don't kill me, I'm a family man and my children are still young, please don't kill me, it was the Sheikh…the Sheikh ordered us to lay an ambush against you knowing that you will try to escape, please save me and my family!" cried the soldier.

"So, you too are a servant of Sheikh Misbah, what a shame," said Abu Muntasir.

"He ordered us to catch you and take you back to him, we did not realize that you were such a strong fighting squad, it is amazing how you all fight with such a rare talent, now that my fellows are dead, please don't kill me, I will let you go in peace, let me go and face the consequences in the hands of the evil Sheikh, if I don't go there, then my family will suffer greatly," pleaded the soldier wetting his clothes with tears and sweat.

"So, you mean that Sheikh Misbah knew of our plan and that was why he sent you to attack us," Abu Muntasir inquired.

"It was the spies whom he sent to your house, they reported of seeing you preparing to flee the village, however, they reported to him too late," said the soldier, adding: "The beggar you chased away from your home was a spy, your sending him away caused him to fail to note your running away at the timely moment."

"How did you know we would take this route?" inquired Maalim Mikdad.

"It was only by guessing, many people who attempt to flee from our village normally take this route because it is deserted, so we thought you would do the same," explained the soldier who was still bleeding from his wound.

"Above all, I have personally been on this route so many times and know all shortcuts and paths that cross the desert, now please let me go so that I should have my wounds treated," pleaded the soldier.

"Let's waste no time with him, let's release him," suggested Muntasir's mother.

The soldier bent down to kiss legs of Abu Muntasir as a sign to beg for his forgiveness and his realize.

"Alright, we will let you go. However, we would like you to send this information to Sheikh Misbah; we're running away from our home and village not because we don't like the place but because we don't like his behavior. He needs to repent to Allah and mend his ways, he should remember that his days are numbered," said Abu Muntasir.

"And, you should remind him that Allah is not pleased with people who just follow their lustful desires to the extent of wanting to marry girls as young as their own granddaughters, destroying their lives and their future, his behavior of turning himself as the only male member of the community is displeasing to all the people, many more will continue to run and escape from the village," added Maalim Mikdad.

"Now, tell us, which is the fasted way that will help us get out of this desert the earliest, the sun is already up and all thanks to your interference," Abu Muntasir said in his military tone.

"From here take the route on your right hand side, after a brief moment the path will pass between date palm trees and rocks. Do not fear anything. This place is always very calm. But it is full of Jinni's and monsters, at some other moments they may even call you by name, just ignore them, keep going.

Whoever responds to such a call then he or she shall disappear and will not come back to you again," explained the soldier.

"There is another route; it is longer, full of desert sand, hot and hilly. It will take you much longer to get to the other village, this route is calmer and usually there is no problem to travelers, it's up to you to decide the route you wish to take," said the soldier.

"Okay, I believe you, and we'll decide which way to take, now take leave, and remember if you betray us in any way, we shall have a chance to avenge ourselves." said Abu Muntasir.

They helped him climb on the back of his camel and saw him leave descending down the hill.

"Congratulations guys, you did put a very good fight, I'm amazed by the skills and capacity of your daughters Maalim Mikdad, who has trained them? They are very good at fighting," said Abu Muntasir.

"Well, ever since their mother died, I took their care and development into my own hands, I've been training them secretly, I didn't know that this training would prove useful someday, I thank Allah for his guidance," said Maalim Mikdad.

"It is amazing, I'm not sure we would have defeated the soldiers if the two girls were not around and had not fought the way they did," said Muntasir.

The two girls were quite, with their heads bent shyly. Secretly, they thanked their father. And they went.

"Once Allah decides to bestow you with His grace, no one can stop Him. I believe that our journey will be okay, even though it will be full of obstacles, let's not give up, let's have faith," said Abu Muntasir.

"Now, we need to select one of the two ways to that will help us get to our destination, what have you got to say, remember, we don't have time," said Maalim Mikdad.

"Well, on my side, I think let's take the route that is full of scary creatures and incidents, because in life we come across many terrifying things and incidents, but it only takes courage to overcome them, so, let's take this route, if you will please," suggested Muntasir.

"I support Muntasir's idea, we've already proved ourselves capable of facing any challenge when we fought and won against those soldiers, we therefore can face any challenge," said Abu Muntasir.

"Yes, that's it," said the other members of the team almost in unison.

They continued with their journey after having agreed to take the scary route.

"I had to make my son to take an oath when I decided to secretly teach him military techniques, how about your courageous daughters, you haven't told us all about them," inquired Abu Muntasir.

"Abu Muntasir, I'll briefly tell you about my origins. My family is from the Persian Gulf. Most of my relatives are members of the military there. They have fought in numberless wars. This has been the case for generation and generation. And when some came to these regions, they even started a small place where they could make weapons. These included spears, swords, military armaments, arrows, shields and knives. By then I was still very young. However, I also learnt the different activities. It occurred to me that every person in my family had to learn military techniques, be it women or men, we all learned the skills. Therefore, I too had that obligation of teaching my daughters martial arts skills," explained Maalim Mikdad.

"Ooh, I'm pleased to learn of all this. I thought I knew you, I was wrong. I only knew you one bit, that of being a Quran teacher and nothing more. Thank you for opening up to me. I'm glad that we have become this close," said Abu Muntasir.

CHAPTER THREE

(Mr. Fairuz and the mysterious horse)

NOW DEAR READER, I WILL take you back to the beginning of this tale to Fairuz bin Haddad at the neighboring village. As I already explained to you, members of his family include his mother, his wife, his son Saqr and himself along with their horse that they called Antar. Let's pay attention to the story behind this horse and how it came to live in Fairuz's home.

Many years back, by then Mr. Fairuz was still young and was yet to beget his son Saqr. On this particular day, he left his home for work. He carried his axe and climbed on the back of his donkey before heading to the wilderness. To get there he had to cross a stretch of a desert.

While he worked looking for firewood he tethered his mare and gathered some grasses for it to feed on. He worked until noon time when he took a brief break during which he drank water and ate some dates, a slice of bread and drank some camel milk that he carried in his leather pouch. As he sat down for his meal, he heard sounds of an approaching animal. He was startled, he didn't know what to expect. He feared that it could be a foe. He decided to hide behind a certain tree as he looked towards the direction from where the sound was coming.

He was surprised to see a horse running towards where he was and no one was on it riding. When the horse got very close to where he was, it stopped and kept looking at the supposedly lone donkey under the tree. Fairuz decided to wait a little longer. No one could be seen coming. So, he decided to come out of his hiding. He slowly approached the horse. The horse looked a bit terrified. As Fairuz moved a step towards it, it also made one step backwards away from him. Fairuz realized that it would take him a very long time to get hold of the horse if he were to continue in that way. He decided that the only way to attract it was to give it some food and water.

So, he collected the remaining of the food and water and showed them to the horse. It remained standing where it was fixing its eyes on him. It didn't take it long to realize that what Fairuz was offering to it was food. So, after having smelt it was food, it did not move backwards. Fairuz went to where the horse was gave it the food and water to drink. He gently patted it on its neck.

"Hey, hey, hey! Don't you worry, I'll not harm you," he kept saying to the horse.

After having eaten the food and drank the water, the horse made as if it just remembered something, it turned its head towards where it had come from and made some sound with its nose as if indicating danger.

"Don't you fear, there is nothing that will harm you," Fairuz told the horse. But the horse did not stop making gestures signifying that there was some danger approaching.

Then all over the sudden, some objects in the form of birds crossed the air where they were. They were moving at a very high speed such that it was just like the blinking of the eyes. This told Fairuz why the horse was in so much fear.

Then, as if what they had just seen was not enough, there was a sudden wind whirl that raised a lot of sand and dust. That was when the horse proved itself to be so mysterious. In less than a second, it grew wings and started talking:

"Be quick, climb on my back, there is a great danger approaching, there are enemies coming, now get on."

Fairuz was stunned. It was his very first time in his life to hear an animal talking like a human being. He didn't think twice, he quickly mounted the horse leaving behind the donkey and the firewood he had collected already. The horse started flying like how a bird would do. To Fairuz, this was like a dream. He was so much afraid. He had only read in books that people could also go up there into the sky. Now, it was all happening for real.

"I understand that this is like a dream to you to experience what you're experiencing. But all this is possible with the help from Allah. I'm not like any other horse. I'm a good jinni. I was turned into a horse by my close friend who is also the king of the kingdom from whence I come. It is a very long story. I will narrate it to you later once we settle down. Now, tell me, where do you stay?" the mysterious horse told Fairuz was in a frozen state.

He gave the horse directions. The horse started descending. It landed on a rock that was not very far from the village. It told him that it would be good if no one saw them.

"If people see you flying on horse's back, they will start poking you with numerous questions. This will cause you a lot of disturbance. I hope you understand what I mean, no?"

"I understand very clearly, and please allow me to name you Antar, and I'll be very happy if you will live with me and pretend that I'm your lord. My name is Fairuz bin Haddad." Fairuz said.

"I'm pleased too and will stay with you as my lord, and I like the name, however, make sure that no one comes to know of this secret. You human beings are very selfish creatures and never wish one another well. So, you should not talk with me in the presence of other people, if you do, I'll understand but will pretend not to hear," Antar the horse said.

So, they continued to Fairuz's home. The horse looked normal just like any other horse.

Another big surprise was still in store for Fairuz. When he and the horse got home, he found his donkey and cargo of firewood that he left in the wilderness already there.

He whispered to Antar the horse, "Do you see what I'm seeing as well?"

"Ooh, yes. It's the Jinni's servants I had commanded. They have done their job. But don't you fear anything, this is a good sign that they are beginning to recognize you and that you and I are very close. They will keep visiting you from time to time and will always attempt to do certain things to you, but since I will be here with you, they won't harm you. So, just continue with your normal business with your family," Antar responded.

Queen Farna Bash

"Thank you Antar for your encouragement. Unlike you Jinni's, I'm only God fearing and will therefore fear no other creature. I only adore the Sub'hanahu wa taala, He who is above everything else, Lord of the lords," said Fairuz.

So, Fairuz took Antar and tethered him near where his donkey was. He quickly went inside and found his mother and wife doing well with their normal activities. None was aware that the donkey and the firewood cargo were already outside the house even before the arrival of Fairuz.

"Hallo, I'm home, how are you here?" he greeted them.

"We're fine my lord. Everything here is okay. All in all at a certain time we felt a strange cold wind engulfing us, it made us feel very cold. But the moment was very brief. Then everything returned to normal," explained his wife.

Life went on well at Mr. Fairuz's home. Antar continued to live with them and they were always discussing issues together. Mr. Fairuz used the extraordinary nature of Antar to try and understand matters that faced him. So, he would consult him on almost everything. All in all, he also sought the advice of his family members.

One day Antar was in a very jovial mood. Mr. Fairuz was surprised, so he asked him, "What's so special today that your face is beaming with pleasure, what is the secret?"

"I'm happy my lord. A friend of mine is going to visit us. He is so bright that this entire place will shine so brightly because of the beauty of my friend."

Mr. Fairuz did not know how to take the news, who could this strange friend, is he wondered to himself.

"Antar, can you please explain this, who is this friend of yours and where is he coming from?" he inquired politely.

"Would you really like to know my friend's name," Antar asked.

"Ooh, yes indeed, and I would like to know more, like since when have you been friends, and how come you never mentioned him before?"

"My friend is Saqr, and he is coming by the will of our God grace Sub'hanahu wa Taala," responded Antar the horse.

Mr. Fairuz was perplexed, "How come you speak about where he is coming from while a few moment ago, you were saying that he was on his way here?"

"I'm sorry my lord, it seems my proverb has not been understood; now I'll make it plain clear to you. It is that Lady Ramsey is pregnant. Out of this pregnancy a beautiful son will be born. He will bring a lot of bright light with him to this household and in your life. This young man will be an exception by all means, physically, in habit and even intellectually.

"You will name him Saqr, please don't change this name. Once he reaches the puberty age, he will do wonders that no hero has never managed to do before. And there shall come a group of people who will be running away from a brutal ruler in the neighboring land. One of them is your close friend and a person who was kind to you. Receive them whole heartedly, because their coming to your house will bring you blessings.

"However, you shall also taste a hard time because of receiving these people into your house, it will be fighting with this distant evil ruler and his allies. As for this group, they will face many difficulties before getting here. So, it will be Saqr and his allies who will help these people. Now, I'll end there for today my lord. The rest I'll explain to you in future," finished explaining Antar.

Days passed and Lady Ramziya gave birth to a son just like how Antar had predicted. On that same day, Mr. Fairuz named the new born baby Saqr to fulfill the promise he made to Antar. The baby's face radiated a lot of light.

Mr. Fairuz went to pray in the mosque to give his thanks to Allah. He raised his hands to heaven and said, "Yaa Ilahi, Rabby wa rabb ssamaawati wal ardh, I, who is your obedient servant thank you for this wonderful gift and great love to me, please My Lord, receive my thanks giving and that of my entire family, thank you for making our household shine with this wonderful little angel whom you have safely delivered to us. Alhamdullilah wa salaat alaa sayyidina Muhammad wa aalihi wa as'habihi ajmain."

He finished his prayers and rushed to his friend, Antar, being full of joy and happiness.

"My friend Antar, your friend has arrived just as you predicted many months back," he said amid laughter.

"My lord, I'm happy for you. Light has come down on your household, remember our God said, if you are thankful to Me, I will bless you and if you are not, I'll punish you. Let me just let you know that this boy has come with many more blessings. Now, make sure that the money that you earn through hard manual work should be invested in educating this new guest, both religious education and that of this world. This is the only way through which you will help make him useful. Once Saqr reaches the puberty age, he will accompany you in all that you do. His physical strength will help you a lot.

"Above he will be very obedient to you. And there shall come a time when he will ask you to rest. Do not refuse him his request because there will come very tough incidents that only him will manage to tackle them. He will never fail in anything. Do you understand?"

"Yes, I do," responded Fairuz thoughtfully.

Days passed and Saqr grew up into a healthy and well mannered young man. He grew very fond of Antar and at the same time kept helping his father with his duties and continued with his studies. So, this is how generally Antar the horse came to be part of Fairuz's family. So, now we will turn back to Maalim Mikdad and Abu Muntasir. Let's follow them and see where they have gotten.

CHAPTER FOUR

(Face to Face with the Evil Jinni)

YOU WILL RECALL THAT MAALIM Mikdad and Abu Muntasir and their group had chosen to escape and take the dangerous route that passed by desert. They had walked for almost the whole day. It was now time for prayer. But from a distance they could see a green point that looked like having many palm trees. It was certainly an oasis or at least that was how they perceived it.

So, they decided to go there where they could take a rest after a long journey in of crossing the desert. To their surprise, upon getting at that oasis, they found several old rags spread on the ground ready for use for prayers. The entire group climbed down from the chariot. They tethered their horses. Then they prayed and prepared themselves to eat. So, they ate dried dates and bread. Fortunately for them the water at the well was okay for drinking.

"Maalim Mikdad, I've been thinking, you said you have a friend at the other village where we are going, suppose he has gone away on a trip or whatever reason he is not there, what else shall we do?" inquired Abu Muntasir.

"My friend Abu Muntasir, you have every right to ask that question, and I can understand it very well given that you are a soldier by profession. As a religious teacher, let me remind you that Allah surpasses all reasoning; He will show us a way. If He protected us against all the evil that we have come across with so far, He will also take care of us in such an eventuality," responded Mikdad calmly.

"Mikdad, thank you for your response, you're quite right, sometimes for us soldiers, we mind too much about calculations and planning and the like. Well, I'm satisfied by your response. Insha'Allah, we shall be okay," said Abu Muntasir.

They made sure that they had enough rest before embarking back on their trip. When it was time to leave, they felt highly refreshed and ready to face the desert again.

After having been back on the trip and had travelled for about an hour, they started hearing people talking. These were in some kind of a conversation.

However, all they could hear were people's voices. They did not see anyone. As they progressed, the voices also followed them. Still they did not see anyone.

Abu Muntasir was disturbed by the voices, however, as is always the case with all soldiers, he told his colleagues: "Don't you fear the voices; you will recall that the Sheikh Misbah's spy had warned us of such things. So we need to keep calm and strong in heart, we are yet to see the bad misfortunes that will follow us."

As if in response to what he was saying, a sudden gush of wind came from the opposite direction throwing the horses in havoc and making their progress almost impossible. The wind was full of sand and they found it very hard to breath. The best they could do was trying and cover their nostrils and eyes so that they could continue breathing and seeing.

All over the sudden, a dark cloud hovered above them covering the entire narrow valley through which they were passing. All they could do was to try and control the horses that had been thrown into panic. The catastrophe lasted for about a quarter an hour, then suddenly, they heard a clacking voice addressing them: "Ha, ha, ha, ha, today … yes … Today is your end you corrupt souls, you've brought yourselves to your end, there will be no escaping."

Then the cloud started turning into smoke that spiraled at a very high speed and descended towards them. It made a spiral shape. Then, the shape split into two as if two parts of a door parting from one another. Out came a terribly looking creature whom they have never seen their entire life. It was red in color and had many scars all over his body.

Maalim Mikdad muttered in Arabic: "Audhu billah mina shaitani rajiym, Bismillah rahmani rahiym, hasbiyallahu wa ne'ma-l-wakil." If I'm to tell you how this creature looked like, I won't find enough words to describe its physical shape accurately. However, this is how I can say: it had long horns that protruded from its head, it's eyes were very sharp and penetrating, some of its big front teeth could not be contained in its big mouth, it's head was hairless, it's entire body was covered by long reddish hair like it's skin color and had very long nails matching its fingers. Anyone having a soft heart could faint on seeing it.

All members of the team, except the old lady, jumped down with their swords ready in their hands. The terrible creature said in its ugly voice: "This is my property, no creature passes here without my permission. It has been many years since the last person attempted to set their feet here. Now that you've brought yourselves here, I'll extinguish you. I'm the great jinni known as Khurkush Majangar, I'm the ruler here, and I'm the king here. Before I finish you tell me why you wandered to this part of the world, my dominion? Tell me, why?"

Muntasir requested permission from his father and Maalim Mikdad to address the Jinni, "I know what I want to tell him, and so, please let me speak with him." The two granted him with permission.

"Ooh king of these valleys Khurkhush Majangar, we are not aggressors, we are travelers who have lost their way. We don't know much about this desert. We don't know the paths of the desert so well. We chose to pass by these narrow alley valleys to try and protect ourselves from the scotching sun. Please calm your anger down. Give us permission to pass here peacefully. And we promise you that we will not again pass here."

"Ha, ha, ha, ha, you have trespassed in my dominion, you must be punished accordingly," Khurkush Majangar responded with his ugly voice.

Suddenly, the chariot in which Muntasir's mother was in started being pulled forwards at a high speed. Muntasir who was on the back of the lone horse decided to live a chase.

CHAPTER FIVE

(Malika Farna Bash)

NOW DEAR READER, LET'S TURN back to Saqr and his father.

On this particular day, Saqr went out to work as usual leaving his ailing father at home. So, he went to the shed in which they kept their camel and took him out. When he entered the shed, he was surprised to see Antar the Horse being in a restless condition.

"What's wrong with you dear Antar?" he spoke to him softly as he stroked him on his back. 'Only if we could talk to each other … it's unfortunate that we speak very different language from what animals do,' he thought to himself.

"Only if you could speak in a language that I understand, look I'm being late. I want to go to work and come back in time for my studies," he was now speaking to him softly as if talking to a friend.

To his utmost surprise, Antar responded: "Saqr, don't be surprised that I'm talking. You'll understand some day, as for now; there is something very urgent that I want you to take care of. If you don't act now, there are people who will die and they are new in this area. You must do as I'll tell you.

"Pick seven hairs from the tip of my tail. Use these to tie your head so that they cross your forehead. Then climb on my back and hold me very tightly on my neck. Then we will fly together. Do you understand?" Antar said in almost a commanding voice to Saqr who was completely stunned to hear a horse speaking to him.

"Hey Saqr, wake up! Do as I told you. You'll understand the rest later," Antar brought Saqr's mind to the present.

Saqr quickly moved to Antar's tail, and picked seven hairs from it. He tied them around his head across the forehead. He climbed on the back of Antar. Immediately Antar grew wings on his ribs. He started trotting before taking off into the air. They headed to the desert.

As they flew, Antar explained to Saqr who he really was. "Your father is a very honest person. I had ordered him not to tell anyone about me. But today I had to tell you who I am."

"Now, let me warn you. We're not going to have an easy time where we're going. But today is the day you are supposed to demonstrate your brevity. All in all, do not fear, have peace of mind.

"As of the moment, there is a young man struggling very hard to save his mother from the hands of the evil one," Antar said.

After a certain moment, the land below started being visible. "Get prepared; we're going to help this young man in this war. Pray to Allah so that He will help us defeat these enemies, okay?" Antar said.

"Insha'Allah, He will protect us from all danger and will help us save this young man and his mother and the other guests," responded Saqr putting all his trust in Allah.

"Remember our enemies are Jinnis. I know them well. Their leader who is the most evil is known as Khurkush Majangar. He is their king and has a huge army of Jinnies. I grew up in this land among them. But they consider me a betrayer because I decided to help a human being whom they wanted to kill, and this is none other than your father. Therefore, I've also become an enemy to them. I decided to deflect because he was so evil that no one experienced mercy in his hands." Antar explained.

Then they landed on a piece of land that was full of vegetation. "Here we are in the land of Jinni's. You don't see anyone here, but Jinni's are all over. So far they have not noted your presence. I'm covering you with the seven hairs that you tied to your head. They can only see me," said Antar.

They could hear sounds of all kind, especially voices speaking in all tongues of the world. "This is how it is, whenever you hear voices know that they are sleeping, and when it is quite, they are awake," explained further Antar to Saqr.

"Before we attack them, we'll need to find allies as well as find out what happened to the guests, whether they are still alive or they are dead." So, they passed among trees and over vegetation covers. Antar sniffed here and there and looked up one tree. Started digging with his forelimbs then looked up the tree again. Immediately there came down several little creatures, dwarfs. They came closer to where Antar and Saqr were standing. These had their heads covered in cloths. They knelt down and put their hands on their chests and greeted: "As salaam Aleykhum."

"Wa aleykum salaam, where is your Malika, Farna Bash?" responded Antar.

"I'm here my lord." Immediately descended down from the tree a big bird. She was in the shape of a very beautiful bird (Peacock) Tausi. She bent down her head to pass his greetings to Antar.

"Your greetings have been accepted Oh! Farna Bash, now tell me, how are my parents and other elders, I've very little time here," inquired Antar

"My lord, it is very sad. Ever since you left this place. The king, Khurkush Majangar has become even more evil. Current news has it that he has captured a young man and an elderly woman. They are now locked up in remand and are being punished heavily. In fact no human being who care across this part of the land who escaped from his wrath," explained Farna Bash.

"Yes, I know about that Farna Bash, and this is exactly what took me back here from where I live with this gentleman and his family. The two human beings are related. The young man is a son and the woman is his mother. They and the others were guests to my lord and his family. Now, I would like you and your comrades to help us out. We must defeat Khurkhush Majangar and save people who pass this route," said Antar pleadingly to Farna Bash.

"My lord, it's up to you to just give us a command and we will act," responded Farna Bash.

"I'm pleased to hear that ooh good servant of my parents and elders of my tribe," said Antar. I'll repay your good deeds. As for now, please go down to the valleys to give a helping hand to the companions of this lady and her son. They are overwhelmed by sadness because they think that the two are dead. Please take the human form and pretend to be lost travelers. Take them through the paths in the desert where they will be safe from this evil Jinni Khurkhus Majangar. Secondly, please send a messenger to my relatives so that they will prepare themselves to help me in my war against this evil one.

"I'll be waiting here, I'd like you to be as quick as light in implementing these orders," said Antar in a pleasing yet commanding voice.

"Yes, my lord I'll do as you say," responded Malika Farna Bash.

Like the speed of light, the strange creatures to which Antar was talking vanished.

There remained only the tree that was there when they arrived.

Now let's turn back to Maalim Mikdad and his company after the chariot carrying Muntasir's mother was pulled away.

"Help, Laa ilaha illa llah, the chariot, the chariot! Give it a chase, there is someone inside," they shouted in confusion.

Muntasir did not waste time, he kicked the horse on which he was riding and started giving a chase.

Abu Muntasir was confused. He became totally restless, he was muttering words that amounted to some sort of prayer: "Ooh, Allah, help your believer, save her from this evil, save her son, the tests you have made to descend upon us are too much for us."

He threw himself on his knees. He cried with bitterness that no one had seen before doing that. The two were his most invaluable presents.

On his side, Muntasir, whenever he drew closer to the chariot, it would speed up and leave him far behind. In the end it vanished from his eyes. So, he opted to follow the marks that it left behind on the sand in those narrow valleys surrounded by rocks on either side. Steps made by the groves of his horse echoed many times adding to things that confused him.

He walked for a long time till he felt that the horse was now very tired. It was sweating profusely on its neck.

"Dear horse, I know you are very tired, please I beg you don't give up in finding the chariot that carried my mother, please don't give up!" he talked to the horse.

But after a certain moment, the horse came to a standstill. It refused to move on and besides its legs was shaking. Muntasir was confused. He climbed down from the horse's back. His heart pained him. He started calling out his mother, "Ummy, yaa Ummy, my good mother!" Tears rolled down his chicks. His heart became so heavy that he sat down lamenting, "Ooh Allah, help us during this troubling times, we've run from one evil hand and fallen into another. Please save my mother. She is totally alone with no one to protect her except you.

"Dear horse, I know you're too tired to move on. I'll keep moving. So, when you feel like it follows me behind," he said to the horse.

He started walking following the tracks left behind by the chariot. After walking for some time he saw from the distance the chariot. It was no longer moving forward. His heart beats doubled. Was his mother still in that chariot, or was she somewhere else, was she still safe? He wondered to himself as he moved forward tumbling in the desert sand and rocks.

As he drew closer, he saw that the horses that pulled the chariot were okay and so was the chariot itself. But his heart almost stopped beating when he didn't find his mother in it. Had she fallen out on the way, if so, how come I didn't see her? He questioned himself trembling. He didn't know what to do or whom to ask. He was surrounded by an empty desert; he was deep in the valley with high rocks on either side.

On raising his eyes up the steep slope on his right hand, he saw a Bedouin man descending a narrow path on the back of a camel. Another camel followed him from behind. He felt hope pumping back in his heart. The Bedouin man came straight to where he was. He did not greet him. He studied him for a moment before saying: "I'm only a servant. My lord has sent me to pick you from here to where you will find your mother. So, climb on the back of that camel and follow me. Now choose if you want to see your mother follow me if you don't want you may do as you decide. Remember, I'm not a human being, I'm a Jinni.

"Alright, I'll follow you, but on one condition. Order these horses and the chariot to turn back to where I left my colleagues," Muntasir found his courage and said.

"Your request has been granted, now climb on the back of this other camel and follow me," said the Bedouin man.

As soon as Muntasir was on the back of the camel, the horses started moving back from the direction that they came from. They were running at a very high speed, just like they did on their way there.

Going up the winding path on that steep face of the rock was not an easy task. It was extremely dangerous. However, Muntasir's desire to save his mother overcame his fear. So, the two of them made a single file. None spoke to the other. Only sounds made by grooves of camels could be heard.

The scenario above the rocks was very different from the one below. Here there grew trees and grass, it was rather cool compared to the situation in the valley. Muntasir felt revived in body and in spirit. They passed under tree shades and entered into a large cave. By the entrance to the cave, there were several guards. They were huge in shape and jumped from place to place with their weapons ready in hand. The Bedouin who came along with Muntasir made signs to the guards and one came forward to where they were. The Bedouin indicated to him that he should escort Muntasir to their king. So, Muntasir climbed down from the back of the camel.

The entrance to the cave was so huge that even four elephants could walk in together. The guard, who escorted Muntasir walked ahead, then followed Muntasir and behind him four more guards lined up two on either side. In the cave, Muntasir witnessed a lot of things that he had never seen in his life or heard about. At some points, he would see just half the shape of a human being passing by. Others had human forms but heads of other creatures. All these were very scaring but Muntasir prayed to Allah and felt courageous.

Their journey ended in a huge court like room. All over the sudden, he saw the Jinni whom they saw at the time they set their feet in that part of the desert. It was none but Khurkush Majangar. He was seated on a raised chair.

"Now young man have you realized how much power I have got? I'm very angry with you human beings. I will tell you why I'm angry with you.

"Many years ago, there came to live here a tribe of other Jinni's. These were sheikhs who were highly educated. When they came to live in this part of the world. They found my ancestors here. These ancestors felt it okay to welcome these newcomers. However, they were different in habits to us. We felt no mercy for human beings while they felt mercy for them. They came all the way from the land they called Shaam. It was also said that they were servants of Prophet Suleiman bin Daud. When he died, that was when they scattered to different parts of the world.

"Now, why do I hate them? There came a person by name Mohammed. He brought another system of beliefs called Islam. So, these neighbors have been instrumental in spreading this faith. The faith preaches things that we don't agree with. So, they even converted a lot of my tribesmen into this faith. They even work peacefully with human beings. By then my ancestor was in power. I was still young and therefore had not much said. So, even though I was there when they came from Shaam, still I couldn't do anything to stop them from staying here. However, I was very much attracted to another youth of that tribe in many ways. So, I gave him the name of Saahib and he was pleased me to call him by that name. From him I learnt a lot including information of where they came from, that is, Shaam. I also learnt the dates during which King Haroon Rashid and his minister Jaffer Barmaki ruled. This minister was later killed by King Haroon.

"There were many tales including the adventures of Abu Nawas and others. I learned a lot of interesting things from my friend Saahib. It was that I was not happy with the spread of Islam. My friend Saahib did spread Islam. Many of our followers converted to Islam, including my parents. I didn't like the way these foreigners were changing our ways of life.

"So, I organized a revolution and dethroned my parents whom I locked in jail. To this very moment they are still there. I pleaded with Saahib to stop following the teachings of Mohammed and I promised to give him all that he wanted, but he refused saying, 'I'll never exchange the benefits of the afterlife for the earthly benefits. Sayyidna Muhammad (s.a.w.) has brought us all a new light, why should we go back to the old ways that even Allah doesn't like?' That was what he told me. I became very angry.

"So, I told him, 'I give you seven days to decide, you follow my orders or you disobey me. And know that if you choose the second option, I'll kill you.' But he responded in a strong-headed manner, 'Why give me seven days, even if you give me seven minutes, I'll not change my word, and I'll never forsake our prophet Mohammed and follow you an evil Jinni. Do whatever you want to do with me. I'll always follow this new light.' I fumed with anger and immediately ordered all those who believed like Saahib to change their forms and that of a horse. So, they are in that way to this day. But Saahib managed to escape. I was informed later that he was living among you human beings. Now that you've heard enough about me and my fellow Jinni's, I believe you want to know whether your mother is still alive or not."

Khurkush Majangar called out to one of his servants, "Take him to go and visit the old lady whom we captured today. Lock him up with her. Punish them in similar manner."

As he was being taken to where his mother was, they passed through many underground chambers. They came to one chamber. An iron grilled door was opened and he was pushed inside. At first it was totally dark and so he could not see. But after a short moment his eyes became used to the amount of light that was there. At the same time he heard a person sobbing quietly and in pain. He did not know the person yet. Then all over the sudden he felt that he was being pierced with long nails just like what thorns would do to the human skin.

This trend continued for a long time. He attempted to clear things but failed. In the end he could no longer take it. He realized that the Jinni's were at work fulfilling their orders.

"Please have mercy on me, I'm old and cannot manage this punishment," Muntasir heard his mother cry out.

"Mother, is that you, mother, mummy," he called out in the dark.

"Muntasir, is that you my son," his mother responded.

"I've come to rescue you mother, I must rescue you from the hands of these filth, evil creatures," Muntasir said.

"Don't say so, my son, where are you I want to embracing you," Muntasir's mother said.

So, they used their hands to search for each other. When they finally found one another they embraced.

"What bad luck has befallen us my son, we've have been experiencing a lot of terrible things, ooh Allah, hear our cries," said Muntasir's mother amid cries.

"Mother stops crying, we'll find our way out. We're in the hands of the terrible Jinnie whom we met with at the beginning of this pass way. All this land is under his dominion, do you remember him?"

"Yes, I do my son."

"The reason he has captured the two of us is to revenge against human beings for living with his enemy. It is a very long story. May be I shall find time another day to narrate it in full to you. Let's not lose hope. We shall be saved." Muntasir encouraged his mother.

Dear readers, please forgive me whenever Khurkush Majangar mentions the name of Prophet Mohammed without adding (s.a.w.). He had no respect for our Prophet. I hope you understand what I mean. So, let's move on

CHAPTER SIX

*L*ET, S GO BACK TO, where we have left Antar and Saqr when they reached the tree where they met Antar's old friend Farna Bash. As they were waiting for the response of the message Saqr has earlier requested to be sent. It did not take long till the messenger arrived with full report. First and foremost was the message sent to Antar's parents, who were still located in the same mountains? They were still in the same transformed shapes of horses as was Antar. The message began with greeting, "Salaam Saahib", and he was greeted back with "Aleykum Salaam, please enlighten us with how my elders, brothers and sisters are doing. The messenger responded by saying, "Dear friend, don't worry, they are all doing well and were very happy to hear that you are here. They are just worried about your presence here because they do not want you to face any danger or be harmed, and even worse, Khurkhush Majangar's awareness that you are near. Firstly they beseech that you take extra care in this matter and secondly they have said that in a short time, a very fierce worrier from your family will arrive. The one you know and adore very much. And that will only be your cousin Saharzena. She has been commanded to attend to your concerns and needs. Thirdly your parents want you to know that if you have come to avenge Khurkhush Majangar for what he has done to all of you, then they are ready to join you in battle. Even if it means risking their lives or elimination of the whole tribe in this evil land of poverty.

Antar listened quietly and then said, "Well done for sending back such fulfilling good news". He then immediately turned towards His friend Farna Bash and told her, "I did not come here to start a battle. For the outcome of any battle is tough and the price to pay is very high. You can never tell who may lose their lives. It is not in my intention to risk my people's lives for my sake. If I am to battle, then it will only be between Khurkhush Majangar and me. I will not allow anyone to be suicidal for my sake. On the contrary, I will rather be at stake for my masters. So now I will request my master's son to reveal himself before you, so you can get to know and greet him".

(From the beginning of the fourth line, I started to translate from this date 30-5-2015)

42

Saharzena fighting Janjara Mansha

With that said, Antar turned to look at the invisible person on his back and said, "Oh master Saqr, please untie the threads around your head so that my allies and supporters can see and acknowledge you". With obedience Saqr un did the threads of the tail from his forehead, and before everyone Saqr became visible, the most handsome and well body build young man, everyone there were stunned by the good looking of this young man, some said "Oh! God the creator" and other said "Sub'hanallah", and then Anta introduced him to them and said "May I introduce to you my master and my friend Saar, May I ask all of you to give him his respect please" and everyone there of those little people kneel down with their hands on their chest and bow, as well as Queen Farna bash who also bent her head down to give her respect to this young handsome man, and all said "Salaam Master Saqr" and Saqr replied their salaam by also put his hands on his chest and bow to them, suddenly there were hoofs sound heard, and within a short while came such a beautiful white horse, very young and beautiful looking, the horse then stood with her hind legs and snored loudly, and then she walked slowly to where Antar was and start to sniff to each other, and then shake their necks, this is their way of greeting, then Anta said "Greetings my fellow cousin" and the white horse replied "Greetings my uncle son, it is indeed a great pleasure this day for us to meet again after a very long separation my dear cousin" and Anta replied "Yes indeed, even to me it is a great pleasure to see you again Saharzena, my uncle's daughter, you have put pleasure and happiness in y heart by seeing you again after a very long separation time, May I please beg your forgiveness for bothering and calling you this urgent hour, but it is important and necessary" and Saharzena replied "To serve you is not bothering my cousin, but a pleasure, and even if you had bothered me then that will be a cheap bother as to us in our family you a very priceless member cousin Saahib, Our parent has instructed me that I should obey all of your commands without arguing, without questioning, please cousin Saahib, command me and I am all at your service" and then Antar told Saharzena "there is a village somewhere below eastern side of these mountains, that village is very close to Empty quarter, there is where I live now with my Masters, and this figure you see him on my back is my friend and son of my master, and his name is Saqar ibn Fairuz ibn Haddad, there in their village now we have left three people and all are alone, his father who is not in good health and his mother and his grandmother, the evils are trying every now and then to come and harm them but they could not and all because of my presence there, and those are none others but are the army of Khurkhush Majangar, but my fear is that, now I am not there, that place is no longer safe to stay alone by themselves, if Khurkhush Majangar will get information that I am not there now, he can send his evil army and attack my master and his family, I want you this moment Saharzena to go there and give them protection, as you are very well known as warrior and the best fighter in our family" and Saharzena replied "I understood and I obey Oh! My cousin Saahib" and within a second Saharzena open her wings and fly high in the sky.

May I request you my dear reader of this book which contains many adventures, that we should return of where we had left Maalim Mikdad and his companions when the chariot run away with Muntasir mother in it, Abu Muntasir still was in agony and crying like a child for his family, Maalim Mikdad went to help him to sit down, but poor man he could not control himself with such a shock of losing his family in front of his own eyes, and he said "Oh! My God, my poor wife and my son Muntasir what kind of miseries will they face, oh! Allah, I beg you to protect them from all the evils of Jinnis and human beings" Fardhana and Fardhada all the time were with their uncle Abu Muntasir just to give him moral support and to cool him with sweet words and prayers to God, just in a little while Fardhada saw a camel caravan coming their way, and she point it out and said "Uncle Abu Muntasir, there are people on the camels coming this way" when Abu Muntasir heard that there are people coming, he gain strength and wipe out his tears on his face and sat properly and look at those coming caravan, yes it is true there are people on the camels coming this way, and he said "we are not sure about these people, who they are, are they friends or foe? we must take serious precaution on them, but also it could be they also have lost their way and headed this direction of many miseries and evils, but first let us find out the true about them, if they lost caravan then we should warn them to turn back and not to proceed this way of evils, and if it is possible to ask them to help in taking us out of this place" and they all agree to that, When that caravan reached them, they were five people on their camels and two other camels carrying their goods,, They stopped and greet "Assalaam aleykum" and they were replied with "Aleykum salaam" then they asked "Gentlemen, we have lost our way, is this road behind you will lead us to the Empty Quarters village?" and Maalim Mikdad answer them and said "No, this way will lead you to hell, no many others are using this way as it has many evils happenings, and that is the same reason which we have encounter in our journey by using that way and that is why you have seen us abounded all by ourselves and without any help" and then they were explained of all what has happened to them, and the Arabs said "we are sorry to hear of those misfortunes, but now after hearing it we have to change to other direction and avoid going on the same route, and you our brothers have to come with us if you please so, we cannot leave you here all by yourselves after what has happened to you, and may Allah protect those who misfortunes fall upon them" here is then there was hardship to decide, either to follow or not follow them, as up to now there is no any sign if these are good or bad people, but even though, as that place also is not safe, how then they can spend more time in such a place where there are Jinni's and Evils, and in the end they agree to follow those Bedouins with their camels, before they mounted the camels, they heard the sound of the cart wheels coming their way, and when they look at it those it was also still far away, Abu Muntasir said "Maalim Mikdad, that cart and horses they resembles our chariot and horses" and everyone stood with interest to observe it, and Fardhana after observing properly she said "Yes uncle Abu Muntasir, that is our chariot and the horse, but I see in driver on it" then the chariot slow it speed and stopped of where they are, Abu Muntasir was the first one to rush and see in it if there is anybody, and poor Abu Muntasir he was so disappointed when he find that chariot was empty and nobody inside, not his wife not his son Muntasir, he was so broken hearted and drop himself on the chariot step, here is where Fardhana went to cool her uncle and said "please uncle Abu Muntasir, do not lose hope, none of us have any knowledge of why these all misfortunes fall upon us and for what reasons, but to Allah one should always believe in him and hold his rope of hope and never otherwise, please uncle do have faith that your family is still there somewhere and alive, I have faith that there is some good news ahead of us and sooner we will hear it" Abu Muntasir then raise his said and look to Fardhana and said "Yes my dear niece Fardhana, what you have said is true, as there is nothing hard and tough and for better than to maintain patience, as Imam Ali bin Talib said this about the patience, [I will be patience until patience itself know and understand that I am a patience person] these are very wise thoughts, so I too will try my best to be patience, yes Fardhana let us except the will of Allah". And then said to other "As our transportation has come back, then we will use it and travel together until we will get our way which will take us to our destination".

But the real fact is, those Bedouin travelers were not really travelers but they are Queen Farna Bash loyal servants, changed into desert travelers just to guide them out of that place, they were sent them there on behalf of Antar who requested his friend Queen Farna Bash to save and guide those lost guests of his master Fairuz ibn Haddad out of that most evil place, Though Fairuz have no knowledge that there are guests coming for him.

Butterfly people

Now my dear readers, let us go back of where Saharzena was sent to safeguard the Fairuz family, what has happened when he reached there? She flied until she saw that place which Antar has described to her, she went down but not exactly near that house but away distances from the house, just for one reason, to check and see if those or any evil are around the place there, she found the place to be so quiet and no sign of evil around, she decided to remain somewhere there and keep watching, she stayed a little far from the house eating the grass around there. Now it is better to go back of where we have left Antar and Saqar in the Kingdom of Farna Bash, up in the mountains, where they are neighboring with the Kingdom of Khurkhush Majangar on the other side of those mountains. Khurkhush Majangar was in his cave palace, well guarded by his evil Jinnis, and was enjoying very much the crying of tortures which his human beings prisoners were producing during their suffering of tortures, those tortures voices were to him the most entertaining thing and never miss it in any day, that morning when he was enjoying his morning entertainments, came some of his spies and inform him that in these mountains there are strangers arrived but do not know which part of the mountains they have arrived, Khurkhush shout with anger to his spy and said "What kind of Jinni are you? Is there among us Jinnis if he what to know something he cannot? Go now quickly and bring the right information before I take your life right now, GO" Within a split second thy spy disappear and came back to Khurkhush to report, and said "Oh Mighty one, the news I got is that Saharzena is not here in the Kingdom, she must have gone somewhere a short while ago, this is for the first time Saharzena dare without fearing for her life live the place without permission, I have my doubt Oh! Mighty Khurkhush, that there could be a connection of her disappearance with human being somewhere" then Khurkhush Majangar said to himself "Since when you Saharzena to show me you're being ignorance to this extent? There must be something else involved here, Go and summon Janjara Mansha to be here quickly, GO" and the spy left the place, and within a few minutes there was wind of dust entering the palace cave of Khurkhush Majangar, and that dust wind then circle the palace room quickly and turn itself in a huge cobra never to be seen, and then the spoke and said "Mighty Khurkhush summoned Janjara, and Janjara is here to serve you Oh! mighty one, please command me and I obey" and then Khurkhush said to Janjara "Janjara, for long time now you know that Saahib has left us here in our Kingdom and went to live somewhere in the village near the Empty quarters, in a house firm which belongs to one named Fairuz, Saahib is living with this Son of Adam, but the place is well guarded is strong, penetration is difficult there, I want you to go there and find all about who is living in that house of Fairuz, and if it is possible I would like you to snatch anyone you can get in that house but without harming in bring here to me, but for any security reason, you had found that this mission is impossible and could not do anything there as that might put your life in danger, then I want you to abound this mission and came back safe and sound, and I will send another brave and strong servant to accomplish this job, understood Yaa! Janjara Mansha? If you have anything to ask or say then say it or leave this place now and bring me the good news, GO" and Janjara Mansha turn again into a dust wind and disappear from the room.

Now my dear readers, let us go of where we have left Saharzena grazing outside the Fairuz house, but since Saharzena was there watching and guarding the place, if is there any evil happened or will happen?.

CHAPTER SEVEN

(Saharzena challenge Janjara Mansha in fighting)

*F*AIRUZ MOTHER WENT TO COLLECT dry sticks for cooking, and all because her daughter-in-law Ramziya, always after cleaning the whole house, she is the one who cooks, but this morning she wanted to go earlier to and do the cooking and all because her husband Mr. Fairuz was not feeling well as he was suffering with fever, Ramziya wanted to cook milk porridge for him, as well as cook for him soup with bread, this soup is delicious and can give him strength, she went and ask her husband about this day menu, would he prefer these food or he has other suggestion? And then she got that "thank you for the soup but I would prefer if you will cook for me Harris (wheat cooked with chicken soup) as now I feel more better then when I was this morning, yet what about Saqar? Did he not return yet? "and she replied "No, I do not have any information yet about his return, maybe today he went further far distance to fetch the dry tree logs, or he took a rest somewhere and fell asleep, let give him more time, he will be back safe God willing" then the house door was open and enter Saqar grandmother, and she said "do you know what did I saw outside?" and Fairuz was stunned and ask "What did you saw outside mother?" and she said "what I saw and which surprise me is that, in the stable all the camels are there, none of them is missing and only Antar is not there, secondly there is another white horse outside grazing the grass and all by herself and no rider" here then Mr. Fairuz surprisingly said "This means that Saqar did not went to cut the woods today, and he must have taken Antar with him, then where did he go and for what purpose? This is not kind of his habit to go anywhere without informing us, then why today this mystery disappearance? I have my doubts that there must a very important mission which has caused them to leave without informing, but as long as Anta is with him, then fear not as he will be well protected, but let's hope so that that is so. Regarding this second white horse outside grazing, this is what surprise me, but allows me to go myself outside and check her" and Mr., Fairuz though still is weak with fever, he manage to stand and slowly went outside to see that horse without her master, and when he reached a t the house door, yes there was a white horse seen from a little far away, but that white horse when she saw there was a man on the house door, she raise her neck and start shake her head up and down, this action has reminded Mr., Fairuz what Anta has told him about the behavior of horses that if a horse want to call you he do that by raising and lowering his head, Mr. Fairuz then understood that that horse is calling him to go near to her, he then started to move slowly and head toward that horse, The horse was watching Mr. Fairuz's movements when he take his step by step to reach her, and when he reached within remaining steps close to her, Mr, Fairuz said to the horse "Oh! You beautiful strange horse, please make sign to me if you will understand of what I going to ask you, just nod or shake your head on any question I ask you, Did you lost your way? "And the horse shake his head as a sign of "No" then Mr, Fairuz took more step forward till he can touch that horse, and ask "Oh! You Beautiful horse, do you know anything about my son Saqar and my horse Antar?" and the horse nodded with her head as a sign of "Yes" then Mr., Fairuz raise his hands and touch horse chicks and smoothly tendering her, and ask "if then you know something about Antar and Saqar, then that means that you two are acquainted" and here is where that horse replied with humanly language, and said "yes Abu Saqar, we are acquainted" and Mr., Fairuz heard that horse can speak humanly, he then said "Please, if you have come with any message to deliver to me then tell me so cool me and my soul" and before she could replied, they heard horse hoofs sound coming to their direction, and the white horse said to Mr., Fairuz "before I answer to your question, please sir, those horse hoofs are from the chariot of your guest who are coming to visit you, please Sir, go and welcome them as they have come from very far away and experiences many difficult on their way to come here" and then that white horse in details of about those guests who they are and what misfortunes has befallen on the them, and after the long explanation to Mr. Fairuz, the guests were already on their land, with four people inside, but their conditions were worse, as their faces and all their bodies were covered with dust and became un recognizable, and also they were so tired that all their strength were drained away from their bodies, then Abu Saqar called loudly "Yumma! Yumma! Please come all to receive our guests who have come far away" and the house door was opened and two ladies came out to help their unexpected guests, then they were took inside to rest and given water to drink, and after a short rest, Abu Saqar told his family that "These people are our guests, from this day they will remain here with us, they need great care to be looked after, please prepare food for them so they can gain strength, as well as water to wash their bodies" then Fairuz mother said "I will go and milk the animal so to get fresh milk for them to drink" and Ramziya said "I will go to arrange a place for them to rest and sleep and then cooked the food for them, but my dear husband, is it not better for you to go and slaughter one of those small animal for better food for our guests?" and Mr., Fairuz replied "That I will do, and that was a very good suggestion my dear wife, for the guests to give them best of the available food in your house, you better go and do your part of the job and I will play my part role of the job" then Mr. Fairuz came back in the living room of where their guests were resting, but was yet in good health as he was staggering, not walking properly, then one of the guest saw him that he was not walking properly and near to fall, he quickly went and help him to walk and called him "Mr. Fairuz" he was stunned when he hear that that guest know him by his name, and he replied "Yes Sir" while looking at his face, and he find that person still with dust on his face, but seems to be very old person, older than all of those other guests, and the old man said "I know that in the condition I am now you will never recognize me" he was talking with difficult as he was so tired and also hungry, as well as the heat of the desert which was in high degrees, then he said "I am your old friend Maalim Mikdad" and Mr, Fairuz when he knew that among those guests one of them is his old friend and his teacher, he jump with joy and hug him strongly to his body and said "Maalim Mikdad! Is this really you? Oh! my God, I did not recognize you completely, please Sir, do forgive me" Then they sat down and Maalim Mikdad narrate to him all the adventures which begin from their own country of why they have run away there because of that evil Sheikh who want to marry every young of his subject no matter how old is he and how old is she, then he introduce his neighbor Abu Muntasir and his two daughters Fardhada and Fardhana, and then Mr, Fairuz said, "Sub'hanallah, if you did not mentioned to me now that these two young lads are girls, then I would never recognize them with that outfit they wear, I am sure that there is behind it main reason for doing that" then Maalim Mikdad complete his story by telling the remaining of adventures which has befallen on them, and how they have lost two important people the wife and son of Abu Muntasir, and then of those lost Bedouins who came to their risqué and brought them till Maalim Mikdad find the way which led them here, here then Mr. Fairuz turn to Abu Muntasir and said to him "Abu Muntasir, that is a very hardship and bitter fate which has befallen on you, but Abu Muntasir, know that we have not reached the end of living life in this world, life is still ahead of us, yet I believe and have faith that this all fate Allah want us to experience, let us all have no that faith of what has disappear will not appear again, but sometime when we propose to do something for our own good and best, God dispose it, for other reasons we do not know, but could be for our own good and not the worst, let us hope and pray to Allah that this fate will turn better for us and not against us, I believe and have faith that your family will return safely to you Inshaa'Allah, it is true that the evil doers are plenty but also Allah protection is here to protect us, Allah never ignore those who have faith in him" suddenly they heard a horse cry and running of the hoofs from one side to the other, Mr, Fairuz went outside to check of what is going on outside and has left his guests to rest there in the living room, but when he was outside, he could not see anything as there was dust in all places, and poor visibility is all in front of him, and the white horse is not to be seen but his snoring and make sound loudly, and she seem to act mad, Mr, Fairuz decided to enter that cloud of dust just to get more visibility vision of that horse of why she acts strangely, but Mr, Fairuz got his shock of the day of what he saw, as there was a huge snake, very huge with wide body and very big head, and has raised his head with open mouth and tongue in and out, the snake was trying to strike and bite the horse, but that horse was very clever as in every strike the snake tried the horse is dogging it the best tactic, and sometime raise and stand with her hind legs and fight that snake with a loud crying, though that was a very fierce fight between these two animals, but in reality, Mr. Fairuz was in fear, so much fear that if that horse will be killed then what will happen to him and all his people in the house, then with luck the horse forcedly kick that cobra with her front legs on the Cobra's body and then raise again forcedly kick again the Cobra with her from legs until that cobra felt the pain of those kicks and began to lower his head down with lower profile, the agony he is suffering is too much that even to breath was difficult, and then the horse when she got a better chance she circle that cobra and then stood up and with force she kicked the cobra with her front legs on his head, and that was a fatal blow that finished the life of that cobra, and then the horse cry loudly with her head raised up, and then surprisingly that cobra raised his body and open his mouth and strike heavily on the neck of the horse, and that was quite a bite as blood start to come out from that bite, but the horse was clever and she also turn her neck and open her mouth and bite that cobra on his neck too and pull it while her front legs were on top of that cobra body until she cut off the cobra head from his body, after did that she stand up with her hind legs again and cry loudly while her head was directing up in the sky, then it was cum and old the dust start to disappear and visibility return again, Mr, Fairuz then saw clearly of both those animals, the pride horse who has won her war and that dead cobra lying on earth with no head on his body, then the horse slowly came step to step towards where Mr, Fairuz stand, and the sign of that cobra bite pain start to show as she was not moving properly, Mr, then hug her head and kissed her chicks, while he was thanking for showing her bravery fight against that huge evil Cobra, but while touching her lower part of her neck, he felt the wetness, and when he look at his hand there was red blood on all her hand, this gave Mr, Fairuz a shock and said to the horse "Oh! beloved horse, this evil cobra has bitten you and you are bleeding" and the horse replied "I know dear Master, and his teeth are so painful in my body, but have no fear, as he is not an animal as you think, but he is a very brave and tempered Jinni who always turn into Cobra if needed be, he is also one of the loyal personal servant of that evil King of all Jinnis, Khrkhush Majangar, that is the place of where I came from, this evil Cobra was sent to investigate here if I am with you in this place, as they have found out that I have left that Kingdom without warning or asking for permission, also he was command to harm you too, but today was his last day to live, now I want you dear Master, to listen to me careful so I can tell you of who am I and why I am here.

My dear Master, by name I am called Saharzena, Saahib is my cousin, he is alright with your son Saqar, he requested me to be here so give you all protection from the many evils surrounding these area, we all know that if Khurkhush Majangar will find out the I am here of where Saahib came before, he will send his evil servants to harm you or me, as long now as your guests have arrived, please master, go and be concern about their welfare, they need you now, and I will remain here to give you protection, be sure no evil will dare to touch you as long as I am here, until I get another order from Saahib of what to do next, he already received the message I have sent it to him, after I have killed this evil Jinni known as Janjara Mansha" Mr, Fairuz said "But Saharzena, your wounds are bleeding, and the poison will kill you Oh! dear Antar cousin, tell us what should we do to remove that poison in your body so you can survive" then Saharzena replied "Worry not much my Master, it is true I suffer much pain out of that bite, but his teeth contains no poison, as Janjara Mansha is only a Jinni and not a real Cobra, please go to the kitchen and fetch the wooden ash, and I will go and look at some herbs so you will grind them together and paste it on my wound, and I will be alright" and that is exactly what Mr., Fairuz has done to that wound on Saharzena shoulder, then Saharzena explained in details that Saqr is in safe place with Antar and are protected by the friends of Antar (Saahib), and now as she has finished killing Janjara Mansha, then they should wait to experience more evils from Khurkhush Majangar as this will pain him and anger him so much, then she said "My master, now you know all about me and all the information of your son and Saahib, please go and inform your guests that Abu Muntasir family are alive, and is prisoned by Khurkhush Majangar in his palace, but we will do all our efforts and means to get them out and join them together again" then Mr., Fairuz said to Saharzena "thank you so much Oh! you Good horse Saharzena, for sacrificing your life in protecting us from that evil Jinni, and thank you for the best news you gave me regarding the Abu Muntasir family, May God protect you too Oh! Dear one. I also have one request from you, please from now on do not stay far away from our house, you can stay in the stable the same place Antar using it to stay, please Saharzena this is my personal request from you" and Saharzena said "Thank you Master, without doubt I will remain here and sometime there in the stable, because my mission does not allow me to be on one place only"

BACK TO FARNA BASH KINGDOM

Let us now go back of where we have left Antar and Saqar there in the Kingdom of Farna Bash, what has happened there when Saharzena sent her message by crying loudly with her head facing the sky, that was a message sent to Antar to inform him of the killing of Janjara Mansha, these were their own way of those horses Jinnis of how they can communicate, by using their own telepath, and by that time Antar was waiting g for any message coming from Saharzena, as he knows that Khurkush Majangar will send his evil servants there to do evil things, that is why he chose the best of the best fighter in their family and that is none other than Saharzena, because the reason of Anta and Saqar to be there on the mountains meeting Queen Farna Bash and sending message to his members of his family on the other side of the mountain where there is the Kingdom of Khurkhush Majangar, this message was sent so to others should be involved in the plan of how to attack this evil Jinni Khurkhush Majangar and destroy him completely so to rescue those who are prisoner by him, as this Jinni is very wise and clever and it is not easy to remove him from those mountains or free those who are imprisoned by him, only if there is a weak point on that Jinni side, and yet, no one knows what is his weakness.

Antar and still Saqar on his back, when he received that message from Saharzena about the Janjara Mansha killing, he also stood up with his hind legs and cried loudly head up in the sky, and then step down on his four legs and said to all who were there "My brothers and sisters, there is good news, Saharzena has wipe out one of the most stubborn evil servant of khurkhush Majangar, she has killed Janjara Mansha, but the question here now, how can we penetrate in that palace cave of Khurkhush Majangar to rescue those who are still imprisoned by him? that palace cave is well guarded by his special force, the unseen force, here we need a very wise discussion" Queen Farna Bash then said "Saahib, it is true that we have here a very limited time, of how we can save those who are suffering in that cave palace jail, and those are none other but your master guests, my advice to this matter, I think we should delay our actions against Khurkhush Majangar for now and look at the other angle by studying the matter more, we need an inner person who can supply us with more information's, a person who give us more secret regarding that cave palace jail, and especially some information concerning Khurkhush Majangar weaknesses, I still believe that for now we should abound our plan, I am so afraid that instead our plan to be successes should turn into failure" and here is when for the first time Saqar spoke "I completely agree with Queen Farna Bash suggestion, her's is very wise suggestion, I think Yaa Antar, we should go back and sit with the elders and discuss these matters in more wisely way, perhaps in our discussion with them one can get better solution to our problems of how to find a better way of fighting this evil, King of Evils Khurkhush Majangar" then they all agree to postpone their war plan for now until after they will discuss it with their elders at home, and then Antar and Saqar left the Kingdom of Queen Farna Bash and return to their village.

My dear reader, before we left the mountains of both Kingdoms, lets us find out about the conditions of those Prisoners in Khurkhush Majangar jails, those we know them and those we do not know them who they are, in one of the cell hole where prisoners are kept, there was on old man but healthy wise, though Khurkhush Majangar tortures his prisoners, but he does not deny them good food, be it from fruits of fresh meats of differences animals, from camels, cows, goats as well as mountain goats who known as Arabian Tahir, that old man is now for a long in these jails of Khrkhush, what he has done to deserve these torturing punishments?, Please read the following chapter and find out yourself about the life of this old man.

CHAPTER EIGHT

(Sheikh Shammaakh invitation)

IN HIS TIME, SHEIKH SHAMMAAKH was a well known figure in his home town, as he was a very well known among the business men there in his town, he had a very huge farm land, where he has many kind of crops and fruits trees he has planted himself, as he always enjoying agriculture as a hobby as well as an occupation, in his farm land there trees like dates palm, olive trees, Fig trees, water melons plants, as well as vegetables, in summer he always harvesting Dates, water melons, and in winter another seasonal which are producing only during winter. Sheikh Shammaakh had a son, the only son, but unfortunately his wife died a very long time age, he took all the initiative to bring up his son by himself only, he is full name is Shammaakh ibn Khalduwn, he is called Sheikh only because he is a wealthy figure in his home town and very helpful to the others, kind and giver to those who need his help, he has quite a big land of his farm, and Allah has blessed it with what he has grown and planted there.

Sheikh Shammaakh has so many business friends who buy from him his crops products, so many horses carts daily are coming into his farm to pick his products for transportation either to the main city market or to the neighboring countries, he was very generous person and help those who asked for his help, he has built so many tents in his farms, tents for resting, tents for his guests to sleep in with, tents for other functions such as religious or socializing gathering but never for any evil gathering, but of all these tents were used to give shelter to those who are coming from far away with their caravans to buy his crops, so they get a resting place or a place to sleep with, he was so popular in these regions for his low prices in selling his products so the moments he harvest them should be sold quickly, these caravan of buying Sheikh Shammaakh products which are coming in his farm, does not only getting the place to rest and sleep only but also they are provided with all the foods during their stay there, these generosity of Sheikh Shammaakh is some of the reason that Allah always blessed him with profitable business and always more and good plantations of his products always are increasing.

Sheikh Shammaakh son name was sheikh, he took every care of his son, though he did not getting married again after his wife died, but he spent much of his time to look for the welfare of his only son, he provided him with a nanny to look after him and teachers to teach him so he should learn of which are compulsory for making him the most educated child, yet Sheikh Shammaakh wanted his son to learn more about Islamic affairs, so he was looking for the best teacher who can take care of that one main issue, an Islamic teacher, someone told that in a neighboring country there is a very Islamic teaching teacher, this teacher himself has learn abroad, but this teacher also it is not easy to get him excepting every and each student to teach, as he has already many students to teach, as he only go to their home to teach as he has no any teaching classes anywhere, and most of all his students are the sheikhs and landlord children, not because he chose that but for his own security he is forced do, that he should come in their home to teach them,

Then Sheikh Shammaakh got these news about this well known teacher, he wished that this will be the perfect teacher for his son Shaikhan to learn much about Islamic affairs as well as the holly book Qur'an from him, so he sent his message to him on the other side of the border, this message was a special invitation as well as request for the sheikh to come on one of the special night of religious function he does every now, and he will be one of the speaker to his guests, as he invite many of his friends to come for these religious functions, the answer he received is that the teacher has much about Sheikh Shammaakh and his generously to others, so he has accepted Sheikh Shammaakh invitation and agree to come and be one of the speaker on one of these night, as long as the messenger of that invitation will be one of the guest and which he always attend these functions of Sheikh Shammaakh,

Here I would like to point out my dear readers, that this teacher is none other than Maalim Mikdad and his friend the horses and chariot owner, but please bare in your mind my dear reader that this was not that time of Sheikh Misbah ruling but during his uncle ruling who was Sheikh Mbaarak, but as he bare no a child to take his place then after his death the ruling went to his nephew Sheikh Misbah, I hope now my dear reader you have understood the generation difference here.

Now let us remain at that old generation of Sheikh Shammaakh during his nights in his farm land with his guest's friends. When that day of religious night came, all preparation were made to make that function possible and without any obstacles, the servants were very busy to do the cleaning of the tents, places for the guests to sleep for those who will remain there till next day for their journey back home, food and water supply, carpets for the guests to sit on as well as all necessary required things, nothing were missing there in camp, guests started to arrive for this function, part of the Sheikh Shammaakh farm land was in the desert, so all tents were erected there on the desert sand side, Maalim Mikdad and his friend arrived at that night function, and Sheikh Shammaakh went and receive and welcomed them personally, and took them on their selected private tent, to rest until the time of the beginning of that night function,

After the rest of that night, all the guests were gathered on one big tent which will be the function tent, the opening of that night function begin with reciting with some verses from the holly Qur'an, Maalim Mikdad was the main speaker of this night gathering, topic was all about religious matters, and Maalim Mikdad topic for this night he chose to narrate a tale concerning Prophet Joseph (Yusuf) and all about his brothers jealousy on him on why their father show more love and concern on him then others, though this tale of Prophet Joseph is common as it written in some of the holly books, like Bible and Qur'an, but the way Maalim Mikdad narrated this tale of the prophet, one's really enjoying hearing it from him, many invitees have really enjoyed this night and especially the chosen subject of Prophet (Yusuf) Joseph, and after the function some of the invitees returned to their homes and those who came far away from other neighboring countries have to remain and spend their night there with Sheikh Shammaakh as his personal guests, as tomorrow is Friday, a holiday for all Muslims, Sheikh Shammaakh has arranged a big lunch feast there in his farm for those guests who have remained there, as even the Friday prayers will be prayed here in the farm, and in the morning for those who have remained there, woke up and prepare their day having breakfast and then Sheikh Shammaakh took them around his farm land in his horses carts and show them around all his farm, and they really have enjoyed it, they returned to the main tent and sat to chat, among the guests there were three Arabian gentlemen, these gentlemen wear difference clothes then others their dresses were so colorful with some gold thread and stitches around them, they mostly speak classical Arabic, Maalim Mikdad could not denying himself just to look at them, as they were still young and very handsome, here then Sheikh Shammaakh spoke to his guests and said "My dear brothers, I have to thank each and every one of you whom have except my invitation to be here from last night for that religious evening which we all have heard Maalim Mikdad narrating to us the Tales of our Prophet Yusuf (Joseph), and as today is Friday, I request you all to remain here with us and complete this day with Friday prayers and then feast will follow,

Today here we have guests from many difference places who have come to attend last night function, as it is our fore parents tradition that when you guests in your home then you must introduce those guests to one another, so allow my dear one's to introduce you to others, if I will begin on my right hand side here, I have these three brothers who are the princes in their homeland, and they are His Highness Prince Sheikh Nijaad-Nuwr, Sheikh Fat'h -Nuwr and the last one Sheikh Nuwr -alaa Nuwr, these young princes are living somewhere bordering the Empty Quarter desert on the mountains of those area which are known as Moon Mountains, my relation with their family begins many years back, and they always attend here many of the functions I have arranged for many years now, and now for the first time, we have a special guest who is known as Maalim Mikdad you all had the privilege last night him on his prophets stories, and if it was not for my old friend Mr. Khamzah who took all initiative to deliver my request of the invitation to Maalim Mikdad, then maybe Maalim would never have been here thanks should be to you Mr. Khamzah, to speak the truth, my invitation to him not only just to narrate in our majlis but also I had personal request to ask him, so Maalim Mikdad I take this opportunity in front of all these people to ask and beg you to take my son Sheikhan and teach him the Holly book Qur'an and many of our Islamic religious affairs, Maalim Mikdad, like you had except my invitation to attend last night function, I request further more from you to except my son as your student and teach him of what compulsory needed to learn about our faith Islam, you will do a great favor to my son Sheikhan to be educated Islamic affairs, Maalim Mikdad, this is only a request from to you and not a forced burden I throw on you, if it is possible I will be most thankful person in my life"

And then Maalim Mikdad replied Sheikh Shammaakh and said "Thank you so much Sheikh Shammaakh, but first allow me to thank Allah for his kindness to make this gathering from yesterday to be possible, and to allow us people of difference races and tribes be here in reciting from his holly book what he has asked us to learn from it, gain and understand that holly book, and we did recite from it and it is in my hope that others who were here from yesterday and us who remained have gained from that book teaching, these arrangement though were prepared by us human but in fact it is Allah preparation that he wanted us to be and teach other of what we have learned from his teaching, so to have faith in Allah that he is here and exist and never believe otherwise, if Allah would not like this gathering to be then it would never have been possible for us to be here, but it has been arranged, it has been possible for people to come from many parts of differences regions to come here and it has been done perfectly from yesterday till the moments of where I stand and speak. Sheikh Shammaakh, when a gentleman asked another noble gentleman a favor it is a shame to deny his request, this is our traditions and culture which we learned from our parents, no matter how difficult or hard the request is, as that hardness does not over weight that respect and love you have within your heart of that requester friend, I personally respect you from that day I have received your invitation through my friend Mr. Khamzah to attend this gathering, I believe I too have the opportunity to meet you and others and make new friends, and I did make friends here from yesterday, and you among the best of a friend I have gained here, as Sheikh Shammaakh, you are an example of a gentleman among the gentlemen, and if you were not then in this place we would never meet those people among the high class people excepting your invitations to be here, we saw here Tribes Sheikhs from the low land and those from the higher mountains were here, Princes as well as scholars and clerics, all have attend here, this is to me proof enough that what a noble person you are, and for that, I have come to agreement to except your son Sheikhan as my student, I will put all my efforts to make him learn and earn the best of my teaching so for him to be one of well educated student, but there is one major problem with me, that I cannot accommodate him in my house, as I am not yet married and living all by myself, your son need more company of younger people of his own generation to be and live with, he need more parental care and not only teaching, and I am not yet matured in that category, if you will arrange for him to be and stay with someone else who has a family then I have no objection to take him as my student, now after I have thank Allah, and answered you on your request, I take this opportunity on behalf of myself and on behalf of us here whom you have invited and gave us your best hospitality with your brotherly atmosphere, and the best place to stay and enjoyed our time here, and above of all Sheikh Shammaakh your love and concern on each of us, I say thank you Sheikh, thank for yesterday and for today and thank in advance for your tomorrow" and then Maalim Mikdad went and sit back, and here is where Mr. Khamzah request permission to speak, and permission was granted for him, and he said "Maalim Mikdad, I as a close friend to Sheikh Shammaakh, I will take full responsibility to open my house door and my family to allow Sheikhan to live with us in our house during all that time you need to teach him until that day you say enough, yet, the final decision is in the hand of Sheikh Shammaakh, if he allow his son to be living with us then me and my family have no objection at all to take him

living with us" Sheikh Shammaakh was so much pleased and happy on that
decision of his friend Mr. Khamzah, then Sheikh Shammaakh was so pleased
and so happy for Maalim Mikdad to except his son Sheikhan to be one of his
student, he immediately called one of his servant and told him to come closer
to him, and then he spoke softly in that servant ear and asked him to leave.

And when the noon time came they were ready for the Friday prayers which
Maalim Mikdad will be the Imam (Leading the prayer), Maalim Mikdad
preach that Friday prayer and lead all the people who are there in that Friday
prayer, while all servants were preparing sufra (White sheet for eating on it on
the floor) for the feast, and everybody after the prayer went to the other tent
where the feast will be eaten, and what a feast, Sub'hanallah, many kind of
foods were there, rice, biryani, pilau, tandoori chicken and bread, many kind
of fresh fruits, fresh juices and on top of that fuala of coffee with dates, figgs,
and other dry fruits, and after the feast the guests were ready to leave the camp
and return to their homeland,

And here is where Prince Nijaad-Nuwr of Moon mountains Kingdom
got his chance to face and talk with Maalim Mikdad, and he said to Maalim
Mikdad "Maalim Mikdad, it is a pleasure and a great honor to meet you for the
first time my dear Sir, your higher knowledge of Islamic education is like a light
in the heart, as we who have earn a very limited in this field of education so
when we get that chance like this one here, we regard that chance like getting
one food grain and added it in your bag, with no doubt Maalim Mikdad allow
me to thank you personal on my behalf and on behalf of my two brothers, for
this opportunity of us hearing you how much knowledge you have obtained,
one can judge you just in your preaching yesterday when you narrate that
Tale of Prophet (Yusuf) Joseph, we understood how big this ocean is in your
mind, we wished that even for a few days if you could also pay us a visit in
our homeland on the Kingdom of Moon mountains, which is just two days
journey from here, our will people will benefit more and understand much of
our faith Islam, please sir do find some time and days in future to visit us, your
invitation to our Kingdom is open Maalim Mikdad, any day any time you are
welcome to visit us, if for any reason you have decided to pay us a visit, then
there will be no problem for you to find someone in informing us your visit"
then Prince Nijaad took from his younger brother Prince Fat'h-Nuwr a cage,
and said to Maalim Mikdad "Maalim Mikdad, in this cage there are seven
pigeons, these are my couriers, in their legs each, there is silver chamber so to
put your written message and then allow him to fly free, and the pigeon will
deliver that message to our Kingdom without any problem, I am talking about

sending your message just for your visit to us, No Sir! But I am talking for any need you require from us; just send your message to us in one of these pigeon, believe that from this day we have a build a brotherly bridge between us, forever to remain" and then Maalim Mikdad said to Prince Nijaad "Thank you so much Your Highness, my many thanks should be to you all three brothers for your kind invitation to me to visit your Kingdom, that will be a great honor, and God willing if that day will come and I am able to travel, then know that for sure I will pay you a visit to your Kingdom of Moon Mountains" and then Prince Nuwr alaa Nuwr had an chance to speak to Maalim Mikdad, and said "Sir, Maalim Mikdad, I request you please to accept this small gift form us three brothers as a key of opening a new chapter of our relation here today, just for you to accept our friendship and built this brotherly bridge between us and you, is quite a huge gift and can never be replaced even with bags full of diamonds and gold, and all because wealth cannot buy friendship and love of someone, wealth can of course buy something or many things only, but true friendship, love and faithfulness and fairness can get you a good friend without buying him, and that we have find it from you Maalim Mikdad when you agree to pay a visit to our Kingdom and our people in a near or any future time, please Sir, do not deny to accept this small gift as a token of our newly built friendship relation" then Maalim Mikdad, raise his hand and just touch that covered unseen gift which was carried by four healthy servants, as a proof of accepting that gift, then Maalim Mikdad said "I swear to Allah, my young friends, that this is more than too much, in the beginning of us knowing one another was quite a great gift, enough to remain forever in our whole lives, there was no need for such a big heavy burden gift, I found myself now I am in debt with you and I do not know when I Mikdad will be able to repay you with such kind of gift" then Prince Fat'h-Nuwr replied "Mali Mikdad, between us there is no debts and payments, if there is payment then the payer is the one who took a loan, but Sir, you did not take any loan from us, only your good will and your knowledge of education of how you have maintained high standard of Islamic affairs knowledge which many of us need to learn from it, that is a bright light which can brighten a dark heart, we only seek from you Sir, that please help us and our people to give us more of your undimmed light into our hearts too" and then Maalim Mikdad thanks these three gentlemen for their kindness and for their friends hipness, and then bid each other farewell by hugging and kissing on each other chicks.

Sheikh Shammaakh has instructed his servants to make sure that all the gifts of these two very important friends, Maalim Mikdad and Mr. Khamzah to be loaded on an extra horse cart and be taken with them in their journey back to their homeland, he then with a young un matured boy with him, he then said to Maalim Mikdad "Maalim Mikdad, I am so obliged to thank you for excepting my request of taking my son as one of your student in teaching him of what I wanted him to learn, and you did turn me off but you raise your hand and keep it on your chest as saying yes, though a small tackle was there but the tackle was solved by my friend Mr. Khumzah, Maalim Mikdad you are a noble gentleman among the nobles in your deeds and your habit, my thanks should go to Allah, for making your journey to be here and for us to built this boundary strong wall of our friendship never to be broken or allowed it to fall, this wall is the foundation for us to also built a stronger fort to remain forever as a sign of goodwill and our friendship, that fort which will never give any chance any of our enemies to penetrate inside it, yet this wall to needs more solid materials to make it survive to the future, and those materials are, faith, understanding, sacrifice, patience, struggle and most of all great love, these are the mostly needed building materials to make this wall of our friendship to remain strong and forever. Those who would not like to see us as good friends will raise among others to make sure that this wall should fall and never to remain, just of no any good reason but for their jealousy and hate rage, Maalim Mikdad, let us be alert and strong to safe guard this wall so to remain and not to fall by their very mean reasons.

Maalim Mikdad, lastly allow me to remind you that my son Sheikhan is the only child I have, and to me he reminds me of his late mother, she has left this child to me and it is my responsible for me to see the Sheikhan get all the necessary education in his life and what he deserve so to accomplish the wish of my dear wife, Today I put this child into you two responsibility, you and my friend Mr. Khumzah, as also your child not only mine, please take good care of him, and feel him as I feel him, and if he cross his boundary then punish him too as he deserve it, he needs to learn from you a better and a right direction of how to live his life either we are alive or dead, he need to learn more in respecting others so he too can earn his respect from others, he need to learn of how to chose between the forbidden and the excepting of what Allah has taught us from his holly books, because in reality he is half orphan and as long as he is not in my care and in your care than he is completely as full orphan, but you two are also hi parents and from you two I know and have full faith that he will earn his protection from you, I have no any doubt in your care, as Mr. Khamzah has said here that his and his family are all his from now, now, I give you my son and put him in your care, please decorate him with honor and respect so he can also learn of how to honor and respect others, give him of what you have and he has no right to demand of what I use to give him, he should eat and sleep of where your family eat and sleep Mr. Khamzah and otherwise, he should work as you do and no all the time servants to work for him" and then Sheikh Shammaakh took the right hand of his son Sheikh and put on between two hands of his friends Maalim Mikdad and Mr. Khamzah, then he produce two bags full of money (Dirham's and Dinars) and gave each of the bag to each of his two friends "please my dear sirs, let it be accounted that I buy favors from you but I take care of what is necessary to make the wheel life turn and never to stop, this is compulsory need, we all know, and if there is need for more expenditures, please do not hesitate to inform me, and every month you will both will receive the same for Sheikhan welfare. Lastly, there is life but also there is death for all of us, either on me or on you two, let be understood that Sheikh has his own home to live, as well as nanny to take care for him, that nanny who has promise me that she will live all her life to care for Sheikhan, she is a loving, honest, kind and like mother to Sheikhan, and she has requested that if she will die to be buried here in on this land, and I have excepted her request, now, I have no further talking to say but I beg you two noble friends to pardon and forgive me if I have said anything wrong or if my tongue have slipped, but do not take with you of what that I have coursed to hurt your feelings but take out here and now even if you to vomiting it on my face, I will never have any grudges against it but will be pleased that you have left here with clean hearts.

I have said and said much, and even did not gave you any chance so speak, I beg your pardon for that but before we depart one another here now, if for any reason lace among you has anything to say then say it now, but do not leave this place and there is a heavy burden within your heart coursed by me or anyone among us here, as this is the right time to clean our hearts" and as there were no one who said anything, Sheikh Shammaakh then signed to his farm Forman, and here came a horse cart full of many items as gift from him to his friends, Maalim Mikdad and Mr. Khamzah, some fruits from his farm, some chickens as well as other gifts, and he said "please except from these few gifts for both of you to remind you of what this farm does produce, please sirs, I only need your expectation and that will please me most, the driver of this cart will follow you to your hometown and after rest will return by himself, have no worry on him as he is trained to the" Then Maalim Mikdad hold both hands of Sheikh Shammaakh and said "My dear Sheikh Shammaakh, I speak now and Allah is my witness, that I will put all my efforts to teach Sheikh and get him the best of education so for him to be the best of the best, I ask Allah to give longer life and good health so to fulfill my promise I gave you now" and then Mr. Khamzah also gave his word to Sheikh Shammaakh, and said "My dear friend Sheikh Shammaakh, I promise you now and Allah be my witness, that Sheikh will stay with us in our house with my family with all better and all good, and he will be a son to me as he is to you, for that have no fear or doubts, may Allah give us all longer life that we shall meet again god willing in good health, and Insha'Allah you will be mostly please with the teaching results of Maalim Mikdad of which Sheikh is going to seek it from him, know this, that I have no boy in my house but only a daughter who she is the same age of Sheikhan, from this day there will be another man in my house and my daughter has got a brother to look after her, I will be less of giving thanks if I will not thank you Sheikh Shammaakh for all of what you have giving us, I am not talking about the things but about the hospitality, the love, the care, the concern from you personally and all who were serving you, May Allah protect you and give you longer healthy life and for us to meet again and again, and allow us to live Sheikh Shammaakh, as we do not say good bye but we say farewell oh! Good friend of ours" and then they hugged and kissing and left Sheikh Shammaakh and his son bidding farewell to one another, and Sheikh said to his son "My son Sheikhan, bear in mind and know that from this moment these two gentlemen now are your parents, respect them more than you did to me, love them more than you love me, obey them more than you obeyed me, if you guard your language and respect to others, they will do the same to you, learn with ability and put all your efforts in your education to know and understand the knowledge of our faith and of other important subjects, live with them with good manners and in return they will do the same to you. I have all the faith in you Sheikh that you will successes to earn a better knowledge for yourself, I know that you will safeguard my advice to you, and then Sheikhan replied his father, and said "Yes my dear father, your advice will remain as a treasure in my mind, with all my life I will safeguard this advice within me, I ask you please father, just calm down and have no fear or any doubts on me, your son is going to earn a better knowledge and will come back with it, that is for sure, I promise you dear father, only give me your blessings and pray for my success" and Sheikh replied "My prayers and my blessing are with you my son, always" then they hugged and Sheikhan climb the horse chariot, and that caravan left the farm heading to their hometown, with them they took Sheikhan.

My dear reader, though you may find that I have taken much longer time and space to write much about Sheikh Shammaakh, sometime it is for more entertaining, or for better understanding, for me, it is to make you read this book and enjoy it in every page of it and never feel bored, to me it was necessary to go back to that generation of where this sheikh how he used to live. Please dear reader, be patience and learn more about this sheikh, as there are more to come concerning him and his life and particularly of how the Arabs of Empty quarters they used to live.

The caravan of Maalim Mikdad and Mr. Khamzah has arrived safely in their hometown, Sheikhan went to live with Mr. Khamzah, and so Maalim Mikdad will daily come here to teach him.

Let us now continue to follow up the adventures of Sheikh Shammaakh of how he became a prisoner of Khurkhush Majangar, but before that let us go back to this generation to Mr. Fairuz house with his guests and what has happened there now.

CHAPTER NINE

(Saqr and Antar returned home)

IT WAS IN THE AFTERNOON, when Anta and Saar landed on the mountain a bit far away from their home, just to avoid be seen by others so their secret should remain a secret, they head to their home unseen by others, and when they reach home they find everything were normal here, Saharzena knew that Anta and his master are returning, and when she saw them they are coming it where she stands on here hind legs and cry loudly that horse cry, those who were inside the house heard that cry, Mr. Fairuz said "what is wrong with horse, this cry is not normal there must be something there, let me go and check outside" when he was outside he saw her still standing on her hind legs and less crying, but when she saw her master Mr. Fairuz, she started to shake her head left to right as well as up and down, Mr. Fairuz move slowly to Saharzena and when he reached her he asked in his lower voice "Saharzena, is everything all right? I found you at not normal way" and Saharzena then replied "yes master, I am not, but even you should be the same, and all because even those in the house will be like me more active" and Mr. Fairuz inquired more information from her "can you please be more specify about these changing and activity please?" and Saharzena answered "those are not evil or sad changing master, but they are changing full of joy and happiness" and then she stopped speaking and turn her head to look at those far away trees and said "look master under those tree there who is coming" and Mr. Fairuz turned his head to look and saw that there is a horse coming and a rider on it. But after a moment he recognized them as Antar and Saar, Mr. Fairuz then was the first to show joy and happiness of those changing like Saharzena has predicted, he called "Saqr! Saqr! My son" and then he look up in sky and raise his both hands and thank his God, and said "Thank you so much Oh! Allah" and then his runnel after them and half the way, and Saqr were calling his Father "Yubba! Yubba! (Father! Father!)" And when they were close enough, they hugged each other with joy and kissing each other much and more much,

That night the house was full of happiness and joy, and Mr. Fairuz went and slaughter one of his animal as elm for the return of his son whom he did not know where he went and why, then Mr. Fairuz introduce his guests to his son said "My dear brothers and daughters, this is Saqr, my only son" and then he introduced individually each of them to his son Saqr, then Saqr said to his father "Yubba, thank you so much for introducing to me your guests, I am honor and happy to have them in our house" then he took his father aside and talk with him "allow me to explain to you of why me and Antar sudden disappearance without warning, it was necessary to do that, as we also took part to go somewhere of where we can get some information concerning our guests.

From Antar, I have all the information regarding my uncle family disappearance, that was the main reason that we have to go somewhere in that mountain kingdom of where some of Antar's friend live as well as the other side of that mountain is where Khurkhush Majangar live, I am so sorry father that I had to live immediately without your permission or even informing you of where I went, but there are time when one cannot do that if it is beyond limit, we went to discuss the way of how we can save and get them out your family my dear uncle Abu Muntasir, but unfortunately I have to say that the situation there was so tough and impossible, as the place is well guarded by Jinni's, at the end we came to conclusion of returning here home and discuss these matters with you our elders, maybe will find any solution of some way of how we can create an army of our own and go fight Khurkhush Majangar 's army, maybe from you elders of wisdom you may have some better idea of how we can help and save Abu Muntasir's family, Yes my dear sir, like you too, I believe that Allah strength is more powerful than any other, but these strength are not somewhere where can go and get them, but only Allah himself he can share them with us if he wanted to be, and if he say BE for sure it will BE, by saying this, it does not mean that I do not depend or have faith with Allah, NO! that is not my intention, but what I believe is that I prayed and begged to him to give us any way of how to help and save those who are in the hands of evil one's, and give patience those who are in the hands of Khurkhush Majangar" then Mr. Fairuz said "yes, I understood you very well my son Saqr, and what you have said is perfect, as there is no one who command Allah, but Allah is the one who can command us, the will of give and not to give is his and not ours, wither he will answer now or after many years that prayer we asked him grant us, is his will, but for sure he will answer as he promised us that, ASK FROM ME AND I WILL GRANT YOUR WISH, Thanks should go to God, for he has answered of our demands and requests in our lives, he has answered of ours and of those before us, those who have faith in him and those who did not have faith in him but believing in something else other than God, yet he gave and give and will never stop to give,

Though we have to know that not all faiths are excepted by God, he has mentioned in his holly book the Qur'an, that the only faith to God is Islam, no other faiths are regarded as religious to God, and God mentioned in his holly book Qur'an that Muhammad is the last of God messenger and what he has come to teach us should be excepted as God's teaching and not otherwise, but we human being are very stubborn and argumentative, it is not easy for all of us to believe of what we are told, those who have other faiths before us believe in what their fore parents believe in their faiths and their messengers and not other, and that worshiping idols and statues is wrong and forbidden, that is to follow to wrong path and go astray, though you may explained to them with proof, they will never believe in that, and for those who agree and have faith in believing what the last messenger has said, are the winner and are walking on the right path, that straight path which will led to heaven.

Let us not be disappointment, but let us hold that rope of Allah's faith, Insha'Allah that day is not far where all our prayers and begging's from Allah will be granted as well" this conversation was between Saqr and his father only and nobody else, but after this conversation, Mr. Fairuz told his son "Saqr my son, your uncle Abu Muntasir though he is trying hard not to show his inner pain and agonies, but within him he is suffering a lot, go my son to him and give this encouraging news, maybe it will release his pain and agonies in his mind and heart and will give him relief, Go my son" and Saqr said "As you wish Yubba, but to I will prefer that we all sit together and talk about what we had decided up there on the mountain Kingdom, as where there are many and elders, one can learn a wisdom or two, better will never leave empty hand" and Mr.Faruz said to his son "it is true of what you have said my son, a sitting together between us all, men on one side and women the other, no doubt that some better and wise idea may be born in one's mind, let us call for a sit down now to discuss of how we can conquer a war with Khurkhush Majangar and save our people"

Now my dear reader let us go back a little when Antar and Saqr have arrived a few hours ago, Mr. Fairuz when he saw his son has come back with Antar, he rushed to them, but what about Antar? What he has done? Let us find out now. Saharzena was in the stable running from one side to the other for the joy of her cousin returning safely with Master Saqr, and when Anta reached the stable door, he stands with his hind legs and cry loudly, and so Saharzena did the same, they stands together and cry loudly as a sign of joy and happiness by seeing each other again, then they came close to each other and smelling each other nose, and then they scratch each other's neck by their teeth. These are the attitudes of the horses when they met as showing sign of happiness and joy to each other, then Anta in their own language said to Saharzena "Oh! My dear cousin, Thank you so much for your bravely by destroying that evil Janjara Mansha, the wounds on your neck prove as sign enough that there was a very tough fight, though Janjara Mansha wanted to accomplish his mission by killing or taking prisoners all who are in our master's house, but by your bravely you have conquered the war, thank you so much Saharzena, and also Queen Farna Bash congratulate you on your victory" and then Saharzena replied her cousin and said "Oh! my dear cousin Saahib, you are the only friend and cousin who always be with me, since our childhood we are together, even before our transformation into these forms, of being turned into these animal shapes by Khurkhush Majangar, your love and your protection was always there when I need it, and I cannot repay you of what you have given me in my whole life, I will always serve you till my last breath, dear cousin Saahib, it is our fate that since that day Khurkhush Majangar when he got angry, turned us all with our parents into these forms of horses, this is our punishments from him, but we will not all our lives as animals, the day will come and we will turn back into our original forms, and Insha'Allah, by the will God, Khurkhush Majangar will be destroy and no more another evil will take his palace, he is the first and will remain the last.

God create this world for us all the world nations to live together in peace and harmony and without discrimination or oppression from one nation to another, between citizens to other citizens, between neighbor and another neighbor, this world should not be a place to create enemy and foe between us people, but we should believe in friendship and create a friendship so to understand between us and make this world a safe place to be and live, let us all forgets about our skin color, our languages, our religious faiths, but let us help one another in respecting each other and no matter in what we believe but as a human beings that this world is for all of us, no matter how big or small our nations are, let us wipe out all those who use their power force to destroy those who are weak and poor and maintain no powerful force, let us respect God for what he has given us, the most spacious earth land for us all to live on till that day we have to leave this land for the better place to be and to live, The heaven. This is my dream of what kind of a world I wished we all should live, Saharzena" then Saharzena replied "your dream are so sweet dear cousin Saahib, Oh! God, please allow that world to really happen so we can live with harmony and peace and loving each other, please God, gives us longer life so to witness that kind of world if you will allow it to be, but dear Saahib, you did not explained to me of what you all have decided regarding of our plan to attack" Anta replied her and said "It is true that I did not explain to you about the plan, and all because of the pain and suffering we all are suffering from the torturing we are daily experiencing from Khurkhush Majangar and his evil army. Our last decision we all agree that we should not rush as we are not strong enough to fight Khurkhush and his army, we decided to come back here and seek the advice and opinion of others, such these new arrived elders whom among them their loved ones are also prisoner in Khurkhush jail, and secondly we did not yet get any information regarding the weakness point of Khurkhush Majangar, so we can use that weakness as a weapon to destroy him, so here we are back and hope to get any wise opinion from these elders, as they said, where there are elders you will always get a wise builder" then Saharzena said "I remember once I heard from our parents during their conversations that Khurkhush Majangar does not like small creatures such as insects, lizards, spiders, scorpions and others, he is afraid of these creatures and hate them so much, he cannot bear their presence anywhere, and most of white he is afraid of is that large spider none as lion spider, if in any place there these kind of spiders, then Khurkhush will never go to that place at all" and here is where an idea came into Antar mind, and said "Saharzena! My dear cousin, you have mentioned very important issue here now, but it is better to inform these good news to our young master Saqr so to tell others, maybe this will be one of the right solution to use as weapon against Khurkhush Majangar" then Saharzena said "I think that is good idea, we better call young master Saqr now and give him this news" and Saqr agree and sent his calling to Saqr which he already taught him, that if he hear him calling with that kind of noise, then he should come quickly, and then Anta sent his message by making that noise.

Inside the house, they have already sit down together for discussion when Saqr heard Antar's calling, he excused himself from others and rushed outside and went to the stable to listen to Antar regarding his urgent calling, and as usual when he reached to them, he greeted them and they returned his greetings, and Saqar slowly touched their heads while listen to why he was called, and Antar gave him that information from what Saharzena has remembered, Saqr said "This is very useful information my dears, Saharzena you have done very well, may Allah blessed you, I will go and tell others about these information, please allow me, it is true what our ancestors have said that [every stronger has his weakness]" and Saqr rushed inside to tell others about the news he has received,

Inside all the others were there sitting at their places as he left them, and then Mr. Fairuz open the meeting by explaining to them of what they are planning to do to save Abu Muntasir's family, and he added "I have to inform you all that, the family of Abu Muntasir is still alive, though it has been hide by Khurkhush Majangar in his cave prison, this is what the latest I have heard from Saqar after his coming back from his trip from those mountains of his horse Antar friends, who have informed him of this news" here is where Abu Muntasir raise his hands up and thank his Allah for such hopeful news of knowing his family is still alive, he said [Alhumdulillah] and all others shown happiness and thanks Allah for his blessing of saving Abu Muntasir though they are still under the captivity of Khurkhush Majangar, and everyone congratulate Abu Muntasir for this great news, and within a minute Saqar enter side with another great news, and he told others there still in their meeting sitting "My parents and my family, just within a short time when I was outside attending the horses, Saharzena has informed me something very useful and important, the news is about Khurkhush Majangar, I understand from those news that Khurkhush is afraid of little creatures, he does not like spiders, lizards, Scorpions and others poisoned creatures, he cannot stand them wherever they are, to me this is a very good point of finding the way of how to use these kind of creatures in attacking Khurkhush" Mr. Fairuz then tell others "I have one point to clear to you all, this is very important for you to know as long as you are living here with us now, just now Saqar mentioned the name of Saharzena, Saharzena is the name of that white horse outside and Anta is the name of the other horse, they are cousins, Antar and Saharzena are not really animals, but turn into animals by the power of that evil Jinni Khurkhush, in reality they are also jinnis, but not evil jinnis, their parents except Islam faith in where they live up there in the mountains of where Khurkhush Majangar live, this action of becoming Muslims has angered

Khurkhush and to punish them for their action turn the whole of their families into animals and mostly horses, they have run away from Khurkhush Majangar domination and came down here to live with us, I have to tell you this facts that I do not want to rise doubts in your mind of we get information's or how we could travel as far as!long journey and came back soon, Antar and Saharzena are flying horses as well as they can speak humanly but only to me and Saqar, and this is how Saqar how he got this information just now from Saharzena, I hope now I made myself and the situation very clear "and Mr., Fairuz gave them the story of how Antar came there and why he runaway from Khurkhush Kingdom, and also how Saharzena was sent by Antar here to stay guard in protecting them during Antar absent and how Saharzena fight that big fight of life or death with Janjara Mansha and won the fight, here then everyone filled safe and courage for being protected by these two kind friends, here is where Maalim Mikdad said "this is a very important news Saharzena has deliver, and it is a very good point to sit down and discuss it, as I see it, this is quite an effective to use in fighting Khurkhush Majangar, but the question is how to use these weapons?" Abu Muntasir then asked "surpose there will be a war to fight this evil Jinni up there in his Kingdom, how can we who cannot fly or climb those mountain of Khrkhush Kingdom join hand in hand to fight him?" Saqar replied Abu Muntasir question and said "Uncle, do not worry regarding how would we be there, all those who can fight using any weapon will be there inshaalla" and Maalim Mikdad added "but let us not forget that we are not going to fight with human, they are difference creation, they are Jinnis" Abu Muntasir said "it is true of what you had said Maalim Mikdad, those Jinnis are quite difference with us, there fighting power, there shapes are quite difference with us, but these all Jinnis were human slaves some generation back, and up to this time they some of them are still human slaves, used to do evil thing, Prophet Solomon was there king and has command them by the power given to him by God, I have faith that Allah will be on our side to give us protection or find a way for us to fight and win this war against these evil Jinnis, let us not put fear and be weak in our hearts, let us be brave and think of winning only, our parent has told us in their wisdom thoughts [If you have decided then go ahead and put your faith in Allah] Faa idhaa azamta fatawakkal alaa Llah" here is where Saqar point out another important issue and said "Forgive me my elders, but up to this minute we did not find the solution of how we can enter in that cave where our relatives have been prisoner?"

Dear readers please let us now stopped at this chapter and open other which concern other issues about TALES FROM ARABIAN AND PERSIAN DESERTS.

Zarza speaking to the animals

CHAPTER TEN

(Zarza bint Aarish meets with Human beings)

NOW PLEASE DEAR READER, LET us go back to that time of where Sheikh Shammakh where he had invited friends in his farm for the religious evening gathering, the night of where Maalim Mikdad preaches to gathering invited friends of Sheikh Shammakh.

In their kingdom, these Jinni's when they want to come down to where human live, they have to seek permission from their King, this does not concern all created Jinni's but only those who are living in those mountains of where Khurkhush Majangar rules, because Zarza is among those who ruled by Khurkhush Majangar in his mountain Kingdom, none among his subject or among servants are allowed to leave the Kingdom and come down of where human are living without obtaining permission from him, and if Khurkhusha Majangar permit any one of his subject, then he or she must abide with his rule, that if he want to come down to where human being are living then he should come down before sundown and he must return before sunrise or viceverser.

That particular day was the day Zarza is allowed to live the mountain and come to visit where human is living, when she went to Khurkhush Majangar to bid farewell that today is her day to come down, Khurkhush Majangar asked her by saying, "Zarza, till when you will remain unmarried again? you are still young and very beautiful and very obeying Jinni, but it does pain that in the whole of my Kingdom you could not find a replacement of another male Jinni who could take the place of your former husband after his death, what has happened to your husband was a matter of a duty to his King, he died to protect the honor of this Kingdom, he did sacrifice himself for protecting me, he was a very good fighter and a perfect guard, but unfortunately sometime in a matter of a challenge, one become very clever and powerful then the other, and your husband has lost in that challenge of fighting for higher position in his duty against other, as you know Zarza, that in my ruling if I would like to promote any of my guard, he must accept the challenge of facing his opponent in a fighting, the winner can take the position, and that is exactly what has happened, and your husband lose in that fight and has been killed, though that winner did came to you and asked your hand in marriage, but you had refuse him, now Zarza since that time, so many years has passed away and you are still alone and do not want to remarry anyone else again, up to when Zarza you will remain in this kind of life? Please Zarza, make another decision and get married"

Zarza then replied Khurkhush and said "Oh! King Khurkhush, please I ask you, do not eat your heart for my sake, if in all this your Kingdom there is no one man who has attracted me, then take this words as a promise to you that the earth is wide enough and on this planet earth there are billions of other living creatures not only here in your Kingdom. When the right time will come for sure I will find that man of my love and I will never return here in this Kingdom without him, and know that, there is nothing which can stop me to get of what I want, not even you y6ou your Majesty Khurkhush Majangar, remember this Zarza Aarish you are talking too, and without fearing you, as I am not like other, and when Zarza speaks, her words will never fall down, when Zarza gives her words those never changes but remain as they were told, now I promise you that from this night of where I am leaving here to go down to earth and seek of what I am seeking, if I will not get it this night, then know that Zarza Aarish will never come back to this Kingdom until I will get of what I am looking for, this I promise you, now choice is yours, either you deny me not to go to earth or either you allow me to go so I can do of what I have promised you of what I will do"

Khurkhush replied back and said "I will not stop you Zarza Aarish, as for so many years you have suffered in pain and agony within you for losing your loving husband, if you will get of what you were looking for, then just give me my respect by telling me who is he and from which Kingdom he is coming from, if I will be pleased with him then I will allow you to marry him" then Zarza ask Khurkhush in tactic way "anyone of whom I want, your Majesty?" Khurkush answer "yes anyone, but I have to know and be satisfied with him too" then Zarza said "I have accepted your condition your Majesty as word of honor from you, where there is a will there is a way" then Zarza bid farewell to her King and fly away into atmosphere.

Zarza fly high that night, please herself to enjoy the weather and the beauty of that night, she passes many stars of differences size, but she could not fly high above and beyond the clouds limit, as Allah kept so many angels as guards to prevent any evil not to penetrate beyond the limit line, though was an evil Jinni, but has faith of her own, as she know nothing of religious so she do not perform any praying, Zarza when she got of what she want of circling the atmosphere of the millions of stars in the sky, then she decided to go down in lower profile where she can see the earth better, with full speed she lower herself down until she saw very far away on the earth there light and camping with so many people around, still in the air, curiosity start to itch her mind, she want to know what is going there, why there so many people here and what they are doing in this night in these big camps, now slowly she came down to that camp and land on the dates palm tree, looking and investigating of what these people are here for, and what they are doing in this night, gathering together in this huge camp?, I have to stay here and watch these human beings and find out for myself their reasons of being here together, she saw those human beings sitting surround in that camp and facing each other, one big of a circle, and then wonderful perfumed she smelled coming from that camp, the smell was coming from the smoke which these people have kept many small things inside it there are burning coals and while sitting the servants are keep on putting something in those burner and produce this very beautiful good smell, she really enjoyed that smell and wished will never finish, [in fact these were the naturally perfumed Uud sticks which many of the Middle Eastern homes and places are using it to fumigate their homes so to get that good smell, and originally these Uud sticks as well as Uud perfume are coming from Far East countries, and they are very expensive according to their quality and grades] then she saw one among those people stand and start to say something, he gave a short speech to well coming the guests, here Zarza understand that that person was host and he was welcoming his guests to this evening gathering, Zarza interests and curiosity to know more has increased, so she stayed put and watching and listening. After finishing his speech that host person went to sit and another person came and stand on his place, this person was wearing long bear on his face and wearing turban and a long (Busht) black clock, like many of there were wearing but differences colors, as these are traditionally national dress.

This second person spoke about tales of Prophet Joseph [Nabii Yusuf] in a long way, explaining to the guests of whole what has happened to Prophet Joseph, all his suffering just by jealousy of his brothers, while explaining the story, he was also referring to the holly book the Qur'an, verses by verses in each his explanation and translation, Zarza was listening with very keen interested, emotionally she was taken away of the story of Prophet Joseph, Zarza then said to herself "how wonderful for these human beings in memorizing these stories of so many past generation in their hearts and still preaching them to their present generation, while we Jinni's only knows that our parents were slaves of Prophet Solomon, nothing more do we know about other prophets or about other God's teaching, I think the time has come for me now to learn more about God's prophets and his teaching, what God would like us his creation to do not and what not to do" Zarza was watching everything and movements of what these human beings were doing to each other, she saw after the old man speech, people were served food on big copper plates, cooked food as well as many kind of fruits, she saw that before eating servants come with [Taasa and Birka] small basin and kettle of water, passing to each person to allow them washing their hands, following another servant with dry cloth as towels to dry their hands, she saw all of these human being tardyons and their way of living life which has impressed her so much, in whole of her life she never had chance or wanted to remixing her life by living with human beings, though she knows that there are other God's creations who are known as Human being, but did not bother at all to come down to earth and find out much these human creatures, and this is exactly what has happen during that night of Sheikh Shammakh when he invited his friends into his farmland for the traditionally Islamic teaching gathering, the was the same night where Zarza Aarish came down to earth and witness the human way of their living.

Yet! Zarza was not fully satisfied for just of what she has witness and heard, she wanted to know, see and learn more from these human beings, she then decided to go down somewhere where she can see and hear more, she thought maybe if she can get just any chance to mingle with these human beings so she can understand better their way of life, their tradition, their culture and more, and what has attracted her more is that fumigating of Uud smell, that smell really did drive her mind made, suddenly she heard someone calling with loud voice "Darwish!" "Darwish" "where is this Darwish hiding, can someone please go and find this Darwish and bring here so he can serve the guests please?" That voice was of Sheikh Shammaakh himself searching for one of his servant by the name of Darwish, This gave an idea to Zarza, in her mind as she is a Jinni can see thing the way she want to see but within limit, as God did not gave them many powers but gave them powers within their limit, Zarza was looking at that Darwish in her mind and saw him he has been taken away in asleep somewhere in a farm, Zarza saw this as a good opportunity and decided to her chance, she went where that Darwish was and saw him he is in a deep sleep, she then transform herself into Darwish shape and with his same clothes, and rush to where the big guests camp is, when entering the khaimah she saw so many people sitting down around that camp (Khaimah), when Sheikh Shammaakh saw her as Darwish, he called him by a hand sign, and Zarza went to sheikh, and Sheikh said "Where were you Darwish? people have finished their dinner, they must be served with fruits and sweets and black coffee, and lastly the Uud incense and rose water sprinkling, go quickly and follow others by giving them a helping hand" and Zarza replied "Yes Sir" and rush and went of where other servant are, waiting to be order of what to serve the guest, leader of the servant told Darwish "Darwish, as usual, you will be serving the Uud incensing to the guests, everyone go and take your thing to serve" Zarza follow other, and when she was given the Uud burner with that smell of Uud smoke coming out of it, she could not resist that, and her body start to shake and her eyes closed, until she felt someone gave her a spank on her back and told her "Hey! Darwish, wake up, follow the others, be after that rose water sprinkler, after he is sprinkling, it is your turn to incense guests with this Uud burner, Yallah" here is where Zarza learn that this is part of human beings traditions, to sprinkle rose water and incense guests with this Uud burner, and what a beautiful tradition is this. She wished she will always be part of these humanly tradition or learn more, as she enjoyed every moment of that evening.

Zarza served the guests with Uud incense very well, to each individual person until she reached where the three Sheikh brothers from Jabal Qamar were sitting, she look at them with their colorful Arabic dresses they are wearing, looking so smart and handsome, and these sons of Sheikh were Sheikh Nijaad, Sheikh Fat'h Nuwr and Sheikh Nuwr alaa Nuwr. Zarza notice some odd thing here, whenever she send an incensener to any of the guest, they kneel forward and use their hand as sort of fan and do the best to make that smoke of Uud smelling go much to them and so inhale it, this is something never she saw or experience before, Zarza forgets herself, instead of moving forward to other guests she just remain there in front of where Sheikh Nuwr Alaa Nuwr was and just looking at him without even taking his attention away from him, until that Uud smoke was too much for Sheikh Noor Alla Noo and start to choke him, he begin to cough, then someone came and take away Darwish (Zarza) in front of those guest, though Darwish (Zarza) was not there again, she was so much attracted to the last of the three brothers, who is Sheikh Nuwr Alaa Nuwr, she could not take away in her mind that very good looking and handsome face of that person, when Zarza was not longer in the camp serving, she went outside somewhere and sit down without been seen, in her mind she said [In whole of my life, I have never see such a handsome young men like that three brothers, and that last one was more than the others, others always said that we Jinni's are so beautiful and handsome than human beings, but to me I* said no Jinni can be as more handsome than these three brothers, I do not know what has happening to me now, why can't I forget the memory of that young man in my mind, am I in love?, has my heart been effected by this good looking young man? Oh1 my God, please help me, Zarza Aarish has found that person she was looking for, that young man will be my next husband.

That night function completed well and many of the guests start to live the farmland and go back to their homes, others who came very far away remain there in the farm as guests of Sheikh Shammaakh, Zarza Aarish make sure to know which of those small camp those three Princes were kept, because she has decided that this night she must win her love from that young Prince, she must meet him in private somewhere else, she went camp after camp until she heard their voices talking came from one of the camp, she stopped there and listen, but her presence there have caused more problem, as some of the animals start to be unsteady, camels and horses notice the presence of that Jinni and start to make noises, this will be not a good action in this night, so she went in where those animals were tied under the tree and said to them "I know you animals have felt my presence here, that is why you are afraid and started to make noise, but know this, I am not evil Jinni, I have come here with my good intentions and will leave here with the same, please I ask you to be calm and allow me to be here with you without anyone of us hurt the other, is that o.k." there was a camel who was tied on one of the palm dates tree, he was all by himself no other animal with him, he also felt the presence of a lady Jinni in the camp, she saw her moving around here and there but just was watching and did not move of make any noise, when Zarza finished talking to other animals, he answered her by his own animal talking where animals and Jinni's come understand one another, he said "Oh! daughter of Jinni, it is not easy for us to take your words as solid and firm and word of honor, and because you Jinni's do not speak truth always, your words means nothing to you, you always say this but do that, prove to us with swear to Allah, that you did not come here to do evil things but your presence here are only for good intentions" Zarza then went close to that camel and said "I swear to God, that I did not come here with evil intentions, my intention to be was just coincident only, but after what I saw here, I became attracted to these human way of life and more" then Zarza kneel to that camel ear and told him of how he has been attracted to that young gentleman of three bothers.

Then the camel said to Zarza "Oh! You daughter of Jinni, that is the son of one of well known Sheikh in these area, and those are his elder brothers, they are living on the mountain known as Jabal Qamar, their father is a ruler of Jabal Qamar, they came here just to except the invitation of this farm Sheikh who is a family friend to them, and I am is personal rider of that young Prince, and you said to me that you find him as the right husband to marry you, I cannot say anything about that, but what I know that his elder brothers did not marry yet, then how he the young one can get married before them, I have my doubts here" then Zarza replied the camel "Oh! You good camel who is always carrying the person that I have suddenly love, please feed me more information regarding these three brothers, I beg you please give those information, I will drop down to hold your feet if needed be and I swear to God that I will do that unless you tell me more about these three Princes, know that your Master has attracted me so much and I think that I have fallen in love with him, what is his name please?" then replied the camel "Oh! you daughter of Jinnis, when you mention God's name from your lips, you made more lenient and kind to you, but first of all let give you a history about us camels, it among my ancestors who had carried Prophet Muhammad (s.a.w.) on his journey from Madina to Mecca, when majority of the Qureishis had converted to Islam and refused to worship idols and images, then the Qureshis have decided to built a house for Prophet to live in it with his family, they asked our Prophet to find a suitable place of where he would prefer that house to be built, but Prophet Muhammad (s.a.w.) he did not decided himself but gave that privilege to our great great grandfather, his personal camel, to chose the right place of where his house should be built, So Prophet Muhammad (S.a.w.) told the Qureshis that, [my camel will be the one to chose, he will walk and wherever he stopped then that is the place he chose for you to built that house for me] and that camel obey his Master who was our Prophet Muhammad (s.a.a.w.) he walked step by step and all the Qureishis were behind following him, until he came to the place where he stopped and did not move another step, and here is where Prophet Muhammad said to Qureishis [That is the place where my camel have stopped, you should the house for me and my family], so you see Oh! Daughter of Jinnis, of what position are we camels to many of Allah Prophets? We did deserve them and obey them and in return the credited us as part of them, and until this day we are under their protection and serving them well, they love us, they trust us, they live by drinking our milk, they are like our own children to us, and all of these circle of life are the will of Allah that human being are part of us and we are part of them, even if they slaughter and eat our meat, it is also the will of God, and there are others who eat of what God has forbid, yet they pretend to ignore the law of God and do of what they wish till this day, all these command are the will of Allah, but let me ask you now, can you bare to be obey full to human like we did?" And after short hesitation, Zarza answered the camel, and said "Ahh! How much I have enjoyed today for the first time in my life, when you were narrating me those past stories of your ancestors serving that Master of all Masters Prophet Muhammad, yes my dear friend, I am ready and willing to serve the human beings, and at this moment in front of all these other

Animals and in front of you my friend, I announce myself to follow the faith of Prophet Muhammad, and Allah and all his angels may be my witness, and Allah has heard me this moment, and Allah willing, he will allow me to be among the Muslim" and here is where the camel and all other animal around there with one voice they called "Allahu Akbar! Allahu Akbar! Allahu Akbar! And then all the animals there knelt down put their heads looking down to earth, they action has surprised Zarza, looking around she saw all camels, horses, goats, sheep's as well as cows knelt to their knees and their faces are looking down the earth, she asked "Oh! my friend, you good camel, why you all knelt before me while I am not human but a Jinni?" and the camel replied "No my friend Zarza, we did not knelt before you, but when you have announce yourself to become a Muslim and accept to follow the teaching of Islam and follow the faith of Prophet Muhammad, then at that moment the sky open its doors and many of Allah angels came out of those doors looking down, when you pronounce the shahada of Islam, that is the sign that Allah except you as a Muslim Jinni from that moment, that is why we all knelt before Allah for opening his sky doors, it is a very rare thing to happen, I believe now you a Muslim Jinni woman Zarza Aarish, but not forget that every now and then to mentioned Allah from your mouth".

Now I am pleased and satisfied with you, and from this moment we are friends, but very good friends, welcome to the right path to Allah and his forgiveness, and to answer your question regarding my master, now is the right time for me to give you your answer, and your first answer is my master's name is Sheikh Nuwr Alaa Nuwr, what is your next question" Zarza then replied and said "First allow me to thank you Oh! Dear good friend camel, for all lot I have learn from you and kept me in brightness where I was living my life in the deepest dark, I f you had not spoken that first time when I was speaking to other animals to calm down because of my presence here, I think maybe I would have missed many of benefits and understanding of other God creations of how they are living with their culture and tradition as well of their faith in believing to Allah the creator of us all, I am sure I will gain more from you and other whoever they will be, for now I do not have any other question but be wear that I am here in this farm with you just going around from here to there, if I need to ask you again, I will come back to you my dear friend" and the camel replied "You are mostly welcomed, anytime you wished so".

Next day was Friday, Zarza was still there but invisible, no one could see her, she remain observing every and each movements of the human of what they are doing, she saw how the guests were served their breakfast in the morning, she saw all the people of how they attend their Friday prayers, she saw when many of the remaining guests start to live the camp for their journey back to their home, She heard it all when Sheikh Shammaakh asked and request Maalim Mikdad to be the teacher of his son Sheikhan, while trying to pursued him with sweet gentle words, and how Maalim Mikdad explained his situation that he is living all alone, Zarza heard all these conversations, and here where Zarza realize that This old man Maalim Mikdad he is well educated and a teacher who teach others all about Islamic affairs plus other worldly education, then she said within her mind [I have accepted Islam and all this religious really went deep through my mind, and I have witness here many way of how Muslims performed their duty of worshipping Allah, but I obtained zero education, I know nothing about this faith, I wished if I can the chance also to learn and be educated by him, such a man with higher knowledge. But how I can be educated by him when I am not human being like them but a Jinni? Those who had such knowledge there in our Kingdom all were arrested, tortured or turned into animal by that evil Khurkhush Majangar, Khurkhush Majangar has kept us in darkness, away completely from the right civilization of having freedom of faiths and expression, he did not want us to know that there is power beyond and every each of us are entitle to believe and rely on that power, and that is the power of Allah, Khurkhush Majangar did not allow us to learn and be educated in learning that by living with other Allah creation, especially the human beings, we will understand and learn much of how to live with harmony, love, friendly and peace, but he always make us believe that human beings are the enemies and they will never friends to us, now I found that it is true, it is completely difference, he did all these just to blindfold us and he should remain in power all his life by himself only, only one yesterday night, I had an opportunity to hear and learn about the life of Prophet Joseph, and it was such an interesting life story, and I have enjoyed every moment of it, I wished that I will get other chance of learning more about other prophets and their life stories, and these human beings by themselves arrange such gathering to teach one another of what has happened in the past, and what Allah always want is, for us all human beings and Jinnis to believe in him, and to deny of what he has forbidden and to except of what he has allowed, and to follow the teaching of his prophets, only that much, is it not these what they call the sea of wisdom where one should threw himself into and gain a lot?.

I swear in the name Allah, that I Zarza Aarish, will never return back to Khurkhush Majanga kingdom until I gain, learn and earn of what I am looking for, and in the higher respect so I can teach my children of what is right to follow and what is wrong to avoid doing it, I have made my mind, and so I have made my decision and so it should be done, please help and guide me Allah,

Last night I have removed that foolishness cloth of which I used to wear all my life, but I threw it into the fire so I cannot wear it again, but now I am wearing another new cloth to protect and guide me from the darkness to the brighter light, and I swear to Allah that my next husband will never be among the Jinnis but from the Human beings race, and this young man of whom I have fallen in love, Inshaalla by the will of Allah, he will be my next husband],

When it was noon, Zarza saw that every one go and wash their hands and legs, as well as cleaning their mouths and wiping their head with water, then they all has enter in one of the empty camp and form straight lines, and one of them then went in front of them and start reading verses from the holly book, Zarza want to know more about these activity, so she went to his friend the Camel and ask him of why these human doing that, his friend camel then said "Oh Daughter of Jinni, this is not the right way for two Muslims when they met without wishing one another, in Islam, wishing by saying [peace be upon you] as a cumpolsary thing to do, and the other party will answered the same [Peace be upon you too]" then replied Zarza "Oh! my dear friend, within a short time since we came to know each other, I have a learn a lot from you, if there was in my whole life the best of a teacher who taught me much of life, then I swear to Allah that there is no better one then you, you are my first teacher of whom I have learn of what I have no idea about in all my past life, and God's willing you will never be the last one but I hope in future to get another who can teach of what I did not learn before. Now I take this opportunity to wish you in an Islamic way, Peace be upon you my friend" and the camel replied "Peace be upon you too Oh! Daughter of Jinnis, how did you slept last night and how did you wake up this morning, I hope that you have slept well and woke up with your better health" then Zarza said "We Jinnis, do sleep when we want to or remain wake without sleeping, it is our nature way of life, we feel no differences at all if we sleep or not sleeping, but to speak the truth my friend, last night I slept very well, with that breezing I really enjoyed my sleep, I did not woke up until when I heard someone among those Human being called [Allahu Akbar Allahu Akbar] that loud voice did wake me up, then I wanted to know what is going on, why this person calling loudly then I saw everyone was preparing himself to wash his hands and legs and stand in one line and start to pray as I have see they were doing the same yesterday at noon, and that same person was in front leading others and all remaining people stand still with respect and manners and their faces are looking down, and that leaders in front with his melodically voice was reading verses from the holly Qur'aan, nobody shake or turn but all were quite and listen to that leader reading, then he bent and they all follow him the same, and when he knelt to the ground they also did the same, Oh! My good friend camel, please teach me more so I can understand better about these Human beings" and the camel answered, and said "Oh! you Daughter of Jinnis, those human beings are preparing themselves to worship Allah, they have to do that five a day, every day the whole of their living lives, but not only Human are the only one who are command to pray but even you Jinnis among those who must perform the same, as Allah said in his book the holly Qur'aan [And we have created you Jinnis and Human beings to pray and worship], and that loud voice you have heard is the voice of the Muadhin (Caller for the prayer) in every mosque in the whole world there must one, who is duty to perform is climbing the mosque Minaret(Tower) and call the people that the time for praying is now, as praying accord to the right time is compulsory for each of you Jinnis and Human, and prayer is one of the Pillar of Islam, there are five pillars, the first is to believe that Allah is the only rightful God and Muhammad is his messenger, and praying is the second one, and give alms is the third one, theAlms must come from your halal earning, so there is a percentage from the profit you get to be given to the poor and to those who are in need, and fasting in the whole month of Ramadhan, is to deny yourself in eating and drinking anything, before sunrise and up to sundown, and not only that but also to control yourself with sexual temptations for the whole fasting month, this is the fourth one and the last Islamic pillar is performing Hajj in Makka and Madina {if finance situations allowed you} and also there are conditions about the Hajj pilgrim, this is the information about Islamic pillars, and regarding the prayers, the person who was in the first row, is known as Imam, he is the responsible person to lead all those who came here to say their prayers, he reads verses from the holly Qur'aan and the others just listen and kept quiet, but follow him in what other action he is doing, to bent and to kneel, that is also part of the prayer, now tell me Oh you Daughter of

Jinnis, have you learn anything from this information I gave you?" and Zarza replied "Yes, my dear friend, I did learn and gain a lot from today's teaching, of how Islam faith teach others of how a believer of this faith should live his life in what to believe and what not to, in what is Allah teach us to do and what to avoid doing it, take it for example like give of the Alms, this is a great thing to do in life, helping those who are in need, from what you have earn in your working with or from your business profit, I find this is a very good teaching, where I came from only oppressors and those who maintain more power are the one who can enjoy life, no one care for other at all, Oh! my dear friend the camel, you have opened my mind and allow me now to see of what I have never seen in all my past life, it is true that Islamic faith teaches of what a God creation should do in his life and what is forbidden and not to do all his life" and the camel cut her off by adding "Not only that, but it is Allah who command his creations through his Prophets and his holly books and not for Allah benefits but for us his creations, we should learn and understand and do of what have been asked to do and avoid to do of what we have been asked not to for our benefits and never for God, it is Allah who brought his holly books through his messengers for us to read so to learn and understand his teaching for the better living life, here on this planet and there in heaven for the life after death, it Allah who has decided that a creation must believe his creator and obey him by worshiping him, and our creator is none other than Allah himself, there is no any power greater beyond or above him, Allah is the only one to be worshiped and none other, and to believe and worship other than that is to go against him and in Islam that we called [Kufr], as Allah is the creator of earth and the sky and what so ever is living in and on it, he has created all Angels, Jinnis, ghosts, animals, insects and all the creatures in the seas and lakes bigger and small, he created those who are visible and those who are not seen by the naked eye, and all these are his belonging, we all my dear friend, are belongs to Allah, we are his slaves and he is our Master, the only Master and no other (God) than Allah, that is why, my dear friend Daughter of Jinni's, these human beings are making themselves more concerning in obeying God, and here I am referring mostly to these followers of Islamic faith, they are very strict in their daily prayers, in their way of bringing up their children, in their cultures and tradition not do actions beyond the teaching of their Islamic faith,, that is why there are many mosques in the world than other religious worshiping building, they were worshiping Allah from the time of Prophet Adam to this present time. Now my dear friend, I have explained to you in details and in very longer way so to make you know and understand why Muslims are so concern in obeying the God, for all of what he has taught us to be and to follow through all of his Prophets, beginning of Prophet Adam to the last Prophet who is Prophet Muhammad who has introduce Islam in this planet earth by obeying the orders of his Allah.

And Muhammad was given this mission of deliver the message of Allah to all us human beings, and he did so, and till the of the living life of this planet earth, all human being must follow the rule of Allah by obeying that Muhammad is the last messenger of Allah and what he has deliver has deliver on behalf of Allah of which he was commanded to do, and so in open language there is no other God to worship other than Allah, Allah is the first and Allah is the last God to be worshiped by all human beings, and he who do otherwise he mislead himself on the direction which is not acceptable by Allah, so he should know that he is committing a sin.

I have explained you in details Oh! Daughter of Jinnis, all the importance of why all God creations must worship him, Allah, and now it is your duty to perform all the daily prayers and obey of what you have been asked to do and avoid of what you have been denied to do from teaching of Allah through his holly book Qur'aan and through those who have learned before you" and Zarza replied "yes, it is true my friend, that within a short time, from yesterday till this hour you had spent much of time teaching me and gave me many of the information concerning worshiping God and much of the information concerning the Islamic faith, thank you so much my dear friend, I have accepted to believe the Islamic faith and choose myself to also a follower of Prophet Muhammad, all because of your teaching my dear friend, and I intend to remain and learn more about this faith so I can allow my heart to be stronger in my belief of accepting Islam and never came back out of it"

And the guests of Sheikh Shammaakh start to leave the farmland to go back to their homeland, Zarza then she saw her friend the camel was brought for his master, ready for the journey of going back to their mountain Kingdom of Jabal Qamar. She saw when the three Princes bid farewell to Sheikh Shammaakh and everyone of them climb on their camels with their servants and guards for that journey back home, but these farewell bidding did effect the inner feelings of Zarza, as she do not know that is she going to meet again with these wonderful Princes of Jabal Qamar or never, but how is that going to be possible, when I love one of them? No! Never! That I will never allow to happen, this only opportunity for me to get of what I

Liked and loved, I will follow their caravan to where it goes, till I know what is the end of this growing love within my heart.

Prince Nuwr meets Zarza Aarish

Zarza then fly up high in the sky without been seen as she made herself invisible, and all that time she is in the sky was looking and watching every step of that caravan of three Princes journeying toward their homeland Jabal Qamar, and her aim was if she will up in the sky she can see the earth very clear and know of where to land if needed so, before the Princes caravan at that place, this will give her a chance and excuse of what to do or of how to attract the attention of these three Princes so they can notice and like her,

When she was still up in the sky, she has found out that the caravan to direction of crossing the desert instead of passing through the wadis (Valley), but also she saw from the sky that the path they took is leading to where there is an Oasis, here is where Zarza understand why this caravan has decided to cross the hot desert instead of passing under the wadis, because she also saw that very far away from that Oasis, there are huge mountains, it could be that is where their destination is, said Zarza in her mind, she knew then that as long most of their means of traveling are riding the camels, then for sure these people know of what they are doing, they have crossed this desert purposely so to have a rest at that Oasis and from there then, they can to continue their journey to those mountains, [what a clever idea], and then Zarza said to herself, if this caravan is going to where I think is going, then this is the right time for me to reach their first before and wait for them, what will happen after, only God knows, but I pray to you Allah please, allow me to have my dream come true, let that young Prince fall in love with me so he can be my next husband"

Though Zarza was still flying in the air watching that caravan's every movement, and make sure that caravan is heading to that Oasis, when she was certain that it was heading there, she then came down and landed on one of the palm tree there, she decided then to transform herself in a beautiful and colorful bird who know will ignore to look at her, and she start to sings most beautiful melodies, The caravan of the three Princes was heading to the same oasis where Zarza has already landed there on a palm dates tree in a shape of beautiful singing bird, this a common place for Sheikh Naajid and his brothers for their rest before leaving to their Kingdom Jabal Qamar,

When their caravan was so close to that Oasis, for the first time in their lives they heard that singing bird melody coming there from the Oasis, they all were so surprised, who is singing this so beautiful melody, what kind of creature is this, while coming close to that place, their eyes were searching for that singing one whoever maybe, Sheikh Naajid said "My brothers, do you hear of what I hear coming from the Oasis?" and his brothers replied "Yes Oh! elder brother, we heard such a beautiful singing bird melody coming from those trees from the Oasis" and the youngest Prince said "Yes, and it is so entertaining, you would want to hear it without stopping, such a wonderful singing I never heard it before all my living life, but who is the singer, defiantly this is not human singing, but could be of a bird, but why not go more closer and find out for ourselves who is the owner of such rich miracle voice?" and slowly step by step they were going closer near those palm dates tree, and all their eyes were searching in the between the palm dates leaves, until they reached exactly under those huge palm dates trees and stopped, but yet could not find who is this singer of very effectively melody singing, here they were taken away and have forgotten completely that they are tired and need to arrange their camps for resting, every and each one of them was hypnotized with that singing, the important thing here was not that melody only but is to find out who is this melody maker and why they could find and see him? suddenly they Prince Nurw Alaa Nurw, said "Sub'hanallah Jalla Jalaalahu' come my brothers, come you all, I have found who the melody maker is, look there near the bunch of the dates fruits, not only her voice but even her body and look is so beautiful, that is a she bird, who are very rare in the world, I have learn about that in school, from my teacher, these kind of birds can live for so many years and survive all the climates. During the hot summer seasons they immigrates to these parts, and mostly in these mountains areas as they are very shy and do not like to mix with other spices of birds, they prefer living by themselves only, and before winter they immigrate to other cold countries, that is why these creatures are so rare and if it happened that you have found one anywhere, then count yourself that you are a very lucky one to get the chance of your life, like what we all did now, so gentlemen, count yourselves that you are among the luckiest who had this chance to see with your own eyes, the Queen of all rare birds in this planet earth"

And everyone was stunned and shocked for what they have seen in their own eyes, the creation of God of such a beautiful creature ever they have seen in their whole living life,, she was so beautiful, so colorful with her soft puffy feathers, you cannot take your eyes away from looking at her, this is God creation, as our ancestors has said [Allah is beautiful, loves beauty and always create beautiful creations] Sub'hanallah. Everyone and everything was calm and quiet, not even a hiss sound from any surrounding there but that bird dominate all their minds of all those who were there from that Princes caravan, no steps movements, no animal movements, but only the concentration of those present mind in listening to that beautiful creature's melody, they have reached that moment that to forgot completely that there camps to be erected and food to be cooked and compulsory duty of worshiping Allah, as the time for that has been matured long ago, suddenly came a high speed wind that made huge dust and shaking of those palm trees, and the animals started to be unsteady, and they saw that bird flown away high in the sky and never to be seen again, and they hope not.

Here is then is where everyone realize that there is a hush wind, and were trying to hold themselves till that wind did calm down slowly and everything came back to normal, but they have missed that melody singing and the presence of that bird, all that surrounding area was like an empty egg shell without its York, and everyone trying to make himself busy by doing this or that but his mind is all in that bird. The camps were erected, and after a short rest and refreshing and saying their prayers, they all sat down all for their evening lunch (as this was their first food of that day), and that night they remain there camping at that Oasis, after their evening lunch, Sheikh Najaad asked his brothers "My brothers, can we entertain ourselves tonight, can someone Wanna please?" (Wanna is a singing of the [Bedouins] Normads, when they sit together in the night around a campfire, they like to sing their Wanna melodies with strong love words or poems of praising something, Sheikh Fat'h then request his younger brother Sheikh Nurw Alaa Nurw, and said "Yalla Oh! Sheikh Nurw, please Wan wan for us tonight" and Sheikh Nurw Alaa Nurw said "Insha'allah, I will do the Wan wan" and then he begins to sing his melody while playing his musical instrument known as Rabaab, and his Wanna, his singing while composing at the same time, like many of well known Bedouin Wanna singers used to do, and he said while following the tune he was playing, this is his poem:-

I saw it in my life I saw it difference kind of beauties
It is the will of God to spread them in many parts of the earth
This is the art creation of our Master, the almighty God

He has created them, I said in many shapes and colors
The tall's and the widest the thins and the fats
But what I have seen today Sub'hanallah! Sub'hanallah!

That bird of its kind so beautiful, so colorful
Who can sing such a melody which entertain the heart and the mind
A bird never have I seen before, very rare of its kind

Oh! You, rare of all birds please come back, let us meet again
Your body creation no where one can find
Suddenly you have disappear and made me suffer within

If it was wealth the reason to bring you back
I would have spent all my wealth, just to get you back
Even if I will return to be poor but be with you, I do not mind

Oh! You beautiful rare bird I send to you this message
I swear to Allah, I am helpless for a strong love entered in my heart
And I have no choice as you have made me a sick person now

Please hear this message if you are closely and near
I miss you; I envy you I cannot stand any longer
I need you, Oh! Queen of my heart please come back, I am waiting for you.

And here is where Prince Nur Alaa Nur completed his Wanna, and
everyone there applauds and cheers for such a creative composition, within a
short time he has composed and sing it his poem regarding the beauty of that
rare bird, then said Prince Najaad "Really my young brother, you have been
effected by the beauty of that bird, I personally do not blame you, as she is
really a beautiful creature created by God, she has everything one would die to
get her, her beautiful creation, her colorful body, he melodically singing voice,
yes, she is something one would like own and have, I am sure that whoever will
be able to get that bird, then he is the owner of a very rare creature in the world,
but my dear Brother, I would advise you not keep her much in your mind,
you better try to forget her, as it is not easy to get something of you do not
know where it has began and how it will end, we know not much about that
particular bird, we are here in the wilderness, and suddenly we are attracted by
the so beautiful melody coming from the singing bird, a very rare bird that we
have learn it only from the school but know nothing much it, this is a little bit
wear, how can we believe that is really a bird? As always here in the wilderness
there are other living creatures living here, she could not be a bird but maybe
another of those God's creation as well, My dear younger brother, I ask you to
take precaution of yourself and be careful in what you like and dislike in your
life, this is my advice to you my brother" and Sheikh Nur Alaa Nur replied "It
is true my dear brother Sheikh Najaad that the bird have effect me so much
that I wish I could own her and always to be mine and on my side, looking at

her and listening to her melodies only, but among all what has attracted me most is her eyes, do you people have noticed that her eyes though were little but they are completely in difference category of the bird eyes, her eyes were in human shape rather than in the bird shape, they were in light blue color, if this bird was available anywhere in the world for sale, I would go and buy it and have her as my own, but it is true of what you have said my brother, it is not advisable to love something of which you do not know anything about it" and Sheikh Najaad said "and that exactly is what I want you to do, try to take her out of your mind, now it is the time to have a sleep so we can wake up early, as after the early morning prayers we will be living for our journey back home, good night everyone" and all they replied "wake up with Allah blessings" and all they went to sleep.

In the middle of the night, Sheikh Nuwr Alaa Nuwr woke up suddenly, he did not know what has awaken him up, he sat down and looking around, he saw his brothers were all in a deep sleep, he kept sitting there on his sleeping place listening and looking here and there, but there was nothing but only the emptiness of the night, he did not know why he has woke suddenly like this, after few moments waiting and listening, he heard a sound of Rabaab musical instrument coming from far away, the player of that instrument must be very far away, but surprising of all, there was a singing voice, a soft singing voice of a lady, the voice was so entertaining

So melodically, so soft, combining with the Rabaab, Sheikh Nur Alaa Nur could not resist anymore, he stood up and went outside the camp to check and see if there is anybody else heard that sound and voice, he found everything was normal, the guards were there but sleeping and the campfire is burning, he decided to go back to his camp and change into normal cloth, took his sword and came back outside and find his horse and ride on it and move out of there slowly following of where that voice is coming from, all by himself and without fear, but with a brave heart he wants to know who in this middle of night could be playing Rabaab and Wan wan, this is really a strange thing to happen in this wilderness and at this time of hour, a place is where there is no civilization exists, he lead his horse slowly following the voice and the music sound, he went step by step while he was carefully listening which exact direction the Wanna and the Rabaab sound is coming from,

That night by good chance was a full moon night, so it was clear vision, he can see things clearly, he went with horse until he reached a place where there was a desert, he stopped there, and here he can hear that Rabaab clearly, and the voice of a woman singing with Rabaab, this is was the poem he heard from that singer:-

I am that one the same one A proud of a woman
I am that one I am also I have lived all alone
I am from there the same place far away I came from and you the same
the same one why I should not want you
And you look at the same place look but do not stop to look

I and you are the same that man and a woman
Know that I am the same do not bother to get tired
Me and you are those who should build and not to break
You are that you the same one enter in my heart
And not other one the day I saw you you have upset my mind
My love, know that do not rush I am waiting, please come

This strange night singing, sung by unknown singer, in this full moon night, which has spread his light all over this sea of desert sand, where there is nothing more than two or three palm dates trees, did surprise Sheikh Nuwr Alaa Nuwr, then he started to ask himself while his eyes were searching here and there, looking for what he has come for, looking at the figure down the dune sand of the desert, sitting all by herself with just a campfire in front of her and a Rabaab in her hand, playing it,[why this poem has complication to understand, why should this singer to be here in such a place and such time, all alone by herself, singing for her love who is also not here or is strange to her, who is this strange night singer? And why at this strange place and strange time? I have to get answers to these questions, and the only person who can answered them is only that singer] Sheikh Nur Alaa Nur when he saw that there is someone in the middle of the sand dune down below, and all by herself with just a campfire in front of her and still singing her song while playing the Rabaab, he decided to go down slowly to her, so to ask her of this strange singing in the middle of a night at this strange place and all by herself, he then walked slowly behind her, when he reached her from her back he wished her with "Assalaam aleykum" but that strange figure of the night, did not answer the salaam, but keep on singing like there was nobody came, this attitude did surprise Sheikh Nur, why is that this strange lady of the night did not answer his wishing?, he decided to repeat his wishing with louder voice "ASSALAAM

ALEYKUM" here is where that lady of the desert night, stopped playing her musical instrument and raise her hand as a sign of not to be disturbed, while she was just looking down in front of her without looking to who is this person who come in the middle of the night to disturb me with my enjoyment, Sheikh Nur then thoughts, maybe he did not show her good manner and have angered her, he said "I am very sorry if I have caused you any discomfort whoever you are, it was not my intention to interrupt you and your enjoyment, but I have no choice after hearing your singing in the middle of night, I have to find out who is this strange midnight singer" after said this, here then that lady lower her hand, and raise her face very slowly and look at me, but when Sheikh Nur saw the beauty of that lady, he was shocked, how come such a beautiful young lady could be in such place, in the middle of the night and in the middle of the wilderness of the desert and all by herself alone, though she had covered her face with very soft see through cloth, as part of the Islamic tradition, women do wear hijaab in front of men, as protecting their moral respect.

As there was a little wind in that night, her were flying high and sides, that make sometime to expose her face more, Sheikh Nur has nothing to say but just to look and admire the beauty of this strange lady of the night, while their eyes were looking to each other, and after a long silence and no one speak but just looking to each other, then the lady cut off the silence, and said "without any doubt, you must be a surprise person by so many things you have witnessed this night, and in your mind now, there are many questions you want ask me and get their answers, yet there are among those questions, you are asking what kind of a creation am I, am I a human being?, an Angel? Or maybe even a Jinni, and secondly, there is this must be answered question, how come a girl like me to be in a place like this and at this time of a night, all these questions are running in your mind and are seeking their answers, and those answers only I can give you, yet I agree with you that it is strange for such a beautiful woman like me to be at the place like this and at this odd time of the night, and thirdly, still to be answered is, why I did not reply to your both salaams (when you wished me) for that I ask your pardon and forgiveness, as it is not a gentle and respect attitude to ignore someone else wishing, now, allow me please to give all other answers which are bothering and itching your mind, first of all, I reply you now your wishing, WA ALEYKUM SALAAM, why then I did not answer your salaam from the first time, my reason for that is, I wanted to put in you more uncomforted and make you more inquisitive, so you should find me as a complicated one, or rather odd one, I wanted you to be a little disturbed with my attitude, so you can try to find more about me, and that is exactly of what you did, as you did not leave the this place but keep on yourself to remain here and without fear, though you do not know whom am I, will I be friend to you and charm you or will I be an enemy and harm you, is this not true my dear sir?" and Sheikh Nuwr replied "yes, what all you have said is true, and still I am in that condition of curiosity to know more about you, who are you?, please tell me more" then Zarza said "Ok then, now please be patience and sit down on this carpet of sand, and allow me to give you all the explanation in details, of who am I, and why I am here in this wilderness all by myself,

Before I tell you all about myself, please allow me to tell you much about you and your concern, by name you are called Prince Nur Alaa Nur, you living up there in Jabal Qamar, now you and you brothers are returning home after attending an invitation of a religious function which was arranged by your family friend Sheikh Shammaakh in his farmland, and the speaker of that function was one called Maalim Mikdad, now tell me, is this true or not true?" and Sheikh Nurw replied "it is absolutely true" then Zarza said "Now I will tell you with a true tongue, who am I, and never will I hide a true at all.

I am a Jinni, my name is Zarza Aarish, I am coming from those south mountains which are near the Empty Quarters deserts, I am a widow, it has been a long time now since my husband has died, I am living under ruler of Khurkhush Majangar Kingdom, this is a very cruel Jinni, and have no mercy at all to anyone, this Jinni do not like at all good deeds but like to harm and torture others, he is enjoying doing that, he is against anyone who believe in God, what has taken me away from him till being here at this place, is a very long story, but in short, I have promise Khurkhush Majangar, never will I get married again with another Jinni, if God has written in his book that I should be getting married again, then my second husband will be among the human being and never among the Jinnis" Then Zarza explained in details of all what she has seen in the farm land of Sheikh Shammaakh, and how she came to know him and his brothers and many others who were there invited in that function, and how she had met Sheikh Nur camel and talk a lot until the camel has able to pursued her to believe in Islamic faith and took the shahada of becoming a Muslim Jinni woman, and also she explain of how she was attracted with the three brothers, especially their national dresses, she concluded by saying "but it was you Sheikh Nur that have entered in my heart, as you are the most handsome among you three brothers, and you are still young, you are the first human being that I have fallen n love to, it is you Sheikh Nur who is my choice to take that place to be my second husband, it is you and only you and nobody else who can take my love, this all tactics of me transforming into a singing bird, was just to find away in attracting you to see and notice me, or of me singing here in this night of hour is just to find a reason of bringing you here so I can that chance I am looking for of telling you who am I, and how much I have been effected by your look, and that you are person of my dream, that I have fallen in love with you and if there will be another next husband, then that husband to me, is no one else but you and only you. If I would not have done this, then for sure you would never be attracted and there would never be a better a chance for you to come and meet here, this exactly what I did want to happen, if did happened, and now you are here, and you have learned the truth, the whole truth and everything about me, and I did not hide nothing but speak out all in my heart regard you and me, now Sheikh Nuwr, the decision is yours, either you accept me as your friend and a future wife or refuse and dump me and leave this place and never to see you again all my coming life, as for me this was a very hard tusk to open my heart and speak all about my inner secret of my love for you, and there is no better witness to all these more than Allah and all his living angels, but also you better know this fact, if for any reason, you will not be mine and refuse to accept, then there will be no any other woman in your whole life who will be yours, this does not mean that I put fear or challenge or force in you, but we Jinnis, never would like to share our love with anyone. You can give me your answer now or later, but I am around here waiting and watching you and you movement till that time you will decide to give me your right answer, the truth answer and never the forced one, you will not see me but I will see you wherever you go with your brothers, and if you need my presence, just call my name and I will be wherever you are in glimpse of an eye" though it was dark in the night but the moonlight did help Sheikh Nuwr to see the beauty of that Jinni girl Zarza Aarish, he then said to Zarza, "Oh! You beautifull Jinni girl Zarza Aarish, it is not easy for me at this moment to give you the answer, that answer which you need and which will please you, as it is a heavy burden for me, which you have put in my heart, this a matter which concerns life relation, and not only that but it also concern a relation of two difference God's creation, between a Jinni and a human being, remember that we have been created with difference sources, with differences capabilities, you can fly, you can be invisible, you can see of what is not here or in front of you, but me as human being, maintain no such power and capabilities, tell me now, how then can we live in equal life? you can enter in any house without permission or even inside a human body, I cannot do that, as I have no such power to do that, my power has limit and

Saqr hide behind the weeds and saw the two swans

cannot go or do beyond that limit, but I swear in the name of Allah that I have no any personal objection as you are very beautiful woman, any man will be proud to have, I have no objection to marry you, but for sure in front of us there are many obstacles which can deny us to reach our goals, I ask you Zarza, I beg you Zarza, let us not rush on this matter now, let us give an opportunity a chance to find a solution to our problem, let us be patience and find a solution by thinking which is the right and the best way to pass through in reaching our destination" then Zarza replied "I think I did not make any mistake when I allow my heart to chose you as my life partner, you are really a gentleman and honest person, you are really direful person and without fear, and yours is a very clean heart, this I have found with these moments we are here together and during all our conversation, yet! After all you know that I am not a human being but a Jinni, yet you stand firm with unshaken foundation which have hope and determination, yes' I agree with you, that we should not rush in this matter and must be careful and watch all our steps, I agree with your advice, let us give patience a chance to produce nice sweets and eatable fruits, and this relationship which we have created today let it be strong and firm to remain longer and hope it will produce better Results. It is true what others have said that patience is a key to a relief, I agree with completely and I will be among who had experience the patience" and Sheikh Nur replied "God will, that will be, and I promise you Zarza that I will be with you, remain with you and will never avoid you, no matter what circumstances will occur ahead of us, our relation will be stronger and remain longer until that day relief will be born for us to join as husband and a wife" and Zarza said "I respect your judgment very much, I know that it is not easy for any other person to conclude his decision the way you did, just in a very short that we have agree to each other to be and remain friends, without force percuation, as love is a free choice for anyone to except or not to except, I will wait till that day my love also grow in your heart as yours have already grown in mine, but I will bid farewell this life without you be mine, this I promise you" and Sheikh replied "Inshaalla (God will) Zarza, Let us give time a chance to decide for the better and never for the worst for us, though our ancestors have said that TIME IS LIKE A SWORD, IF YOU DO NOT CUT IT THEN IT WILL CUT YOU, and I said TIME IS A PILLAR OF PATIENCE, IF YOU DO NOT RESIST WITH IT THEN IT WILL SPOIL YOUR INTENTIONS" then Sheikh Nuwr raise his both hands and open them, it was an invitation for Zarza to enter in those hands, and Zarza after a short hesitation understood the intention of his love Sheikh Nuwr and closer and hug him. Then Sheikh Nur notice a very strange odour, and asked Zarza "Your body odour, has a differences smell, it is very nice and appealing, this is something new to me Zarza" and Zarza replied "My dear Prince, we female Jinni's who are kind and have faith in God, smells like this, this is our secret and a gift from God, we hate very much dirty and bad odour".

And here we should stop on this chapter my dear reader of this story of TALES FROM ARABIAN AND PERSIAN DESERTS, and go to other chapters which are concerning with other issues, especial those issues which we left behind, let us go back.

CHAPTER ELEVEN

(A big lake on top the mountain)

AFTER SO MANY DAYS PASSED away, and still the problem of saving from the jail of the Kingdom of Khurkhush Majangar, the family of Abu Muntasir could never be done, and all because the situation was very hard and that place was heavily guarded, and how can be possible for only few human to fights the whole army of Jinnis in that Kingdom of Khurkhush Majangar, even of how to destroy Khurkush himself was not yet possible, and so they delay the matter for the time being until other future time if the situation allowed, but Mr. Fairuz and his family has kept his friends and their families in their home like they are all one family, while they are kept their selves in patience waiting for the right opportunity, and the right day and time so to take their action against Khurkhush Majangar and save Abu Muntasir family,

On the other hand, Saqr did not waste his time, he started to take Fardhada and Fardhana out for hunting, and them of how to hunt small animals, like gazelle and rabbits, as well as some eatable birds, they were just like brother and sisters, and on the other side they taught Saqr of how to use sword in fighting, this was a daily routine for them, until Saqr was a very good sword fighter, and all because Saqr has so much interest to learn of how to use sword in fighting,

One day, in their daily routine of going out searching out for the dry trees to cut them for firewood, this particular day they had taken another difference route, they went until they reached at the place where there are huge tree, they enter under those trees and came to a place where there was a lake, plenty of water, as there was a waterfall coming up from the mountain, pouring that water in that lake, they stopped there and dismount on their animals, they have enjoyed seeing the sceneries of that place, as there was plenty of tree shadows, and the sound of the water falling up from the mountain, this was the right place for them to rest a while, really that place was like heaven, and Fardhana said "What a beautiful place this is", there were also wild desert flowers alongside that lake, that really add more touch of beauty to that place, and then Fardhada add to her sister comment, and said "It is true my dear sister, this place is really heaven of earth, the only thing that surprise me and make me to curiosity is, why there is no a single human soul here, or even an animal, or even feet marks of others to be here, why is this place is so difference? Does this mean that there was no body before us who came here or knows about this place? "And here Saqr said "it is true of what you said Fardhada, it does make sense, why there is no any feet marks on the sand, not human or even animals? This is something to be surprise and also has created doubts" and then Fardhana said "My dear brother and sister, do not forget that when the wind blows into differences directions, caused the reasons of taking sand with it and cover the land, could there were marks before but they have been covered by the desert sands" and Saqr said "That could be so, yet I think we better camp here, have our prayers and then we lunch here and then after that we should start exploring this place, we should divide into two groups, a group should follow this lake on the right and the other on the left, and maybe we meet around the other side of this lake, if by any chance there is no passage to pass through then we all should return here where we began, agree?" and they all agreed to the idea.

Then they made their camp there and say their prayers and then have their lunch, and after having their lunch, they were ready to explore the place, they mount their animals which were camels and as they have agreed each part took their direction, Saar follow the right route and two sisters follow the left route, their aim was to reach on the other side of that mountain, the mountain which the water is coming and made fall, they thought that maybe there will be a way around that mountain so they can meet there, after quite a long journey while looking here and there, and their hope was maybe they will find someone on the way, a human being of an animal or even a foot print of a human, but unfortunately they did not find anyone, neither any foot print, not even a small animal like rabbit or bird, it took them about half an hour to reach beneath that mountain, they decided to go around that mountain maybe they will find away where it will take them to climb up, but when reached behind the mountain, they did not find any way, and it was not possible to go around that mountain, as it was the end of the road and one must turn back, then Fardhada said to her sister "Don't I said before that this place is completely out of civilization, no human no animal, quite a strange place this is" and Fardhana replied "I said maybe there were feet print mark but maybe because of the wind dust they have been covered, but now I think I too was wrong, this place is completely out of human beings and other animals as well, as you have said this place is quite a strange place for one to be" then they decided to return back of where they have camped, as their exploring journey did not produce any result,

They turn and return to where they had their camp but could not find their brother Saqr there, he did not return from his journey yet.

Saqr on his side, he continue his journey of exploring the place on the other side of the lake, until he reached beneath that mountain which the water falls from it, he did not find any possible way to climb that mountain, but curiosity and determination was eating his mind, he is not that kind of a person who except defeat easily, he refuse to abandon his mission without getting of what he has come here looking for, he decide to dismount his camel and look around if there is any possible way he can climb that mountain so to satisfy his mind of where the water coming from, he searched many places of the mountain to find out if there is any possibility of climbing by himself only without his camel, fortunately he did find a place where there was a tree grow very close to that mountain, he climb that tree, branch after branch until he was on the top, and from there he did find a place where he can put his leg on the side of the mountain which he hoped that he will be able to climb the mountain up to the top, luck was on his side, he was able to climb that mountain though with difficult but he manage to hold this stone and that branch and those bushes, slowly and step by step he went up, though it did take all his energy and longer time but at the end that did pay off, and Saqr manage to reach completely on top of that mountain, but when he look at his hands he found that some of his skins were off, but he care not as long he reached his target, then he heard some birds singings, and there was so many long grasses with flower trees, he stated to pass through those grasses and came out the other side where he found a big lake, a very wide lake where you can see up to infinity, colorful blue water, many flower plants on the edge of that lake, the weather was chilly and cool, he walked through the edge of that lake between flower plants and until he came to a place where he can view down of that mountain, very far down there he saw his two sisters were riding back with their camels, he assumed that they have waited longer enough and got tired, and have left before the evening and darkness caught them here, he then decided to explore the place walking back inside those long grasses just to take precaution not to be seen by anyone if exist here, what he was looking for the source of the water, whey they are coming from, as he saw a big lake here but no waterfall, so follow the edge of the lake yet still inside those long grasses until he reached at the end where the water fall down, as he was lake level he could not see what is exactly in the center of the lake until he should be somewhere above, so he decided to find a higher point near where he was so he can climb up and see the lake from above, fortunately there was a tree a little distance away, he decided to go there, he climbed that tree up above and when he was at the higher point he look down in the lake, and he find the secret of where the water come from, as he saw that in the middle of the lake there is a spring which produce water inside the lake, many bubbles are coming from that spring, he solved his puzzle mind to know of where this water is coming from above here on top of this mountain, a place where there is no another higher point only here where he is now is the highest, he climb down the tree, and went to find a place to sit while watching the place and still hiding behind those higher grasses,

Time has passed and within few hours there will be darkness, but the weather and the colorful blue water of the lake has made him to forgot that he had left his two sisters down there, remembered his sisters, he know that the time to go back to them has come so he stood up preparing to return the same way he came from, then suddenly he heard a sound of bird wings flying in the air, he look up in the sky and saw where that sound is coming from, it was a very huge white swan with black mouth, so huge than any normal swan, Was huge nearly to a shape of an Oyster. The swan was flying in lower profile and circling the lake, when this bird open his wings, add more beauty of his shape, and then after circling the place the giant swan slowly start to land on the lake and remain floating, and then before came to a stop, he open and close to dry his wings with high speed, and Saqr saw all this actions of this huge God creation which he never saw like him all his life, while he is still behind the grasses, Saqr was asking inside himself [what has brought this giant swan here? a place like this where there is no more creature of its kind here? I will remain here hiding and watch this swan till I know what has brought this swan here] still behind those tall grasses, Saqr was just watching and observing every movement of that bird, he saw then he was scratching under his wings with his mouth, and all other places of his body, sometime he will submerge his neck inside the water and only his legs and tail remain up, and then come out and shake his body to dry his feathers of the water, then Saqr thought in his mind, maybe this bird came here just to enjoy this place where there are no more animals or to come here for a swim, and then with a few seconds before Saqr answered himself he heard another wings sound in the sky, he look up to see and saw another swan of the same kind was flying above in the sky in lower profile, and was ready to land on the lake as well, he landed on the lake and then came slowly where the first swan was, this second swan was all in black and red mouth color, and when he reached where the first swan was, then they hug with their necks and scratches each other with their mouths and make sounds like talking to each other, Saqr was all the time watching them behind the grass, suddenly he remembered his sisters, as time passed away, but what can he do now, he cannot come out or move from his hiding place, a small movement can draw attention to these two birds, so he decided to remain there calm and just watch these birds of next will be, and in his mind was asking himself [where are these two coming from? and why then this particular place is their meeting place? if these were immigrates birds, then for sure they will be more than two birds, but only these two birds know the secret of this particular place] but then after a long enjoying the water, the birds suddenly started to swim simultaneous heading toward a small white sand beach very near of where Saqr was hiding, Saqr here then decided to go more lower profile so not to be seen, he was afraid to scare them, maybe if they see him they will go away, the birds swim up to the beach and came out of the water, and then they face each other and open their wings and speedily open and closing them, and raise their heads up in the sky and cry so loudly, and suddenly Saqr was shocked of what he saw, as those birds continuous to make noise slowly they start to change from swan to a human being shapes, until both of them changed completely to a human shapes, a male and a female, and both they wear very expensive well decorated clothes, and when they were completely human, they stop shaking their bodies and stop making noises, then the lay down so tired from that transformation of turning from swans to human, Saqr still asking himself [who are these creations?] After a short rest then they sat down and hold each other hand and hug so tightly to each other body, while they were crying with pain and agony, and Saqr noticed tears were falling in streams on their chicks, these unexpected actions from these two, really have upset Saqr's mind, he do not know what to think and what to assume, what strange things has happened to me this day? [asking himself] then he started to count hem, first the strange wilderness, second the string waterfall mountain, third, these strange creatures on top of this strange place, and lastly the transformation of these swans to human beings and why this painful and tortured crying? and then they stopped hugging and the young man said something to the young beautiful lady, but Saqr could never understand what they were saying, as they were not speaking in Arabic but another language, and that language sound more like Afghani or Turkish or Farsi, though Saqr could not understand what he was telling his lover, but I have to explain to you my dear reader what the talking was about, he said "My love Nazniyna, this our meeting day today after completing the whole one year of pain and torture with very hard and bitter patience" and Nazniyna replied "Yes my love, and hero of my heart, Oh! Shuhur jaan, this our day after one whole year in torture in pain, in thirsty of your love my dear, this today is that day of another meeting" this all conversation between these two strange lovers, Saqar did not understand what they were saying, but the action after that was, the young man then wipe the tears on his lover chicks, and then Nazniyna did the same to Shuhurjaan, and then again they hugged so closely and each one calling the name of other "My dearest love Nazniyna" and "My dearest love Shuhur jaan" this is prove to Saqr that how much these two love each other, but he then understand that something must have happened to that turned them into this the swans, could be something like sorcerer or some magic have turned them like, and they come here just to relief because they know that here is where they will transform into their originality so they come here, but yet Saqr do not who these people are and from where they are coming from, are they originally human beings who were turned into swans? Or are they Jinni's or other creatures who are not animals and not humans? These were the questions running in Saqr's mind, he does not know of where he will get their answers, but he said that "I will remain here until I see their end, what will be after this"

Naznina and Shuhurjaan remain there and enjoying their love with talking and laughing till near the last light of the evening, and Saqr remain where he is just watching and investigating their movements, for the whole night these two were enjoying their love, and when the sign of early morning shows to appear, then these two lovers stand and facing to each other and raise their head up in the sky and start to make noise like when they came, and slowly the transformation begins and turn them again into the swans, and then they enter into the lakes and start to fly away high above in the sky until they disappear, and this was a full moon night, the vision was possible. Saqr then had a chance to come out from his hiding place, and then he went where those two lovers spent their whole night and he sat down, allowing his mind to recall all that night events of those two strange creations, he then notice in front him on the sand two shinning objects, he picked them up and check them, they were two finger rings, they were so beautiful and were made one in silver and the other in gold, he assumed, the silver ring had a black gem and the gold ring had a diamond gem, and there were nice decorations on both rings, skilled with high professional art work, Saqr then put them in a safe place in his cloth and hide them firmly, then he decided to return home, he was afraid not to put too much worries into their parents, he then climb down the mountain the same way he has climb up until reached down, and he did find his camel was still there, he ride his camel and headed home.

When Saqr reached home, he went first to meet his friend Antar in the stable, and there he saw those two camels which Fardhana and Fardhada rides, he got relief in his heart to know that his two sisters have returned safely home, Antar and Saharzena stood with their hind legs, as greeting to their master when they saw him he is back and safely, as all at home were worried for his not returning last evening, he enter the stable and went and tight his camel and gave him water and food after a long journey, then Antar and Saharzena both of them came to him and put their necks on his shoulders showing their love and how they were worried for him too,

And they both said "Thank God for coming back safely, master" and he replied "Thank both of you for your concern on me" then Antar asked Saqr, "Oh! Master,

Did you met any problem yesterday that has holds you to come back? "And Saqr answered "No, there were any problems but there was something unusual happened to me for the first in my life" and then Saqr told the whole story of what has happened yesterday to Antar and Saharzena, and in the end he produce those two rings and showed them, then Antar looked careful at those rings and said "My dear Master, what I am going to tell you now, will be something very hard to believe, in the past, before I have been transform into this shape of a horse, I heard my grandparents talking about the Tale of a young Persian Princess, who fell in love with a poor young man, and that has caused quite a big misunderstand between King Kismat ibn Shahzara and her daughter Princess Nazniyna, King Kismat was a powerful ruler and dare full who ruled without any fear, as he was a King who maintain to keep Ruhanis and the Jinnis, he command them and these Ruhanis and Jinnis were afraid of him, the love story of which his daughter and that young poor boy, did not pleased him at all, he did tried very much to warn her daughter about her love affair with that young poor boy, but the young Princess was so deep in love that she care not all of her father warning and continue her love with that poor boy, King Kismat was not against the marriage but was against the choice of her daughter marriage to a poor family, this is will bring shame to his family and his all Kingdom, and even may caused embarrassment from his subjects and his neighboring countries, this is what he was afraid of, if their secret of love making will come out and spread, that will bring big shame to King Kismat and all his family as well as his all Kingdom, how can a Princess of Persia fell in love and want to get married with a simple poor young boy who has no Royal blood, the ignorance and the careless of his daughter as well as her stubbornness, was not bearable by King Kismat, he then decided to stop this childish game of his daughter, he find his own way of how to stop this shame in his family,

Then one day he called his daughter in his chamber and told her that he agree to allow them get married but in condition, that their wedding will be in secret without inviting people and it will take place in one of his palace which is very far away near the border of his neighboring country, and after their marriage, they are not allowed to return here in the capital of Persian Kingdom where King Kismat live but to remain all their lives in that palace with all necessary needs and all the servants and guards needed, and a piece of a big land for their cultivation including farmers and workers for that land, that will be the price they will have to pay to King Kismat Shahzara so give his consents to their marriage, the second condition which King Kismat gave his daughter Naznina is that, not her and all her children will be entitle to the throne of Kingdom of Persia, as that moment they will get married, their relation will be cut off between King Kismat and his daughter

Nazniyna, then he ask her "Do you Naznina agree to these conditions?" and poor Nazniyna for the sake of saving her love she had in her heart over Shuhurjaan, she agree to sacrifice all that she had and accept to her father conditions,

King Kismat Shahzara, then secretly took these two young lovers until they reached in his palace near the border of their neighboring country, he provide them with every necessary needs, include all the servants and guards to protect them, next day in the early hours of the morning, he asked them to come with him in his horse carriage, they went far crossing the desert until they reached where there was a big mountain, he asked them to get down from the carriage and follow him, then he start to climb that mountain in the hidden paths, these secret path to climb that mountain only him knows them, three of them climb that mountain following the secret paths and King Kismat was leading the way until they reached up that mountain where they find a big lake full of water, in the middle of that lake there was springs where the water came from, that place was so silence and there was no any other creation, but plenty of long grass and wild flower near the edge surrounding the lake, then they sat somewhere near the beach, and King Kismat then he told them of his intentions of why he has brought them here, he said "I swear upon my Allah's name, and in front of this great lake which is a witness to what I say, that if you two or any one among you, in any day in your living life you will go against my orders and against the conditions I gave you regarding keeping secret of your marriage, and if for any reason this secret leaks and spread, then know for sure both of you will suffer the punishment of transforming you two in other creature than human being, and you will remain to live that life in prison separately and never together, and in each year and in the same date I will transformed you, you will be released in that prison so you can come and meet here for just one evening and one night, and before the early hours of the morning you must leave this place and return to where you are prisoner, and this will be your way of life the whole of your lives till death do part you or if my heart changed and forgive you, this will a punishment for not obeying if you will disobey my rules and my instructions, now tell me, do you still want to get married and put my name in shame?" then Nazniyna replied her father "yes Abbajaan, to the marriage and no to put your name in shame" and they all return to their new living palace.

After their marriage ceremony completed, King Kismat called these two lovers and said to them "Today I believe that the power of love is much stronger than the power of blood relation, today I believe that love can sell even the blood relation cheaply just for the sake of buying love relation heavily, from this day, I have wiped you Naznina from my heart and from each member of our family, just because you did not value us more than you have valued your love, but know this Naznina, any day you will try to cross border of my country and go to the neighboring country, then you and your this lover will suffer heavily, your only way to live in peace is to remain here in this palace without to be seen or known that you are Naznina the princess and daughter of King Kismat Shahzara, you are not allowed to invite strangers here in this palace, be very careful to obey me and my rules, but if for any reasons your presence here will known by others and the news will reached me, than know for sure that same day I will punish you for the rest of your living lives, this is I promise you, and so I have said it, and so it should be done" and then King Kismat marry the couple himself in Islamic manner and in front of all the servants as witnesses, and then he left them there and he returned back to his Kingdom in the capital of his country, and so my master, this is the tale of Princess Naznina and her father King Kismat Shahzara, but it did not there, as Shuhurjaan and Naznina lived there happy life in that palace until they start to feel bored, now they want something difference in life, they want more of what they have missed it, they lived there with all the facilities and fulfillments of their demands, but what they were missing is there social life, they missed their friends, relatives, seeing of outside world life, even some of the food which they used to get when they were in the capital, and all of this is because of the love they allowed to grow in their hearts.

In the neighboring countries bordering this Kingdom of King Kismat, and in particular those countries which where Shuhur jaan and Nazniyna were living in their palace, there is a yearly festival which their people have created themselves, this festival is known by the name of LOVE YOUR NEIGHBOR, there are events for seven days, and it goes around, each year this festival is in one country, fortunately this year festival was in this Kingdom and in particular in this area, people bring their products to sell in those area chosen specially for the festival events, also there are local folklores, cooking food competitions, handcraft works competitions, for years now these events continue of more than five countries participation, also their games competitions, as well as holly Qur'an memorizing competition, for seven days the festival events are in each country and according to their programs which they have agreed together these neighboring countries, just to exchange many things and show their love to each other, and that is why they have name their festival LOVE YOUR NEIGHBOR.

This festival events were very rare things to Shuhur jaan and Nazniyna, all their live never had a chance to experience such a thing, the envy to go and to see such a thing were eating them in their minds, they would like to go and see for their selves, and maybe have fun and enjoying, or buying something from their neighbor products, the festival was so huge and big with so many people participation and thousands and thousands of visitors, so Shuhur jaan and Nazniyna changed in simple clothes just to hide their identity, and went there and really they did enjoy in everything they saw, they went to see differences competitions, and enjoyed the cooking of their neighbors and bought so many things for themselves, all seven days they attend this festival events without missing any day, and on the last day of the events, Nazniyna completely forgot herself, who is she and from where she is coming from, as that day they went where handcraft makers displaying their products, when they reached at the jeweler shop and saw many products which were made of silver and copper, here is where they saw those two beautiful rings and liked them, so they decided to each a ring of his/her like, She bought a silver ring for her husband and he bought a gold ring for his wife, and each one gave that present to his/her love, the shop owner of those rings, had his doubts on these two young lovers, he had found these couple buying very expensive things, they must be rich people, so he started to ask them some questions "you young couple seems that you are really in love to each other, and maybe coming from the rich family, from which

Family is you, who are your parents? What about if you ask them to join with me in this business, there is high profits in jeweler business" and Nazniyna replied, "No thank you, our family are no interested in any business, they are well to do and have plenty enough without entering in business" he then asked "Who are your family my dear young lady, that he do not want to earn more in business, then what they do to earn their earning?" and here is where Nazniyna forgets herself and without realizing she quickly answered "I am a Princess of this country, I am a daughter of Shahenshah King Kismat Shahzara and this is my husband" and here is where Shuhur jaan got a shock of his life, what have my wife done? And he gave her quite a look of warning for what she had done, revealing the secret of their identities,

Nazniyna when she saw her husband was shocked and looking at her with alerted open eyes, here then she realizes here mistakes, [oh! God, what have I done?] She raise her hands and cover her mouth and was shocked, and fear start to go through her mind, she then knew what a great mistake she did, why she had reveled their secret? And today without being careful she have spill the beans, quickly both of them left the place hurry and rush to their palace, and when they were at their palace, Naznina was not happy at all, she was all worried, all her happiness have disappear, her heart was full of fear, she does not know what will happened in the next coming hour, she cannot even sit one place but going there and coming back here, and then she went to her husband and said "Please forgive me my husband, please forgive the bad mistake I have commit, I have put you in suffering all your coming life, from now on you will never be safe or find happiness but only suffering and torturing and all because of me, because of my stupidity mouth which could never control itself, Oh! My God, what have I done, what have I done" and Shuhurjaan came and hug her and said "Yes Nazinina, that was your greatest mistake, I am not worried about suffering or of all the punishment your father will give me, my worries are only you my love, I do not know how will you be able to bare to take those coming suffering, and what kind of suffering will those be?" and here is where Naznina release her breath and felt a little comfort from the courage words which Shuhurjaan gave her.

They keep on living their life in that palace, though they were trying to ignore of what will come, Yet as they do not know of what will happen next, they tried their best to live their day to day life without thinking of what will happen tomorrow.

After three days pass by and nothing happened, they took it as they are safe and nothing will happen, the curse of King Kismat will not come to them, but unfortunately, on the same third day night, Naznina dreamed her father came to her with great anger, and he was so mad, and she saw that he was provoking her with strong words of anger, he said "After all, you did of what I warn you not to do, Eh? And you ignore of all the circumstances which will come to you, but I swear to God Naznina, like you had anger me, from now on you will never find peace of mind or happiness at all, and from this moment you will never see your husband again, but only once a year on that mountain which I have taken and show you, and you will meet there not as human but as animals and then you will transformed into human for a limited period of the whole night, and before sunrise you must return of where you will be prisoner all your living life, there will be no one among human who can help you in this punishment but only me, and that when my heart cool and my anger wiped from my heart and my mind, then maybe I may consider give you both your freedom, pray to Allah that I will live longer, because if I die then I will die with that key of retuning you into your original human being forms, and the I chose for your meeting with your husband will be on 14th of every dhul hajj, in Islamic calendar, that will be a full moon night so at list there will be some vision, and you both will be transformed into big swans, where you will be able to fly and to that place on the mountain for your annual meeting, and remember Oh! Naznina, this is the lowest punishment I gave you, thank your God I did not give you my worst punishment" then Naznina woke up from her sleep sweating, and fear control her mind, and her heart beats faster, she put her hand on her chest and recite the holly Qur'an verse just to cool and sooth her heart not to beat faster, and when she got her relief then she woke her husband Shuhurjaan to tell him of all what she dreamed of, but she did not find him on the bed, and not even in the room, where is Shuhurjaan gone? She went and asked the palace guards if they have seen her husband, and they said "we did not seen him come out from the house" she went back to the house and search in every and each room, but in vain, her husband is nowhere to be found, here then where she has put back of her hand on her forehead and cried loudly "Shuhur jaan! Shuhur jaan! I have lost you my dear and all because of me" and then she drop herself on the ground while keep on crying and hit the ground with her fists, this is where she remember, what a price to pay for just a little foolish mistake.

Antar conclude telling his story of King Kismat Shahzara and her daughter Naznina "And so my young Master, this what has happened to Princess Naznina, and according to these two rings and two those two large swans, I could say that my dear master you are the only Human being who was lucky enough to witness with your own eyes the existing of those two young lovers, Shuhurjaan and his loving wife Princess Naznina, and all that has happened because of your determination and stubbornness and you always do not like to be defeated" and Saqr replied "Masha'allah, this really is a happy and a sad story of these two young lovers, and which has so painful ending, now I understand and remember the language which these two lovers were using when I met them, was Farsi (A Persian language), these two are coming from that country which is located on the east of Arabian peninsula and as is known as Persia, and now with no doubts, all of which I had witnessed today and all of which you Antar had narrated to me, I must tell all of them inside, so they two believe of what I have seen last night, maybe from your tale Antar, another thoughts may be born of how to create a success fight of defeating Khurkhush Majangar, forgive me my friends, I have spent a very long time here with you, but it is the time to wipe the tensions and fear in the hearts of those inside, allow me to leave you, But Antar, that was quite a lucky day for you to get the chance of hearing from your grandparents the tales of King Kismat and his daughter Nazniyna".

And then Saqr leaves the stable and went inside the house to meet his family after the whole night disappearance, and he found his family all were sad mood, and all because of him not returning the whole night, and when all they saw Saar has returned safely, everyone atood and rushed to greet and hug him, and happiness has returned in that house again, after all the greeting and the hugging and the kissing on the forheads, Saar has this to say "After the Isha'a prayers, we all will sit down and I will tell you the whole story of why I did not came back last night here" and everyone said "Insha'allah" (God willing).

After their prayers and dinner, they all gathered in lounge to hear what Saar has to tell them about his last night disappearance, and then Saqr narrated his story step step from the moment he leaved the house with his sisters, and how they found that strange place where there was no any living creature, and how they decided to divided in group and how he was able to climb that mountain and what he has found up there on the mountain and what strange birds who landed there in that big lake, and how they transformed into human beings and how patience he was to hide for the whole night behind the bush of weeds and how before sunset those two swans return transforming into their swans again and what he find their two forgotten finger rings, and produce them to show to prove his story, and then he told them the story of King Kismat and her daughter Nazniyna, Abu Muntasir then asked Saqr "Oh! Saqr, how come for you to know this story of so many years back?" and Saqr replied "It is true my dear uncle Abu Muntasir, how come I will know something of the past while I am still young, but my dear uncle do not forget we human being have learned a lot, we have learned of the past and of the presents, we have learned of Prophet Adam and Eve, yet we were not there at their times, and this is possible now through those who preserve the history, either through writing in the books or narration from one person to the other, do not get surprise know about King Kismat, I am sure among there are who knows the history of King Solomon and Sheba, Sultan Harun Rashid and Aba Nawas, all these possible, by hearing from those who have heard the stories before me" and Abu Muntasir said "True my son, this is how we build our life histories, to tell others of what has happened today and to hear from others of what has happened yesterday and this is how our history remain to told to those who not heard what has happened here" and then Maalim Mikdad said "as for me, I have never heard about this story of King Kismat, though King Kismat is still exist and still ruling his country, and it is true that he is the most powerful king, fearless and brave, warrior, yet he love his people and he is very helpful to his subjects, he is kind at heart, but he is never afraid to remove that which will stand on his way, and also it is true as I have heard, that King Kismat Shahzara, is keeping and commanding Ruhanis and Jinnis as his private army, and those who are making him so fearless and powerful"

And for me to know about King Kismat, I am sure there are among you who knows the history of King Solomon and Sheba, about Sultan Harun Rashid and Aba Nawas, all this is possible, by hearing from those who have heard the stories before me" and Abu Muntasir said "True my son, this is how we build our life histories, to tell others of what has happened today and to hear from others of what has happened yesterday and this is how our history remain to told to those who not heard what has happened here" and then Maalim Mikdad said "as for me, I have never heard about this story of King Kismat, though King Kismat is still exist and still ruling his country, and it is true that he is the most powerful king, fearless and brave, warrior, yet he love his people and he is very helpful to his subjects, he is kind at heart, but he is never afraid to remove that which will stand on his way, and also it is true as I have heard, that King Kismat Shahzara, is keeping and commanding Ruhanis and Jinnis as his private army, and those who are making him so fearless and powerful"

CHAPTER TWELVE

(Impossible marriage)

*M*Y DEAR READER OF THIS book of TALES FROM ARABIAN AND PERSIAN DESERTS, we must allow ourselves now to live all about the lives of Saqr and his family and return back to that time of we have left off, the time of those three Princes brothers who were traveling back to their home town Jabal Qamar.

Early next day, the caravan of three Princes left the oasis and headed to Jabal Qamar, but Sheikh Nuwr Alaa Nuwr was not in happy mood, and all because he was thinking of how he can face his parents regarding his intentions of getting married to his love the girl of his choice, how can he explain of how he met this girl, the worst part is he is a Prince and this girl is not a member of any Royal family, but also she is not a human being but a Jinni, these all are matters which for sure will be a reason to rise complications, though he was traveling with his eyes wide open but his vision was zero, no vision in those eyes, and his mind and his heart are all beating fast and he have no hope that his request will be granted, he begins to change in his habits, even his brothers begin to notice that their young brother is not normal, he was not concentrating, he is all in upset mind, here then his elder brother Sheikh Najaad asked him "Eh! Nuwr, are you alright my young brother?, I Notice you are not in normal condition, are you not feeling well? Is there anything you ate and has upset you? Or is there something happened to you of whom we do not know? Tell us dear brother, we might help you to overcome your problems" and Sheikh Nur replied "yes Oh! elder brothers, there is a reason for me to change my habits, there are things which occur suddenly last night, and those thing is like a big burden in my heart as well as my mind, and I do not know of how to overcome them, and with all respects to you my brothers, since that time which has changed me and until now, I have failed to get an excuse of how to explain it to you my brothers, I am just stuck in that web of which I cannot untied and free myself from it, I am afraid that in front of me there must be unpleasant which will happen, even those unpleasant

116

words from your mouths of which will hurt my feelings, I am afraid to listen to them, and I hope you will not say anything" these all conversation was going between these brothers while their caravan was in its movements, here then Sheikh Najaad hold his camel and stopped it and said "May God forbid in every evil, did it reached this stage my dear young brother, that you are hurt inside and you have things which we do not know, and yet you kept quite all this time without sharing your problems with us, is this possible for you to do such a thing? What kind of problems that have occurred between last evenings to this morning which has changed you to this level that all the way you do not speak with anybody, and habits have changed, and yet you could not be able to involve us your brothers so to sit and discuss together and to try and find a solution of how to overcome your problem, you could not share your pain and agony or your worries with us, but why? are we not brothers?" and Sheikh Nur replied "It is not that my dear brother, not to that extent that I will ignore you my brothers, for what has happened to me, has no reason at all to avoid and not to share my problems with you, but I request you, I beg you, be patience with me until we reached home, then we will sit together and I will all tell of what has caused me to change in habits, this a promise to you my brothers, and without you my brothers, I am nothing, I always depend on you on many things in my life, let us continue our journey safely and all the good blessings will be there at home waiting for us, I pray so" and Sheikh Najaad was pleased with his younger brother answer, and they continue their journey until they reached their Kingdom Jabal Qamar.

A very hot reception was waiting for them, as they were excepted this day to return, everyone in their Kingdom was there to receive them, all the roads were decorated and people were on the streets to receive them, their parents were so happy for their return back home safely, but all this happiness and celebrations did not cheer up at all and make Sheikh Nuwr happy, and all because every past minute he was thinking how to overcome his problem of explaining his love with Zarza Aarish to his parents, he remain so quiet and sad, he was remembering last night of how he met Zarza Aarish for the first time, and what a beautiful woman she was, but the main problem here is, how can he pursued his parents and make them be satisfied that he want to get married with on beautiful girl he saw on the way coming here, and yet, the girl is not a member of any Royal family, also is not a human but a Jinni, how can they be pursued to except his demand? So that beautiful woman should remain his all his life in legal manners (Halal), here is where the main problem lies. When all ceremonies completed and everyone returned to his home, then

Sheikh Nur was summoned by his father who is the ruler of that Jabal Qamar Kingdom, to attend a meeting, he quickly obey the call and hurry to go and see his father for what his was called off, when he reached there, his father was not alone but with all his advisers as well as tribal chiefs of that Kingdom, he wished by saying "Peace be upon you" and they all answered "Peace be upon you too" as their culture and tradition allowed them to do, he kept his right hand on his chest and bowed to all of them, and then went straight to where his father was sitting and kissed his hand and forehead as a respect to him, and said "Peace be upon you dear father" and his father replied "Peace be upon you too my son" and then Sheikh said to his father "You have summoned me to be here Oh! Dear father, and I am here, command me father, what do you wish me to do?" and then his father said "I have been told that you are not feeling well my son Sheikh Nuwr, that there is something bothering you, I want you yourself to tell me my dear last son Nuwr, what is that bothering you, and make you not to feel well?" and Sheikh Nuwr replied "May God give you health and longer life dear father, that you will always be and stand with us when we are in need, but please do forgive me Oh! Dear father, but I need you to promise me, if I will give you my secret of what is that bothering me, and put them under your feet, that you will not put your feet on them but will take them with your own hands, this is my request to you my dear father, will you please promise me that?" and then his father replied "My dear Sheikh Nuwr, I found that your conditions are hard to swallow, as they force me to do something without consideration, I do not think that you have the right to do that, but that right is mine, I have to give the condition and not you, now tell me truly, how come you my son to cross out of your boundaries and give me conditions before listening to your problems, and that I should not through away you demands even if they are against our traditions and cultures and the safety of our people and our Kingdom?"

And here then Sheikh Nur through himself on the ground in front of his father and all his father's adviser cabinet and said "do forgive me my dear father, I did not do that to show ignorance to you or superiority, but the fear which is in my heart command me to request you that you should not lose your temper after you will come to know that which has changed me in my habits and deny me of my happiness, that is my main reason of begging you of not put your feet of what I have to tell you but to take it with your hands and put it in your mind for consideration and fair judgment and all because I am afraid when you get angry, and I do not want make you angry and lose your temper, instead of solving the problem then I created more, the problem of which is eating inside me, in my heart and my mind, if there is anyone who can help me then it is only you my dear father, I do not have any bad intentions within me but just my intentions are to be allowed to live with what I have love it, Please father, do not get angry if you come to know of what is that I love, I only ask for your blessings and keep your mind and your heart very cool and tender so I can feel free to you in details of what that has changed me into a difference person" and then his father replied "If there is a way to avoid my anger, then I promise you that I will listen your story with a cool heart and a consideration mind, I give you my words in front of all these people present here, my dear son Sheikh Nuwr" then he explain to his father everything in details of how he came to see that bird of wonder with his singing melodies, and how come he heard someone in the night playing Rabaab and how he went to search in the desert and met Zarza bint Aarish, and that is the reason of his habit changing as he is so much in love in that girl and he want to get married with her "And now I am asking for your consents to marry her, my dear father" After hearing all the tales of his son, Sheikh al Kabir, has this to say "I do not know where to begin in giving you the proper answer to your problems my younger son Sheikh Nuwr, I do not know how to weight this happenings that they are blessings or evil doing, but it is not easy on my side as your father as well as a leader of the nation and ruler of this Kingdom of Jabal Qamar, to judge you fairly and without being one sided, it is not easy for me at all, but to give you an answer of my judgment, that I will sure will, and that is what exactly you are excepting me to do, is it not?" and Sheikh Nuwr replied "Yes dear father" and then Sheikh al Kabir said "Now hear this of what I have to say, and it should be written on all our history books, so to remain for our future generation.

As a Sheikh of all tribes and as a ruler of this Jabil Qatar Kingdom, so here I speak openly that your marriage will not be possible, until there is clear evidence from our religious scholars that there are proofs from all the books of God that this kind of marriage is allowed and excepted by God, a marriage between a human being to a Jinni, one has been created by blood and flesh of which it's originate is clay and the other who is created with fire, I have no other choice but to forbid this marriage completely, as it did never happened before, generation after generation and it will never be allowed to happen in this generation, I am so that I can never help or be with you on your request, this the time one should judge fairly according to the law of Allah, and the time of pleasing one person against the whole nation, as I do not want to commit myself in taking the wrong step and Allah tomorrow on the day of judgment count me wrongly and send me in hell because of you my son, also remember that not any parent will allow to marry or be married by someone who no one have and know his or hers background, I want you to be brave, I ask you to be brave, not to get angry with my decision but to take the answer and weight it in your mind that am I write or wrong in my decision? take my place and act as judge to your own son who will come to you on the same request, what will your decision be, will you allow such marriage or will you not permit it?,

May Allah help me and guide me not to make any wrong decision that will anger him and put me in the hell fire for that wrong doing." And then Sheikh Nur replied his father "I understand of what you have told me father regarding your decision, it is true that this is quite a challenge for you not to take any wrong decision, here is where wisdom and justice is needed for anyone who judge fairly without being one sided, you are a leader of our nation father, and citizen always follow the steps of what their leader does, one have to be careful in his judgments and decision making, and you have that decision after using your wisdom and fair judgment, and in the history of this nation never before were accused of being unfair, all the people respect you for what you are as a leader who stand on justice, and I now respect your decision on me and I obey it, but Oh dear father, I promise you this, here now and in front of all the cabinet of your advisers, if it is not possible for Zarza to be my wedded wife, then all my life there will be no other wife for me who take her place, and also here this dear father, my relation with Zarza will not be cut off, but will be stronger all my living life until that day we human beings will be allowed to wed Jinnis if god will permit, so I have said, so I will stick with my decision. I beg for your pardon your Highness, and I also beg the pardon of your advisers cabinet, I ask your permission to live this place now" And here is where Sheikh Nur leave that place with tears in his eyes and heavy burden of anger and disappointment in his heart".

Immediately after sheikh Nur left the palace Diwan (court), One of his father's adviser ask permission to speak, and he said "Your Highness, Our young Prince is not in good shape but also in very dangerous position, in this condition, any young man like him could even harm himself or even the unexpected things, here it need wisdom to deal with this kind of situation, just to cool him down until his heart relax and realize of what you had told him was the right judgment, and for his own good, Let us ask others here in this Diwan who have any experience of this kind of situations to speak and advice us of how we can help our young Prince in his mingled himself in falling in love with another young one, and not to a human but to a Jinni" And the Sheikh replied "I agree with you, it is true of what you have said, the only problem here is that kind of his choice to the girl he wants to marry, never in my life did I heard or witness a marriage between a human being and a Jinni, not in the past and never this generation, it pain me so much for my son to get involved with this Jinni girl, the question here now, is, how can we help him to avoid this marriage with this girl?" then another of the Sheikh adviser asked permission to speak, and he was allowed, then he said "All the books of God have mentioned the creation of these creations, and God said in his Holly Qur'an [I create human beings and Jinnis to have faith in me and do the prayers] yet in all those four books, not even one of them mentioned the existing of marriage between us human beings and Jinnis, still among them there are very obeyed and religious mind Jinnis, who also performed their faith duty regularly as they are commanded by Allah like us, and if it was allowed this kind of marriage, then during the ruling of Prophet Solomon that could have happened, but not history and not Books of Allah have mentioned that to happen, then this is clearly that a marriage of this kind did not occur before for many fundamental reasons, like those who will be born from these kind of parents, will be in which groups? Will they be human beings or Jinnis or a new creation of Humanjinni? We human beings are known as children of Adam, what their children then will be, from what source they come from? There are many differences between us human beings and Jinnis,, we get sick we are cured by Hakims, but what about them do they get sick like us, these are the many reasons that Allah did not mentioned regarding the marriage between us Human and Jinnis, and I do not think this is allowed, and I as among an adviser to your cabinet, I personal object to this marriage as well as the relation between them"

Sheikh Nur when he left the palace court of his father where he was summoned to present himself for a special inquiry regarding his habit changing, he was broken hearted and all his mind was disturbed, he was a person with full of pain in his heart, he then went to the stable and took a horse and ride out of the palace yard rushing into the wilderness, he went far away and until he find a place where there is a shadow of tree and stopped his horse there, and then his dismount his horse and went and sit under that tree of where there was plenty of shadow, all his mind was upset and his body was shaking with anger, and his eyes start to shed tears and then suddenly he shout with all his voice power and cry out his anger, he then called "Zarza, Zarza, come please come" he then felt someone touched his shoulder and a voice said "I am here my Prince, your Zarza is here with you" and then Zarza appear in person and came and sit near Sheikh Nur while holding his hands, and Sheikh Nur still his body shaking and tears falling down his chicks, said "It is not fair, I swear to God it is not fair at all for what they have done to me, how can I be able to explain to you what my father and his advisers cabinet has decided on our marriage planning, please Zarza forgive me, for our marriage will not be possible, as my father did not approve the marriage between us, and Zarza put her hand on his mouth to stop him continue speaking, and then she said "My Prince, all that I know, as I was there but unseen, I heard every and each word which every one spoke about our relation, though you had left the palace court but also the advisers had their saying, I heard all what they had said.

But my dear, please allow to release these tensions which are within you, please be cool and think, and do not get more angry, let not the bitterness within your heart and your mind grow bigger, that will not help but will lead you to the disaster, here is where wisdom and better knowledge is needed, if I as a Jinni did understand their objection stand, then why not you?, I found that their objection reasons of not for us two to get married is very sensible, why we should not be allowed to get married is all because of we are two difference creations, you are a human being and your sources are coming from Adam and Eve and these two first human beings were created from sand clay, while my sources are created from fire, this is the will of Allah, it is impossible for two of us to create a family and live in harmony, we are differences, you have to agree my dear, and all I came to understand when those advisers explained in details of why human beings and Jinnis cannot live as a family, and they were so concerned about your condition, as you were there in great anger and have sworn in front of them that if we are not allowed to get married with me, then all your life no one will take my place and you will marry no other than me, this call did put fear in them as they are afraid that you might harm yourself or harm others, Now is the time for you to think, consider and give your mind more energy to function well, so to come with the right answer of how you can tackle your personal mind to produce for you the understanding solution, same as I have now, think and think to be able to understand of why before us this kind of marriage never happen, there must be very good reasons behind it, reasons not from human but maybe from God himself. Now I want you to do the same as I did and then give me your answer"

Kismat Shaharyaar at the hunting ground

Two arrows hit the lion

Here then Sheikh Nuwr allowed his mind to reduce its tensions and study of what Zarza has advice him to do, he begins to understand now, of why his father was against his marriage and why those advisers also did not allow this marriage to proceed, he then bent his head and look down on earth while thinking, after moments passed by, he then raised his head and look at Zarza while his face was all changed, he has wiped out all his anger and some shinning appear on his face though not with a smile but with no hard feelings on it, he then said "It is true of what you have told me Oh! Zarza, there are time it is not possible to do the impossible, one cannot go against the nature of how things they are created, and we human beings sometime force ourselves to do thing against its nature, or against its principal, which is wrong, the outcome results sometime is not except able by our society or by the will of God, for example, if God has allowed animals also to get married, will the marriage between a donkey and a cow will be allowed? Definantly not, as it is against its nature. Yes Zarza, one must be brave and not to be weak against his willpower, if his willpower will be weak then this will lead him to play many wrong roles out of his living life, If a human today dare to face an angry lion in front of him then why he should be afraid to face the facts and the truth? Yes Zarza, if it was not for you to make me understand the facts nature of how things they are created and should remain that way, then I do not know what kind of condition I would have been, Thank you Zarza, for your advices and for your wisdom, but still there is something bothering my mind about you Zarza, why you did not show any sign of disappointment or anger, when you are also affected on this situation?" and Zarza replied "Because all my angers wiped off by the wise explanation of those old people who are your fathers advisers, what they have said did make sense to me, that the one reason of why I could not show any anger as I did understand the facts of the situation of how it is, and I have believed in it and then I went and sit on the praying matt somewhere and raise my hands to Allah and ask him to guide me and help me to overcome that anger within me, this is what my friend the camel taught to do when one is desperate, then I followed you up to here to try and make you understand as well, so you also can forget this relation idea of us getting marriage, so now I ask you too my dear love, face your Allah by sitting down and pray and ask him to guide you too, so you too can have that relief in your heart and take the matters as how they are in their natural way and not to force it into unnatural way, only God who answer his creation prayers, though I am a Jinni but I do believe in God and his commands, though I have chased to fall in love with the most expensive human in my whole life, thing that exist but you cannot reach to it, also I will sit again and pray and beg for the forgiveness, as I swear to God that I will not again be married to another Jinni but only to a human being, which now I find it is not possible.

Yet it is true now that we could not create our own family, but we can remain very good friends all our living life, and we can help one another in any necessary needs" and Sheikh Nur replied "Yes Zarza, true what you said, if that was not possible than our friendship is possible, we can be friends all our living life, I promise you in the name of Allah that I will remain loyal as a friend to you, for better or for worse"

And then they depart with hugging to each other, and Sheikh Nuwr gain his strength and many of his inner agonies soothes away, and he became the same Sheikh Nuwr with full of energy, and all of this became possible because of the wisdom of Zarza to encourage him to be strong and wipe out all his pain inside him.

Sheikh Nur climb is horse to ride back home so to go and beg forgiveness from his God as well as his father for the last words he has said in front of all the advisers in that palace court, but before he leave that place, Zarza has this to say to him "I have no choice but to return of where I have come from in the Kingdom of Khurkhush Majangar, but know this, that since my arrival here in this humanly world, I have learn a lot and experience much with my short living period of being with you human beings here, I have came to know of many things I did not know before about you and about your faith of worshiping Allah, I have converted myself into Islam all because of what I have seen with my eyes and hear with my own ears that of which I had no chance to see and hear before, and the thanks should go to your camel who open my mind and educate me by explaining to me each and many of your traditions and cultures and your faiths, also if it was for Sheikh Shammaakh's that night religious event, maybe you and I would never be possible to met and be friends, and Sheikh Shammaakh is a very kind and generous person, many of my thanks should go to him, but let me tell a little about Sheikh Shammaakh, let me predict to you about what will happen to him in future, as you know that Sheikh Shammaakh has sent his son to learn about Islamic affairs as well as other knowledge which will make him an educated man, he will learn well and will help his father to run his business, but something bad will occur to Sheikh Shammaakh, as Shammaakh will disappear and no one will know where he will be, but that will not for a very long time, but he will suffer a lot of where he will be, if you will listen to me very careful, then he will come back, he will be prisoner by our King Khurkhush Majangar in his mountain Kingdom.

There is a young boy living in the desert of Empty Quarters, he is a poor boy and still young now, but when he will be matured he will be a brave dareful young man, who do not fear anything, something will happened with him and his family at that time of being a young man, something not bad but very dangerous and adventurous, he will survive this dangers with the help of friend who will appear in his village inexpertly, if it is possible on your side, then when that time will come, be ready to get in touch with this boy and join hand with him in his missions of helping others, and one of those who will face major problem when that time will come, will be this man Maalim Mikdad, because of his daughters, he will face hard circumstances of running away from his country and seek refuge in that Empty quarters family of Saqr family with others, the time is not yet now, but I gave you that information of what will happen in near future, so I have predicted, so you have to keep in your mind till that time will come, and you will be informed. Remember that we Jinnis sometime do know of what will be coming ahead of the time, this is a God given power we had, as I saw of what will happen and to that poor family of an

Honest man and his brave son, I have shared with you the secret of the future before it will happen, hide this secret in your heart and tell no one, but wait for me, as when the time will be ready to take any action, then I will let you know, and if it is possible on your side, you too can participate to help those who will suffer and will be prisoner by our King of Jinnis Khurkhush Majangar, did you understand my dear Prince?' and he replied "Yes Zarza, I understand very well, I promise you that I will keep this secret in my heart until that day you will allow me to take any action under your instruction," and Zarza then said "Close your heart and mind your tongue not to reveal this secret, I now wish to bid you not farewell but till we meet again, and if for any important reason you need me, then just call my name and I will be beside you with a glimpse of an eye, see you Insha'Allah," and Sheikh Nuwr said

"Goodbye my dear friend, and the only creation I have loved and within a glimpse of an eye" and Zarza vanished.

CHAPTER THIRTEEN

(King Kismat bin Shahzara bin Shaharyaar)

(During his youth time)

KING SHAHZARA BIN SHAHARYAAR, HAD only one son and he named him Kismat, he loved so much his son that he wants him to grow rapidly and learn quickly, he want to send him abroad to gain more knowledge and experience, knowledge of army, fighter with swords, knowledge of Islamic affairs as well as the knowledge of foreign affairs, as it was his plan that His Kingdom should be a friendly country to all nations of the world, he hates war and bad diplomatic relation with other nations, this was against his policy, he believe that love your neighbor and he will love you, that is why he prefer the idea of his son Kismat should go to the outside world and learn from them so when he come back he will be a ruler who have many ideas and information's of other people, so it may help him to create a Kingdom of which respect and live with peace with others, in the beginning he send him to neighboring countries of Sham, and that time those countries were known as Biladshaam, Badyaarab, Hijaz, al Jazeera and land of Palestine, and when Prince Kismat went there, he put all his efforts to learn well and understand the culture and traditions of the countries he had been schooling, he had made many friends, and was very handsome and charm, so many others liked him, he had a very good reading mind and memories, he learned quickly and most of his teachers did love him and he gained that title of BEST STUDENT OF ITS KIND, though his mother tongue was Persian (Farsi) but he dare to learn and command the Arabic language very well, especially with many of his friends there in the Land of Sham.

One of his best hobby was hunting, he likes hunting's, he spent much of his time during his holidays with his local friends there in the Land of Sham to go hunting, he is a very good archer, when of the best in his country Persia, and well known best archer in his country, in his holidays he will follow his friends who knows the many places of where to make a good hunting for Gazelles or birds.

Butterfly people

One day, during his holidays, he was invited by his friends to go for hunting in the wilderness, the invitation had made him so happy as he has envy it for a chance to go hunting in this land of his friends, and also it has been long time since he last went for hunting, and also he wanted to know the nature of that country's hunting, what kind of animals do they hunt, he left the town of where he is studying with his three rich friends with their servants and camping equipments, they went into the mountains and passed many valleys until they reached that hunting sport, where there is a stream of water passing through near the a mall forest of long trees, here the servants made a camp and they dismount on their animals and rest for a while.

Prince Kismat's friends were the children of well to do business men of that country, by names they were Marjaan, Qeis and Ridhwaan, after a long rest then they decided to go for hunting the same day after having some hot red tea known in those part as [istikhaan], this tea is cooked with combination of tea leaves and Safron, some likes to add a piece of a slides lemon as to add taste, the cooking port of this tea making is known as Samaawir in these parts, after having that tea which has stimulate their bodies, then they enter that nearby forest for hunting, riding their horses, they took their arrows and bows, and the servant they have their lances, in this country, hunting has its regulation and tactics, for some reasons, they do not call one another with voices but imitate animals or birds sounds to draw attention of one another, everyone chose particular sound so to recognize who is calling.

Qeis was the best guide, he knows these places like he knows the marks of his hands, he is also one of the best hunter, when they were inside the forest shadow, they move slowly with their horses, step by step and careful listen to the sounds of animals, while looking and searching with their eyes left and right until they came to a place where there was a stream of water running by, some of the hunted animals were sometimes coming for a drink of water here, always the hunters never go together side by side but they keep their distances to each other, here then suddenly Qeis halt and signed to Kismat to stop and to keep silence, he then pointed out and asked Kismat to look to his left, as far away a long side the stream there was a group of gazelles came to quench their thirst, Kismat saw those gazelles and signed to Qeis that he saw them, then Qeis signed to Kismat to dismount on his horse and tightened him at the tree while they will walk slowly, kismet understood and did the same, they cross that stream very slowly without disturbing those gazelles, slowly they took their weapons and keep them ready for any immediate attacking, here then Kismat when he find the right place and a good position for his hunting, he signed to Qeis who was far distance that he will be the first one to attack, and Qeis understood and agree, and then Kismat to his position and stand firm while raise his arch and aim and the largest male of them all and release his arrow which went exactly to his target and hit that male gazelle on his chest passing through to his heart, and make him to jump up and then fell down near that stream, here then Qeis rushed to slaughter that gazelle before it died, as in Islamic, it is not permitted to eat a dead animal meat with slaughtering with pronouncing IN THE NAME OF ALLAH, THE MOST MERCIFUL THE MOST GRACIOUS while slaughtering, and when Qeis reached the animal he found him still breathing, he quickly remove his dagger from its cover and completed the ritual, and then Kismat arrived to check the animal, yes that was quite a big male gazelle with plenty of meat. Qeis then request Kismat to bring the horses there so they can carry the animal on one of the horse, and Kismat obey that and went to bring those horse, he came back walking with horses, but before reached the place of where Qeis and the animal was, the horses denied to move and started to make noises, and pushing back Kismat, though he know much about horses habit, he tried to cool them but the horses completely denied to go forward but pushing back, then suddenly he heard a big roar of a wild animal, coming from where Qeis was, that roar really did shock Kismat, and quickly he tied the horses on the tree and rushed to where Qeis is and saw what was that roaring, as he was near the place he found that roaring was coming from one big strong lion, the lion was facing Qeis with his dead gazelle, the only reason that lion did not attacked Qeis was that Qeis had his lance ready in his hand and ready any time fight for his life from that roaring lion, that lion was only looking for a chance to grab that killed gazelle, as he was very hungry, and this place is his kingdom, Kismat find a chance and penetrate under the trees until he reached that position where he can see that lion clearly, he remove his arrow and put on the bow and aimed to his target who gave him his back as he was looking to Qeis, when Kismet sense that he was ready for realizing his arrow he called the lion by whistling, the lion got surprise by that sound and turn to see what is that sound, he saw that there is someone else here, he turned completely facing Kismat, and that was exactly why Kismat called for, just to get the lion attention so he should turn and give him his chest, and Kismat realese his arrow and it went directly to that lion chest and penetrate inside his chest to its heart, the lion felt the pain of the arrow and cry loudly with pain, and then send another arrow which enter in his right eye giving that lion more pain and here is where Qeis had his chance and came rushing with speed, lance in his hand and attacked that lion by throwing his lance into

King Kismat arrived at the desert mosque

that lion stomach, this added more fatal blow to the lion and the lion cried more and then it fell down with pain and blood coming out from his wounds.

Marjan and Ridhwaan while on the other side hunting, hey heard that agony noise of the lion suffering with pain, they were worried and concerned, as they did not know what was going on the other side of that area where Kismat and Qeis went for hunting, they decided to stop hunting and go and look to where their friends were hunting and to find out what was that noise all about, maybe they are in trouble and need their help, when they have reached where Kismat and Qeis were hunting, they have found that beast already dead and understood now who was that making noises, and Kismat and Qeis were alright, they help one another to carry both animals on the horses and return to their camp, then the servants immediately start to skin both animals, one foe food and the other for its fur skin, as that was very rare and expensive thing during that time in that country.

They spent their night there camping and enjoying every moment of it by feeding and feasting with plenty of meat and sleeping there till morning, Kismat when he was in his camp tried to sleep but could not get any sleep, he tried his best but the sleep was not his companion this night, as sleep itself tried its best to run away from him and let Kismat to be alone by himself only, he tried this side and that side and forcing his eyes to remain close but all in vain, he could not sleep, as his head denied to bring any sleep, he waited and waited and then after some time still closing his eyes but without sleep, he heard voices from far away, voices like people talking, he sat down on his sleeping place and concerning and listening to know and make sure is that voice are of people or whoever they are who, then he thoughts maybe the voices are of the servants and night guards chatting by themselves, and then slowly the voice started to fade away, and then it was all silence and no more voices, he then woke and sat up listening and watching the flames of the campfire images dancing its shadows on the tent, then he decided that is better to go outside for a short while, maybe the outside chills will help him get back his sleep, he stood up and put on better clothes and went outside to enjoy the chilly night, when he was outside, he found every servant and guard are all asleep, none of them are awake, this did surprise him if all these guards and savants are asleep then who is guarding and protecting this camp?, he then where the fire was still on and sat beside it just to get warm, he then look at all the sides of that camp just to check or maybe see something awake or moving, then he heard again that voice he heard before, people were talking from far away, but he could not understand their language, and do not know what kind of language were they talking, as they were not talking neither Arabic and neither Farsi, here then something he felt in his mind, and he felt some doubts running in his head, who these people talking? What language is this? And where are they? He then stood up and went into his tent and change into perfect clothes and took his sword and starts walking following the direction of where those noises where it was coming from behind of the tents, he did not wake anyone of his friends neither any of servant or guide but went alone following those noises, the voices did lead him into the woods where he enter inside the darkness of those trees, but fortunately that was a full moonlight night, but the more he goes further the more the voices are clear and closer but no one is there, only voices of people talking and in a very strange language to him, this became very strange and wear to him, with wide open eyes and his hand on his sword he looked around, every angel of where he was but could not see those who are talking, suddenly those voices stopped to talk and the place was silence again, then some thought came to his mind, maybe those who talking are trying play game with him, and he have no time for any game now, he decided to return to his camp, on his way back he felt someone press his right ear very hard, he thought maybe that was a jungle insect tried to bite him, he quickly raise his hand and clean his ear to scare that insect, when he did that then he heard that voice again but now talking in Arabic "you are hurting me" Kismat then asked "who are you talking without being seen and why you pressed my ear?" and the voice replied "Please my dear sir, bring your hand very close to your ear" and Kismat obey that order without fear, when he did that then he felt something jump on his hand and then the voice said "Now my dear sir, you can look at me" then he brought his hand in front of his face so to look at that thing which was on his hand, and he got a shock of his life, as what he saw on his hand is something in a shape of human, wearing local Arabic clothes, a robe and a turban and local shoes but has wings on his back, but above all, that human shape figure was just the size of his hand, he was very small just like a size of a pigeon, and he was standing on his hand looking direct to him, then Kismat said to him "Yes I saw you" then the little man bow his head with his both hands on his chest and then raise his head and wished by saying "Peace be on upon you my dear sir" and Kismat answered "Peace be upon you too little man, but to me you are something to wonder about, how come you are so little in size and you are as same in creation as me?" and that little man replied "Sorry my dear Sir, but I am not surprise at all in finding you in wondering of my shape, as I am not a human being, and I do not live here on this earth land, I live upon a higher mountain nearby here, that mountain land is the Kingdom of my queen, and

I am not alone but I came with my fellow men, we are known as Butterfly people, though you do not see them now because we are capable to be invisible and visible any time we want, we have carry with us a massage from our Queen to you, a massage of thanks for your bravery of destroying and killing of that beast which has disturbed and denying us coming down here, and not only that but also he has killed many people here among you and also among us, peace was available here because of that beast, but there is a question here your mind might have it, why in particular my Queen should thank you while we are not those people who living here on this Kingdom? The answer to that question is that even this gazelle are among her subjects, although we all know that you people are hunting them only for food, but you do not wipe them, this is except able, because even us we do use their meat as our food too, these animals are living with us up there on the mountains in our Kingdom, yet they are coming down here just because of these kind of grass which only grow here on this land, those grass are specially for these animals, as they contains some liquidity and that liquid is kind of medicine which make these animal very healthy and strong, and also that water stream which pass through that grazing area of where our animal come to feed, is essential for making these grass grow faster and plenty, that beast has killed many of our animals until he put fear to many of us, and only few dare to come down here just eat these grass for their food as well as their healthy gaining,

My queen also has instructed me to extend her invitation to you, she said that you will give her a great honor if you will except her invitation to visit our Kingdom, any possible day in your living life will be except able to her, as that will be one of the greatest day in the history of our Kingdom, but there is a condition here and you must agree to that condition, otherwise you are not except able to come, and that condition is that you must keep secret all these events of meeting us here and of coming to our Kingdom as guest of honor to our queen, until she will allow you to tell others about us and our Kingdom, now my dear Sir, before I disappear, do you any question you need an answer to it so I can help to give any information you need to know?" and Kismat then answered and said "yes I do have some questions to ask you Oh! you little man with such a wise and sweet tongue, my first question is, why you Queen among all us here, she choose me and only me, My second question, why your companion who are with you here did not show themselves until this moment so I can believe of what you have told me is true?

And the last question is, how your Queen did know about us and about our hunting here, and then sent you to deliver her thanks massage? I ask and request you to give my three questions and answers, please dear little man, go ahead as I am finish with my questions" the little man then answered and said "My dear sir, Oh you brave and dare full young lad, we of butterfly people Kingdom know much, by the will of God we can see or hear of what happened if we want too, we are not human like you but we are like angels though we are not angels. Now, if I have to reply your

Questions, the first answer for your first question is that, it is of your bravery and fearless which made you to face that fearful creature and destroy him just to save your friend who was in a great danger of being attacked by that lion, and it was your arrow which went through the heart of that lion and make him suffer with pain and then your friend finish him with his lancer. The second answer is that, why others who came with me did not show up so you can believe me that what I have told is the truth, yes sir for that I beg your pardon that at the that time I did not present them to you but now is the right time do that" and the little butterfly man clap his hands and many little butterfly people appear before him, the old, the very old, and the young ones, the n he completed to answer the third question, and said "our Queen has the power to know so many thing, not as a magic or witchcraft but as the power given by God, we too believe in Allah, we perform all the duties of the same faith you follow, our queen can see of what you cannot see and know of what you do not know. For such a long time now, this creature has bothered us by killing these gazelles, which also is one of the main sources of our daily food, it is true that we also are God creations but we do not maintain such strength and body power like you human being as we are created in very small body shape, though we fly and can disappear and appear by our own will which we have been given by Allah, but that is not power enough to fight such powerful and stengthfull creature, and this was our main reason of always being Allah to send us any one who can destroy this harmful creature who has caused us so many disaster and fear in this land of where we get food for our living, Allah has answered our prayers and brought you and your friends to come here for hunting and finish off this evil creature, and our Queen saw all of your bravery in her vision and that is why she has send us to find and meet you and convey her massage of thanks for what you have done by killing that disturbing lion, Now allow me your Highness, to present to you all others who came with me in front of you" the little butterfly man then called in his own language, and many little butterfly people appeared in front of Prince Kismat, he was so stunned and surprise to see such wonder of God's creation which he never saw in all of his life, so many butterfly people of all ages flying in the air with their colorful dresses, and all of them then together they bow their heads just to give respect to the Prince and said "Peace be upon you dear Prince Kismat" and Price Kismat reply them by returning his greeting and said "Peace be upon you too little butterfly people" and the little butterfly people then said "Oh dear Prince Kismat, what should we do to serve you just to show our gratitude and thanks for the brave action you and your friends have taken just make our living life batter by killing that fearful lion who had bothered us for a long time" and Prince Kismat replied "Thank you so much for your kinder heart, but for the time being I have no service or favor to ask you, but maybe in future if need come to request your help, I might ask for it, but I will ask you to take with you my greetings and my thanks to your Queen, and tell her that the message she had send to me of invitation, I have accepted with open heart, and when the right time will come, I will let her know that I am ready to pay a visit your to Kingdom, I also hope that you will let me know how to send my message to you, I thank her for praising me so much for what I have done but there are brave people in this world who are clever and brave more than me, also please return mu greetings and my many thanks for her, tell here her secrets will remain secrets, I promise not to tell anyone until I am permitted to do so, for the time being all your Kingdom secrets will remain in my hearts and will be lock to get out from there, farewell my little butterfly friends and safe journey to your homeland, the little butterfly man then asked. Prince Kismat then return to his camp and enter his tenet without anybody knows that he has left the camp that night, he then fell asleep till morning.

Days went by and Prince Kismat completed his study in that Shaam country, and he passed well, he waited until the time to return to his homeland was ready, then he remembered the promise he gave to Queen Farna Bash through her messengers little butterfly people, that when a suitable will come he will sure request a permission to pay a visit as he has promised, here then he did as he has been what told that when he is ready to come and pay a visit to the Butterfly people Kingdom he should this and that and the message will be conveyed, then that night when Prince Kismat was on his way home from the mosque while riding his horse, he felt someone has pinch his ear, he understood that the messengers now are here with him, he then raise his hand up to close to his ear and a very small little butterfly man jump on his hand, he then brought his hand in front of his face so to see who is there, but this time it was not the same old man who used to bring and take all the messages but a very young lad, the young lad then greeted the Prince and said "Peace be upon you my dear Prince Kismat" and Prince Kismat replied "Peace be upon you my dear young lad, a messenger from Queen Farna Bash" then a butterfly man said "Your Highness, you have called, and I have been sent to obey your call, tell me sir, what can I do for you at this moment?" and Prince Kismat then said to the young lad "Thank you so much my dear young lad, I have no service to ask you but only to convey my message to your Queen, tell her that Prince Kismat have completed his studies and I am planning to return to my home country very soon, but before I do that, I would like to complete the promise I gave her that when I am ready to visit her Kingdom and her people then I will inform her, for me now is the right to do that, and please convey my personal regards to her" and the little young lad of butterfly people answered "Thank my dear Prince, I heard and understood your message, I will convey your regards as well as your message to my Queen, is there any further services you need me to do?" and Prince Kismat told him "no my friend, thank you" and the little butterfly man then disappear in the thin air.

Prince Kismat then head his way to his home, he sat at the place where he will be served his dinner, before he was served he felt someone touch his right ear, he knew that the messenger is here, and before he could send his hand near his ear the little butterfly man came in front of his face while still floating in the air, the little man then greeted the Prince and said "Peace be upon you my dear Prince" and Prince Kismat replied "Peace be upon you Oh! Messenger of Queen Farna Bash" the little man then said "My dear Prince, many greetings which I have been to convey to you from my Queen, she taked me to tell that it will give her a great pleasure of your visit to our Kingdom, she also said that she was counting days and hours waiting for your visit to the Kingdom, she also said that on Thursday evening all of her subjects will be waiting for your arrival to their Kingdom, and there will be a special envoy to escort you to the Kingdom, you will have to go behind Hudhayma mosque, there is a hip of desert, you will go there with your horse and wait until the envoy will arrive to take you, please my dear Prince make sure that no one else should know about this trip to our Kingdom, Now I have to live you but if you have any question or further services which you need me to serve you, please my dear Prince do not hesitate but command me and I will serve you" and Prince Kismat said to a little man "No, there is no other service but please convey my personal regards to your Queen, and tell that on Thursday evening I will at the place for a journey to your Kingdom, I will be there with my horse only. That will be day of a great honor for me to visit your Kingdom. Farewell little friend till the day of our journey"

On Thursday, Prince Kismat was coming from the mosque after night prayers (Isha'a) and was heading to his home, and his home is not far from the mosque, and as he was a Prince, there was a tight security of many guards who guard his place, he then ordered for his horse, and it was brought for him and he rode it towards the Hudhaiyma mosque, the place he was told to be, when he reached there the place was quite, very quite with no any movements, behind the mosque was a desert and a hip of desert sand, he drove his horse on that hip of the desert sand and climb with his horse on top of it and wait and then dismount on his horse and sat on the sand, some minutes passed by and there were no one coming, but with a few minutes his horse started to be not steady and move to the left and right, he then stood up and touch his horse his chicks just to cool him down, his horse was very obeyfull, he always obey his master on every thing he told him to do, then the the weather started to change, as there was a dust storm far away and was coming his way, that dust storm then beginning to circle while coming down from the sky above, but the surprise part of that dust storm is that it did not made any sound or sending dust in the sky but slowly continue to come down from the sky while still circling, and then that circling sand storm start to move toward where Prince Kismat was, this did not scare him at all but with keen interests he was watching that sand storm of what next step will be, though to him it was something to wonder about as this was his first time to witness such a thing, then Prince Kismat felt his ear was pinched and then a little butterfly man came in front of his face, this was the very little butterfly man who came to him n the first time, he said to the Prince "Peace be upon you my dear Prince Kismat" and Prince Kismat replied "Peace be upon you too, Oh! you messenger of Queen Farna Bash" the little butterfly man then said "My dear Prince, may I ask you please to climb your horse and ride him toward that circling dust storm and enter through it without hesitation or stopping please, your safety and your protection is on my neck, please do not fear or worry, God willing your journey will as simple to go and be back in one piece" then the little butterfly man vanished in the thin air. Prince then mounted his horse then he bent his body down until his mouth reached his horse ears and spoke to him with no one has heard, and the horse then shake his head as a sign of obeying his command, then the horse started to move step by step toward that wind dust storm circling, and when he reached there the horse without hesitation or fear enter the in the dust storm and disappeared, but Prince Kismat when he just in the dust storm he then find himself on the other side there was a big garden with huge trees, and many of little butterfly people standing on his path on both side of that path waving their hands as a sign of greetings to the Prince, all they ware colorful dresses with turban on their heads and robe designed with many gold or silver paten, and all these butterfly people hand lamps in their hands and were latten and so bright, here then he stopped to admire the beauty of this scenario, then one of the butterfly man came to him and asked to follow him while he was still floating on the air, and Prince Kismat obeyed him and command his horse to go further and follow that little man, and all on his way while moving ahead, there were so many butterfly people with their lights in their hands waving to the Prince, then further ahead he saw that there was a big tree and below the tree there was a platform, that tree was all decorated with things which Prince Kismat could not know what was it but so colorful and were twinkling, and that tree was exactly at the center of end of the road.

All the way these little butterfly people were greeting Prince Kismat by waving or bowing at him, the further he went the more people are there, when he reached some few yards before the tree his horse stopped to move, then the same messenger who came to explained to him regarding this trip, came to him and said "Your Excellency Prince Kismat, may I ask you to dismount on your horse and go of where the platform is under that tree? Because our Queen is envy to see and welcoming you" and Prince Kismat obeyed and dismount on his horse and slowly walked toward the platform, there he saw there was a well decorated Royal chair which was painted with gold color, but was facing the right side and not the road, and in front of the chair on the other side, there was sort of a short pillar, the size of the chair, this pillar also was well curved and decorated with gold color, then suddenly he felt that the whole place was covered with completely silence, no movement or even a hiss sound to be heard, then he heard in the air there was a sound of wings flapping, he looked up and saw there was a big bird coming down slowly while flapping her wings, and when she reached down on the platform she landed on that decorated pillar, and that bird was a big well built peacock and then open her tail to demonstrate her body beauty, then Prince Kismat did notice that the peacock wear a crown on her head, that crown was sparkling with diamonds and other valued colorful stones, the crown did fit her head very well and gave her another look, and that all the little butterfly people bow their heads down as a respect to the peacock, after resting within a few seconds, then the peacock talked and said "Peace be upon you all" and everyone including Prince Kismat replied "Peace be upon you too" then the Peacock said "Your Excellency Prince Kismat, I now welcome you on this land which is over the mountain, unseen and unvisited by any one before among you human beings, on behalf of myself as a Queen of this Kingdom, and on behalf of all my subjects who are living in these very limited land which we called our Kingdom, I take this opportunity to welcome you in our Kingdom. These maintains mostly were ruled and still in the parts are ruled by the Jinnis, these Jinnis came in these area so many years back and dominate these mountains by force and take some of many parts of these land and make their homeland, thank God they left us alone in our Kingdom and did not interfere with land. The Jiniis are living the other side of these mountains, I do not want to go much further in details in explain to you all about Kingdom, our people and as well as our neighbors the Jinnis, but I did want you to know in just few words of how we live and with whom we are living so you will have exactly image of how we live in our Kingdom, you have given us a great honor Oh! Prince Kismat by eccepting our invitation to come here, you have made our people and including myself very happy by your presence here, you are a real gentleman, and you have proven that to us that you are realy a son of a King, who keep his word and never againts it, and we today all of us here are so happy that you have made it to come and be here among us in this historical voyage you have taken by accepting our invitation, and for that we all say thank you Prince Kismat, Please your Excellency, welcome to our land, to our Kingdom of us the little butterfly people, with all open heart Oh you son of a King" then The big peacock turn to address her people and said "Oh my dear people, my dear subjects, today I take this opportunity to introduce to you that brave man who destroyed and killed that enemy who always denied us happiness and destroying of food, it was this man here before you and his friend who has managed to kill that lion face to face and without fear, with his powerful and full of strength heart as really the son of King, he has saved us from that evil creature, that creature whom for many days and years was destroying our hunting by killing many of those gazelle whom we depend as our main sources of food, for many past days no one came forward to help us with that problem until Prince Kismat dare to do that, though he did not did for us when he went for hunting, but coincidentally he did to save his friend as well as saved us, but he did what others could not, but I also believe that it was a will of God that has sent him there to face this giant creature face to face and kill it so that we could get relief as well as food to eat,

Without any doubt we must give him all the respect, all our love and show him our appreciation for his bravery, from me this is an order and not a request, this son of a King has come as he promise to be here in our Kingdom, he has fulfill his promise to us, and all of you have seen him with your eyes, and now I want you all to fulfill your promise" and then all of them with one voice replied "we will and we are under your obey Oh! Queen" And then there was a big feast of many kind food, especially difference type of fruits as well other cooked food especially made foe Prince Kismat, Prince ate and enjoyed the feast and thanks his God for that, after a little rest Queen then asked his people to do of what she has instructed them before to do, then everyone leave that place and came back quickly carrying each of them a parcel wrapped with clothes, also there were bundles of clothes made out of silk and other materials in difference colors, then the Queen said "your Excellency, I have to asked you a request and you must agree and without objecting, if you do that than know for sure that you have please many hearts of my people, in these small bundles there are gifts which are coming from my people, they are there way to say thank you to you, they have insisted to me and ask me to pursued you to except and never to refuse their gifts to you, and if you accept them than it means that you have gave them a great honor and respect, and if you have decided not to accept their gifts to you than know for sure that they will regard that you have dishonor them, I personal advice you that you should not refuse their gifts, now, if you decided to accept the gifts then just put your hand and touch them, and if you decide not to accept them then you stand and turn yourself the other side, now choice is yours, do of what you have decide to do" all the little butterfly who there for his visit, concentrate their eyes on him only, watching his every movement, and all the time he was sitting there on the VIP seat his right hand every now and then was used to touch or scratch his beard and moustache, while his eyes were looking at those little parcels, then suddenly his stopped to look at those parcels and his face at the little people and look at them, he look in their eyes of those who were closer near him, then he said "In the past few days I did not give you my words or my action regarding these gifts, because I was asking myself within me so many question regarding this situation which surround inside my mind, the answers I got are these, my heart replied me and said [it is my nature as a heart that I like good and beauty things, and I hate dirty and bad things and I hate bothering, if you will not accept these gifts from these good people, then know that you will break the hearts of so many of your hosts, you will also destroy their love on you and maybe create an hate between you and them]. Then I ask my soul, and this is what answer I got from my soul [my dear sir, I soul, it is my nature that I desire everything, I always demand things to be mine, I always like you to get and not to miss and I do not like when you are generous to others but others never pay you back their generosity. If these gifts you will accept them then know that this will be a debt on you and you must pay back]

Lastly I ask my clever brain of its opinion regarding these gifts, this is what my brain answered me [It is not you who have the right of the last saying, the last decision on this matter has your horse, he has that right to decide for you, go and ask your horse and let him give you an answer by his action, whatever it will be you must agree with him] it is here where I agree with my brain rather than my heart and my soul, that I should allow my horse to decide for me fairly, whatever his action will be then that should be regarded as my decision, I now ask you all that please bare with my horse, that there should be no disappointment on his decision, but should be regarded as fairly and should be accepted by all of us, do I get your approval on this matter? Will you all agree on my horse decision?" then the Queen said "To speak the truth my dear Prince Kismat, that is a wise decision, I did not know before that you will maintain such kind of clever decision, you are truly a son of a King, on behalf of myself and my subjects, we all agree to that decision, go ahead and let your horse be the judge of this decision" then Prince Kismat went to his horse and speak loudly to him that everyone could hear "My dear horse, I request you to go to those gifts parcel and be fair with your judgment, if you decide that I should accept or I should not accept them, then show us your sign please by shaking your head as NO or raise up and down as YES" then the horse turn his head to the right and look at those little butterfly people and then to the right and look at them too, then he look straight forward to where Queen peacock was and look straight into her eyes, then both were glazing at each other's eyes, then he turned and look to his master Prince Kismat, then he started to move backward, step after step and then stopped, after a little pause, he then went forward toward the platform and stopped of where those gifts parcels were, he the bent his head down to those gifts and with his mouth he picked one and then came backward until where his master was and turn his head and give that gift he picked and gave to his master, and Prince Kismat accept that gift and took into his hand, then all of those who were present there shouts with joy and claps their hands, and all they know that because the horse has accepted their gifts, and then here is where Prince Kismat said "I think without doubt, my horse decision has pleased you all, and on my side I have nothing more than to respect my horse decesion, and with open heart and all the respect I have received from you and all your love to me. Ma y God bless you and your Queen, and may God protect this land of such a very kind and beautiful people, you will remain in my heart, and I will never forget the foundation which you my dear Queen of butterfly people has created, this foundation will remain firm between us and I will remain as a good friend to you, and I assured you that when you will need my help I will be willing to help you and your people my dear Queen of this kingdom, as our relation will remain forever, and I speak this on my behalf and on the behalf of my people, thank you your majesty" and then Prince Kismat requested to be send home as he has consumed much time of this night here, Her Majesty The Queen, then said to him "I thank you very Prince Kismat, for all that you have done for us, those good things which you have given us within a very short time of knowing you, your speech was enough foundation of which you came here today to built a strong relation between two of us, all my people have shown openly how much they have appreciate your visit and how much they have liked you, will always obey you Oh! Prince of Persia, we will always be with you in any need you request us, wither that need will be for happiness or for sadness, but please we also ask you never to forget us, we can see you in your absent, we have that God given will, so know that we always are there on your side, any day you need me in particular for your service, just touch your right ear and call my name FARNA BASH, and my messengers will be there to listen to your request and your call. Thank you once again Oh! Son of the great King of Persia, let this be so long and never farewell, so we can meet again and again" and then Prince went and mount his horse and all his gifts were in one big bundle which was mounted on the back of his horse behind him, and those small butterfly people took him at an open place where there was a green land and has stopped there, and the same wind of dust storm came again to where he was and took him and his horse and within a minute he just find himself at the same place of where they have took him on top of the sand dune behind the mosque Hudhayma, he then guide his horse to return back home.

Sheikh Shammaakh Accept The Invitation

CHAPTER FOURTEEN

(Disappearing of Sheikh Shammaakh)

*I*N THIS CHAPTER, LET US go back to Sheikh Shammaakh farm; let us find out how things were with him after his only son left for studies. After some past years, one day when Sheikh Shammaakh was about to take his lunch, he sat on eating mate with many kind food surrounding him, he took the first gulp and then stopped eating, as he remember his son Sheikhan who is in another land for his further studies, as well as remembering his late wife who is no longer with him, and all because these memories came when he felt the loneliness all by himself even no one to eat with him during anytime on his sufra, sadness filled his heart and tears came down on his chicks, no one among his family now even to talk with, he felt now that this life by living all by himself without any member of his family has become very difficult to bare, though he force himself to face life as it is, yet memories never stopped to torture him, he then decided to stop eating and went to another room, though he did try to control holding himself of these suffering but there are time when even one try to control himself sometime he fails as even that controls sometime dissolve within his body, then a thought came to his mind, why not he travel and pay a visit to where his son is studying in that neighboring country, he will also get a chance to see and meet his old friends, he then took a paper, pen and ink bottle and sat somewhere and write a letter to his friend who take care of Sheikhan,

That at the end of this month he will pay a visit to see them, he also added in his letter these words [if there is a need of anything here, or any other services they would like him to do on their behalf, they should not hesitate to inform him before he start his journey] he added also [reply of this letter should be given to my messenger who brought to you this letter] he then closed the letter very well in a sheep skin and tighten with a thread and call on of his servant and handed over the letter and ask him to deliver to his friend, he asked him to leave the same day today and wait for a reply of his letter, and the servant who took that letter prepare himself an ride his horse to send that letter, and next day he was back from his journey with an answer of that letter, and the letter said this:-

In the name of Allah, the most gracious, the most beneficiary

> *Dear brother Sheikh Shammaakh,*
> *Peace be upon you,*
>
> *Many thanks to you for the arrival of your messenger who brought with him your letter, frankly the letter has open our hearts with joy and brought happiness in our family as well to your son Sheikhan, especially when mentioned that you are going to pay a visit to us, your visit here will brighten our hearts and our house, we are looking forward to that day of your arrival. You have made Sheikhan a very happy person when I told him about your arrival.*
>
> *With our regards and many thanks,*
>
> *Your brother*
>
> *Khamzah.*

After reading that letter, Sheikh Shammaakh called for his head of the servants and tell him to prepare for a journey, after five days they will leave here heading to his friend neighboring country where Sheikhan is studying, he instructed him to arrange a caravan of many camels who will be carrying many gifts for his friends there. When the day of the journey arrived, every neccessary things were taken, enough food and water, tents and utensils and firewood for cooking. After the morning prayers on that day they have started their journey to his friend's country. The journey was cool as the weather was very chilly, as this was journey of a caravan so it may take more time to travel, so in the evening they have reached that village,

They choose a place somewhere where there is a desert and make a camp there, and then Sheikh Shammaakh sent a messenger to his friends to tell them of where they have camped. Then Mr. Khamzah and young lad Sheikhan ride in a horse coach with a driver and follow that messenger to lead them of where they have camped, Sheikh Shammaakh was so happy to see his son who by now has gain weight and became a young lad, they hug and kissed one another many times, then Sheikh Shammaakh went and hug his friend Mr. Khamzah, and then invited them in his personal tent with a cup of coffee and dates and with other fruits which Sheikh Shammaakh brought from his farm, then Sheikh Shammaakh requested Mr. Khamzah to allow Sheikhan to remain with him in the camp until the day he will leave there, and Mr. Khamzah said "Oh! my dear brother, Sheikhan is your as well as I just your servant to serve you, you do not need my permission for his staying with you during your stay here, as this is quite clear that if you did not ask me Sheikhan himself will remain here with you, as he has miss you so much and then Sheikh Shammaakh replied "Oh! My dear brother Mr. Khamzah, I cannot repay your kindness even with all the wealth of Prophet(Aaron) Qaarun, for helping me and gave me a necessary hand of taking care and look after Sheikhan, when he need someone to look and care for him while fighting for gaining education, if it was not you than for sure Sheikhan would never been here today, it is a matter of respect for me to thank you for helping me carrying this heavy burden on my behalf, allow me to thank you more and more as that is a gentle way to show an appreciation to a gentleman like you, for this I will never forget you all my living life. In this world today there are very few of your example that can come forward and sacrifice their life for the sake of others, believe me my brother, not me who can repay you but always in my daily prayers I will kneel before Allah and beg him to repay your kindness and generosity and may tomorrow on the day of judgment I will ask Allah to forgive and wipe all your sins if so ever you have commit them. Thank you once again my dear brother Mr. Khamzah" and then Mr. Khamzah thanked Sheikh Shammaakh for his blessing prayers and said "Thank you Sheikh Shammaakh for your prayers to God on my behalf, may Allah accept them for both sides, yours and mine, as we also will never forgets your generosities, always you are with us, in good and in bad, your example is that example that others should follow as well, you help who in need of help, you have a very generous heart to give, you give those who have not as well as those who have it, you give that who is helpless as well as who manage to look at himself well, you give to believers of God as well to those who do not believe in God, your name always on the lips of so many for your good heart of caring for others, for me, it is my luck to have this chance of being one of your close friend, and trust me with your son as my own, though it was a big responsible but for your son to be among my family has brought blessing in my family and mu house has brighten with his presence, he is a kind of a young lad who is like his father, he care for others, love the neighbors young lads, generous in giving, kindness is among his nature, faith of believing in God is among his daily routine matter, education is his love, truth is his language, cleanness and perfuming his body is among the first priority of his nature. All these time we have been living with him he never even once showed me disrespect, he is always humble to us he chose his words when he speaks or answering, he respects himself before his respect others. Sheikh Shammaakh, believe me if I tell you that I envy you to be blessed with such a child, I wished that I too would have bare a child of his kind" and Sheikh Shammaakh replied "My dear brother, it is true that I am the logical father of Sheikhan, but know this, that even you is a father to him, you have taking care of him with your family like your own son, a father who for him such a wonderful teacher who have teaches him so much, it is you also who during all the time with you shown him which path to walk to and which to avoid, it is you as his parent who taught him of how to mind his tongue and how to us his language where there others, all these teachings may only comes from the love of a parent to his child, and I also believe that Sheikhan himself will never forget you and your family for the love and care you have gave him, to him you will always remain as his parent and your family as his" and then they conclude this conversation regarding Sheikhan and begin other topics.

Sheikh Shammaakh stayed there for seven days, and decided to leave the area, he then asked his servants and the whole of the caravan to return back home as he has decided to go and pay a visit to his friends in there mountain Kingdom, and those were Sheikh Naajid and Sheikh Fat'h and Sheikh Nuwr at their Jabal Qamar Kingdom, He has decided just to take his horse coach with just two of his bodyguards, this time journey did not need to cross the desert but Jabal Qamar was very nearby to where his friends country is.

They travel in their coach until on the way they saw an old man who's one eye is blind and a long stick to help him walk was in his hand and was standing all by himself waiting for someone to give him a lift, the old man then signed the coach to stop, Sheikh Shammaakh ordered the coach to stop and listen to this old man of what and why he signed them to stop, the coach tried his to stop his coach and it did at the feet of that old man, then he asked if they can give him a lift, but Sheikh Shammaan has his doubt this old man, first this old man did not wish but demand a lift only, secondly, what has made man of his age who need a stick to help him would walked all alone by himself in this wilderness where there is nobody while also his one eye is blind, these two things were the main reason of his doubts about this old man, but he prefer to listen to his needs, Sheikh Shammaakh asked him up to where he would like to be taken? he said that when he will reach his destination on their journey then he will disembark there, and this was third reason which has made Sheikh Shammaakh to be more concern and doubtful about this old man, but he did try to ignore these doubts in his mind and he welcome the old man in his coach and they continue their journey. In the coach the old man then begin to ask and question Sheikh Shammaakh "Gentlemen, from where are you coming from and to where are you heading?" and Sheikh Shammaakh answered him "We are coming from the south of the desert and we are coming going to our friends on Jabal Qamar" then he requested "How about this day you all to be my invited guests in my humble home?" and Sheikh Shammaakh answered "Thank you so much my dear sir, thank you for inviting us in your humble home, but unfortunately our journey is long and need much time to travel, may we ask you to pardoned us and thank you so much for your hospitality" the old man then said "We are near now to my home, I will not take much of your time but only a few seconds, or is it because I am a poor and a blind person that is your reason which made you to ignore me and my invitation, or because you are wealthy people and you have plenty?" that answer has stunned Sheikh Shammaakh, he did not expect such a strong words to be used by an old of his kind, but he answered him and said "No! my dear sir, that is not true and it is the reason of not excepting your invitation in your home, but the truth is that we would not like the evening to meet us on the way but to reach our destination before the sun goes down, and secondly my dear sir, we are not those kind of people who practice discrimination to others, that is completely not our tradition and manners, our faith is to respect every and each human being no matter what color, tribe or faith he believe in, and to you my dear sir, we have respected you as parent to us, but after all, we ask your forgiveness if you feel offended for any reason, and we are excepting your invitation and will come to your humble home, and we all my dear sir, under your obedient" these sweet and wonderful words did really pleased the old man and then direct the driver of where to stop the coach, somewhere in the wilderness where there is not even one building structure, and the driver obeyed the command and wait for more command from the old man to where he wants the coach to be stopped, then the old said to the driver "Do you see that small mountain ahead of you, if reach there then stop" and the driver of the coach did exactly of what he has been told, and when they have reached that small mountain he then stopped the coach, then the old man disembark from the coach and requested Sheikh Shammaakh to do the same, and he command Sheikh Shammaakh driver and guards to remain there in the coach, then the old man and Sheikh

Shaammaakh following behind him, the circled that mountain to where the entrance is, and the entrance was behind that mountain, there find a gap of where a human can penetrate, here then the old man request Sheikh Shamaakh to enter with him inside that mountain using that gap, he said "Please you good and kind sir, do enter in my home, this is where I live" and Sheikh Shammaakh really was surprised that how a human being live inside the mountain, he hesitate first but then he decided to follow that old man inside his home, but when he was inside that mountain house of that old man, he met with more surprise, as inside that mountain was something completely difference from one's expectation, inside that mountain was all decorated with so many kind of decorations, from the brass and copper products and from so much beautiful wooden chests, and on the floor were well decorated and expensive carpets, and many old oil lamps were hanging on the walls and were listen, and after old man requested his guest to make himself comfortable at the sitting place where there were many back and sitting pillows, he then pardon himself to Sheikh Shammaakh and live that place and enter inside the other room, all that absent time of the old man, Sheikh Shammaakh was so confused, his mind was boiling inside regarding this old man and his odd manners and the way he is living, his mind was telling

Him this [who is this old man? Why is he so difference with others? Why he did not wished us when we first met him on the way? Why is he here all alone and no one else in this mountain? Oh! My God, who is this human being?] Then sudenly the door curtain was opened and a very good looking young man enter at the sitting room, he ware very good and expensive dresses which were fumigated with Uud and local very expensive perfume like Misk, Hal uud and Ambar, the young then wished by saying "Peace be upon you Sheikh" and Sheikh Shammaakh replied by saying "Peace be upon you too" and all that time of disappearing of the old man, Sheikh Shammaakh was standing looking and admiring the decoration of that place where he was waiting the return of old man, then the young man welcomed Sheikh Shammaakh by saying "Please sir, do sit and feel free here as your second home" and he sat first and follow Sheikh Shammaakh, after they have sited, then they each were looking at each on the eyes, here then Sheikh Shammaakh notice that even this young man is one eye blind, as same side as that old man, the young open the conversation by saying "My dear sir, I know that there so many things which has suppressed you since you entered this humble house of mine, but may I request to not to get yourself into suppresses as much are to come ahead, and this place is well known here in this area as the house of funny surprises, but allow me sir, to cool down your mind in explaining to you of why these odd things will happen here and there and now and then. First of all you better know that I am that same old man who brought here, and I live in this home all by myself, question in your mind now is how I came here as an old man and turn into a young man, yes I agree with your mind thinking that this action needs an explanation, my answer to that mind thinking is that first you must know who am I, am I a human being or a Jinni?, My name is Manamdaar Bandar, I am originated from the land of India, I have come here as a student to learn about witch crafts and magic's by those well known teachers who are living here in this land, by good chance I had an opportunity of getting a very good teacher, but one day by accident he died when he was trying to mix some chemicals which has burst in his hands and I lost my eye, what next I did is to bury him in a grave, and this was his house where he used to live, as he has no wife or children here, I inherit this house and his work, now I am living here for many years all alone by myself, if I get bore living here where very rare people to approach and pay a visit, I turn myself in an old man and roaming in the wilderness or in the villages nearby waiting sometime of the travelers and asking them for a lift and bring them here in my humble house, and for your information my dear sir, here in the house I keep Jinni's as my servants, you do not see them but they see you, I use them to serve me for many difference purposes, even for those who are sick and need treatment I use them to treat those sick visitors, after they are under my command and they obey me well, whatsoever I command them to do they will do.

One day among this loyal servant, he took me flying to the far away mountain, and there on the mountain there was a Kingdom of the Jinni's, the whole mountain were occupied by them and with their King, he introduce me to a very young Jinni as his close friend, he was a son of the King, and this young Jinni who was a prince

Was a very spoiled and stubborn lad, he hates so much those who believe in religious, he has also another friend among the Jinni whose parents were immigrated from the land of Sham, for many years those Sham Jinnis came to live in there Kingdom, but after that Prince of Jinnis got very much squinted with his new friend from Sham, his friendship with my servant started to thaw, he begin to lose interest with his old friend and be friendly more with his new friend from Sham, when my servant find out that he was ignored much, he loosed his interest to live on the mountain and came here down on the lower land looking for a better master to serve him or her, and met with my master and agree to be his servant and he still remain till this day. Then one day we got the information that Prince of the Jinnis took over the power of ruling from his father, and he imprisoned all his parents and those who disobey him, and every and each who is a believer of any faith as he was a religious hater, but his new friend Jinni from Sham was so much worried, as he and all his parents and those where came with his parents from Sham were believer of Islamic faith, they were the followers of Prophet Muhammad and follow his faith, these actions then turn these two friends not to remain in understanding at all but they were turning unfriendly against each other always, and lastly the Prince Jinni who is now became a King of Jinnis mountain Kingdom requested his new friend from the land of Sham to be his second in command by being cruel to those who have faith in believing in religious and those who follow the path of Muhammad and in particular these human being who have brought faiths to others, but the new young Jinni from Sham refused to be part of tyranny ruling of his friend, the new King who took power and imprisoned his own parents, and for his refusal to take part and be his second in command to torture those who believe in religious faiths, made him so angry and called upon him and told him that "If you refuse to be part of my ruling with torture then be wear that I will torture you and the whole and each member of your family" but he said "I cannot betray my own faith, I believe in God and I follow the path of Muhammad teaching as I have inherited from my ancestors, do of what you want to do but I refuse to be part of your cruelty and tyranny ruling" and with these words has made the new King of Jinnis very angry and then has turn his friend from Sham into a horse including all members of his own family, and all because they too were believing in God and started to follow the faith of those other Jinni's from Sham. He then declare himself as the rulers of those mountains and his parents Kingdom will be his Kingdom as he is a new King now known by the name of Khurkhush Majangar.

My dear sir, I have explained to you in details of all where I have come from and of how I am living here, but before we go further of more conversation I think it is better we get something to eat so to please our stomachs as well as something to drinks so to wet our dry throughts" then he asked his guest to follow him inside to another room where every kind of food in the plates were layed on the (sufra) eating white cloth, the food were so plenty that even ten people will never finish it, here then the young man said to Sheikh Shammaakh "please sir, choose the place to sit and make yourself comfortable and enjoy your food" Sheikh Shammaakh then said "is it not better to invite those others who were with me to join us?" he replied

"There is no need for that, as they were already attended and are sleeping heavily in the horse coach" by these words, more doubts raisin in Sheikh Shammaakh mind but he said nothing but obey his host by sitting down and have something to eat, who have cooked this feast and who have served and brought here, he do not know, but he ate to feed his belly enough. Then they return back to the sitting room, Sheikh Shammaakh then request permission to ask some questions, his host permitted him by saying "Please go ahead, ask" then he asked "When we first so you on the way, and you have stopped our coach, you did not greet us, now my question is, is this your habit or your culture?" Manamdaar then replied "It is true during that time as I was in that shape as an old man, I did not greet you people, but here as a young man I have greeted you and you have returned my greeting back, were you not satisfied with this greeting as a young man as you prefer that greeting as an old man as a perfect and worth greeting?" and Sheikh Shmmaakh replied "Yes sir, I am satisfied, but I was only surprise of why when we met first you did not greet as it is a natural way to do that" Manamdaar replied "Forgive me sir, I agree that that is a Muslims tradition to greet one another when they meet, but I am not a Muslim, I am a Hindu, yet I did not deny you a greeting now when I have transformed into a young age, though it is not my tradition but it is yours, as we Hindus have our own way of greeting when we meet.

Antar meets Zarza Aarish

I now realize that this matter of greeting have touched you much, then for that mistake I made, I ask for your pardon and forgiveness, I do not want you to think of me otherwise, Did I get your forgiveness my dear sir?" and Sheikh Shammaakh replied "There was no need of asking pardons and forgiveness here, as this was a matter of reminding and correcting only, especially when one sense that there is missing thing somewhere in between, I have felt that and that made me to feel uncomfortable and unsatisfied within me, that is why I raise this issue of asking you so I can get the right answer to satisfied my conscious, I also thank you sir, for your open heart in telling me the truth of what your faith is, that you are a follower of Hinduism faith, though there are many differences between our faiths, still you have welcoming in your humble house in our tradition and culture that if you did not tell me that you are not in the same faith as mine, then I would have believe that you are a Muslim, to me, I regard all these hospitality as a great gift from you that I will always remember you Mr. Manamdaar as a gentleman, and now after I have accept your invitation I ask your permission to live this place so I can reach my destination in time before darkness meet me in the way" and here is where Manamdaar show his true face, he said "There is no need for you to travel again as you have already reached your destination, as your guards and driver have already with someone else, someone resembles you perfectly, and they do not know that the person in that coach is not their master but my Jinni servant, Haa! Haa! Haa!

My dear sir, you are now my prison, you have no other choice but to obey my orders if you prefer to remain alive, and if you will choose to be stubborn and disobeyful, then for sure know that you will lose your life one way or the other,

As you will be taken away and sent to Khurkhush Majangar, it is where your next remaining living life you will spend. Know that I am one of his loyal servants, I am here kept by him and this is my main reason of being living in this wilderness all by self just waiting for people like you to pass through so I can perused you to believe that I am just an old man and have nothing in common but just spending life here, in fact that is not the right me, I am the servant of that King of the Jinni's Khurkhush Majangar who hate you human being and will do anything to catch and torture people like you, that is why he kept me here so catch people and send them to him for his amusement, Haa! Haa! Haa!" and here is where Sheikh Shammaakh was so much shocked and disappointment for such a bitter news, as the person he thought to be a friend turns out to be a foe, and suddenly there were iron chains fall from the room roof to the ground, and those chain then by itself move up to where Sheikh Shammaakh was and start to tide around his legs and his arms, and Sheikh Shammaakh could not bear the weight of those chain and he fell down on the carpet which was decorating that room, and then that carpet rolled and put Sheikh Shammaakh in the center and imprisoned him, even breathing was difficult for him and after a few minutes he has loosed his conscious. Time has passed away and then he felt that that carpet was rolling and it opened and he was again out of the carpet but on a difference place, he saw himself not again in that small blind man house but he was in a big hall and that hall is not a man made building but it was sort like a cave, there were no sunlight inside that hall but only torch light which were hanging on the wall of that cave, then suddenly the chains which were binding on his body opened and fall down from his body by itself, and he felt a free man again, he then stood up slowly and look around that cave which he did not how he have come there, though his heart was full of fear of this such a place, and in fact the place itself truly is scary, especially by things done without anybody to be seen who is doing it, and then within a few minutes he felt the cool breeze coming inside that cave, from where the breeze come he do not know, that breeze enter the hall with black smoke and then that smoke started to transform itself into a form of a human shape but huge in size, a very scary figure with horns grown on his head and long hair and beard and an awful smell, this huge figure than spoke "And who you might be, answer?" and with fear in his heart Sheikh Shammaakh replied "I am a traveler, I have been caught by an old one eye blind man, then I was bind with these chains and was rolled in this carpet and I did not know what came after that, only when I open my eyes after have been released I found myself in this strange place" Khurkhush then said "this is a good work of my servant the one eye blind man, do not worry, I will keep you in a very good place where you will enjoy your stay here with us" and then Khurkhush called is guards and said "take him put him with others in the cell, and the torture should be the same, come-on, take him away quickly out of my face" and they took Sheikh Shammaaakh and was thrown in prison cell like an animal and without showing him any respect.

If we come back and try find out about that coach with an imposter of Sheikh Shammaakh, the coach went its journey to Jabal Qamar until reach its destination, there the guards of Sheikh al Kabir, welcomed and treat the coach guest with all respect and then went and the information inside the palace to the Sheikh of the arrival of the coach of Shammaakh arrival, The three sons of Sheikh of Jabal Qamar then went to the coach to welcome Sheikh

Shammaakh, but unfortunately when they open the door of the coach there was no one inside it, the coach was completely empty, the three sons of Sheikh demand an explanation from the guards, but poor people they have no any idea of where their Sheikh is and how he have disappeared, then they have a long explanation of how they met the blind man on their way to come here, and how he insists to take them to his residence and how he insists to except his hospitality by have the dinner in his house, and then they saw the Sheikh left his host and came the coach and enter the coach and they have left the place with their sheikh inside the coach, this information has caused many doubts and fear in the mind of those three princes, in conclusion they have to send this information the higher council of ministers. SheikhAl Kabir, when he heard of this bad news of disappearing of the Sheikh Shammaakh who was guest to in his Kingdom, he felt the responsible of his disappearance as Sheikh Shammaakh was coming to visit them here, how a person can just disappear in the thin air without any knowledge of those who guard him and under their own nose, the situation has denied them happiness but also made them to be more concerned, then Sheikh Al Kabir he instructed his cabinet to arrange for a such party and go back to follow the same route of where the Sheikh coach has taken and look everywhere and leave no stone unturned together with his driver and guards, and also he instructed his two elder sons to be among those who go for the search, Then the searching force left the Kingdom in search of the disappearing of Sheikh Shammaakh following the same route.

In behind they have left their younger brother Prince Nuwr Alaa Nuwr by himself, as his father did not want him to go because of his young age, he then excused himself from that council meeting and went out and took his horse and ride away to his regular place of where he always meet his love Zarza Aarish under that huge tree, he dismount on his horse and went under the tree and called "Zarza Oh! my dear Zarza, please come quickly" and immediately he heard a voice answering him "Yes my dear Prince, Zarza is here and under your obedience, please tell Zarza of what service or need you require and Zarza will obey your command my dear" and Prince Nuwr said "Zarza, a bug misfortune have fallen in our Kingdom, and this misfortune has coursed my father and all his councils so much concern that he have to send my two brothers away in searching of the solution which has coursed this misfortune, and that Sheikh Shammaakh has disappeared on his way to visit us here on the Jabal Qamar Kingdom, I beg you Zarza please do help us to solve this situation" and Zarza said to Sheikh Nuwr "Insha'alla, but I request you to close your eyes and then count in your heart from one to twelve and then open your eyes" Sheikh

Nuwr obeyed Zarza and then closed his eyes and start to count from one to twelve and then opened his eyes but saw Zarza still she is there in front of him standing, but before he could say anything, Zarza speaks "My dear Prince, I saw Sheikh Shammaakh, but he is very far away and not in a good place and not in a good condition as well, he is in prison and being tortured by the army of Khurkhush Majangar, he was cought by Khurkhush Majangar spy while on his way to visit your Kingdom, and his guards and driver will never know about his disappearance as there was a resemblance of Sheikh Shammaakh who enter the coach from that evil Khurkhush Majangar servant, he used one of his Jinni servant to take a place of Sheikh Shammakh as his duplicate, the guards thoughts that they were traveling with their master, This is that generation which I have predicted to you that it will come, now it has come, but I thank you so much that you of what I have advice you to do, that you should not take any action without my consent, thank you, you have performed your duty very well, and this is the fact about what has happened to Sheikh Shammaakh" and Prince asked Zarza "Oh! Zarza, what can we do to help and save him, this a very kind gentleman and who was our guest to be?" and Zarza replied "my dear sir, I will not lie to you or give you any hope, but Sheikh Shammaakh has been hold in a very secure and very hard to reach him place, for just me by myself I have no means or power to reach there, but nothing can stop me to be there, I think now the time have come of which I told you before in the past, that you must create a force by yourself and including others to form such a tough group which can be able to sacrifice themselves even to die but save others, I have faith that if we will be able to pursued other group to join us then we can have more strength to fight this war against Khurkhush Majangar and his army of jinni's which are so powerful and have many tactics more than you human beings" then Prince Nuwr said" Oh! Zarza, you have put me in a very hard situation in this moment of grieve, even though, I would not thanking you for this latest and quickly news you have given me, but the question is, how can we get other groups so make them understand our situation and pursued them to join us? While they will know that a war against Jinni's is a very hard tusk and risky?" and Zarza replied "My dear Sir, in your own language there is a saying which says [if you had made your mind to do it then go ahead and do it] and in Arabic it says (Fa idhaa azamta fatawakkal ala llah), now if you my dear sir, have made your mind to go ahead and sacrifice your life for your guest Sheikh Shammaakh and others, then you better know that the beginning of your force is starting with you and me, if you agree to this beginning then please put your hand on my and I will put my other hand on your hand and you will put your second hand on all the other three hand to complete the swearing that from now there is no going back but to go ahead until to any end. And me from now I will start my search to find out who among others will be interested to join us and create own army to fight and save those who are imprisoned by Khurkhush Majangar, and please allow me now to leave you and I will go to my first mission to that young man of which I have mentioned you previously who live in the desert with his parent, maybe I can get some idea or help from them" and within a split second, Zarza was not there.

Zarza is welcomed into Mr.Fairuz's home

Zarza then fly high in the sky while heading to the Mr. Fairuz village in the empty quarters deserts, while flying in her heart was asking herself [how I Zarza as a Jinni, can be accepted by these human beings who do not even know me? How can I pursue them to believe in what I have to tell them that it is true? this is really a very hard mission and a tough task but I will return back, I am going ahead and meet these people, be of whatsoever will be] then before landing to her destination where Mr. Fairuz house was, she transformed herself into a very beautiful and colorful little bird and near the house on the tree which was in the animal stable where she saw there were some animals but also there were two horses, a brown and a white horses.

CHAPTER FIFTEEN

(Zarza meets other Jinni's from her same Kingdom)

ANTAR AND SAHARZENA WERE IN that stable, but suddenly they felt and sense the present of their kind is around here in the place, Saharzena then went close to Antar and said to him "Dear cousin, do you sense that feeling like I do?" and Antar replied "Yes my dear cousin, I think there is a guest around here, and this guest is coming from very far away, let us show our respect and welcoming her in a very good manners, and all because she is not a visitor or guest but also a messenger who brought a very important issue of message, her visit to come here to us are of the goodwill and not the evil one, so I ask you to cool down and do not worry" then that little colorful bird came down from that tree and landed on the stable fence, then she started to sing her songs with beautiful melodies, the very entertaining melodies which sooth the mind and the heart. Antar then went close to that fence where that bird was, and so close that they were steering to each others on each other eyes, then Antar spoke and said "If anyone come as a guest, must greet and wish with peace, I did not hear you wished us at all, are you not in the nature of wishing others with peace?" And that bird stopped singing and then again look into Antar eyes and said "Saahib?" when Anta heard his old name called by this bird, he was stunned and surprised, as no one knows this name except those who were in mountain Kingdom of Khurkhush Majangar, then he asked "Oh you bird of which I do not know you, but I know that you are not a real bird, please I request you to show up yourself in your real form so I know who you are, as when you called me by my real old name, I know now from where you are coming from, Please I ask you to easy the situation and make the matter as simple with any difficult" and here is where Zarza transformed herself into a really herself as Zarza the Jinni from the mountain of Khurkhush Majangar Kingdom, Antar when he saw that bird was Zarza Aarish he spoke "Zarza Aarish, you?" and Zarza replied "Yes Saahib, it is me, Zarza Aarish" then Antar asked "even you Zarza are among the Khurkhush Majangar group and spy? After all what has happened to your

163

husband?" and Zarza answered "No! Never was I born to be a slave and never will I be a slave of that cruel Khurkhush" then Antar said "Yes Zarza, I believe you and trust you for one good reason, and that is when you mentioned Allah name from your lips, No good Jinni will mentioned Allah, never, but what has brought you here to us Oh! Zarza? Were you brought here to serve anyone? Or is there any problem on your side which you seek our help Zarza?" and Zarza replied "Yes Oh! Saahib, I have come here with a mission, and this mission needs a cooperation of your masters, but before I go further with this conversation, can you please tell me, who is that beautiful girl with you in the same shape of a horse?" Antar answered Zarza and said "I am so sorry Zarza, I should introduce you before, please forgive me, that beautiful young horse is my cousin Saharzena, allow me now to introduce you with her" and then Anta requested Saharzena to come to where they are "Zarza, this is Saharzena, my cousin as well as my partner here with my masters, she had join me here and help me to give protection these kind and good people who lived here all by themselves alone, it is I who requested her to be here with me so to give me a hand in protecting my masters, and it is I who asked her to run away from Khurkhush Majangar Kingdom. Saharzena, this is Zarza Aarish, she was the wife of the head bodyguard of Khurkhush Majangar, and she is a widow as her husband has been killed in a challenge to fight for higher position of which Khurkhush has arranged" and here Zarza interfere And said "Masha'allah Saahib, you remember everything and you did not forgot a thing" and Antar said "a hard and a bad past history no one can forget it" and then Saharzena said to Zarza "I am so please to meet and know you Zarza, though I heard about you before but never had a chance to saw and know you, though we were on the same land but that did not happened there and it happen here" and Zarza replied "And I am also pleased to meet and know you Saharzena, God willing, this our first meeting will remain firm and be friends always for the long time to come, and I hope that this meeting of ours will produce peace and better future for us and our Kingdom" and then all of them together said "Insha'alla". Then Zarza explained in details of all what has happened and why she is here seeking for those who will be willing to join the force against Khurkhush Majangar, and yet she did not know of how to approach these human beings as she is not among them and as a Jinni, so to pursued them to understand the situation and join the force which has just begin with only two, Zarza and Prince Nuwr Alaa Nuwr, Then Antar said "Where there are good intentions, always there are blessings, and you Zarza for coming here today with your mission, is like an answer to our prayers, because for many days now my masters are in the same situation as of that of Sheikh Shamaakh, and they could not resolve their problem because of the weakness of their power strength to fight the army of Khurkhush Majangar, day night they are just looking the way to resolve their problem, and today Zarza, you came here with the same problem and seeking other to join you in solving the same kind of situation, and today, Allah had send you to us as an answering prayer, as we had no other choice but only to wait for the right time so we can react, you have come to unknot that rope which was waiting for the right person like you to be here, you are the answer to our prayers Zarza. Now how to send your message to my masters, please allow me to take care of that, because before you leave this place I will call my young Master here in your presence and give him this message so deliver it to the elders inside the house, These blessing messages which they were waiting for them for a long time now" Then Antar went aside that stable facing the house and made a call with his horse voice, and that was how he send his message if he want to call his young master Saqr, and inside the house when Saqr heard that calling he knew that he is needed by Antar, he then went out to listen to that call from Antar, He went straight to Antar and asked him "Yes Antar, you called me, is there any problem?" and Antar replied "Yes young master, there is a very important news which have arrived here within a short while, and that is why I called you" and Saqr said "Please go ahead and tell me about the news, I am listening" and Antar begin "My dear Master, the patience we took for a long time now regarding the problem of how to save our people from Khurkhush Majangar prisons, today we have a key way of how to save those people, I have called you so you can hear yourself from that messenger who have brought this news" then Antar turned his head toward that big tree and shake his head as a sign to call someone, and the little bird flown from that tree and came land on the fence near to them all, Saqr look at that beautiful colorful bird in front him on the stable fence, he really admired the beauty and good looking of that bird, but yet said nothing but just looking at the bird, then Antar said to the bird "My dear bird, I request you please transform yourself into your originality so my master can see and know you of who you are" and within a split second that bird transform herself into a beautiful young woman who wear her oriental dress and a veil covering her face, only her beautiful eyes were exposed, then Antar said "My dear young master, the lady you see now in front of you, she is not a human but among us Jinni's, and her name is Zarza Aarish, and she came here with a message, I will allow herself to deliver her message to you" and then Zarza bow her head down to greet and give respect to Saqr as a master of her friends Antar and Saharzena, and then Zarza explained all about Sheikh Shammaakh and how he was caught and have been taken prison in the Kingdom of Khurkhush Majangar, and also the reason of why she came here seeking others help to join the group against Khurkhush Majangar. Saqr after hearing in details of the reasons of why this young Jinni lady came here to deliver her message, he was so confused and could not speak or say anything but was frown with so many questions in his mind, here then Antar noticed that his young master was not very impressed with what he has heard, he said "My dear young master, I know what has bothering you now, but I beg you please, be trustful and wipe all the doubts and curiosity in your thoughts, as we Jinnis knows one another well, did you forget that I told you before that in this land here no evil Jinni can dare to come or penetrate to harm you as long as we are here? Zarza has come with goodwill and fair intentions, and what has just deliver has prove that of what she has said is truth, please my young master, just to clear your doubts go inside and ask the elders, especially Maalim Mikdadi when he will heard about Sheikh Shammaakh he will really be shocked" Saqr then showed the sign of clearing his doubts on Zarza and he said "It is a duty of any human being to have his doubts on matters he knows not about its beginning or its end, and for me to act this way does not mean that I have ignore Zarza and her mission but I have to have the right picture in my mind which satisfied my conscious, but now day, one do not know whom to trust and whom to avoid, as situation now days are really scary, just take example of Sheikh Shammaakh, he trusted the blind man and has ended in being captured a prison and taken Khurkhush Majangar as Zarza has just said in her message. Please Zarza, do forgive and understand me well with good intentions and not otherwise, as this is our first meeting to know each others, and before today I had never heard anyone among these two between Antar and Saharzena mentioned your name, please pardon me if for any reason I have hurt your feelings" and then Zarza replied "My dear Master Saqr, I know you before you were born, I knew you were coming and what kind of a man you will be, and what you will do in your whole life. I have mentioned you before you were born to my friend Prince Nuwr Alaa Nuwr, and to prove my tongue is true, you will have to wait till that day when you will have the chance to meet Prince Nuwr Alaa Nuwr of Jabal Qamar" and then Saqr said "I repeat again to you my dear Zarza Oh! Daughters of Jinni, please do not punish me for my mistakes of having to doubt you, if you think that I deserve more punishment than this that will teach me not to repeat again the mistakes, then I ask you please do punish and I will bear no grudges against you at all, but if it is possible for you to forgive me then let us clear our hearts and allow a bygone to be a bygone:" and Zarza replied "My dear Master Saqr, who am I that you request from such a high profile forgiveness, I was not disturbed and never was angry on your doubts on me, as it is not possible for anyone to trust ones word to a person he knew no before or never met before, what action you had taken was right and justice, I came here as a stranger, seeking the right people who can join our group for helping those others who are suffering in the prison of Khurkhush Majangar, I only ask you to have faith with me and trust that I am here with good intentions and never the evil ones, I swear to God that you did not disturb me neither angry me on your doubts and suspicion on me, and because it is not easy for one to believe to anyone whom you do not know, as I have come here with my good intentions I only ask you please go inside and inform the elders that I am here as a guest who came with proposal of helping those who are victims of Khurkhush Majangar and take their opinions, if by any mean they did not except me as a goodwill ambassador then I swear in the name of Allah that I will leave this land and vanish and will I not come back even if you slaughter one hundred camels. And if I will leave this place without you people listening and consider of what my mission is for, then remember that all your life you will remain as you are and nothing and no one else will dare to come up and render his help and your people will suffer where they are. Please my dear young master, go inside and announce my present and tell them of my mission and I am waiting for your answer here with these two as my witnesses" and Saqr left the stable and went inside to deliver the message to his parents which was delivered by a Jinni called Zarza Aarish.

When the elders of the house heard about this very good and surprise news which they have never expected that someone will come with such hopeful news, then the elders ordered Saqr to welcome this Jinni lady in the house so they can sit and discuss these important matters together, and all together they agree not to show any fear or disrespect to this important guest as she is not a human being, but to give her respect and show all the love as same as any guest whom to the house, until she will know and find out that we human beings are good and friendly people. Saar went outside to welcome the lady to their house, but unfortunately when he went to the stable Zarza was not there and not to been seen around, he asked Anta and Sahazena of where is Zarza, and the replied that she is no longer around and do not of where she has gone, Saqr was very much disappointed with this attitude of

Zarza, leaving the place without informing or bidding farewell, why she has made Saqr as a fool by sending him inside to inform the elders of her arrival and then disappear, this made Saqr also angry, and it did show on his face, then Saharzena came to her young master Saqr and said "My master, do forgive me please, but I have to tell you the truth, that you did not do good the way you deal with Zarza, especially to doubt to her with her mission and show it to her on her face, that was not fair, that was your mistake and has caused a wound in ones heart, and I do not think that there is a medicine to heal that kind of a wound, and even if that wound will heal but the scar will remain for a long time in her chest" suddenly Saqr raised her hands and shouts "Enough! Enough! Please stop! I cannot bare longer these pain and torments in my heart, Oh! My God, what have I done, why I allow my conscious to guide me wrongly, Oh! My God, please forgive me and beg forgiveness for me from that lady, I do not know how I can wipe those wrong doing I have done to her" then Saqr cover is face and allow his eyes to release tears to drop down on his chicks, and then he drops down to his knees still covering his face with tears running still, and then he felt a hand touch his shoulder, he opened his eyes and look, who was that person touching his shoulder, and he saw that person was his father, Mr.Fairuz, Saqr was shocked to saw his father was there, and his father then said "Stand up Saqr, wipe your tears and follow me inside the house" Saqr then stood up, wipe his tears and before he follow his father inside the house, he went to Antar and Saharzena and hug them closely and said "I made a mistake Antar and Saharzena, I beg you two, please do not get angry with me with my foolish mistake which came in my mind, I swear to God I regret my mistake, I regret it so much" and when Saqr enter inside the house he found all men were sitting one side and female on the other and all were looking at him when he enter the house and nobody spoke anything but were silent, he then stopped to go further and asking himself [What has happened here within a short time? Why all this silent? Why all these people in this condition] he then asked "Is everything alright here? Has anything happened during my short absent?" and his mother replied "Yes, everything is alright in exception of you are not alright" and Saar asked his mother "Why am I not alright mother? What is wrong with me?" and his mother answered "the wrong with you my son is that you have became lack of respect, lack of our tradition and culture, lack of showing guest our hospitality, even faith and trust begins to disappear and in its place doubts and suspicion are feeling in the heart, and this is what is wrong with you, now tell me, can you supply us in this house these missing things of which I have mentioned them to you so we can live happily as we were?" and then Saar answered his mother and said "Yes mother, if these thing are available I will sure do all my best to get and bring them in our house, but these are very rare things mother, where will I get them mother" and his mother replied "If you are willing to go deeper and search for and bring them, then I would suggest to sink deeper in yourself, in inner of you by wiping out doubts and suspicions and also by minding your tongue and respecting those whom you do not know them but came for you as your guests, do not rush to judge before you give others time to prove themselves as genuine and not fake, consult with others who had learned more than you maybe by doing this you may reach your destination. This the first in our living life Saqr that I see you slip your step and fall on the wrong path, and now I am sure that you regret of what wrong you have done, am I right or wrong?" and Saqr replied" It is true, I regret so much of what wrong I have committed, but mother! How come you know all of what wrong I have done and I did not tell you?" and his replied "The one who have good intentions and her love on us, she is the one informed us of your behavior" and Saqr asked "who is that could be mother?" and his mother first paused and said "Zarza Aarish" and Saqr really was shocked to hear his mother mentioned the name of Zarza, and with a big surprise asked "you said Zarza Aarish mother?" and his mother answered "You seem to be very much shocked when I mentioned the name of Zarza Aarish, I mentioned her is because she came here to us with a goodwill, to seek the help of how to save those friends and relatives who are suffering in hand of Khurkhush Majangar, but you my son, spoil things with your attitude of doubts and suspicions, by mistrusting her as an enemy or not a friend, Thank your God for her not to take any reaction against you for her soul is clear and clean on her mission and really she wants to help us human beings against that evil Jinni Khurkhush Majangar, and if her intentions were not pure and good, then know that for sure none of us would be able to help our loved ones, and they will remain there till there death, and never will we be able to meet again with them. Pardon us my son for not giving you a good face but a frown ones because of that mistake you had committed with realizing that mistake could cause a serious prize to pay. Now, without hesitation and in front of all of us here, I am asking you to kneel before all of us and beg for forgiveness for what wrong you had committed and never will you repeat again that mistake" Here then Saqr drop to his knee and touch his mother's feet and said "I swear mother, I did that begging for forgiveness, but I will keep on begging for forgiveness even if is a thousand time, even if the whole of my life living begging for the mistake I did to Zarza, I will do it mother, tell me where can I find Zarza and I will go search for and drop to my knee as I did to you just begging for her forgiveness" and his mother said "No need for you to leave place just going to search for Zarza, Zarza never left this place, Zarza is here for a mission as a goodwill ambassador, without delivering that message to our elders and get the result of mission, then Zarza has no plan to this place, she is our guest and will remain so till the end of her mission, Zarza came to me secretly and introduce herself and explain to me of what has happen before coming here and until the way you ignore her in not a good manner but with you doubts, Zarza wanted you to learn and understand our manners, respect, tradition and our culture of how one respect his guest if he comes with good intentions unless otherwise, Zarza wanted you to be a very good young man, as she believe that this mission with you will never be successful, so allow me to call Zarza and you must beg for her forgiviness" and then she turn her face to inside the house side and called "Zarza my dear, please come and meet your young brother Saqr" and then Zarza came from one the house room covering her half face and only her eyes were exposed, and then Saqr in front of all kneel down and ask Zarza for her forgivness and said "Please Zarza do forgive me" and Zarza said "Stand up Saqr, you a man, and a man never became weak but always strong, be of what I always know you how you be, a clever young lad and direful and without fear, I have faith in you and I know that the matter was just like a slip of a tongue and you had no bad intentions on me, but a mind of doubts and suspicion was running in your head that made you to ignore me and not showing a respect. Believe me if I tell you that I do not have any grudges or anger against you, but I did want you to learn and change your habit way of life in becoming a better person with the right judgment and never otherwise, that is why I did not leave this place but remain here to complete my mission in delivering the message to these elders so if they accept our group to join yours, so we can work together as a team to help those who need our every help. I thank all members of your family for accepting me as Jinni in this family, joining hand with human being, maybe for the first time but welcoming me with all the love and respect till I do not feel that I am different but as same as anyone here in this house. And now I think it better for us to sit in and discuss the situation step by step till we reach the best of solution of how we will win our mission".

King Kismat had a meeting with Queen Farna Bash

Then Immediately, the sitting of meeting between two, the ladies on one side and the male facing the ladies on the other, and Maalim Mikdad chair the meeting "In the name of Allah, most gracious most beneficiary, My dear ones, today is that where the signs of blessings showed up in here in this home, this is that day which with patience we were waiting for it that something should come up to help us resolving our problem, but with Allah blessing the day have arrived and that is today, but not only the day, even the messenger who will bring this blessings has been chosen by God himself, to guide us and tell us of which and how to do in our planning for saving our people from the hell of Khurkhush Majangar, I would not like to take much of your time of which you need it to spending it in discussions of your future plans of searching and opening many doors in your minds so to penetrate and reaching for a solution of these main problems, now, I take this opportunity to invite this surprise guest, to take the table and complete with discussion in how and where and when we should go for our strike against Khurkhush Majangar and his army so to save our people who are suffering in his prison. And then every and each one of us have the right to share his or her opinion not matter how old is he or she, My dear lady Zarza Aarish, please take the lead and tell us of what you have come to tell us" and Zarza started her speech by begining with "May peace be upon you" and everyone in that meeting returned "May peace be upon you too" and she continued by saying "without doubts, allow me first to give my many thanks to Mr. Fairuz and his family for excepting me as not one among as a human being but a Jinni, to be here and join this family and all others in this matter of very important matters regarding the disappearance of your loved ones, secondly I have to thank my chance of luck which Allah has given me to be able to travel from very far away and found this village of where I have no knowledge who is living here but has decided to take my chance in approaching to who human will be living here and if possible sharing my thought and the reason of my mission, luckily I have come to the right place and to the right people who are suffering the same problem of which they are waiting for the right time and the right messiah who can give them the right advice or the right direction in how to overcome these problems of the same kind, and thirdly o have this chance in meeting again with a very well know scholar Maalim Mikdad of whom I have met him once somewhere in other place without him have any knowledge that I saw him preaching in one of his friend gathering, as well the chance of meeting this noble gentle who had sacrifice his life and job just to save his neighbor, what a gentleman this person is. Abu Muntasir, you are a noble gentleman among the whole of the world gentlemen who deserve to be called a gentleman, and I Zarza Aarish, bow my head down as a respect and honor to me to meet you in person, Insha'alla your patience which you have kept till this day will be relieved by the will of Allah. I have to inform you that a problem has raise somewhere in the mountains of Jabal Qamar, and this is the main reason of why me I have to come here seeking and searching not for the help but for those brave people who are willing and ready to sacrifice their lives for the sake of saving others. Sheikh Shammaakh has disappear on his way to visit friends in Jabal Qamar, but we know that has been captured by a spy of Khurkhush Majangar and now he is in his prison, and he is suffering very much and tortured by Khurkhush Majangar army. Please I request you to give me more time so I can explain myself of my past and from where I have come from and who really am I" and Zarza explained in details of all her life story and how Khurkhush Majangar took the power from his parents and put them in jail, and how he met Prince Nuwr Alaa Nuwr and his brothers and how he was attracted to him but could never fulfill her dream of marriage, and how she and Prince Nuwr form this group of salvation to go and save Sheikh Shammaakh "And this is what has made to come here looking for those brave ones who can dare to sacrifice for the sake of other. Maalim Mikdad, you have given me the right of the counsel in this room, but I have come to end of explaining the reason of my visit here and all about myself without hiding anything, then I return this chair back to you so complete of what should be done and to hear others opinion as well, my strength is very limited if you compare our group and that of the Khurkhush Majamngar's army, but it is not the few that should worry us, as they have said [Kam min miatin qalilan ghalabat miatun kathiyra – How many few hundred won against how many thousands hundred], my dear good people, it is not those weapons made out of steel can destroy Khurklhusha Majangar and his army but here we need to use that weapon which Khurkhush do not obtain, and that is the weapon of using tactics knowledge and wisdom, we must find other groups to join us so to add more strength. Maalim Mikdad, please take your chair" Maalim Mikdad then took the chair and said "My dear ones, I believe in what Zarza has said is completely true and fact, we cannot won this war just by ourselves, we need more strength from others as well knowledge of tactics and wisdom as Zarza said, we must here now think and come out with the answers of who we should pursued others to join us" then Saqr raise his hand in asking permission to speak, and he said "My dear elders, am I permitted to ask a question to my sister Zarza?" and he was told yes you are permitted, then he asked "My dear sister Zarza, is it possible on your side to send a request through Prince Nuwr to request his father in joining us?" and

Zarza answered "No, it is not possible, because they will ask him of how he came to know of our group and our aim, if it is a matter of sending a messenger then why not sending elder people to approach the Sheikh al Kabir himself then sending a young one? you better think more wisely, send a man and not a child to this kind of mission, I will take the responsibility of escorting the messenger for his protection" and Maalim Mikdad said "It is true what Zarza has said, this not a mission of sending a young one and from the same place, this mission needs one of us elder to go to Sheikh al Kabir and ask for his help in joining our force, I am willing to go to Jabal Qamar and deliver our message to Sheikh al Kabir, as we have a very old relation between us, I think he will respond positively on our request" here then Mr. Fairuz add "It is true and this is a very wise decision, Only Maalim Mikdad is the right person to go to his friend Sheikh Al Kabir for this mission, but......?" Mr. Fairuz hesitate a little, and all members rushed him to complete his sentence "but how many of those out of army of Sheikh Al Kabir that they will be able to add the right of the right and perfect force to fight this war" Zarza then said "My elders, do not forget that it was the two of us who begin this plan, so whatever the extra people will get will add the extra strength and power in our force, and that is what is important to us" Here then Saqr stood of where he was sitting and went to where his father sat and speak slowly in his ear, and Mr. Fairuz nodded as a sign of agreeing of what suggested to him, then Saqr asked permission to leave the place for a short period and went out of the house.

Saqr went directly outside to the stable to where his friends Antar and Saharzena were, and explained to them of all what has been said by the elders meeting, and he pledge to them to give him their opinions and advise, Antar said "My dear young master, thank you so much for your concern and your love on us, and for also in including us in what is going inside, frankly, you need more power of force than that of what you think can help, and that force power you will get it from only one person, and that person is King Kismat Shaharyaar of the land of Persia, he is well known figure for his good striker in using bow and arrows, and the only one who can help you to reach and perused him in joining the force is Queen Farna Bash, if would like my advice and opinion, we better go to Queen Farna Bash and explain to her about this mission and also request her to take our messenger to King Kismat, I have faith Queen Farna Bash will never refuse us with request, she also tired with everyday troubles and spying in her land by this cruel Jinni Khurkhush Majangar." These news did pleased so much Saqr, then he accussed to Antar and Saharzena and went inside to inform the elders about what he has heard from Anta. Saar explained in details to elders inside the house in details, here then Zarza said "Farna Bash is a Jinni queen who lived on the other side of our Kingdom, this Jinni can help us, she has the ability to help us by seeking help from others, it needs a special envoy from us to go and deliver our plan and request from her" then Saar request permission to speak, and he was allowed he said "I request this mission to be given to me my dear elders, as I know of how to reach where Queen Farna Bash is as I have been there before, and elders all agree that Saqr should be their messenger to deliver the request to Queen Farna B ash. They all agree that they will stop their meetings from now until Saqr returned from Queen Farna Bash Kingdom. Saqr went outside to the stable and informs Antar and Saharzena of their new mission, Anta said "My dear young Master, I think we should start our mission this moment without delay, but before that, allow me to send information to the Queen of our journey to their kingdom" and Saqr said "Very good, you better do that now, and then we can start our journey to Queen Farna Bash Kingdom" and then Antar raise his head up in the sky and cried with that horse voice and send his message, and then said "Climb on my back young master" and Saqr climb on Antar back, and before they leave he called Saharzena and said "I do not need to tell you Oh Saharzena of how to take care of yourself and all our masters, I know how tough and dare full guard you are, but please take of yourself and all our masters and this place" and Saharzena replied "please my dear cousin, worry not much, as nothing can dare to come here as they all know who is here, I have already sacrifice my life to be here and guard this place, go in peace and return with peace" and then Antar and Saqr rode off that place and went somewhere where nobody see them and Antar open his wings and fly high up in the sky. When they were in sky, Saqr asked Antar "Tell meAntar, have you any confidence of these little butterfly people can fight Khurkhush Majangar army?" and Antar replied "My dear young Master, never judge a person's ability by his size, but by his capability, by his know how, by his talent, we know nothing of how powerful or their secret weapons are, even power of their Queen, but let's allow time to decide that, when the time will come then every and each one of us will show and prove how good or an able fighter he is" and then they slowly landed on the land of Kingdom of Butterfly people, and when they reached at that big tree of where Queen Farna Bash meets her guests they found the place is empty and no one to welcome them, this has surprised them, why such a reseption?, here then Antar raise his head high in the sky and start to smell the air, then he said "Queen Farna Bash is not here in her Kingdom, she has traveled to very far away, and as long as there is no one here to meet us, then for sure something is not right here, now what do you think of this situation, should we leave this place and return or remain here, young Master?" and Saqr replied "To return without getting an answer for what we have come for is not an advisable solution, and also to remain here without seeing anyone is also not the right thing as we do not know for how long we will wait, I do not know of how to overcome this situation, I cannot give any answer" and then Antar said ": It is not the nature of Queen Farna Bash, that if I send her a message of me coming to her Kingdom and not being here, there must be some emergency thing happened here, let us wait a little more and see what result time can produce, maybe it may produce a hopeful result" suddenly they heard the sound of a big bird wings up in the sky while landing, and then Queen Farna Bash was landing on that big tree and followed by her subjects, many of them behind her also came down and land on the earth, and then Queen Farna Bash said "My dears, Saahib and Master Saqr, first of all forgive me for not being here to receive you when you have arrived here in our Kingdom, but it was very necessary for us to leave this place, we got some information that Khurkhush Majangar wants to send his army to attack our Kingdom, that is why me and my all people went to a hiding place and leave this place empty, all of that because we want to save ourselves from this evil Jinni, after all, please be welcome to our Kingdom my dear friends, please feel free to ask any services from me and you will find Queen Farna Bash under your command, willing to serve good friends" and Antar answered "Thank you so much your Majesty, first please allow me to wipe any doubts in your mind that we are not happy for not finding anyone here to receive us, as in life there are time that things could come up with notice or one's knowledge, and for that reason one have to cancel or changes all previous program with notice, thank God you have come back safely and met us before we have left this place. Secondly, the main reason of our visit here and this time, that e have come here to ask you a favor, an important matter favor which can save others lives, and all regarding this favor, I will let my young master Saqr to explain it to you" here then Saar explain in details of all what has happened to others who are in Khurkhush Majangar jail, and what elders has decided to do under the cooperation of Zarza Aarish and her companion Prince Nuwr Alaa Nuwr of Jabal Qamar, and also of what assistance Queen Farna Bash can assist to the exits force. After Queen Farna Bash hears of all the plain and what has happened to others, she said "First. Allow me to thank my God Allah, for all the blessings he gave us, Today for the first time after a very long time my ears hear that language which it was waiting to hear after a very long period, to hear that there are braves in this world still remaining to face any evil which oppressed others, evil such of what Khurkhushs Majangar is doing to us peace and harmony in living a stable life, but yet, I agree that there are things which do come to their own time, though patience was a very bitter piece to swallow, what has denied us to fight him was our own weakness of not uniting together so to be strong and face this evil Jinni, but yet, Allah has his own plan at his own time, that now he allow us to be strong and create a force which can fight this evil Jinni, frankly, I thank the person who has thought of this plan, to win or to lose let us allow time to tale, but to try to do something practically with good intentions, that is what should be counted for. On my side, myself and all my subjects we are supporting this mission and are ready any time we are needed for, and all because this the time for deeds and no more words [And say, truth has come and falsehood has departed, Indeed falsehood is (by nature) ever bound to depart] and regarding that mission of requesting King Kismat Shahzara to join our force, that will not be a problem, I will take all the responsibility personal to deliver this message to him and bring back what answer I got from him, but let me remind you my dear one, there was the time for him then, and now is the time for others, what I mean here, is there was a time during his youth hood which he can handle his weapon and fight but now that time has passed and he became an old and a weak person, there was no any other King of his kind who was born and show the world of how powerful King he was, and he bare a child, just one girl child, and that girl has grown to a woman, but unfortunately she has chosen the wrong path against her father's will, now she is being punished and torture. I will go to King Kismat to deliver this message of the mission, and whatsoever answer I will get from him I will let you know as soon as possible, what I need is just enough time and Insha'Allah when I will be back I will send you the call to come here and visit me so to hear what answer I got from him, or what you my dear ones say?" and Antar replied "I do not know about my young master, but I agree with the idea" and Saqr also said "Even me, I agree with the idea and pleased with it, Please go Queen Farna Bash and deliver our message to King Kismat, and if it is possible on your side to request him to get for us the best of his fighters for this mission" and that was the end of their discussion and Antar and Saqr fly back to their homeland.

When they reached their homeland, Antar went to the stable and Saqr rushed inside to inform the elders of what they have done, he told the elders of all about Queen Farna Bash mission to go to King Kismat, and now they are waiting for the arrival of Queen Farna Bash from her mission and her call. All elders were so pleased for the effort of Saqr regarding his mission to Queen Farna Bash.

CHAPTER SIXTEEN

(King Kismat and young lad Bashash Zaad)

*M*Y DEAR READERS, BEFORE WE continue forward of this stimulating Tales, we have to return back to that time of King Kismat Shahzara when he finish his studies and went back to rule his country, when he returned to his homeland, within a few months his father was not feeling well and died, he then was chosen a king to lead his people and run his country into a prospect one, the country and its people were lucky enough to have such an educated young King who recently return for studying abroad, he created a very good relation with all his neighbors as well as other countries, that was his faith and dream to live with peace with his neighbours, he then took the first step of his life since taking the ruling reins of his country and build a high school for his subjects especially the young ones so to get a better education as he has, but inside the country not abroad, his dream were fulfilled with a support he got from his subjects, the high school was built and many of the young lads got a chance of their life to study in their own country the higher education which every one of them needed, and time pat and time come, King Kismat build more schools as well as higher education schools and spread them in the country, and all because he know and have learn the importance of education.

In his Kingdom, there was a young lad who had a very good standard of philosophy education, he sturdy much and highly until he disturbed his mind, he likes to speak and write philosophically, others in his country thoughts that maybe he is mad or crack, in his nature he has crammed many philosophy poems and thoughts of wisdom and sometime while walking in the streets of his neighborhood he will recite them alone by himself, and this was one of the reason that others thoughts that his mad or mind disturbed, but there are others who will follow him to seek for his wise advises, but in fact he was alright and his mind function perfectly, but unfortunately those who did not like him brand him name of madness just because the way he live. This young lad name was Bashash zaad, one of his habit was to write down strong words on building walls or in a small pieces of papers and distribute them to others, what he writes is words of wisdom and philosophy, such as these which follows:-

1. Even fools sometime does wise things and wise people does foolish things, but who will be willing to believe the wise foolish rather foolish wise?
2. I will have no more burdens to carry after my death as this world itself is a big burden for one to carry.
3. If research was meant to preserve better mankind and not destroying it, then I agree to that research.

And Bashash zaad keep on living his way of life like this always without stopping to distribute his thoughts or reciting in the streets his philosophy poems, news about him then reached to King Kismat from his intelligences and with proof of those papers he wrote and distributes, King Kismat look and read careful at each of those papers then said "so you my officers of intelligence think that this young lad is mad and mind disturbed? I want you to go and request him with my invitation to visit my new palace which I have built in the border with my neighbor, I want you to use your common sense of not showing any force to him but be polite and use diplomacy until he agree to come, and if for any reason he refuse my invitation, then come back and tell me but do not provoke him for any disrespect he has shown to you about me, show him all the respect he deserve as any citizen in my country get, do not let him feel discomfort or think that he was going to be arrested, show him inside the palace, let him see all places around that palace with well good hospitality, take him and show him even my personal bedroom, let him judge the whole of the palace and tell him that King Kismat want his opinion and views regarding this palace and what so ever decoration he have seen in it, now go and deliver this message to him and bring me back his answer, if he accepted my invitation or not, and if he accept this invitation then after showing this palace take him back to his home town and give him the most of valued gifts of which I give my visitors including money so to enjoy his life better, and after three days go again to him and tell him that I would like to meet him and hear his views and opinion regarding his visit to that palace, understood?" and chief intelligence officer replied "Yes your Majesty, I did understand," and then the intelligence force went to where Bashash zaad lives and look for him. After asking the village people of where Bashash zaad lives, they were told that every evening he is praying at his nearby mosque, next day they went to the mosque and found him there, and after the prayers they wait outside for him to come out, and a leader of the group went to meet him so to deliver the Kings message, he explain to him the he is the Kings messenger who came specialy to meet and deliver his Majesty's message, he listen to him very careful and without saying a word, then they told him their mission that they want to take him to Kings palace which is in the border, so he can see it and gives his opinion and views about that palace, he then asked "Is this a command or a request?" He was told that it is not a command but a request, but also that it will please His Majesty the King if he will accept this request as well as an invitation to hear his opinion regarding that palace,

He then said "If you will come tomorrow here then I will give you my answer if I have accept his Majesty's invitation or not, please go now and come tomorrow" the intelligence force of his Majesty the King return to the palace to give answer to his Majesty of what Bashash zaad have said, and his Majesty King Kismat was really surprise for that answer and said "He said that? That you should tomorrow for the answer?" and the officer said "Yes your Majesty, he said we should go tomorrow for the answer" and King Kismat again said "My own subject, I called him and he refuse to come? This is really a history happening here, Ok, tomorrow you must go again to him and listen what answer he will give you" and next day the intelligence group went again to Bashash zaad, they find him at the same place at the mosque, they approached him and seeking for his answer, and he answered them "I have decided to accept the invitation of His Majesty the King, I will come with you to his palace, but you will have to come tomorrow to take me for that journey, be here early in the morning and you will find me I am ready for that journey, now Go" and the force left the place and went back to inform his Majesty of what answer they got from Bashash zaad, and his Majesty King Kismat this time he laugh instead of getting angry, and said "Again tomorrow, this is realy a chap, I do not know if he is a clever or a fool person, or is he testing me with my patience or is he ignoring my loyalty. Anyhow, tomorrow you go as usual and if he comes than take him to the palace allow to see it all of it inside and outside, every corner of it, and including show him and point out of the ornaments which I have ordered them from every corner of world, let him see them and do as I told you send him back with all the best of the gifts and money for him as a gift from me, and tell him that after three days you will go again to take him to come and meet me as I would like to hear his opinion and advice, myself and in front of me"

Next day the intelligence force went to pick Bashash zaad in four horse couch with guards and they begin their journey to the boarder of their country where King Kismat has built he latest palace which can host hundreds of guest for his bigness, when they have reached to the palace, they were welcomed there by the palace guards, and Bashash zaad received a hot welcome from those guards, they took him inside the palace and allow him to go around the palace from corner to corner and answer all of his questions, it took the whole day for Bashash zaad to complete looking around that palace, and in the end they gave him many gifts of clothes, perfume, as well as small chest full of silver dinars, and told him that this gifts are from his Majesty the King for him, and after three days they will come to take him again so to meet his Majesty King Kismat in his capital palace, he was so pleased with all those gifts and was looking forward to meet his Majesty King Kismat Shahzara. And after three days they went to take and brought him to his Majesty's palace here town of where he lives, he was sent to a special room of where his Majesty meets his closed people, he sat there and wait for his Majesty to come, and no later and his Majesty King Kismat came to meet him, King Kismat before he sat down went straight to him and shake his hand, and said "I personally thank you for excepting my invitations to go there far away to my new palace and look around and also to come here to meet me so we can have just a friendly talk between us,

I want you to be frank with me, and please feel easy and free to talk of the facts no matter how bitter it will be I am willing to hear it. Now please tell me, after you have seen that palace inside and outside, what is your opinion and advices about it, please allow me to hear your views" and Bashash zaad said "Your Majesty King Kismat, I will tell you of all of what I have seen in that palace, yes, it is true that I went around it room after room, court after court and find that palace should be known as palace of wonder, for such a decorative work the builders have rendered as well as the decorative things you have brought from every corner of the world and put in that palace just to please your conscious, but I found in there, there are three very important item missing, you have not added them to complete the beauty and the fame of that palace" and King Kismat asked him "Three important items are missing? And what are those three important items missing my dear young man?" and he replied the three missing things are 1. ESSENCE OF HEAVEN 2. VOICE OF THE ANGELS, and 3. BRIGHTNESS FROM ALLAH, these three things are not in there in your palace of wonder, and without them the palace is not at all palace of wonder, but just a building big enough to put things of collection only, until you get these three things then this palace will really be a palace of wonder which you should be proud of" King Kismat was stunned and surprised by the answer he got from Bashash zaad, he then repeated those things in words, and said "Essence of heaven, Voice of Angels and Brightness of Allah, this is very impossible things to get, where one will go and find such things like Essence of heaven? can you please be more specific and explain it to me the really meaning of these three things in an open and clear language please" and Bashash zaad said "Your Majesty, I am just humble person, though educated but I have never worked in any place, since I completed my education I have been unemployed to this day, but you your Majesty is the King of all this Kingdom, and under you, you have so many well educated people who served under you, people like Ministers and advisers, why you do not call them and seek from them the right meaning of these words, they might help you and get you the answer to these quiz's, and if for any reason they have failed to get the right answers, then your Majesty, at that time I will be willing to offer you the right explanation of these quiz myself but it should be in front of them all and not only you and me" King Kismat then said "Bashash zaad, you are giving me so many conditions, and I without refusing them or getting angry on your demand, I always agree to your conditions, now tell me Bashash zaad, up to when you will be giving me conditions and I am your King who should get from my subject any of my demand without hesitation?" and Bashash zaad replied" My dear your Majesty, to you they are demands but to me they are wisdom to open your mind of what anyhow to do next if you need something, please judge right and take these demand as mind opener" and King Kismat said "Mind opener, ok I agree, I will arrange a special session here in my palace and invite of all Ministers and advisers as well as leaders of all the tribes in my Kingdom, and put these three quiz to them, but if I did not get the right meaning, then know for sure my people will be at your door to pick you up and be present here and you will give the answers to those quiz's in front of all the invited people" and Bashash zaad agree to that, and said

"Willingly I will come and be present here, and in front of them I will give you the answers to these quiz's, but your Majesty do pardon me, as at that day there will be many questions from me to them and I need answers and that before I give you the answers to my quiz's" and King Kismat agree to that "But you have to be here, somewhere present in my palace that day, waiting for what so ever results I will get from those people, If nobody gave me the right answer, then I have to summon you in front of them and you will give me the answer I need, and you will get your chance of question them as you want" and Bashash zaaad was happy with this decision and agree.

And when that day arrives, Bashash was in the palace before all the people, he was kept secretly somewhere where nobody can find him, waiting for just the call of his King if all those people failed to give his Majesty the right answers he needs. All the Ministers and Kings advisers were presents as well as leaders of the tribes, but one among all the people knows why the King has summoned them, they just say yes to the Kings call and came as requested. When the right time arrive and the King enter the chamber after he has been announce by the palace staff, everybody stood to give his respect to the King, and after he sat down on his chair, he then begin his speech, and said "My dear citizen, Ministers and advisers as well as tribal leaders of this beloved country, I summoned you all here today in this emergency meeting for a very good personal reason rather than government one, I summoned you to help me find an answer to a quiz of which I have receive it from one of my subject, he gave me a quiz without a meaning, but when I asked him to be more open to his quiz, he gave me condition, and that condition is that you all the Ministers and Advisers as well as tribal leaders should be present here, Thank you all for coming and for obeying my call, it is in my hope that these quiz's will not be a tough task for you to unfold it, please do your best and show me how clever and wise you are, and the quiz's are as follow:-

No.1 Where one can get the ESSENCE OF HEAVEN No.2 VOICES OF ANGELS and last No.3 BRIGHTNESS FROM ALLAH, these three quiz were given to me by that one of my subject of whom I invited him to my new palace which I have built recently, of which many of you know it, so to go there and see that palace from outside and inside and then to give me his opinion and advise if there is anything at all missing in that palace, these quiz's are his opinion and advices of that palace, he think that without these three things that palace is uncompleted it will never be the palace of wonder as I hope it to be, now my reason to summoned you here is to give the right meaning of these three quiz's, and I hope that you will not fail me. Yet, Allow me please to make one point clear here, before I know this subject, I was told about him that this young man is a mind disturb person, I was not satisfied with that report, so I have arranged to test him myself by sending him to my new palace as an adviser who can give me opinion about that palace, this is the answers I have received from him, but now I want the right answers from you my government cabinet as well as my tribal leaders, and this court is all yours for any one of you who can unfold these three quiz's, and the quiz's are:-

1.   ESSENCE OF HEAVEN
2.   VOICES OF ANGELS
3.   BRIGHTNESS FROM ALLAH

And here is where the hall people in that court were full of surprise and do not what to say or answer his Majesty, as no dare to speak of something he do not know of its real meaning, there was no one among all the government cabinet and tribal leaders knows what exactly the meaning of those three quiz's, though they have tried hard but could not give the answers, then they declare to his Majesty that they have surrender, as they have no answers to these three quiz's, and here is where then King Kismat said his strong words "So this it means that this young man is more clever than you all, he is more wise than you all, and he is the one you are calling him a disturbed mind lad, while you are more wise than him, but three sentences of his none of you could not translate what it's meaning. Now tell me all of you, who is strong and who is weak here between you my responsible holding government people as well as you our country tribal leaders, is it him the so called disturbed minded lad or you who are holding such high position in my government and your minds are disturbed? This is a big shame, that no one of you can even try to give me even the wrong answer or incomplete meaning of those quiz, but what I get here from you is just silence and no answer, it means you have left me with empty hands, nothing I got from you which can quench my thirst, just on young lad came out with such opinions in his mind to make me happy, to learn of what mistake I made without realizing that was a mistake, he saw it and point out and gave that chance to correct that mistake so I can earn my happiness, but Alas! None of you could dare understand a simple language of wisdom from that so called disturbed minded lad you have branded on him, now that lad is here and I will call him before you, as this is his condition that I shall call all of you here today so he can meet you and as well as asking you some questions. I agree to his condition and that is why I called you to meet him and answer his all question he wish to put to each of you. Please call Bashash zaad to attend this court and meet heads of my government as they are all will be happy to meet him" and King Kismat remain silence and allow the palace officials to go and escort Bashash zaad to the guest court where all Ministers and Advisers and Tribal leaders were waiting to hear him of what he have to say. then official came back and announce that "Your Majesty King Kismat Shahzara, The young lad Bashash zaad requesting permission to enter in your court your Majesty" and King Kismat permitted Bashash to be allow to enter the court hall of that palace where all invitees were there, Bashash zaad enter and he raise his looking at left and right were wishing the people in the hall with his raising and falling while also bowing while he was escorted by Palace officials to where he will be sitting, and when he was in front of King Kismat he greeted him with bow and then said "Peace be upon you your Majesty and all people here in this place" and all the people said "Peace be upon you too" and then King Kismat point to him to sit on the seat near to him, Then King Kismat open the session by saying "My dear distinguish guests, whom you are serving me and as well as this country, I called you here today in this very important meeting just to help me to disclosed the meaning of three wise words of which this young lad here on my side has advice me so to complete the missing items in my new palace which I have recently in the border, unfortunately, none of you has the ability to give me the answers of those three quiz's of which this young man Bashash zaad, has advice me to get them so that palace will be completed to the standard and can be called the palace of wonder, since that time he gave his advice, I requested him to be open in his language so he explain to me the exact meaning of those three quiz's, but he gave me condition that I should call you all here and here is where he will gave me the meaning of those three quiz's but in front of you all after he get answers from you of what he has to ask, now before we waste more time I will allow this young man Bashash zaad to take the chair and speak to you of what he want to say to you, Young man, the chair is all yours" Then Bashash zaad stood up and speak "Your Majesty King Kismat Shahzara, and all the invited members of the government cabinet as well as all the Tribal leaders of our country, Peace be upon you all" and all answered back "Peace be upon you too" and then he continue and said "It is my duty your Majesty to thank you and all the people who are here now in this court, I would like to let you know your Majesty, that I count myself a lucky person for choosing me to go to that palace far away at the borders and open all his doors just for me, and gave me all the freedom of entering any room I would to enter in that palace of its kind, that palace was built by very talented builders from our country, as well as many decoration from many parts of the world were there to add more beauty and prestige to that palace, but your Majesty allow me now to tell you that was possible to be done by those well talented builders and interior decorators, but... here there is a but, forgive me as I will have to leave this page and open a new page, the page which concern your Government cabinet as well as all these Tribal leaders, because for them also I have some example I would like to narrate totem and seek their answers, as from their answers I will be guided to reach my goal, But also I am requesting you your Majesty to give them all the freedom of speech and without fear, that they should feel to answer me freely" and King Kismat said "They have all the freedom to answer you freely and no fear" and Bashash added "Thank you so much your Majesty for your kind heart, My first question to all of you here, if any one of you has the wealth, and has the intention of building one huge mosque, is he allowed to do so by choosing any land in your Kingdom and built that mosque? 2nd question, will the people be allowed to use that mosque for their prayers if there are important things missing?, and 3rd question, is that mosque acceptable (Jaaiz) for people to say their prayers in it?, I would like anyone of you to give me the answers for these three question please, with your permission your Majesty" and King Kismat then request Adviser for religious affairs to give answer to these three questions, and the adviser stood to give answers, and said "Your Majesty King Kismat Shahzara, I would like to give answers accordingly, 1st, it is not important for anyone who is reach enough to have the power of authority to chose anywhere in this country and build a mosque, this is not allowed, he must have the government permission to get the land and that land must not be anyone property but own by the government, then that land must free of any future plans for other projects of this country, he then can build the mosque after he is allowed and obtain all the necessary documents which will give him the right to use his wealth and build that mosque for the people, either it will be under his authority or he will give this mosque to the government as care taker and under Government authority, 2nd, the answer is No, the people will not be allowed to use that mosque if it is not well equipped, with all the necessary needed things, only the completed built mosque with complete important items, such as water, carpets, lights, Holly qura'ans, Imam, Muadhin and care taker of that mosque, as well as other necessary items are all available then it is up to the authority concern to allow that mosque to be used by the people for their daily prayers, and 3rd, is that mosque Jaaiz to pray in it, my answer to that is, first the authority concern must make sure that donors money is pure money and not forbidden money (Haram), that he earned this money legally, and not by doing illegal ways of earning it, such as interests, liquor business, or earn that money in any way which Allah forbid, if he built that mosque with Halal money than that mosque is allowed for others to say their prayers, or otherwise their prayers will not be accepted by Allah, Wa lillahi tawfiq. And if I for any reason have given a wrong answer, I seek pardon from Allah, and then from you all here, as I am human, no doubts mistakes do occur to us human beings" then King Kismat referred to Bash ash zaad and ask him "Are you satisfied with the answers given by my advisor Bash ash zaad?" and Bash ash answered "Yes your Majesty, I am so satisfied by the answer form his Excellency advisor of religious affairs. Here is my second question your Majesty, If anyone built a Higher school with a high standard building, well decorated and enough rooms to accommodate many students, will this school be ready to educate our children?" King Kismat then request his advisor of Education affairs to answer that question "and the advisor stood and greeted the King and all the people, and said "Your Majesty, my answer to this question is this, It is not the structure that give education to the student but there are so many thing must be there to educate a student, things like Principal, teachers, books, inks, writing pens, security for student protection, toilets in the school as well as water for all who are in that school to consume and as well as available doctor, nurse and medicine in case of emergency, and many more. I hope I have answered well and if I miss anything then please do forgive me" and Bashash zaad then turn to face the King and said "yes you have answered very well. Now your Majesty the time have come to give you your answers, but after we all heard the answers of my questions from these noble advisers of yours, now I request each one of you to preserve in your minds the answers I have been given by both advisors, three concerning a mosque and one concerning a higher school, and let us all go to that day of where I gave you the three quiz's regarding your new palace, I told that there are three major things missing in that palace, and those three were the main reasons of why is that palace could never be called (as you wanted to be) a palace of wonder, and those three things were 1. Essence of heaven 2. Voice of Angels and 3. Brightness from Allah, as these three were not there that day, I did tried very hard to look for them in every corner of that palace but they were not there, as you could have forgotten them your Majesty, and you did ignore how importance those three were, more than all the decoration you had put in that palace which you have brought from every corner of the world, yet these three they did not need to be searched or brought from any corner of the world because they are here in your own Kingdom your Majesty, and they need not any wealth to buy them but only intentions and clicking of your fingers and they will be under your feet your Majesty. You then tried very much to get the meanings of these three missing items, you have called all your Ministers and all your advisers as well as all your Kingdom Tribal leaders just to give the meaning of my quiz's, but it end all in vain as no one of them do understood the wisdom of my language of which used to put in this position, and when you requested me to open those quizzes in an under stable language, here then was my chance to prove to you that you will never get the answers you seek from anyone but only me, but how did I know that? because I had my faith that no one will know what I have create in my mind in just a simple language but corrupted in a quiz, and here we are now, still you remain with empty head without your answers, and when you requested me to be here, here then I knew that I won my mission and you have failed yours, as I wanted to weigh your patience your Majesty, because I wanted to know that, do you have that patience like our ancestors before us? But please do forgive me your Majesty, I did not do this that I show you my cleverness or how wise I am or disrespect you and all these gentleman, No sir, I did this because I want to know more about you, as that King who ruled this Kingdom and I am part of it as your subject, as I have said before that I did want to know you more and better that are you that person whom Allah gave him patience? And if you have, than do you maintain that patience? And if you have maintain it, than as a King who has his own Kingdom, do you use that patience as many of our prophets have taught us, that a believer must use his patience though it is bitter to swallow, yet in that bitterness there is a small hidden seed, and that seed can wipe out all that bitterness if only one knows of how, where and when to plant it, but yet it is a very hard task for one to swallow that bitterness for just getting that chance of enjoying the sweeteners taste of that small seed, and this Your Majesty is that time you have been waiting for, as your Majesty you are a man who maintain patience, you have within you a patience and you know how to use your patience, and if have not, then I Bash ash zaad, will not send here before you all today maybe by this I would have in a prison cell or in my grave, but by that patience of yours your Majesty, I am still in your palace and in front of you, breathing and speaking loudly any way I want, and have been able to challenge your patience so to allow you to taste that sweet seed which was hidden in that bitter patience" in that hall every was so quite, not even the breathing sound one can hear, and all because of that long speech of Bash ash zaad, so interesting so philosophical, so sweet language so full of wisdom, and King Kismat with all others just remain quiet and pay attention of what Bash ash zaad was telling the King's court, and all because every word Bash ash zaad has spoken was so sweet than the other.

Then Bash ash zaad continue his speech and said "Your Majesty, King Kismat Shahzara, to let you know the exact meaning of my first ESSENCE OF HEAVEN of which is not in your palace, because of all around I went in that palace, beginning the room outside and ending inside I did not smell any of our ladies tradition when they perfumed themselves, even a Bukhur (Uud burning) of Uud was not in your palace, what I smell is the essence of wall paintings as well as those new decorative items like carpets and woods items, but never of that woman of decorate his house with the essence of Uud as well as the perfume of which she wear, and all because that palace is still empty without the occupation of a lady of the house. My second quiz was VOICES OF ANGELS, since I have put my feet inside that palace, it was so silence and quite, not even a sound of a bird was inside that palace, what sound I have heard is our footsteps when we walked with your guards, but those angels of Allah of which Allah always gift us, was not in that palace your Majesty, and voices of Angels are not others than voices of the children, that palace was and still empty without the availability of children your Majesty. And my last quiz was the absent of BRIGHTNESS OF ALLAH, yes the brightness of Allah is not there, I only saw the shinning of copper and brass as well as silver items, but Allah brightness is not in that palace your Majesty, and where one can get the Allah brightness, it only begins with a good intentions and end up in real action, as Brightness of Allah are in his books which he has brought them down through his Prophets for us to read and to teach, so to avoid of the evil doing and walk on the right path which is a straight path of Allah of which it has tought us the right things to do which pleases Allah and never otherwise, and those books are Taurus, Zaboor, Ingil as well as Furqan (Which is Qur'aan), there was no even one of the book in that palace, not on the tables or not even written verses from any of those book are on the walls, it is there then that I found that place is in the dark as long as Allah brightness is not in it, can you name that palace as a palace of wonder when he gave you all power and made you to be a King and you had forgotten him, what more wonders can be worth than the wonders of Allah who create a human being from a clay? And here my dear King, I conclude my explanations of those quiz's I have put into your mind were for the best and worth intentions and never for the worst or evil means. Your Majesty, if for any reason you have found me guilty of making this simple matter into a complicate matter, than you have all the right to punish me, and I promise you that I will are no grudges against you but will always praise you as a ruler who loves justice and who loves his country as well as all his people in fairness and without discrimination, and if you have found me that I was fair, and did this for a good intentions and never evil ones than you know yourself your Majesty of what to with me. And here is where I have finished all the reasons of requesting you noble gentlemen to be here so maybe for one reason or the other, you have learn or gain something worth that it may help you in your future responsibly for our beloved country and it's people. And to you your Majesty, I hope that I have given something to quench your thirst for those three quiz's I gave you as now you have got your answers which you were seeking for, it is my hope that you are satisfied now and pleased to learn what is those missing items in you new palace. Thank you you're Majesty, thank you all you good and loving people who are holding difference responsible positions of this Kingdom, May God save our King and preserve our Kingdom in peace and harmony forever."

And here is where King Kismet now stood and address those who were invited, he said "My dear distinguish cabinet of my Government as well as our Tribal leaders,

You all have heard what this young man has said in his very long speech, and how he have given me the real meaning of his quiz in a very long way and has explain it in clear language that we all now know the real meaning of those three quiz's, also my two advisers have answered him very well, also in an open and clear language, his four questions regarding the mosque and the high school, I personal was impressed by the answer given to him, and I am sure that in those questions and answers many of us has benefited and gain some knowledge which maybe we do not know before. Allow me now, to take this opportunity to tell this young lad Bash ash zaad, that those who spread the news about him the he is disturbed minded person, are all wrong and not at all true, I think the fact is, they are the one who have disturb minds, is it possible for someone who's mind is disturbed to lecture like this and with a philosophy language and with wisdom? it is not possible at all, and I think you all will agree with me that this lad Bash ash zaad is a perfect normal person.

I have built that palace and has decorated inside and outside with so many very expensive things brought from many parts of our world, just to give it a recognition that this is the palace of wonder, in my mind and in the minds of those who share with me ideas in creating this palace to be of its example, could not find those very important three missing items but this young lad who many of you think that he is mad and abnormal mind person, saw what we all of us did not see, and today here he have stand and pointed out what those missing items and clearly he is quite right and I agree with him, as our ancestors have said that patience is bitter and very hard to swallow, yes I agree with them, as my patience to reach to the fact was very hard to swallow, but fortunately today I did swallow my patience and find out how sweet was that seed of the patience, and all because of this young lad Bash ash zaad.

Now, as I stand here before you, I make this announcement to you all and the outside world as well, that this young man here with us, by the name of Bash ash zaad I appoint him as my personal adviser in the field of Philosophy, wisdom and knowledge, so I have announced and so it should be writen in the official books and so from now on he is part of this cabinet, thank you so much your Excellency Bash ash zaad for saving me from critics and from committing mistakes of which I had no idea before, and saved me from shame from those who know much like you did, and they could have happen if I have invited many world leaders to come and see what kind of wonder I have built.

Both arrows strikes at the same target

Now hear this my new order and my intentions, that from this moment to those who are concerned and care taker of that palace, to go a hang on the walls of that palace many verses from the Holly book Qur'aan so the BRIGHTNESS OF ALLAH could add more light in that palace, and also I announce before you that I am going to get married very soon and take my future wife to that palace so the ESSENCE OF HEAVEN could spread in that palace, and with Allah blessings Insha'aallah those VOICE OF ANGELS should be heard in that palace, (by the will of Allah) bi idhnillah. I would prefer my advisors to advise me of where should I go and knock the door of that house for me to get the right partner who will share her whole life with me, the time has come for me to live in a family way of life" and everyone in that court room rushed to Bashsash zaad and congratulate him for his appointment by his Majesty to be his advisor. His Majesty King Shahzara did not wait much for his wedding, as his advisors did find for him a well educated girl from a well respected family, he got married to that girl and after a short time Allah blessed him with his first born and it was a baby girl which he named her Nazniyna. Days and years past by and Nazniya was well looked by her father, grown up in a royal family way of life, and King Kismat regarded himself as lucky enough to be blessed by such a child, King Kismat took keen interests in seeing that Nazniyna gets the best of education of many aspects and in particular the Islamic religion, and Nazniyna did show keen interests of learning, she has put all her efforts, morning and evening in spending much her time studying, teachers coming and teachers leaving in the palace just to help and give Nazniyna the best of education. Nazniyna while growing to become a young girl was well educated, but in her mind she had one particular interest, to follow the steps and become like her father to be the best of the archer as a sport, she wanted to be the target shooter like her was, and she have received that teaching from one of the well known teacher in Kingdom, and that was none other than her own Father King Kismat, as King kismet whenever he goes for hunting he took his daughter Nazniyna with him and teach her all the technical of how to become the best archer, and luckily after years passed by and Nazniyna has matured and become a grown up girl, she was one of the best archer in the Kingdom.

King Kismat has in his own palace yard a personal blacksmith who produce all of his Majesty's weapons, he was a very good craftsman, his works are regarded as a high standard pieces of work, he can create sword, arrows and bows, shields made out of iron material, and lances, This blacksmith was known as Ridhwaan, he had only one son who he named Shuhur jaan, because of his highly standard quality of his work, King Kismat took him and kept him in his palace yard and gave a house to live there with his family as well as built for him his workshop to produce the best of the weapons only for his Majesty as well as a monthly salary for his job, Shuhur jaan was a very young lad and has grown up in that palace yard since he was born, he was always a helping hand to his father on his work, but sometime he was allowed by the King to come inside the palace and play together with Princess Nazniyna, as Nazniyna was the only child and Shuhur jaan was also the only child to his family, as they were children still under age, they always play together, as sometime Princess Nazniyna is allowed to come down to the garden yard where Shuhur jaan house also there, they get that chance to be together and play together. One day Ridhwaan went to King Kismat and beg him to allow his son Shuhur jaan also to be educate by the same teachers who come to teach Princess Nazniyna, and all because the palace security is so tight that it does not allowed the residence to go out every time, so this became a very difficult for Shuhur jaan to go to learn outside,

This opportunity was the main reason for these two young children so close and and squinted to one another, until it made them quite difficult to miss one another in a day, in their aquinted relation they did not relies or bother to know and understand the difference between them, as they are children who were brought in same place, learn and play and grow up in the place, to them this was normal, as each of them regard the other as his/her close friend, but in reality there is a difference, a very strong difference between them, like that between earth and sky, as she is a princess who live in that palace and he is just a son of a blacksmith who work in that palace. But in fact this young lad Shuhur jaan, was very good and clever in his studies, many time he who helped Nazniyna in her studies if she did not understand the issue, this closeness and helping hand to her, has created an eternal feeling of love to Nazniyna, she slowly started to like much Shuhur jaan for his brightness of mind and cleverness in his studies.

After many years passed away and the young children grow up to be young lads nearly to be matured, sometimes when Nazniyna wanted to go for hunting, though with her guards and guides, she always seek permission from her father to allow Shuhur jaan to come with them, the main reason for Nazniyna of taking Shuhur jaan in their hunting trips, is that Shuhur jaan was very best archer, he never missed his targets, when he aimed then for sure the arrow will reach it's target, that standard of his perfect aiming was noted down by all those who go hunting with them, those guards and guides who accompanied them, they notice and compare Shuhur jaan as the best archer to that standard of leveling Hi sMajesty King Kismat, the intelligence of the palace, send this news and information to His Majesty the King, this information than raise the interest in his Majesty to know and see for himself of how good this young lad is, as he believes that in all of his kingdom there is no such an archer who can reach his standard, because also he, if he aimed, than for sure the arrow will reach its target and never miss.

Then one day King Kismat arranged the hunting trip, and he decided to take both children, Princess Nazniyna and Shuhur jaan in that trip, When they have reached their hunting place, first they camp there and after the rest they decided to go for hunting, but before going they have divided themselves into two groups, one was laid by the King and he took Shuhur jaan with him and their guards, and the other was of Princess Nazniyna with her guards, King Kismat intention to take Shuhur jaan was just to find out of how good this young lad is in using arch, is he real good as he was informed? so he told Shuhur jaan not to be away from him, he must stay beside him in every step of this hunting, then they enter into the forest where there are difference kind of animals for hunting, until they have reached at the place where far away they saw a group of mixed gazzles, then King Kismat pointed to Shuhur jaan with signal (one of the rule of hunting is to use sign language and not words) of where those gazzles were, then slowly and carefully without disturbing those animals, step by step they moved to find the right suitable place to aim their weapons, King Kismat signed them all to stop there, King Kismat than aimed his arrow to that particular animal he chose to hunt, but before he release his arrow, he turned his head and look at Shuhur jaan and then with signal he invited him to take the aimed and shoot at the animal, but Shuhur jaan politely he put his hand on his chest and returned the offer to his Majesty that he should take the aim, King Kismat then understood that and answered back with nodding his head and took his aim, and with open eyes and without breathing he let go his arrow to hit his target, and the arrow with full speed went straight and penetrate in the neck of that male gazelle who was huge and heavy, and that gazelle felt the pain of that arrow in his neck and jump up and then felt down shaking his legs, then one of the royals guard rushed to where than animal fell so to slaughter him before he died, as this in Islamic law is a compulsory matter, while Shuhur jaan was watching but his arrow was in its bow in case of any emergency, as well as King Kismat already put another arrow in his bow for any emergency need, but that guard who rushed to finished off that male gazelle, before he reached, the male gazelle stood up again and with full of pain but also very angry, saw that there was a mane coming his way, he then aimed his horn to him and was ready to go and attack the man, King Kismat and Shuhur jaan saw immediate the danger facing that guard, and there was no time to warn him by shouting but both of them aimed again at that male gazelle and send their arrows together and hit the target and make that male gazelle to fall down near the feet of the guard, and the guard when he saw that, that gazelle fell down near his feet with three arrows in his neck, he still stood there shaking and his eyes were wide open, as he knew before, that he could not save himself from the angry gazelle who want to revenge, if it was not for those two arrows of King Kismat and young lad Shuhur jaan, than there was no doubts that the guard would have being attacked and maybe even lost his life with those sharp horns of that gazelle. While still standing there, the guard was breathing heavily, even his mind flown away as he did not believe his eyes that animal was besides his feet, then King Kismat and Shuhur jaan and other guards rushed to where that gazelle was and find it was still breathing, and King Kismat ordered other guards to slaughter it quickly before he died naturally, when they reached to where the gazelle was and that guard still standing with his mind off, they shook him so to return his memory back, and then his memory came back and was asked to complete his job of slaughtering that gazelle, which he did.

King Kismat and Shuhur jaan were more interested to know which among the two arrows, his or Shuhur jaan's which made that gazelle fell down, but when they look at those arrows which hit that gazelle, both of them were surprised for what they have seen, something more than their expectation, as both of the arrows hit their target at the same sport side by side on the chest of that gazelle, this means that these two archers in their minds chose the same target and hit the same sport, how this could happen, that is a question which was running in their heads, King kismet then asked Shuhur jaan "what was your target Shuhur jaan?" and Shuhur jaan answered "My target was at that place where my arrow hit, because it is where the the heart is, your Majesty" and then King Kismat was asking himself silently within himself, [is this possible? that two human being as hunters think of the same target and hit the same target at the same time? Is this not miracle? This is very rare coincidence to happen but today it has happen to us, that two archers has in their mind same thoughts, same target and at the same time] King Kismat with this action made him to be satisfied to believe of what he have heard of Shuhur jaan is true, this lad has the ability to be one of the best archer in the world. He then said to Shuhur jaan "My dear Shuhur jaan, today I am satisfied that Allah gave you the ability of a sharp eye and the will of hitting your target, without any doubts you are that young man who have that rare quality of its kind, very few have this kind of quality and ability, and today you remind me of that day during my studies in foreign country of where I have saved my friend from a hungry lion, if it was not for my ability of hitting my targets perfectly, for sure that friend of mine would have been attacked by that lion. Shuhur jaan for this I have seen today and have learned about your ability, I want you to be a bright young lad by putting more efforts in your studies, I am proud to have such a subject in my Kingdom, and such a young man in my palace, from now on when ever I go for hunting you will be on my side with me, and also whenever you show your improvement on your studies then I promise you that I will not deny you more higher education, I will not stop given you further more education until you became a well educated young man who depend on himself and be part of this Kingdom among a future leader like others "and then they all returned home with their prayer.

Many years pasted away, and Princess Nazniyna and Shuhur jaan grown up to be a young lady and a handsome young man, that dangerous age of which many failed to resists the temptation of love, and to these young couple their story was no differences, the more they are together the more the seed of love were grown within their hearts, that has spread widely in them that they could not miss to see one another in a day, and for any reason if one them is not in the palace and has to be away for some un avoidable reason, than that will cause in each of them worries and discomfort and lack of happiness. All these happenings were secretly to each other, as none of them have open his or her mouth to express their feelings to each other, but it was a matter within and that sense of feelings were not yet exposed openly but were suffering silently with their silence love to each other. Their secret love was there but it was just a matter of time when it will be exposed to each other, what was denying them to share their feelings openly to each other was their tongues and mouths, and their hearts were crying loudly, but no one can hear that cry by their ears but only by their sense of feelings, it could be that fear of afraid to hurt one another's feelings on the negative results, that this open feelings if it will occur maybe will reached their parents and that results will be a fatal one, the truth of their silence is not known yet, and they were waiting for the right time and the right moment to tell each other of how painful this love feeling is.

Shuhurjaan sending his letter with an arrow

This love feelings between these two young lads, started to show signs, and the first human being to notice them was Shuhur jaan's father Mr. Ridhaanah, because he noticed the behavior of his son beginning to change, many time he forgets things or sometime he will remain silence and if you call him he does not answer you, he became an up sent minded lad, and some time he will notice his son is not in an easy condition but un comfortable, he will go to the window and look at the Princess window every now and then, these signs were proof enough for Mr. Ridhaanah to doubts his son behavior that there is something bothering him and in conclusion he came to understand that his son has already grown up into young man and this is the sign that he is sick in love, and what he loves is very rare and impossible to love, this is very expensive love where he is not son will not have that wealth as well as that royal blood so to achieve it, Mr. Ridhaanah then said to himself [This is not right, if it will continue then for sure this will bring misfortune and disaster in our family, I must find a way to stop this before it is too late], Mr. Ridhanah then thoughts that he must use wisdom and best way to make his son understand of how wrong his choice of love is, that he must avoid her and wipe out all the idea of his love to the Princess. He then waited for a right opportunity, and then one day while they were having lunch he realize that, that was the best opportunity to raise the issue to his son, after they were eating they set down at the sitting place for a cup of coffee with some sweats, here is where Mr. Ridhanaah got his chance and raise a subject to his son wisely and politely, he asked "Shuhur jaan my son, I think now you have already grown to be a man who can take any responsibility, you can now take my place to be a responsible blacksmith, as we your parents now became old and weak and our energy of strength in our body and minds has drained away, and sign of poor health are begin to appear within my body, we need someone to take this place so to help us earn for our living life as usual, and there is nobody else who deserve to my place better and worth more than you, and all because our King rely very much on the best of craftsmanship, and that is why he find me and brought me here in his palace just to create for him the best of his weapons, and on the other side you are our only child gave have given us and we are most thankful for that, and this means that you will be our inheritor of all that belongs to us, any property as well as any of our skills, if for any reason we will not be able to give our King of what he demand and with his satisfaction, than for sure my son, know that we will not be able to remain here and will be send away and this work will be given to someone else, and believe me son, I would not like to stop serving him for any of his work, or this place to be taken by others and not us, he was always generous and kind to us, see for yourself of how much he likes you, and how much he helped you to earn your education as well as being his second man besides him when he go hunting. What I see here now, that you need someone to be close to you, someone as you life partner to live with, as me and your mother have lived till you came to this world and join us as an ad in our family, now my question to you, what is your opinion if we will get for you a partner to live with in marriage so you too can begin your own family life?" Shuhur jaan at first did not say anything, because what his father has told him has stunned him very much, this kind of conversation was a big surprise to him, and frankly it has made him to be dumb and could not speak for just a short while, and all because it is now quite a long time he had the same intention in his mind but could not find a way to tell his father, he had no courage at all to speak to is father a matter concerning marriage and all because of his highly respect to his father.

Day comes and went by, in his heart there was fire burning his veins and the heat of that fire has made his mouth to be tongue tide, behind the curtain he so well courage that he always said that today I will tell my father of my intention of getting marriage, but if he is in front of his father he has no courage to spill out of what is hidden in his heart regarding his marriage intention, but now the matter has eased itself, all that burden in his heart of how and when and where to tell his father of his intention have come as a big surprise to him, yet, there was something holding him not speak or answer his father on his question, and that is how he can mention to his father that he is ready to get marriage and his future wife should not be other than Princess Nazniyna, than his father speak and asked again "I see that you have remain quite for a long period without giving me your answer Shuhur jaan, do you need more time to think and tell me? And if it so, than let us delay this conversation now, but we should continue again next Thursday, this will give you exactly seven days to think and come out with an answer, and at that particular day you must give your answer on this important matter, or do you have any other opinion?" and then Shuhur jaan answer his father and said "very well father, I agree with this idea, after seven day of thinking I will give you both my answer on this important matter" and here was where concluded this conversation of marriage to Shuhur jaan. But in Shuhur jaan's mind, he wished that this news of marriage would have reached Princess Nazniyna so she could know that if Allah wants him to get marriage than this marriage should only be to her and none other. He then has decided to take a pen and a paper and write this following letter to Princess Nazniyna:-

In the name of Allah most beneficary most gracious

To you dear Princess Nazniyna,
Peace be upon you,

I ask you to accept this letter of mine, the first of its kind in my whole life to send it to you, and all because I had no other choice but to sent it, what has force me to write this important letter which express all the facts about my feelings toward you, is what you can call an open dialoged with true message of how I feel about you.

As children we grow up together, played and study together, but as we grow and matured to a young hood, there is something grow inside me as well and cannot be explained in just simple writing letter, but in letter it may take that message to make you understand of how are my inner feelings on you are, if in a day I do not see your beautiful face in front of me, I felt my heart is torned apart and with no comfort but full of torments, I keep on asking myself several why these torments? Why these uncomforts if I do not see you in a day?, my soul refuse to give me an answer, but my heart has these to tell me [you are hurting me so much when you are not with Nazniyna, I ask my heart again, Why? and my heart answered me, Nazniyna is the only human being who give me pleasure and comfort, so in my whole life I do not want

Anyone else to penetrate in me other than her], My dear Nazniyna, it was not an easy decision to write and send this letter, to it was a very hard task, but in the end I had no other choice other than sending it to you so you will know and understand of how I feel about you in my humble heart, please I ask you not to mistranslate this letter as an act of misbehavior but a piece of paper which represent of how I feel about you in reality.

Today my parents have asked me if I will be willing to get marriage and are ready to find the right partner as my future wife, they demand an answer on the matter and gave me one week to think and give them my answer, of which I said I will, if for any reason they have found that I am man enough to get marriage, than there will be no any other person who can take that place other than you, you are my choice, you are the woman I love and you will be that person who will take the place as my life partner as my wife.

Dear Nazniyna, please helps me by answering, and tells me of how you feel after you have read it, and if you have decide to submit this letter to your parents because you think that I have cross over my boundaries of respect to you, than I am willing to face any punishment even if it will be death, But my love to you is more stronger and more live than the death itself, as I will not stop loving you in my whole living life.

I am waiting for your favorable reply and not otherwise, please.

Yours sincerely
Shuhur jaan

Then he rolled the letter on one of his bow and binding it with thread tightly and went on the roof of their house and aim his arrow with his bow directly to where Princess Nazniyna window is at the palace, and with full strength he pulled the string and realize it, fortunately that arrow went flying and reached its target and penetrate through inside the window. At that time Nazniyna was sitting inside near the window and she saw that arrow hit the wall and fell down on the floor, she at look at what was came through her window, went and pick it up and saw it was an arrow but with a piece of paper bind on it, she open the thread and realize that was paper and open it, she find it was a letter, sat down on her bed and begin to read it from begin to the end, but was not satisfied and re-read it again for the second time, but this time she was reading the letter with a smile on her face, that letter has made her so happy that she started to roam around her room and jump on her bed, and then look at that letter and then with a big smile kiss it hardly without release it from her lips, and release it and then went at the window and look outside and she saw Shuhur jaan was still on the roof of their house and then nodded her head as a sign to Shuhur jaan that his request has been accepted. Then she made a sign to Shuhr jaan not to leave the place and then disappear inside,

Shuhur jaan was just pacing left to right on top of the roof waiting for what Princess Nazniyna will react, and suddenly he heard the force sound of an arrow hit somewhere on the roof, he looked at it and found that it was an arrow with piece of animal skin wrapped on the center of it, he went a took that arrow and unbind the skin and look back to the window and he saw Princess

Nazniyna was still there and waving to Shuhur jaan, Shuhur jaan open that letter and started to read, and here is what was written in that letter:-

In the name of Allah the most gracious the most beneficiary

Dear of my heart Shuhur jaan,

 I did understand very well the letter you had send it to me, the letter which has open my heart and feed it with many happiness, in this day I have come to know of your love to me, this love sickness of which you mentioned it is not only on your side but it has also affected me as well, but it was not an easy task for me to express my feelings as well as my secret towards you, and all because of the many hard obsticals and impossible reasons we are facing in this surrounded well protected environment of the palace, but this day you have done for me half of my ambition of which I wanted to do for a long time, you eased the hardness and the uncomfortable within my heart of which I have been suffered for quite a long time now. My answer to your request is YES, as I also have promised myself that if in my life I will get married than there will be no one else other than you. You are my choice of husband I wished to marry too as you are that person of whom I willing to give all my love and in all of my life. I believe that Allah today has answered my prayers and I thank him for such a wonderful gift of my life, and I hope that he will easy the journey ahead of us with no obstacles or any complications.

Loving you for a long time
Nazniyna.

CHAPTER SEVENTEEN

(King Kismat against his people wrong doing)

J T WAS A USUAL ROUTINE for King Kismat every morning to be in his palace court for meeting with his subjects so to hear if there is any complains or cases to be judged, this routine was family matter, as it was done before by his ancestors. But for this day, King Kismat after arriving in his palace court and after listen to the needs of his people, then he asked if there is any case to be heard, and he was told that there is one case to be heard, he then requested the case to brought to him, and those concerned with the case came to the chamber and King Kismat listen to the complain of the case, three people came to the chamber, two gentlemen and a lady, there complain was a matter concerned a baby child, then King Kismat gave chance to each one of them to speak so he can understand what the complain is about,, then the first person stand to speak, his name was Ghullam, he started to speak by saying "Your Majesty, this lady which came with us here is my legal wife, I married to her with her own will and by the permission of her parents, but before she became my wife she was this other gentleman's wife, but then they were divorced and after their divorced I got married to her, The problem raised when this gentleman who was not in this country for such a long period, came back and maybe was told that his divorced wife bare a child within seven months of their divorce, he claimed that this child is his legal son when he came back from his journey and I did not agree with his claim and I claimed that this child is my legal son, this is our main reason for coming here to you your Majesty so you can judge us fairly and tell us who's child is this boy, is it mine or his?" This case real confused King Kismat, as the subject of this case was very much complicated, as here is where is needed really fair judgment, then King Kismat asked Mr. Ghullam "Tell me sir, how long has passed since she was divorced and get married with you?" and Mr. Ghullam answered "Your Majesty, it was the same day she was divorced and the same day I was married with her" and King Kismat said "I do not understand, how come one be divorced and get married on the same day?" and Mr. Ghullam the explained "Your Majesty, our case of marriage was a long tale, even if we have to explain here in details it will take hours and hours, but for your information Your Majesty, it was one of your court that has came out with judgment of this case on regarding divorce and marriage" and then King Kismat asked "what was the cause of you to go to the court of where the judge gave such un acceptable judgment, neither in our Islamic faith and neither in the laws of our country?" and Mr. Ghullam replied "Your Majesty, I would like in short to explain to you the reason of why we went to court seeking justice. In my profession I am a local herbal as well as spiritual heeler, I cure people by using herbals and sometime spiritual by using the Holly verses from Qur'aan, I have inherit this heeling profession from my father and grandfather, one day this man came to me with his wife [who is this woman] seeking curing for her sickness which she was suffering, she became thin as she did not had any appetite for eating, but since that day she got married to her and for a long period she could not get pregnant, and this gentleman always wanted to be a father, when I professionally check her thoroughly, I could not find any reason which could stop her not to be pregnant, then I started to cure both of them, as I gave some medicine to his wife as well as I gave some stimulation medicine to him so to awaken his sperms and which can give him energy as well, and this to me was just a trial base of which I did hope that it may work, then two months passes by and one day this gentleman came to my house and accusing me of giving him medicine which kills his pregnancy sperms, that I gave him medicine which will not make him bare any child, he also accused me that I did that because I had an intention of taking his wife from him, that was a very wrong accusation he did to a person who had good intention on him and never an evil one, and also to think that his wife who was loyal and never betraying him and accusing her, this loyal cleaned hearted woman who really love him and who is honest to her husband, he then raised a case against me in the law court, and that he demand that he will divorce his wife there in the court and the court must force me to marry her and take all her responsibilities as the woman had no one to depend on, and that is how the judge judged our case, that if he could not prove his accusation against me then he should divorce his wife and I should take the responsibility of taking care of her from that day on by starting in marring her to be my legal housewife, as I saw that the matters were not easy one and has raised doubts and wrong accusation and to save the moral respect of this loyal lady, I agree to his terms and the court judgment, but after some time passed away, he heard that his divorced wife is pregnant, then he started to spread roamers that the pregnancy is his and the born child will be his. These were the main reasons for us to appear here today before you seeking justice for that child, that who is the real father of our child Your Majesty" King Kismat after listen to a long history and explanation from Mr. Ghullam, he then realize his breath and said "I think we learn a lot from your case and the tale of your history you three people, we have learned much about the family as well about our Islamic faith affairs, but yet, your case has opened our eyes and saw of what is going on in this country behind the curtain, that we thought we have educated people whom we trust them to judge this country fairly and with justice, but came out to be not at all fair and are injustice to justice as well as to our people, instead of wiping down all the complication of our people they are increasing them more and un fairly and without justice, they rules beyond the laws of our faith, they do not follow what our Holly books has taught us to do, it is shame, a great shame to this country if there are such kind people who rules in this wrong way, who can put justice under their feet and carrying injustice on the heads, This is today is a day of mourning and darkness and not a day that I am proud to be called the King of this Kingdom, people who rule this country without refer to those who knew better than them, even in the Holly Qur'an it has been written that [ask those who knew better then you if you do not know], yet these people are still remain in the darkness and do not want to come out in the light so other can see them in reality who they are and how they are. How can a sharia law judge give such a verdict to a divorce woman to get married without completeting her hundred days Edaa (Divorced refraining period which is compulsory to Sharia law)? Our Islamic law has been mentioned in the Holly book Qur'an clearly that any divorced woman cannot be married again to another man without completing hundred days of her Edaa (refraining period compulsory to Sharia law), but she can remarried any time to her divorcee husband and if she was not divorced three time. The judgment you had received is completely wrong judgment and is not acceptable in our sharia law, but now it is too late to correct the mistake as if the water has already been splat on the ground then it cannot be collected again, May God forgive that Sharia law judge for his great mistake he had committed. Yet, this did not amend anything of the problem we have in our hands now, but if we talk logical and try to give examples, then I have these questions to ask you and need to be answer:-

If I have invited to you Mr. Ghullam and you Mr. Farah jaan to my farm to help me plant difference kind of fruit seeds, and in each of you I gave only one seed of a same kind of fruit, then I went and dug a hole on the earth and then ask you two to put your seeds in that hole, and daily I go and watering those seeds planting place, until then grow out only one plant, and then that plant grow into a big tree which also produce it's fruits, now here is my question to both of you, what answer should I give those who will come and ask me who's tree is this? Now please give me an answer to this question and I will try my best to find a solution to your problem.

King Kismat arrived at the drought stricken village

King Kismat is informed by the little messenger

None of them could give any answer, and all because of the complication of the situation, then King Kismat when he find that none of the two could give an answer, he then said "I know that none of you will be able to answer as even myself if I would have been on your place I will never be able answer as the secret of those only the earth knows it and no one else, so if we real need an answer to our question then we should ask mother earth and by the will of God, now we must go to the right source which can give us the answer, and that is none other than the person who bare that child which is this lady here who was married to both of you, and for that reason I have to ask this lady to give us accuracy proof enough to pursued us, that that is acceptable by all sides, by sharia law, by scientific law and by logical point of view. If there is any good reasons or proof enough than this is the right time to give that proof of what is the fact and what is not, here she can speak and make us believe if what she has said is truth and nothing more but the truth. Now tell me my lady, That pregnancy you had and bare a child after seven months of your pregnancy, who is the real father of that child? Please tell us without fear or being scare and tell us the real fact and nothing more than the fact, who is the real legal father of this child?" and that woman then first release her breath and then said "Your Majesty King Kismat, here I have no other choice but to speak the truth of where justice can be obtained" and King Kimat said "Please my lady, speak of that justice of which you know and believe that that is justice "and then she continued "Your Majesty, I swear to Allah that the child I bare, his father is Mr. Ghullam" and King Kismat then said "My lady, that is only a say so and not a proof, give us a proof so we can believe that what proof you have is a fact" and then she said "That day when we were in the first Sharia court of where I was divorced by my previous husband and got married with my present husband, I was in my monthly period course, so it means that I was not pregnant and this is one of the fair proof" and King Kismat asked "can we have more specific proof to your saying" and here is where Mr. Ghullam requested to be permitted to speak, and permission was granted to him, and he said "Your Majesty, as we all knows that these are more personal matters to our ladies, as when they are in these conditions they do not reveal it but keep it secret, and act as normal person though they are not, it is only the husband who will know what kind of condition his wife is, and I here today in front of you I dare say that is exactly the condition of how my wife was when we appear in the Sharia court for the first time, I take oath and swear before you and my God that what I have said here is truth and God be my witness" and then King Kismat said to Mr. Ghullum "Mr. Ghullum may you please take this Holly book Qur'an in your right hand and swear again in the same manner and that you did not lie just to hide the truth and want to win this case in your favor?" and Mr. Ghullam took the Holy book Qur'an in his right hand and raise and said "I swear in the name of Allah that the statement which I have said in front of all these people here and in front of you was truth and nothing but the truth" and here is where King Kismat approved that oath and said "now I will take that statement as truth proof of what has being presented here by this lady and her witness who is the present husband as enough evidence that this lady was in her monthly periodically course that day when they were called in Sharia court to answer their case, but here there is another angel of doubt, this is a nature doubts and not scincetificaly doubts, as in nature it is possible for a woman who is pregnant and came be in her monthly periodically course, this is possible, as there were many cases of the same kind before this one, for this reason and I am not against the will of God, but have my doubts and cannot give any verdict, not for you or against you, but still there is no more chance of evidence here which I hope that may help us, and that is to wait until this child is born and allow it to grow and in growing to see which among you two, he or she resembling, in feature, in body marks or in voice, and this is should be the conclusion of this case and God be my witness for what I have said. If for any other reason, there is anyone among you who is not satisfied with the conclusion of my verdict, please feel free right now before you leave this place, and I will be more pleased and happy to hear what his or her inner feelings are, rather than spreading rumors outside, that King Kismat was not fair in his judgment and he has been one sided or deny us justice, remember that I too am Allah's creation, and I am also afraid to any wrong step that will displease Allah, as under me there are millions and millions of my subjects and all and each depend for me to be fair on them in all his rights but who is there among all these subjects of whom I depend on rather than Allah, to you I am ruler but to myself I am a slave of Allah who is serving all of his creation on this blessing land of which we all claim it as our Kingdom, every step of my judgment I take then I ask and beg forgiveness if for any reason I failed my duty": then everyone was quite just listen to their King of what a heavy burden his always carry in his mind just to be fair and justice to his people. Mr Ghullam and his wife and Mr Farah jaan all were satisfied of how their King has judged their case, and left thecourt houe with their hand on the chests while bidding farewell. King Kismat then asked if there was any other listening of complain or case to be judge, he was told "Yes Your Majesty, there is a delegation came from faraway of this Kingdom and waiting just to see you with a very importance message, he then said to bring them quickly inside so to hear what is their problems, the delegation came inside the Diwan court and greet His Majesty, and King Kismat went step by step and greet them by shaking their hands and invited them to sit down, after everyone has sat down on the chairs, King Kismat asked what has brought them so far to come and see him for, then they explained in details of what their problems was that have made them to come here and see their King so to overcome their problems, and their main problem was shortage of water and lack of rain and draught has started to effect their living lives, many of their country wells are dry, citizen have no another means of getting water and some of them they became refugees in their neighboring countries King Kismat got shock of his life to know that his subjects were suffering and he has no knowledge of it, that somewhere in his country there is shortage of water where other place there are rivers and waterfalls where other are enjoying life, he then said to them "Thank you so much for these information of which we have no knowledge of it, anyhow, please be my guests here in the palace for two days and have full of rest and then go back to your village and inform all of my subjects that their King is on the way coming to see for himself of how effective this problem has coursed.

After few days, King Kismat and his delegation left his home town and head to that small town where his people are facing the problem of water shortage, he traveled for two days and reached that village, and instructed his servants to make a camp outside of town of that village and all because there was an old water well at that palace, when King Kismat saw that well he gave instruction that this is the place they will camp, King thought that there could be water inside hat well but unfortunately it was dry. After the camp were erected and King Kismat has a little rest after washing his hands and face, he then decided to go walking outside so to get acquainted with that place, he took with him two of his archer guards, unfortunately on all his way he never met even one human being not even heard any human sound even from far away coming to his side, but what has surprised him most was in all his walking he saw only one small mosque, this gave him a big surprise, because as he knows that his people's faith is Islam then why no more or many mosques around this town, he decided then not to put much worries in his mind but to wait till he will meet with the leaders of this village, he then return to the camp with his guards, and then alone went where that water well was and ask one of his guard to send a water bucket down and see if they can water out of it, but he got nothing, he then ask his guard to tight a lantern at the end of the rope and send it down so they can see below, but slowly as the lantern was going down then suddenly it went off and there was darkness, the guards pull up the lantern, he order them to send that lantern again, and they did but also this time it was the same, the lantern went off again before it reaches down below, then he remembered his butterfly people friends, those subjects of Queen Farna Bash, when they told him that whenever you our us to help you just call us and we will be there for your help, King Kismat then ask his guards to back to the camp and ask them just to live him alone there, when he was sure that he was all alone there, then as usual he hold his right ear and called, and then within a split second he heard a voice behind him, said "Sir, my Master, your servant is just behind you, how you want me to serve you?" King Kismat then turned to look to the one who answered his call, he saw a small figure among a butterfly people floating in the air with his wings, then King Kismat told that figure "Thank you so much for answering my emergency call" and that little butterfly man said "Your Majesty, under the command of our Queen, we are always under your calls, as we are commanded to obey and serve you whenever you need us, Your Majesty please command me of how I can serve you?" Please allow me to thank you more for being here, but before I tell you of what service I need you to do for me, allow me please to explain to you of why I am here in this village which is far away from home town. The people of these village came to me and complain of shortage of water in this village, there is no rain now for that a year, many of the water well are dry, like this one here, I came here to look at the matters what has caused these draughts here, why no water here, I have tried twice to send this lamp here down so I can see below but unfortunatly before it reach below it went off, this has caused doubts in my mind, of what is that which put off this lamp off, and this is the main reason of me calling you people for your help, can you please go down there and try to find out what is there which put this lamp off and if possible find out if there are any water? so also I can try my best to find a solution of how to solve these problem here, and please if for any reason the cause of these water shortage are the main reason of these people doing here, then I would also like to know, whatever message you may get down there please bring it to me, either it will be bitter, soar or sweet I am willing to swallow it" and the little butterfly man replied "Your Majesty King Kismat, I understood all of what you have told and want me to do, Your Majesty, just give a very short time and I will go below and look around and come back with the answer" and King Kismat said "Please go, May Allah be with you" and the little butterfly man then disappear in front of his eyes, and King Kismat stand there near the water well waiting for his comeback, and within a short time a butterfly man came back and as usual was floating in the air and then said "Your Majesty, the journey of which I took to go below this water well looking for the cause of the water shortage problem and why the lantern was twice got off, here then is answer to the problems, Your Majesty, I have to tell you that down below there I met with the guard of this well, and his so powerful and very angry indeed, and this guard is one of the powerful Angel and he is here kept by his masters to protect this well that no one should take the water from it, and so all the wells of this villages there are guards in it, there masters are the servants who obey the commands of God, as they too are Angels, the Masters have taken these actions because of the evil done by your people who are living in this village,

These people here have formed very bad habits and are not obeying Allah as well as not following the path of their faith, they are just Muslims by name and not by deeds, they have stopped praying, and giving Zakaat (Annual income taxation in Sharia law), they even stopped to fast in the Holly monthly of Ramadan as well as even going for pilgrim to Mecca, even building of mosques stopped for many years, that is why you saw only one mosque around here, and that mosque is very old since beginning of Islam, yet! This does not mean that every each citizen of this village has no faith, No! Your Majesty, there are some few who still believe and still have faith in their religion, to them only Shahada is enough, but otherwise all the compulsory religion activities are ignored, and the Shahada is not enough, as Allah did not taught us through his Prophets just believe in Shahada but to follow every step of our religious in actions. Your Majesty, the draught which came to village is only a small part of God punishment to these villagers but what coming ahead is a big disaster, this is the sign that Allah is not at all pleased with them in what they are doing, and if they do not change and drop down in their knees begging for forgiveness and start to return back of where their parents has begins and in action and in real faith, then for sure Your Majesty knows that the curse of Allah will fall on this land, Beware of the warning and do something quickly yourself before you return back home, open their minds and their hearts so they will realize what great mistakes they have committed in their lives, the door of forgiveness is still open, make them understand and so to return to their God and enter that door before it is too late, tell your people not to live but hold that rope of God together so they can continue with their faith and be allowed to enter heaven when they die. My dear King Kismat, Satan is an evil figure who always corrupt our minds to do evil things so we should be part of his gang who will be going in hell with him, he never was and will be a human being friend, but a foe and an enemy to us so we should not be obedient to Allah but only to him. Your Majesty, still there is a time to wipe out the evils of this Satan and to deny him never to be our master but to allow our faith in believing that only Allah is a Master to us and we are his slaves who have a duty to perform for the better and the worse, we all must curse him and remove him in our thoughts and our mind and it's place put our faiths to Allah who will reward us heavily in that day where father will know no his son and daughters will know not their mothers, and that we all will be accounted for what we done or said in this world which has an end. Your Majesty, also the guard of this water well told me to let you know that if you will do your best to fight the war against this Satan, then the following actions must be taken: - First of all, you must make sure that the people this village must completely obey the will of Allah by following what the holly book has taught us to do in being a real Muslim, these people they must Pray, give Zakaat, fast in the holy month of Ramadhan and if possible go to Mecca for their pilgrims, They must build more mosques as well as madrasa for teaching their children the holly book, second, is to completely leave all the evils they have done and still are doing it, like making and selling of liquor, Ribaa (illegal profits which are forbidden by Sharia law), to commit adultery (sex out of marriage bound with children, sisters and other people mothers) to stop lying (Lying is one of major sin), to oppress others in their properties or their belongings, to misuse orphan rights,

And many more sins committing activities, then and only then the blessing of God will return to this land, otherwise then remember that the big disaster is on its way coming to your people and you will be counted as a responsible, Your Majesty, do your best to your people and allow the blessings of God to return on this land and to its people by using even an iron hand to those who will be hard to melt. Before you came here you did not know about is happening here on this land and by your people, but now within this moment you know all the secrets and what has caused this land not be blessed and became draughts, now this responsibility is on your neck, you have to clear all obstacles and leave no stone unturned without fear or scare, no matter in which way you use or rule but you must clean this land from its people sins, until you will get that sign that you have done what you were suppose to do in the best and pleasing way, and for sure that sign will appear to let you know that you King Kismat have done of what your God want you to do, and your sign will that day when you see a dark clouds cover this land and drops of water falls from the sky then go the water wells and if you see them that they produce water than know that that is a sign of Allah blessings and you have done well.

And this is my dear Your Majesty King Kismat, is the information of your service you had asking me to do, I have delivery all of what saw and heard and return back to you of what I have been ask to tell you, and so I have said it all, and so you have heard it all, and I have accomplish my mission but if there is any another one then I am here to serve you Your Majesty, otherwise release me to go back and serve my Queen in our Kingdom" and King Kismat said "No, Thank you, I have no other need of you for now, but I will need your assistance again then for sure I will call you, I wished you a safe return home and thank you for all of what you have done for me. Please give my regards to your Queen and thank her for me for allowing you to serve me in this matter of an important mission, Farewell my dear one, and may Allah protect your Queen and your Kingdom from any evils" and then the little butterfly man disappear and not to be seen. But for King Kismat, the news he heard from the guard of the water well, did put him in many worries as well as many thoughts, he was all very disturbed as he know not of how to deal with issue of these people of the village, especially when he came to know that in his own Kingdom there are those still who are living in an ignorance way of life, they are God's creations and know that God do exist yet they go against God teaching and committing sins, and these are the same people whom they send their delegation requesting me to come here and look at the matter concerning problems of their land draughts, and it themselves who are to be blame for this God's curse on their land, and what will I Kismat can do, what power do I obtained that can make this land to be alive again and water to come. Oh! My Allah, I ask you to give me strength and fair and true saying in my tongue so I can speak with courage and without fear or scare to anyone of them, give me that will of where I can wipe all the wrong doing of my people here, these people who prefer to follow the steps of Satan instead of yours, I swear to you my God, this today will be their last day of their ignorance, either they return to follow your path or either they face my punishments on their wrong doing against you Oh! God and suppressed their souls and harm their children and families." Then Kismat left that water well and went to sleep waiting for tomorrow to come so he can meet his people.

Next day, King Kismat send his special representative to the elders and those who are running government affairs on his behalf, including as well as many citizens should come here at the camp of his Majesty to attend a very importance meeting and discussions with his Majesty regarding their call and request to his Majesty to solve the problem of water in this village. After few waiting hours, many thousands of citizens answer the call of his Majesty

King Kismat Shahzara, and after greeting and wishes, King Kismat start his speech to his people, he begin and said "My dear people of this village, you have called me and I have come to see for myself the problem which facing you regard shortage of rains and water in this village, I know and understand how difficult one can live without water, as water is the main source of life, but before we talk about the water let us talk about you people of this village, to be frank with you, you have angered me very hard for what you people are doing in this village, you have forgotten of where you have come from, you have ignore to follow those footmarks of your ancestors and have chosen the wrong path which is directed by that evil Satan, you angered even God himself for you wrong doings which are the main course of this drought in your land, you have became evil doers instead of faith followers, you have became nothing out of something, you were the best my people but sold yourselves to these worldly leisure's until you have forgotten yourself who you are and from what sources your originality came, instead of kneeling on the right pillars which will hold and support you, you have chosen the weak and unreliably pillars which can crushed down easily, what more better pillars will be then of Allah who told us follow and trust those five pillars and I will reward you with heaven, but instead you have taken the wrong turn and became evil doing people, you have avoid to share your love to your creator and instead fall all your love to that creation who was created with fire, you have forgotten that this same creation was the reason of pursue ding our father Prophet Adam and mother Eve (Hawaa) to commit also the mistake of disobeying our God and had resulted that they were removed from heaven and to this earth which is full of evils, is it not him who refuse to kneel down his head on earth in respect of our Prophet Adam, is it not him that God has cursed for his behavior of not obeying the command of God? how then can you my people put your faith on him and forget God whom has created you, gives you, keep you in health and if you become sick he is curing you, then why this Satan who is misleading you and not God who has shown you that straight path to heaven, Where are your minds? Where are your conscious? Where your courage is's which you have within you? That courage which knows what to take and what to refuse, until today you became weak at heart and agree to fooled by these leisure's of the Satan and betraying yourselves in following him, when today the torture of God have befallen on you then you send a delegation to call me here, What I Kismat can do to stop this curse, do I have that power beyond God's power? Tell me, how I can help you when you are the one who have coursed this, did you think by doing evils and committing sins will not be accounted, No! my dear people, you will be accounted for every and each of the sins you have committed, if you did not pray you will be accounted for, if you have consumed liquor you will be accounted for, if you have committed adultery you will be accounted for, instead of building Madarasa to teach your children the Holy book and building mosques in every corner of you village, you are building leisure houses to sell liquors and other evil business, don't you not think that, that is a big burden of responsible and you will be accounted for?, what are you going tell and answer Allah tomorrow on doom's day when you will be asked about these wrong doings? I ask you, please tell me before you going to answer your God tomorrow, you have became like those illiteracy people before Islam, same like them, and all for what, for this world, you are selling your heaven to buy hell, you are selling your ending to buy this world which is good for nothing, have you no fear within you of God? You are denying your children the best of Islamic education and forgot that we all are shepherds and we are responsible of our families. Listen to me now, I am only saying today tomorrow will be too late for you, I speak to you with harsh warning and with all my anger, either leave these evil doing now and forever or face my punishments before Gods punishments comes to you, what has happened here is a sign that you have angered God, and he has shown you just a little examples of his tortures, but beware, as the heaviest of his disasters do exists and if you will not stop these wrong activities then for sure you better know that King Kismat will never bare you and I will make sure that I will wipe out every evil in this village no matter is the wrong doers even if he will be my own son. I ask you again, I plead to you that stop these wrong doing and return to right path, that straight path of God which he has created for us all, time is still here for regretting and ask for forgiveness, as Allah is most beneficiary and most gracious and he can forgive to those who ask him for forgiveness, please my people do that and do not allow me to raise my anger against you as I will be pitiless on any wrong doing person. I speak to you today before tomorrow, and Allah is my witness and all the angels above the sky and below down here on the land, clean your hearts and wipe out all these wrong doing and live on this land with good intentions and never evil one's so to allow the returning of Allah blessings on you and on this land, from today, you must change your inner you as a matter of compulsory and I swear to Allah that if you will do this, this land will return to its normal way of life and you my dear citizen will survive from this draughts and what you have missed and crying for it, will return back to this land as you will please Allah to do of what he has command you to do in believing and praying as well as holding that rope of faith, destruct all these evil places of where you sell liquors and its place do built Mosques and Madrasa(Qur'an teaching schools) to teach your children all about their true faith, stop these habits of earning profits from rendering money which is Ribaa, Allah has forbidden Ribaa, stop lying and speak the truth, protect the moral respect of your daughters, sisters as well as you mothers and other relatives, you must know that these are your future parents of your coming generation, a faithful person will commit an adultery as he also have a mother, or a sister or even a daughter, and to your women I said this, no respect woman who fear her God will commit an adultery, she will prefer to die and protect her moral respect rather than sell her body just to earn for her living, we human beings are not like animals who meet for pleasure between close relative, daughter and her father or brother and sister, this acceptable by Allah as it is strictly forbidden, whoever did that. it is as same as the person who eats the flash of his own relative, I ask you, is this your standard of culture?, so now and from this moment here today that anyone of you found committing any of these sins again will face me first here before he or she face his/her God tomorrow, as he will be punished accordingly, as same as what Allah has written in his holy book Qur'an that if there three witnesses who saw him/her commit this crime then to be thrown in the dugout of the earth and be killed by stoned.

My dear good citizen, I came here to respond your call, but when I have arrived here I found and understood the main reason of this land problem, no land in the whole of this world that will be blessed by God if it did of what you have done, and I as God's creation warning you again that stop of what evils you are doing and follow on the straight path of Allah which will lead you to a better house, and that house is heaven. I have given you my saying, and God be my witness that I have said and warn you, I have forbid, I have remind of which should be acceptable and which should be deniable, what now has remain is for you my people wither you should stop wrong doing or wither you should do of what has asked you to do, and if for any reason you have come to conclusion that you cannot stop doing of what you have been doing against the will of God, than know for sure that Kismat bin Shahzara will never tolerate these evil doing any longer and my hush punishment will follow to any of you who will go against my saying. Now the choice is yours, I would like an answer from you on what have you decided, which among the two ways you will go back to, the straight of Allah or the bend one of Satan. You have up to this evening to give me an answer, and I will not leave this land until I get the answer or make sure that all the evil on this land is no longer exists. Then all the people started to gossips slowly and talking to each other.

Time went by and by until the time for prayers was ready, and then there was announcement that the noon prayers will be performed by all and then there will be a dua recitation to ask Allah for forgiveness and to beg Allah to return the situation of their village water dryness into normal again, all the people stand and pray with their King the noon prayer and then they sit down reciting Dua asking Allah to bring rain in their village. After the prayer, then the Mayor of that village request permission to his King to speak on behalf of the village people and he said "Oh dear our King, I stand here before you on my behalf and on the behalf of all the people of this village which is part of your Kingdom, Your Majesty, your visit to come here to respond our call to see for yourself what kind of situation we are living here, is a great honor you gave us and this also shows how concerned you are on all of us your subjects, it shows also how much you care for us, what you have said here today is completely true, as there are among us who are so ignorance and just for making some money they have completely stopped to perform their ritual duties of what their faith has taught them to do, it is true some of us have committed higher mistakes of their lives and that just to allow themselves being hypnotized by these worldly leisure's, and all because some of young ones have been going to the neighboring countries and imitate their way of life and try to bring it here in our village, these countries of their culture and heritage is completely difference than ours, even their faiths are difference than ours, they believe of what they believe and we believe of what we believe but we are completely following separate paths of our faiths, yet our young ones are the main reasons of many of these evils doings. Your Majesty, Oh! You Good King, Oh! You father of our nation, we have no other choice but to throw ourselves under your feet and even bury our faces in this land soil and dust, just to hide these faces for the shy we feel for what others who done in bringing on this land shame and ignorance and that is what has caused the draught on this land, we have no other choice but to beg for forgiveness from Allah for what wrongs we have committed, we have no other choice but also to beg your forgiveness Your Majesty for all the wrong doing our people have committed on this land which is under your ruling. Your Majesty, as I represent you here in this region, I here do speak openly in front of these people that I here give you all notice that from this moment, all those evil doing businesses should be stopped, and all our young one are not allowed to travel to the neighboring of where they bring from there evil culture and evil things, and who ever will go against this notice then he should know that there will be no leniency on him but will face what so ever Government has decided on him. Today here in front of you

with one word we all going to bury the wrong doing and open a new chapter
of following the teaching of Allah from his Holly book, what has past has past
and no more come back of wrong doings, and what is ahead of us is to build a
new Era, a new village with all the new mosques and Madrasa to build again
and a new life of living as an obedient citizen who knows well of what his
responsibilities are. You're Majesty, we ask you now, please pray to God and beg
for our forgiveness, as we from this day on will change our attitudes, as always
Allah said in his Holly Book [Ask me and I will grant your requests]. And for
these long speeches I have spoken, I now beg to remain silent you're Majesty.
Then King Kismat said "If you people really ask me to forgive you, than first
you should ask Allah to forgive you, and all because you went against him,
agents his teachings, against your faiths, and you all know that tomorrow in
the day of judgment every and each one of us will be accounted for, for what
he did and what he has said, and for any of your good deed you have done you
will be reward for it and for every sin you have committed you will be punish
for, Allah has plenty of blessings and he love us we human beings, because he
kept us among the top of all his creations, and he has mentioned it in the Holly
Book Qur'an, as he wrote in that book [And I created you as the best of the
creation], but I need you now to satisfy your souls, we are here all together on
this open place of where we had prayed our normal noon prays, and he who
promise to Allah that he will do what he has to do, than he must do it now
as we are not alone here, even Angels of Allah are here with us and they will
be witnesses for every word we have said to each other, what now I am asking
you all the people of this village that you must promise me as you will promise
Allah as well, promise me, with one voice and good faith that what wrong you
have commit in the past you will never repeat it again, I am asking from all of
you to give that promise, and with one voice" Then the Mayor of that village
stood and ask all the people to repeat after him, and he said please repeat after
me all of you [Your Majesty King Kismat, we the people of this village as well
as your citizen hereby vow before you and before Allah, that will leave behind
all the evil doings of the past and follow the right path of Allah's teaching from
now on, and God be our witness].

King Kismat remain there in the village for several days just to make sure
that the changing these people have promised are taking place, in his first
positive action he has order all pawn and money laundering shops to be closed,
he then order that one battle of liquor should not remain on that land and that
whoever is dealing with that business should be forced to close down his shop
and find other means of business so to help himself to survive, he then gave

order to respect all women and said "OUR WOMEN - OUR MOTHERS" whoever will be caught in this un respectful adultery acts should face severe punishment if there are witnesses who can prove that. King Kismat has put all his efforts to make sure the people of that village no longer repeat the past wrong doing but now they are obedient and faith law abiding citizen, for so many days he remained there he saw fruits of his efforts, as there were more mosques and madrasa quilted, and you can hear now the call of prayers from differences angel of the village during praying time, the progress he saw of the changing in that village really did pleased him much, he was satisfied that the village people have understood him well and stand beside him to bring these changes hand in hand.

Then one night he could not sleep, though he tried very hard but never could he find the sleep, he stood up from his bed and put on some clothes and came out of his tent, slowly he went around his camp while the guards saw him but signed them to stand on their duties and bother not about him, he then walked to the distance of where that old water well was, he had his lamp in his hand, and then the thoughts of trying to send it again down to the well was itching him, there was a rope near the well and he tight the lamp with the rope and then slowly lower it down the well, and was looking inside to see if that lamp will go off today as well, the lamp went down as far as its light fed away and then suddenly he felt the lamp reached down below as the rope was now loose and not tight, he decided then to pull the lamp up as he could not see anything in that darkness of the well, while pulling that rope he felt that it has shakes a little bit, he continue to pull and he began to see the light of the lamp begins to show, he pulled the rope until the lamp was visible and still burning, but what has surprised him most was that, below the lamp there was a frog, a big in size frog, his hands were holding under the lamp, and when the lamp was at the level of top of the opening of the water well, that frog jump from underneath that lamp up to that top of the well opening wall, the frog then was just looking directly into the eyes of King Kismat, and King Kismat then untighted the lamp from the rope and brought that lamp closer at the frog and was looking at it, and curiosity began to itch inside his brain; he wants to know who this creature is and what has brought it up here, then they were both staring to each other while the frog every now and then take out his tongue and wipe his eyes, then after a short while King Kismat decided to greet this frog and said "Peace be upon you" and the frog answered in a humanly voice "And peace be upon you too" here then King Kismat realize that this creature is not what it is in its look but could be another powerful creation, then King

Kismat asked "Oh! You God's creation, how you as a frog lived in this dry water well?" and the frog answered "Oh! You good King Kismat Shahzara, before I answer your question, please allow me to give you your message which I am just a servant who has been chosen to deliver it to you. Your Majesty, now I take this opportunity to answer your question which you have put it on me, and that question was, how come I as a frog can live in this dry water well?, my answer to you Your Majesty is, first you better know that we as frogs were created by God to survive living in the mud for even more than a year without eating or drinking, as we are consuming the food which are in our bodies until another rain season when it come and we also come out of the mud and begin a new life, and this is the wisdom of God to his creation, as he can do of how and what he want. Second, I have to deliver to you the greeting and the message from that same Angel who is the guard of this water well, who have informed you of the evil doing of your people and who has warned you of what will happen in future if you will not take any action against the wrong doing of your people, These Angels are the servants of God, and they act when they order to do on whatever the matters, they were kept here on this land to preserve these water wells and to allow not any of your people who were evil doing and were going against the teaching of God forbidding them to get use of this well, but after your arrival here and after your hard efforts you had done very well and have wiped many of these people wrong doing, you have pleased him, and by pleasing him it means you have pleased Allah as well, as it was a very bad situation in that time that many of us have to run away and hide beneath the earth to try and avoid that disaster from God if ever it will come, maybe the disaster which can destroy those who are in it and those who are not among the wrong doing. Your Majesty, the drought of this village was just a minor example of God's punishment to your people, but if he wanted he could wipe out this land and all who are on it like what he did in many parts of the world and even to followers of some of our Prophets followers like Prophet Noah and Prophet Loot and as well as to Pharaoh and his army, but for you to accept the invitation of coming here and witness for yourself what was the main reason of these dryness, and we as messengers to be given the right to inform you the secrets of these punishments to your people, was just to give you a chance of returning that good doing and worshiping of your people to God and stop the wrong doing, this is proof enough that how much God love you and your people and your land, and now the messenger ask me to tell you that you have done well enough by the immediate actions you have taken to clean the evils on this land, today your people are enjoying the fruits from God just by your presence here and did well by what you had been asked to do, no doubt Allah will reward you for what you have done to save your people and made the living here as normal again.

It is the time for you to return back to your home town and have a long rest, as your mission on this land was not an easy one, it was a very hard task mission for you to be able and combat these people in their wrong doing put them straight on the right path again and have faith in you of what you have opened their eyes for and what was wrong and have saved them from more further deserter, the results of your good work is seen by everyone here. But before you leave this land, there is some advice for you and it comes from him the Angel guard of this water well, and from this advices you must take immediate actions, first of all, you must reform of those who are representing you in taking care of this village Government positions, you must change this mayor and many of his cabinets members as they are very old people and are not capable of running this village as it needed to run, you must replace them with more educated young and faithful ones among your army and your personal guards, but these selected young men who will be holding their new positions must be religious minded people, who turned their leisure world in their back and put God's faith before them. Secondly, In your palace compound there is your personal blacksmith whom you have kept him there for his best craftsmanship, he has a son, this young lad is also very brave young man who can use his archer and hit its target without miss, you have already witness with your own eyes of his bravery, he is a very trustful young man, and he likes and love you and obeying you, but there will come an act in the future by him which will not please you, and you will want to punish him, here is your advice from the Angel, please do not follow of what your heart tells you to do but follow your mind and use your wisdom, and be fair in your judgments of where you will be benefited more and where you will lose much, this will be a very hard task mission for you, more tough and hard than the whole changing of your people attitudes here on this land which you have faced, as this young man is very brave and you will need him more to be close to you than others, do not allow him to leave you because he has anger you, this will be a challenge to you that you must under all circumstances to control yourself and all because this young man if he will be given a chance he can prove of how good he is, there will come that day that you will be able to witness for yourself the value of this young man. And if for any reason you could not control yourself and misjudge this young man in any wrong way and allow your anger to overcome you, then know from now that you will lose such a valueless treasure of your life and it will take a very long time to recovery it again. I cannot explain more to you then of what I have explained now Oh! You King Kismat Shahzara. What is coming ahead of your future life is quite a big challenge and a very hard task on you, it is only you who will see it, it is only you who will decide about it, and it is only you who will chose between the right or the wrong of it. Now the decision is yours, either you eat it hot and enjoy it or you eat cold and regret it, the time has come now for you to sit and think and end with the wise decision" and the frog than again wipe his right eye with his tongue, and King Kismat just remain there silent from what he has been informed with that very long conversation from the frog, and what has bothered him most is the second version of the information, regarding that young man who is Shuhur jaan, as he found that information needs more specific explanation so he can understand it well of what the outcome future will bring.

King Kismat summoned Shuhurjaan

King Kismat thanks the frog by saying "I thank you so much for bringing to me these information's from the guard of this water well, every important issue of his message is understood, and I will do my best to fulfill all the gaps of the evils remaining until this land will be clear and clean of all evils done. But the second part of his message was a little bit confusing to me, as I do not know what future will bring, will it be for better or for worse regarding this young man in my palace? Will that future bring happiness or sadness for me? These are the questions which eats my mind and I do not have answer for them, and as you have said that you are just a messenger who deliver what you have been ask to do, nothing more and nothing less, I will pray to my God to help me in facing that future with open and clear heart and never with hot or anger one, and request my Allah to send to me his other angels so to guide me insha'alla" and then the frog said "Your Majesty, Allah has send to you his good Angels on this Kingdom, and it them that who are guiding you for many things without your knowledge, please be more thankful to God Oh! King Kismat.

CHAPTER EIGHTEEN

(Shuhur jaan is summoned by King Kismat)

SINCE THAT DAY KING KISMAT left his palace to go down to the village for the call, his daughter Nazniyna was living unhappy, as to her, her father was everything, her happiness, her leisure, her advice as well as her friend, and all because Nazniyna's mother has passed away when she was just a young girl, she do not remember her mother well, all she remember that it is her father who took care of her, and this was the main reason of not being happy as she missed so much her father, though there are many friends and servants who do their best to serve and entertain her, yet to her she only enjoyed to be near her father. The living life's of many Royal families are not other thinks, they are living more like prisons than free like any ordinary person, they cannot go places by themselves without guards and security check up, they cannot talk or contact each and anyone they want without informing the palace protocol, this is a part of their way of life, only it defer from one nation to other, but in general the Royal family living way of life has its own complications, and it is a very tough life to live with. Now let us continue to our story of where we have left before. We should return to Shuhur jaan regarding his parents of proposing to him to get married.

Shuhur jaan all these days of King Kismat absence in the palace, made him to be unhappy and all because how he can or his father can propose the hand of his daughter Princess Nazniyna for marriage to his son Shuhur jaan, yet Shuhur jaan did not gave an answer of getting married and all because he wanted to tell his father if they want him to get married then they should propose to King Kismat for the hand of their daughter Princess Nazniyna, but he could not, as he do not have that courage to open his mouth and speak the truth that he is in love with the Princess and that she is the only girl which he has perfect for him to be his wife, though he knows that there is quite a big difference between his choice of a wife and him, where is the Princess of the Kingdom and where is the son of a blacksmith, and also he knows that it is impossible for him to agree this marriage between them, and he knows for sure that his request will be denuded by his parents, as this is a King and they are just an ordinary people who are working for the King, This King who is a well known over the whole world for his bravery and fearless, the King who stand for justice, the King who fear not anyone on any matter concerning his Kingdom and his people, the King who stand on fairness and give justice to where it belongs no matter to who. In the end Shuhur jaan could not be able to approach his father and tell him the truth which is grinding in his heart.

King Kismat after returning from that village, one day he was informed that there was a heavy rain fall in that village, seven nonstop days of rain, and all the water wells of village were full of water, and there were even wadi's flowing which has even some road to be closed for the safety of the villagers, some of the small lakes are now full of water and the people are really enjoying these Allah's blessings, and thanks should be given to our King, and that is why the villagers have sent an urgent convoy to pass this good news to King Kismat. King Kismat when he received the news of the heavy rain in the village and that the people there are so happy to get that great energy of saving life which is water, he was so pleased, and the same moment he raised his hands up in the sky and thanked his Allah for such a great blessing, and he said these in his thanks "Oh! My master and my Allah, it is true that you are the most beneficiary and the most graceful, you give to whom you want and deny to whom you want and at any time you want, My Allah, I raised my hands up to you to thank you on my behalf and on my people behalf for these blessings of rain which you have pour them on that land so my people now can begin to live a new life. Oh! my Allah, please protect and guide us and forgive us, for what we have done were against your teaching and we were guided by that evil Satan to act against you, we have realize that and we have correct ourselves never to repeat the same mistakes again. Thank you so much Oh! My God for all of what you have given and for all of what you have forgiven." Then King Kismat remembered that secret of water well guard message which he was told regard Shuhur jaan, he send one of his servant to summon Shuhur jaan to come to him immediately, and within a short time that servant came back with Shuhur jaan in the palace to meet King Kismat, and when Shuhur jaan entered the King's chamber of where he works by himself, he bowed with his hand on the chest and greet the King "Peace be upon you your Majesty, Shuhur jaan is at your presence and waiting for your command, please Sir" and King Kismat answered Shuhur jaan greetings and said "I call you here today in my private chamber just to ask you some questions Shuhur jaan, maybe from you I will get the right answers of which for so many days now were eating inside me" and Shuhur jaan replied "Your Majesty, Shuhur jaan is ready to answer any of your questions with a clean heart" and then King Kismat said "I am so happy to get your kind and sweet answer Shuhur jaan, Shuhur jaan you are a very kind, brave, gentleman and respectful young man, you are one among the Allah obedient person, you are always punctual on your prayers, now my question to you is this: - What have you done or commit secretly, that no one knows it openly or secretly, which have been seen or unseen, either here in this palace or in your whole life even if it is somewhere else and which I as a King do not know about it? now Shuhur jaan, can you please help me to clear my curiosity within my mind that made me feel that you have a secret and need to be told, can you please Shuhur jaan share your secret with me?" now for Shuhur jaan, this was a very hard and tough situation he has experienced, as he has been brought up in a manner of not speaking lies and denying the truth, and as he has a secret which it concern his personal life and which up to this day even his own parents do not know about it, but are doubting on him and all because of his changing attitude way of his life, then Shuhur jaan asked himself, how come the King doubt of our love secret which we did not mentioned it to anyone? Or maybe King Kismat has already got the information of my secret love relation with his daughter and all what he wants to know is, will I speak the truth about it or will I lie to protect my secret love with Nazniyna, this is really a very hard and tough situation I am facing now, and I have no other choice now but to speak the truth, but let it be whatever will be as this is the only chance I have to ask a hand for marriage to Nazniyna, then he said "Yes Your Majesty, as you had put me in a puzzle situation regarding if I have any secret, this has made me to be in doubt of why I should not have a secret, and if I have any then why should I share my secret to anyone, will it remain a secret if I have to reveal it?, yet you asked me your Majesty, that if I have any secret then I should tell it to you. Your Majesty, I have been born and brought up in this palace surrounds, I have been taught many things regarding our culture, our heritage as well as our habits, and among the best habits I have learned is that, never speak lies, I think now is the right time for me to speak the truth. For many days now, I have this secret within me, I was afraid to tell anyone for fearing that it may go against me instead of working for me, and all because I was afraid that the secret I have should remain a secret till I get the right chance to prevail it to the right person at the right time, and this is today is the right time and you are the right person to share my secret with, your Majesty, and all because you have made it easy for me to unload my burden by opening that door of which for a long time I want to enter into it and release all my inner secret. Your Majesty, to me you are as well as a father who took care of me in many aspects since my childhood, you have gave me your love, you have showed your concern in me by grant to me as your best archer that whenever you go for hunting I should be beside you, you have insisted that I should get the best education as same as your daughter Princess Nazniyna, and I have learned about knowledge and wisdom as well as about my religious faith, and yet Your Majesty, I Shuhur jaan, have nothing to give you back, even if I will sacrifice my life for you yet I think that will never cover what you have sacrificed for me in my whole life, as I have this faith within me that I too belong to you, that you own me too. Your Majesty, I had prolonged my talk and yet I did not come to the main point of your question which I did not yet gave you any answer, I ask you and I beg you please do not get angry and lose your temper after I share that secret of mine with you, but use your patience and wisdom and be cool and consider and try to understand why I have kept this secret for a long time now without sharing it with anyone but only you.

King Kismat summoned her daughter Nazniyna

My Lord, your Majesty, this obedient servant is throwing himself under your feet and allow my life to be in your hands, do to me of whatever you want to do and I promise you that I will hold no grudges against you, only I requested your Majesty, to accept my request which was very impossible before to ask it from you, for many, many days but today by asking me if I hold any secret, you have easy the matter for me, promise me your Majesty that after revealing my secret to you that you will not get angry and will control your temper and also you will never go against your promise" and King Kismat replied and said "This promise you asking me to give you Shubur jaan, is a very hard task for me to give you, and all because till now I do not know what that secret is, and also I do not know of what your request is, will it be just a simple request to give or a tough and impossible one to deny, yet I give you my word that I will do my best to hold and control myself if your request will anger me, but I can never promise you that I will allow myself to be just easy in giving of what you will request from me without consider and look at the matter of your request, and I think it is fair deal between us, but you should not bind me of any promise which I can never keep, without weighing your request and allow myself to be the judge of accepting to give or refusing not to give. Now you better stand up and tell me what is your request?" and here is where Shuhur jaan got up from where he has thrown himself on the feet of King Kismat, and he said but with fear and with stammering "Your Majesty, I,,,, I,,,, request,,, the,,, hand of Princess,,, Nazniyna,,,, in marriage" here is where King Kismat stood up and shout "SHUHUR JAAN!!!" and here is where Shuhur jaan was in more fear by that loud shout of King Kismat, he then drop again on the feet of King Kismat but shaking with fear. King Kismat then remember what the frog told him there in the village regarding losing his temper, he then release all his temper and seek inner forgiveness from his God, and then said to Shuhur jaan, "Stand up Shuhur jaan" but with lower and polite voice "Tell me Shuhur jaan, and tell me the truth, what kind of power has driven you, to ask for my daughter's hand in marriage, when you know who you are and know who am I in our positions?" and Sueur jean answered but with his head looking down and still have fear within him but also have courage in his heart, and he said "Your Majesty, my answer to that is, nothing more and nothing less than a true love to her, I love her so much that even I do not know what love is but just feel that I cannot leave this life without her, I always feel healthy and happy when I am beside her and I feel sick and sad when I am not with her" and then King Kismet asked Shuhur jaan "Tel me Shuhur jaan, does she knows that you are in love with her?, does she also in love with you?" and Shuhur jaan replied

"Yes, your Majesty, she love me as I love her" and King Kismat asked "Can you prove to me that she also love you?" here then Shuhur jaan put his hand in a pocket of his belt which holds his dagger, and produce a piece of paper and hand it over to his King, and King Kismet took that piece of paper, open and saw that truly that was a handwriting of Princess Nanina, he then read it and understood that was a replied letter of his letter which he hand send to her, here then King Kismat came to realize that these two young lads have fallen in love in this dangerous age, they have became victim of their age and have thrown their selves in this very tough sea of falling in love which many have failed to swim and cross it, with its very rage waves. King Kismat then decided to remain with patience until he also hear from his daughter of what she has to say about this love affair with just a simple boy, a son of his own servant who has no future and not even a Royal blood. King Kismat then said to Shuhur jaan "Young lad Shuhur jaan, Today I believe that Allah has granted you with a strong and courage heart which has no fear, and all because for you to dare asking my daughter's hand in marriage from me, that is something I would not even predict it and also I cannot even weight it in my mind scale, I keep on asking myself from that moment till now, what kind of power do you maintain or what kind of courage do you have that enable you to ask me the King of this whole land, a hand of my daughter in marriage, but you did dare ask me from that mouth and from that tongue such an impossible thing in my whole living life, as no one dare before even during the ruling of my ancestors. Yes, today I believe that Shuhur jaan you are very courageous young man. As I have given you my word before that I will try my best to hold my temper and anger against you and that I also told you not to bind me with any promises which I cannot keep but promise that after what I will hear your secret than I will decide. I have heard every and each of your word, now I ask you to be patience and wait till you will hear my word regarding your request, and that will boot be this day but any possible day which I will find it match my moods, but bare this in your mind that you had requested from me a very expensive item which even the whole world wealth cannot buy. Know this Shuhur jaan, for now I hold myself not to allow you taste my anger tortures, and yet I did not decide to allow you to taste my patience and blessings yet, but your courage has driven me to consider every and each of your background and to come with a fair answer and give you for your request. I found that you have not just requested me from your tongue and lips but from your deep in the heart and with true faith. Go and explain to your parents of all what has occurred here today between me and you, and tell him not to be afraid, make sure that there is no fear hidden within inner him, if for any reason there will come any reason that my anger will return back to me, then that anger will have no any concern with your parents but will be only with you" and here is where King Kismat asked Shuhur jaan to leave his diwan palace court, and Shuhur jaan left the place with his right hand on his chest and his face looking down while moving step by step backward.

King Kismat meets King Rawaanaz

King Kismat was in his room standing near the window looking outside, he closed his hands behind his back, though he was looking at the outside scenery but his mind was all in function in thinking so many things since he came to know about the love affair between Shuhur jaan and his daughter Princess Nazniyna, he then left that window and went on his room chair and sat down and still thinking, then he has decided to summon his daughter in his room, then he called to one of the palace servant and ask her to go and inform Princess Nazniyna that he want to see her but now, he waited for Princess Nazniyna to respond on his call and come or for that servant to come back with any answer, fortunately he heard a knock on the door and allowed the knocker to enter the room, and one of the door guard enter the room and announce that "Your Majesty, Princess Nazniyna asking permission to enter in your room" and King Kismat said "Princess Nazniyna is permitted to enter my room" and the guard went outside and came in Princess Nazniyna with her head bow down looking at the floor and her right hand on her chest, and greeted her father by saying "Greeting to you and peace be upon you Abbajaan (Dear father)" and King Kismat answered back and said "Greeting and peace be upon you too dear Nazniyna, please do sit down" and Princess Nazniyna went and sat on the chair beside her father, but she could not miss to notice the frown on her father's face, then she asked "You have summoned upon me and I am here to obey your call,

Tell me Abbajaan, how can I be of your service now? Do you have any problem you want me to help solve it Abbajaan?" and King answered his daughter "No! My dear Nazniyna, there is no any problem or service of which I need you to serve me right now, but I have some questions to ask you, and it will please me most if you answer me without hiding and truth out of the real things" and Princess Nazniyna then replied "Definitely dear Abbajaan, ask me and I will speak of the facts and all the truth of what I know about" and then King Kismat asked "I want to know more about this young man Shuhur jaan, what do you know about him, about his habit, his mingling with us here inside the palace? Or if he have any love affair with any of our servants inside this palace? Do you have any information about this young lad?" And Nazniyna replied "No! Abbajaan, I have no any information regarding this lad" and King Kismat continue to ask, and said "as you know my dear Nazniyna, that this young lad is a very good archer, very rare to miss his target, and I want to send him in that palace in the country side and allow him to hold a higher position among my guards, but before I send him there, first I must make sure that this young lad has no friends and connection with others here in the palace with our servants or even with other high ranking girls, now I repeat my question, did you heard or know that Shuhur jaan has any connection with anyone here in this palace before I send him there?" And Nazniyna answered again to her father "No! Abbajaan, more than he being the best archer, I have no father information about him" King Kismat then said "Nazniyna My dear, I feel within me that there are more you knows but you do not want to tell me yet, but know this, if you do not prevail the truth then for sure believe that you will be the loser and not me, and if you will tell me the truth about any affair of this young lad in this palace then that will be a wise decision, and that decision will help to protect you from any doubt I have, now take your time, go and think and tomorrow please come and tell me of anything you know about this young lad and his affairs. This is not a force matter to you, but I insist that you consider my suggestion to you. I have brought you up in that manner that never in your whole life you should speak lies but only the truth, even if that truth is so bitter for other to swallow it, you must speak it no matter what it cost. A gentleman never change his words and so also a gentlewoman, once you said YES then it should remain YES. Now Go and tomorrow I want you to present yourself here at the same time but with an answer" And then Nazniyna left room and her face looking down to the floor and her hand on her chest as a respect to the King.

King Kismat knew when Nazniyna left room that she did understand very well of why he keep on insists about any affair of Shuhur jaan in the palace, she knew that her father was trying very hard to make her to confess of her love affair with Shuhur jaan, she did understand the aim of her father that that was a tactic of informing her that [I know about your affairs] but just to make sure, King Kismat wanted Nazniyna to confess openly to her father that [YES I have a love affair with Shuhur jaan] just like what Shuhur jaan has did, bravely and without fear but with great courage, King Kismat then talked in his soul by himself [tomorrow is not very far, tomorrow I will give my judgment to these two young lads of what steps I will take against them.

I ask you my Allah, give me strength in my heart and give me patience to bear, and give me word of justice and fairness on my tongue so I can judge them fairly. My Allah, I am so much afraid not to judge with fairness and justice, I do not want to oppress any one among them and make you angry that I was not fair in my judgment, send to me your Angels to guide me]. And then King Kismat went to have rest and sleep, waiting for tomorrow to come. In his sleep King Kismat dreamed, and it was quite a wear dream, he dreamed he was again in that same village where he was before, he was standing in front of that same water well near where he has camped and there were voices coming inside that water well, and he was there all by himself without his guards or anybody else. Those voices which came from that water well were calling his name [KING KISMAT! KING KISMAT! DO NOT LEAVE THIS PLACE, STAY WHERE YOU ARE!], And King Kismat remain of where he was, and all because he wants to know who's this voice belongs to and what he wants from me, and suddenly he saw something coming out of that water well by climbing its wall, he gave a sharp look just to find out what kind of creation is that coming out of this water well as it was dark night, then he find a foot that was the same as a frog who came from this water well the first time he was here, the frog then came up to the edge of that water well, but what has surprised most King Kismat was that, this time this frog wear clothes and a robe and on his head there was a golden crown with many beautiful colored jewelry stones, King Kismat was stunned to saw that frog appearing in these costumes, he stay there dumped and just was starring at that frog and the frog was doing the same thing, just starring at King Kismat direct in his eyes, after a long period silence the frog then licked his right eye with his tongue and then he greeted King Kismat "Greeting to you King Kismat" and King Kismat return that greeting to the frog, and then the frog said "I know that you are surprised to see me again but in this costumes, completely difference as you had saw me before, please do not be confused, as I am not that same frog which you have met here in the first time, we do look alike but we are difference creations, as I am that King and guard of this water well who have sent to you my advices, that first frog was one of my servant, I have no other choice this night but to appear before you so we should know better one another and get acquainted and if possible maybe create a friendship between us two, and all because that you King Kismat as one among many many Kings of this universe, many of the past Kings were mostly concerned in their personal affairs rather than looking into affairs of their countries and countrymen, but you King Kismat is a difference kind of a ruler, you always put your efforts more on your country and your people, this we know, as you always sacrifice your time, your wealth as well as yourself just to make sure that you and your people are living in safe, secure and with happiness. In reality I am not a frog but an Angel created in this shape, I have been living in this well since I was born in it, and before me my ancestors as well all of our subjects are living in this water well.

King Kismat I have come to meet you in person so I can thank you for what you have done in this village and the villagers for all your efforts you have put to clean and clear the wrong doings of your people, and you had succeed doing that mission, and this village now is really wipe out all of its evils, the villagers now are good people and they obey all the teachings of Allah, no doubts he will reward you for what you have done, either here in this universe or maybe tomorrow in that day of the judgment.

Now I will talk very important issue, the main issue of me coming to see you. Through my messenger, I sent you information about this young lad Shuhur jaan. This young lad is in love with your daughter Princess Nazniyna. He is a very brave and courageous young man as well as kind at heart; he has very good intentions with you and your family, though it is true that he is not a Princes, he do not have any Royal blood in his veins, he is not son of a rich man, but his courage is more strong than of those Princes and richen children. Shuhur jaan will take care of Princess Nazniyna in very good faith and all because he is deep in love with her and not for what she has but for what she is, a girl of his choice. We know that though it is not for any member of Royal blood to get married to a simple person, and this was that culture of generation after generation of Royal families, I think the time has come that there should be some changes now. I advice you King Kismat, do not refuse or deny them to get married, marry them yourself but because you do not want to put yourself in shame and allow others to talk behind your back, take them out the palace and send them far away from others, maybe in that palace near the border with your neighbor, but give them condition that they should hold and keep their secret of their marriage, that it should not leak out that they are married, and also they must control themselves to go out of their palace and not to be seen together every now and then, and if for any reason they will go against this condition then they should know that from that day they will never live in this world as human beings but in the shape of animals and for a long period. There will come that day where you will need this young man to take a very important mission of which to save others, and all because there will be no more capable person who can perform his duty successfully more than him and other few, as there are some human beings who are in bad condition, they are prisoner and being tortured by the mountains Jinnis who are controlled by their King who is known as Khurkhush Majangar, this young man of yours, will be one of the saver of those who are mistreated by Khurkhush majangar, Please look good at him and take care of this young man and ever show him mistreat or bother him. He did not ask much from you, he only asked for the hand of your daughter for marriage, and this is the will of Allah that those two should get married in the name of Allah.

Princess Nazniyna at the palace

King Kismat, I also know that you have create a friendly relationship with Queen Farna Bash of butterfly people, and source of your friendship begin when you have killed that lion who was the worst enemy, and who has deny them to reach of where they get their food sources, and today it is my turn Oh! King Kismat, I come to you with my request of accepting me too as one of your close friend, a friend to remain and not a friend to dissolve, let us create that kind of friendship which will remain together always where there is happiness of there is sadness, in this friendship we have got nothing to lose but just to gain and a lot, let us together built that fort which will protect this friendship between us forever, that fort which will deny any evil to penetrate within and that fort which will allow all the good and the blessings to remain with us. Now tell me Oh! King Kismat Shahzara, what is your saying regarding my request?" and all that time King Kismat was just listening only but never spoke or interfere while King Frog was talking until he came to a stop, and then King Kismat answered King Frog and said "Oh you very kind King Frog, King that has the power to guard this water well, till now I had no any chance in asking your good name, how do they call you? What name do your parents gave you?" and King Frog then replied to King Kismat and said "Oh you good King, my parents have named me as Rawaanaz, since our ancestors we are the guards of all the water wells in this village" and King Kismat then said "Oh! you good King Rawaanaz, believe me if I tell you that to meet and know you was a great pleasure of mine, I thank you so much for many advices you gave me regarding my daughter Princess Nazniyna and also regarding this young man Shuhur jaan, your advices has entered in my heart and I promise you that I will consider them with wisdom and patience, and come in the end with a solution of the best judgment that will be benefit for all sides, I promise you that my last decision will not be against your advices but perhaps there will be a little to add or a little to reduce, but I ask you please do not get angry with my whatsoever judgment I will give regards these two young lads, Please remember that I am parent to my daughter, and all the rights of a child is with her parents, if for any reason during my judgment I have crossed over the fence with the promise I gave you, then know for sure I did that only because I am a father and I have the right to protect of what it belongs to me as a father, I only ask you to bear with me and not to be disappointed for what and how I will judge this situation which is a tough task in my life. Regarding creating Friendship between us two, that is possible and without any rejection, I accept you King Rawaanaz as my loyal friend, for the whole of my living life" and then King Rawaanaz said to King Kismat "Oh! you my friend King Kismat, if in your living life for any day you need me in any help or service, than take a bowl and put water inside it keep that bowl in front of you and then put your [Shahada finger] second finger from the thumb of your right hand inside the water and call my name, and I will be there within a split second, as you will see my face appear in the water, I can see you as you see me" then King Rawaanaz gave his little hand to King Kismat and King Kismat gave him his hand and they shake, and here is where King Kismat dream fade away, and he keep on sleeping till next day.

Nazniyna this day was not a good day to her, as she feels that this day will bring bad news or misfortunes, in her heart she was so unhappy, and all because every now and then she keep on remember that meeting with her father yesterday and yet another meeting with her father today, and most of it is that why her father keep on asking about Shuhur jaan many times?, and still she was thinking what answer she should tell her father this evening when she is going to meet him again, and the way she has been brought up is that she never speak lies or deny the truth, this is to her will be a very tough evening but she said to herself that there is no other choice but to speak the truth, the whole truth and nothing but the truth and may Allah help me, These thoughts were eating inside her mind, just for this one day she has notice that she has already lost some weight, to her this day is a dark day, as every now and then she is thinking of how to overcome this evening meeting with her father.

In the end her heart reduced the beating speed and she began to feel a little better and with courage, she then said to herself [Why should I carry this fear in my heart which it tortures me? Why can't I speak the truth to my father? What major crime did I commit that I feel myself like a victim? Inshalla I will tell my father whatever he will ask me, I will tell him in truth, even if he ask me about my love affair with Shuhur jaan, I hope that he will understand and will be polite with me]. And this is how Nazniyna conclude her thoughts in her mind just to release those torturing bad thoughts which were going around her mind.

When the evening arrived and after the evening prayers, Nazniyna went to meet her father as she was ordered, message was sent to the King that Princess Nazniyna has arrived and waiting permission to enter King's chamber, King Kismat allowed that Princess Nazniyna should be allowed to enter the room chamber, Princess Nazniyna then enter the room and her eyes were looking down on the floor and her right hand on her chest and greeted the King, she said "Peace be upon you Abbajaan" and King Kismat replied her Princess Nazniyna, and said "Peace be upon you too my dear daughter Nazniyna, you have come according our appointment" and she replied "Yes Dear Abbajaan, I have come as per you request that I should come here and bring with me any answer to your question regarding this young man Shuhur jaan" and King Kismat then said "Before you answer any of my question, I want you to take this letter and read it and tell me more about this letter" Princess Nazniyna then took the latter and saw that it was the same letter she has sent to Shuhur jaan, she then said "Yes Abbajaan, this is my hand writing letter of which I have sent to that young man Shuhur jaan as an answer to his letter which he sent it to me" and King Kismat asked her daughter "May I please be allowed to see that letter which this young man has sent it to you?" and Princess Nazniyna replied "Yes Abbajaan, You can see that letter as I have brought it with me here" and Princess Nazniyna then she brought the letter hidden under her cloth and hand it over to her father, King Kismat then took at that letter and open it and read it slowly and with concentration, then he finished reading it, he then rolled and closed the letter and then pick the letter of which she has sent to Shuhur jaan, which was remaining with him, and give those both two letters to Princess Nazniyna and said "can you tell me now, of what decision you have reached after now I know your secret?" and Princess Nazniyna then replied "Yes Abbajaan, but I will only speak for myself. This is true that with that young man for the first time in my life I have fall in love with, and all because of many good reasons he possessed, he is a gentleman, he is courageous, he is honest and truly love me and without fear while he knows well the differences between us, but still without fear he dare tell me his true feelings of me, and no matter what will happened to him he did not mind but send me this letter which explained each and everything of his true love to me. For me these were enough explanation about him, Abbajaan, these quality made me to trust him, to fall in love with him and to hope and believe that if Allah will, then this young man will be my kind and choice of a husband I can share all my life with. And for you, that was your dream that one day your daughter will get such good and respectful person who will come and ask for her hand in marriage, then I ask you Abbajaan to agree with me that there is no better young man to marry your daughter than this one, Shuhur jaan is the right man to be your son-in-law. I ask you Abbajaan, I request you Abbajaan please take this situation and consider it with politeness and wisdom and not with anger, consider this situation with fairness and good heart and not with that heart that had no blessings, as our future lives are all in your hands. Abbajaan! Your daughter Nazniyna is under your feet, begging for your blessings and for a better future life and nothing more, please Abbajaan consider and come out with fair result which will please all of us and remain with happiness" and all this time King Kismat was listening to his daughter of how she is fighting and protecting her love to the only person she had ever love and for the first time, King Kismat now realize that her daughter has really throw herself in this rage sea which is known as LOVE, and if he wants to save her then he must use wisdom and politeness and the suitable judgment. At the same time he remember what King Rawaazan has advice him, when he met him for the first time and when he met in his dream, then King Kismat asked her daughter "is this how you have decided for creating your future life? To be married by Shuhur jaan you think you will be happy and secure? Without considering who you are and whose child you are? Without consider what this world will be saying about us? Without thinking of where we as your parents would hide our faces away from the people of the world? These people who would like to spread any rumors of others and hide their own wrong doing? My dear Nazniyna, I ask you please, talk to your heart and change your decision and I promise you that I will marry you with best of the Prince who will give you all happiness and name and power to hold, I beg you please accept my offer and forget this Shuhur jaan the son of a blacksmith" and Nazniyna answered her father and said "I am so sorry Abbajaan, but it could be that Prince will be the best person, but for you and not me, but to me there is no other best more than Shuhur jaan, he is my choice and he is the one I want and no other, forgive me Abbajaan, I did not meant to break your heart or to put you in shame in this world, this is not my intentions at all, but I am also God's creation like anybody else, everyone among us has intentions, has choices, and has the right of thinking and choosing and take of what he or she want, and these are gifts from Allah who gave us these privileges as a freedom to do the best but within law abiding and not against his law, and Allah did not did not deny me these privileges, Allah gave me and I accept them with clean heart, and Shuhur jaan is my choice of a man whom I would like to share all my living life with him, no matter how we will live, either as a Princess or just as an ordinary person, I gave him my heart and he gave me his. Please forgive me Abbajaan for not responding to what you wanted which would have pleased you most" Then king Kismat spoke and said "If this is your first and last decision then you better listen to my last decision, Tomorrow you and Shuhur jaan will travel with me to a very far journey in the border of our country, and of what you have wanted and decided to have, Insha'Allah tomorrow will be that day to fulfill them. I have no any other saying to you, let us all wait for that tomorrow to come, you may leave my chamber and Good night" And Princess Nazniyna leave his father's chamber looking down on the floor while her right hand on her chest as a respect to the King. And now my dear reader of these tales, we have to go back of where we have left Nazniya after her marriage in that bordering fetisval of where her tongue slip and mention of whom she is. Now continue to read the story and find out yourself what has happened when Nazniyna and Shuhur jaan returned to their home.

CHAPTER NINETEEN

(Meeting of the three Kings)

KING KISMAT WAS IN A meeting with his cabinet, as usual ever motnng he sit down with members of his cabinet and discuss issues concerning his Kingdom and his subjects, then a messenger came with some news, and he was informed that there is a messenger who came from where princess Nazniyna live with her husband, he then ordered that they should take that messenger to resting house and provide him with all necessary needs, food and water to have a bath and after the messenger has a rest then he will see him when he will complete his meeting with his cabinet members, The servants took the messenger do as King Kiksmat has ordered, and after cabinets meeting was completed with the King Kismat, then King Kismat asked for the messenger to be brought before him in his private chamber, and that messenger turn to one of guards commander of his army who are guarding his daughter and her husband Shuhur jaan in the palace there near the border, That commander was a faithful servant to his King, as well as he was also one of the personal informer to the King, and his name was Dastur Darweish. King Kismat when he found that the messenger was none other than Dastur, he then knew that there is very hush news he might have brought it to him, after the messenger came to meet his King and greeted him, King Kismat then asked him "What important news you have brought this time Oh! Commander Dastur?" and Commander Dastur replied to his King "Your Majesty, what news have I brought, is not at all good news to you, There in the region, news has spread about the marriage of Princess Nazniya got married to a poor family young man known as Shuhur jaan and we have no means of stopping these news to spread more your Majessty, as this one will tell that one and that one will tell the other one, and this is my reason of my coming here urgently today your Majesty" King Kismat when he heard this uncomfortable news which is spreading in his Kingdom, really did made him very much uncomfortable and immediately he changed as anger overcome him, he then asked Commander Dastur to leave his chamber and leave him alone, he then stand and started to pace the room from one end to the other, while his was hitting his left hand with his right hand while pacing, then he decided to leave his chamber and headed to his room, while he was in his room he requested for a bowl full of water to brought for him, and the servant has a silver bowl full of water and kept it on the table, he then ordered every servants who are serving him to leave the place and leave him alone and all by himself, and he has ordered that no one should come to his room for this time until he called, when he was all alone than he went to that silver bowl full of water was and sit in front of it, then he put his finger inside the

The bowl and called "Rawaanaz! Rawaanaz! Please answer me" then immediately he saw the water in bowl started to circle and produce bubbles, he removed his finger and look in the bowl, and then the water stopped to circle and bubbled and slowly the face of King Rawaanaz started to appear in the water, King Rawaanaz then greeted King Kismat and said "Peace be upon you King Kismat, you have called me my dear friend, for sure I think you need me for a very important mission, tell me my friend, how can I be of your service" and the King kismet greeted back and explain to King Rawaanaz of all what has happened about the spreading of his daughter's marriage secret which was suppose to remain a secret, and what he told his daughter and her husband that their marriage should always remain secret and no one should know about it, and also about the warning he has gave them that if their marriage news will come out from them then it will be only themselves to blame for what misfortune will fall upon them, what he was afraid not to happen now it has happened. King Rawaanaz then asked King Kismat "what you me to do for you my friend as you have called me" and King Kismat answered "Like I told and have warned them before that if they will go against my words then they will suffer severely, I want you to help me punish them for their mistakes, I want you turn them from their human reform to swans reforms as my punishment to them, I know my friend that you posses this kind of power, please use them for me so that they will learn and know whom I am" and King Rawaanaz asked King Kismat "Do you think this punishment will be a better solution to punishment them, my dear friend King Kismat?" and King Kismat answered "No! it will not be a solution but it will be a hush lesson to them, and it will also be a reminder to them to warning I have gave them before that if you will go against my words there will be a very hard punishment waiting for them" and King Rawaanaz said "I am not going to go against your wish King Kismat, without doubts I will perform of what you had request me to do, but I ask to go back of where I had advice you regarding this young man Shuhur

jaan, you will really need him in a very important mission which will becoming
ahead of you, it is just of a time, and if that time come and these young lads are
still in these reforms, then tell me my friend, how can this young man help you
to overcome that mission when he is not at all in reform of a human being?"
And King Kismat answered "I quite agree with you my friend but I cannot go
against my own words, what I told and warned them it will be then it must
be, please my friend, I ask you, please let me punished them for just awhile so
they will regret of what wrong they have done" And King Kismat answered
"Inshaalla my friend, I will do of what you had asked me to do, within a short
period these two young lads will transform as you wished into the shapes of
swans, male will be in black color and the female will be white color, and in
ever year only for one day and on the same date they will be able to return in
their natural reforms, they will be human being again but only for only one
night and one day, and before the sun goes down and the dark appear, then
these two will turn again into two swans, and these changes will one be able
to take place at on only one place, and that place is that mountain which is
in the border at Empty quarters deserts, and here is where they will return to
home as prisons again. This punishment will continue until that day you will
decide that enough is enough.

I beg to Allah to forgive and pardon you if for any reasons these actions
you are taking are against the will of Allah.

It was in a midday when Nazniyna and Shuhur jaan were about to have
their lunch, Nazniyna then fell that her condition is not normal, something
wrong within her body, there are some changing she felt that begins to took
place within her, because she started to feel very high body temperature and
begin to sweat much, then suddenly she felt her voice start to disappear, she
could not resists these changing in her body anymore and quickly stood and
begin to flaps her arms like bird wings, Shuhur jaan when he saw these actions
of his wife, fear start to overcome him, and do not of what to do or how to help
her in this ordeal, the inside servants also witness this happenings to Princess
Nazniyna, and within a short period, Nazniyna started to grow birds hair on all
her body in front of her husband and all the servants who were presents there,
she then transformed from human being and into a big bird, and that bird was
a white swan, Shuhur jaan was just watching with fear of this transformation
which it took place in front of him while his eyes were wide open and tears
were pouring from it, because knew why this transformation took place, why
his wife changed from human being to animal, he remembered the warning of
King Kismat when he warned them about keeping the secret of their marriage

that nobody should know about, Shuhur jaan then started to cry loudly while shouting "My dear Nazniyna! My life Nazniyna, look now at the result of that mistake you have done, You are going away in front of my eyes and I cannot help you in anything, you have leaving me all alone by myself now" and that swan fly away out of the window and no one's know where she has gone to, all the maid servants were crying non-stop for this misfortune which has occur in the Palace, Poor Shuhur jaan he became so weak and could not control himself but only crying and crying, he was so disappointed and heartbroken, the male servants came and pick him up and put him in his room and on his bed but still crying with screams of tears pouring out of his eyes and flowing down his chicks and ended on his chest. The news of this miracle happening was sent to King Kismat, and was told of what has happened to Princess Nazniyn, he then acted like he know nothing about, and shows on his face shock appearance and puzzled, though he knew something like this will happen as it is his doing.

Next day, he ordered Shuhur jaan to be arrested and be sent to the prison cell there in the palace, and should not be allowed to see the day light, in other words, should not be allowed to be out of the cell but to remain there all the time until he King Kismat permits. Shuhur jaan spent many day in that palace cell, he never so any daylight, he never knew when was the day or when was the night, to him the darkness of the palace cell is all of what he has experience. Then one day by the order of the King, he was taken out of the palace prison cell and was sent to meet the King, and the King asked all those who have brought him should leave and let him all alone with the king, King Kismat then told Shuhur jaan, and said "Shuhur jaan, after spending the whole year in the palace prison, today is that day where you will be allowed to go and meet your lover Nazniyna, and as I have told you,

Your meeting place will only on that lake on the mountain which near the Empty quarters, you have to travel all the way and all by yourself only, you have a freedom from this hour till tomorrow at the same hour you must be here at the palace, if by any reason you will not come back in time and accordingly the know what punishment you will encounter will be more than the prison cell which you have been kept, did you understand what I have told you Shuhur jaan" and he replied with very low voice "Yes you Majesty, I did understood every word you have said" then King Kismat went to the table and took that salver bowl of water and throw all the water on to Shuhur jaan, and with no time Shuhur jaan begin to transform into a black swan, and then the swan fly away out of the window and disappear. The saw flown away high in the sky and was heading to border of Empty quarters was, he knew the place as he has been there before, he remembered those high mountains and that beg lake on top of the mountain, for so many hours he has filed and he reached those mountains, he forced himself to be there before high speed wind will come and deny him to reach his target, in his heart he was so happy for this one day freedom and all because he is going to meet his Princess Nazniyna, then when he was closed to that mountains he slowly lowered himself down, and from the distances he saw on the lake there was a white swan enjoying her bath, he knew that was no one else other than Nazniyna, he land on the lake and went to where that white swan was and then they embraces themselves with their long necks while making too loudly noises while their heads were directed up in the sky with their long necks.

Among these two, none of them knew that this and on this mountain there is the third person hiding himself behind those long bushes, he came just to explore the secret of these water of which they fall from this mountain and to the other side of his country which has bordered with King Kismat Kingdom, and that third person was none other than Saqr bin Haddad. And by good luck and coincidently Saqr has witness all about these two swans, as he was there before their arrival. And this dear reader is the tale of King Kismat and his daughter Princess Nazniyna. As he lived a very lonely life alone without his daughter, a very sad and tormented life and all because of his stubbornness, though he do not to show it up that inside his heart there is fire burning every nerve of his body, because he misses his daughter very much, he knew that the step of transforming these two young lads was not fair judgment but its effects is showing now that he as a King with a Princess but now is living with his daughter, every day he is going to Princess Nazniyna's room just to torture himself more by sitting there and cry, as he has failed in his judgment to give these two young lad such a cruel punishment and for a long time now, years has passed by and the two lads are suffering in that cruel punishment and all because King Kismat did not want anyone to know that he marry his daughter to his blacksmith's son. Instead of using patience and wisdom he used anger temper, now he is the one who suffer more than those two young lads, as he is now regretting for that action he took on these two young innocent lads, yet still he is trying to be stubborn, as he can forgive and forget and return these two swan into their original Forms, but he does not want to do it yet. He prefer to suffer with agony and pain within his heart by everyday going into that room which belongs to Nazniyna and sit there and shed tears.

Queen Farna Bash had another meeting

And here is where we have come now at the present time of those who prepare to attack Khurkhush Majangar, this is that generation which of where the messenger Queen Farna Bash came to meet King Kismat on behalf of others in asking him to support theory plan of saving those who are in jail of Khurkhush Majangar. King Kismat was there in her daughter's room with his agony when he felt that someone touched his right ear, he knew then that there is messenger came and wanted to see him, he then touched his right ear and a huge peacock appear in front of him, All King Kismat sorrows and sadness then disappeared yet he was very surprised to see Queen Farna Bash pays a surprise visit to him, he then gave her a deserving royal reception by standing and bow to her, and Queen Farna Bash on her side returned the greeting to King Kismat, King Kismat then said "What a great pleasure you have gave me Queen Farna Bash by this surprise visits to my humble palace, without any doubts the reason which brought you here to me must be of very important, and if it was not matter of important you would have to me your messenger only, but by presenting yourself here shows that the matters are very important, Tell me Queen Farna Bash, how can I help you or be of any service to you, Kismat is all under your command, ready to listen and accomplish any of your mission, just let me know of how I can serve you "and Queen Farna Bash replied "Thank you very much Oh! King Kismat, a friend of Queen Farna Bash and his butterfly people, frankly speaking, my surprise visit to you is a necessary matter of a very important issue, I carry with me a message from others, a group of which combined between human beings and some Jinnis, and I am a very close friend with some members of this group, so close like you and me, and that is why I volunteer to take this message to you as they know how close our relation is between us two, their members of their families among those in the group have been imprisoned by one of notorious Jinni in our region known as Khurkush Majangar, up to this day they have failed to find any solution of how they can go in that Kingdom of Khurkhush Majangar and save their loved ones, the last decision they have just a short while ago, they have come to me and ask me to join their group with my people so to gain more strength, as I have been living the other side of mountain with my Kingdom and know how cruel is Khurkhush Majangar, I agree to join them though I know that I will put my people into danger, yet I did not like this idea of Khurkhush Majangar of oppressing people for his pleasure, yet though I agree to join them, still we find ourselves that we not capable to create an army which can fight the strong army of Khurkhush Majangar, this is the main reason for my visit to you, to ask and request you Your Majesty to join with us and make our group army more strong so we can be able to fight Khurkush Majangar and save those who in his prison and are suffering for no crime they have committed. Secondly, is how and which way can we fight Khurkhush Majangar army is where we came to seek your advice and help Your Majesty King Kismat, because your Majesty, you are well known for obtaining one of the strongest army in the region and you yourself have great background experience of war fighting your Majesty, and this not only now but before you were your ancestors in generation after generation this Kingdom has one of the most powerful army in the region since then. As I am a participate and also a messenger of this mission, I would like to hear from you in your own words Your Majesty of what your decision is, are you with us or are you not?" and after listening to a long exp[lanation from Queen Farna Bash, King Kismat then said "According to what explanation you have given to me, this is proof enough that even you and your citizens are not living in a peace of mind and all because of this evil Jinni Khurkhusha Majangar? And this Khurkhush Majangar what he think of himself? That he can control this region by himself only? That he can deny others to live in peace and harmony? He thinks that he obtained all the power on us human beings and you too? Did he think that there wills no one to overpower him? Poor Khurkhush Majangar, if Pharoh could not control Prophet Moses and his people while he called himself I AM ABOVE YOUR GOD and when the day came he agree and said NOW I BELIEVE IN MOSES AND HAROUN'S GOD, poor Khurkhush, he do not know of where is the fact and where is just a dream, I believe that this is the right time for Khurkhush Majangar to learn and know between the truth and the lies. My dear Queen Farna Bash, type message you have been asked to deliver has reached me, and me on my side I think I might join force with a heavy army to fight this evil Khurkhush Majangar, but before I give you the go ahead answer of how to fight this war, I request from you just to give me few minutes so I can discuss this matter with my advisers, after I get their decision and their advices than I can call you so you could come to take your answer, or what do you say Queen Farna Bash?" and Queen Farna Bash the replied "Thank you so much oh! my good friend King Kismat, truly you gave me a wise answer, personally I agree to it without hesitation, you may go ahead and discuss the matter with your advisers and then call me as you have suggested, but if you will allow me please, I have some advice to give" and King Kismat then said "Yes! And without any objection, go ahead" and Queen Farna bash then said "Time is more value to us now, and our ancestors always advices us that TIME IS LIKE A SWORD, IF YOU WILL NOT CUT IT NOW

THEN IT WILL CUT YOU LATER, what that should be done today should not be waited for tomorrow to do it, because tomorrow's opportunity no one can guarantee that it will come or not, my suggestion now to you, instead of calling your advisers and sit day after day for discussion, why don't you contact and take advise of your friend King Rawaanaz, if you will include him in this mission discussion, we might get a better advice to solve this problem. Forgive me for mentioning King Rawaanaz without your permission, as this is your personal matter, but we as other creature of God and not human beings, know more than you do, I know about your relation from that day you two agree to be friends, and that was something did made me very happy, and that is why King Rawaanaz mentioned my name to you that day, because before he ask you to be his friend he came to me and seek my advices about you and it I who insists that you two should be friends, and he took my advice, and here you are today as very good and close friends. I again repeat my suggestion that you better waste no more time but to take immediate action now and contact your friend King Rawaanaz for his views and advices, so also form to take back any answer you will give it to me to those who are waiting for my return among our group and surrender to them what so ever your last answer will be" and King Kismat agree with queen Farna Bash suggestion, he then called one of his servant and ask to bring him that silver bowl with full of water, and the servant rushed quickly and brought that silver bowl full of water and kept it on the table, then he dismiss all the servants in the room and remain just him and Queen Farna Bash, he then put his finger in the water inside that bowl and called for King Rawaanaz, and immediately the face of King Rawaanaz appeared in the water inside that silver bowl, King Rawaanaz then greet to King Kismat and asked the reason of calling him now, and King Kismat then explained in details of all about the visit of Queen Farna Bash and that she came there for mission and what mission is that, and that queen Farna Bash suggested that he should be included in this talk so to give his own option and advices. Then King Rawaanaz asked if it is possible for him to be present in that meeting in person, and King Kismat had no objection as well as Queen Farna Bash, and permission was granted for King Rawaanaz to appear. Then in a split of a second something jump out from that water silver bowl and drop on the chair, and this was their first meeting for such great rulers to be meeting together in one place and to discuss a matter of very important issue regarding of how to help and save those who are in Khurkhush Majangar prisons. The Kings and the Queen then greeted each other in a Royal manner by bow and keep their right hand on their chests, after explanation to King Rawaanaz of the important of this meeting, King Rawaanaz then said "First of all, please King Kismat, allow me to give my personal respect to Queen Farna Bash, for making this day as an opportunity for the first of our Kinghood history that we met together, though between us in many time we do discuss but through our maybe telepath or through our messengers, but this day to me, is one of a great day in my life to had this kind of opportunity of three great rulers of our kind to meet together and sit down in discussion of a matter concerning other who need our help. Secondly, as you have called and include me in your discussion regarding the war of which you want to fight against such a powerful Jinni, then know form now that none of you even including others in your group are capable to fight Khurkhush Majangar with any army, to do that is only to destroy all your people and nothing can be achieved by them, never will anyone can fight Khurkhush Majangar army of his powerful Jinnis army using handmade weapons and people army. Yet, this does not mean that there are no other means of fighting Khurkhush Majangar, the only way of fighting him is to use tactics and fooling betrayal, but among the whole of your army and including yourselves only few among you are capable of doing that, by using tactic is and foolish betraying, and among who can be that, none other than this young man of yours King Kismat, and he is Shuhur jaan, because he is the only young warrior who have a perfect aim by using bow and arrows, but it is very sad that my friend King Kismat up to this day he is torturing this young man for just simple accidentally mistake which is not him but his wife did it, and that wife is none other than the daughter of King Kismat, and to me, these two young lads do not deserve such a hush and very painful punishments, if you want and need to with this war than Shuhur jaan must be set free, as he is among those few I have mentioned that will able to accomplish this mission, if you King Kismat will agree with condition, then include me in this group to be among those who will take part of how to fight this evil Jinni Khurkhush Majangar" and when King Rawaanaz completed his talking, none of the two were able to speak must were remaining silent, but in the end Queen Farna Bash has no other choice but to break that silent, and she said "To speak the truth, I swear to Allah that I completely agree with King Rawaanaz and his condition, because this young man what mistake he did according to you King Kismat is just in marriage a hand of your daughter, is that a mistake? Is it against the will of Allah or against the human nature? But it was only a hard luck that truly there were differences between a Royal blood and a simple person, because this a member of powerful ruler and that one a son of a blacksmith who works for that powerful ruler, but let us not forgets that this is also what Allah has planned for its own good and never for any worst reason, as they have said those before us, MAN PROPOSE AND GOD DISPOSED If what has happened was a mistake, than that mistake was done and nothing can change that or bring the situation anticlockwise, and you King Kismat have already punished these two young lads more than enough and for quite a long time now, you yourself have suffered enough for the pain and agony within your heart by missing your daughter and her love and presence near you. Now time has come for you to realize and release these two young lads in their torturing condition and allow them to live again in their natural reforms. Ahead of us there is a very hard mission which need every and each one of us to participate, and like what King Rawaanaz had mentioned to you before about his prediction of this young man Shuhur jaan, that we need him most in this mission, maybe, I said maybe, perhaps he will be the one who can finish off this evil jinni. King Kimat, please think and decided at this moment now, change your attitude for the better and not the bad, let and allow your mind to bear better wisdom of construction and wipe out those thoughts of distruction here now with your brother and sister, and take our every advice we gave you regarding those two young lads and allow them to live their normal lives as they deserve it. We have no more to say but we are waiting for your answer and what another step you will take on this matter of your children as well as other general issues regarding our mission." And the King Kismat said "I think that is very important issue here as Queen Farna Bash has point it out, I am willing to join this group which has intentions of saving those who are suffering in the jail of Khurkhush Majangar, I am also ready to arrange the bravest of my army of five thousands top of the rank best soldiers to join others in this group in attacking the army of Khurkhush Majangar, now let us discuss here of how we can send our armies up there in the mountain of where Khurkhush Majangar lives with his army" but it is here where King Rawaanaz has explain in details of his idea of how to attack Khurkhush Majangar, he said "Khurkhush Majangar is a simple figure to attack him easily, we all know that he is not a human but a Jinni, and a powerful Jinni, all of his army are Jinni's as well, the creation who have the power of transforming and changing into difference kind and shape of creations, who can be visible as well as invisible, and as well as what kind of other power they have, that we do not know, though we other also are not human and have the ability of changing as well as change other, but we cannot compare ourselves with those power of Khurkhush Majangar army, but yet I agree that there are differences in our power obtaining, we can do of what they cannot and they can do of what we cannot, now here is where the question is born, how can we fight such a powerful army with many differences power which we do not have?, In my idea, I think before we discuss of how to send our army there at the mountains of Khurkhush Majangar Kingdom, it is better first to send some spy there to find of how the situation is there, and if there is any possible way of sending army there and what directions before they will be find out, and also of how he is living and where he is living, as he is the main target of our war, to destroy him is to destroy the whole of Jinnis army in that Kingdom. Now let us first talk here of how to send our spy there so we can get the most valued information about this Khurkhush Majangar of where he is hiding or living and any other information which can help us to win our war. Then Queen Farna Bash said, "My dear brothers, since we have started sitting in discussion on this issue, we have wasted so much time already, just by talking and have not reached to the main issue of our point, and that is of how to save those who are suffering in the jail of Khurkhush Majangar, and on the other side, there are others who are waiting for us to bring the answer of their request from you King Kismat as my friend were mostly depending on you, and now as we are three then the answers from two of you and including myself in this discussion, up this moment we have not agree on any suggestion or agreement of this matter, I think it is better for me to return and inform those who are waiting for the answer of this visit here, and tell them that you people need more information of how Khurkhush Majangar live and where he lives, so if there is any possible means to send a spy there then they should do that, If I will get any answer regarding this last matter then I will return here immediately. Now I ask permission to allow me to leave and return to my home place" and here they all agree on this matter and allow Queen Farna Bash to return and seek more information. Queen Farna Bash then disappear and return to her Kingdom, and King Rawaanaz throw himself in the water inside silver bowl and disappear.

CHAPTER TWENTY

(Zarza decided to fight alone)

Queen Farna Bash when she have arrived back to her Kingdom she find Antar and Saqr were still there waiting for her return with any news, she then explained in details every and each subjects they have talked and what conclusion they reached in the end, and also that they will be another session of a meeting if any news of Khurkhush Majangar of how and where he live and stay most, if somehow someone can get information, Saqr then said "Thank you so much Oh! Queen Farna Bash, for all your efforts you had taken to send our message to King Kismat and his friend King Rawaanaz, all of what is needed is well understood, we all go back home and inform our elders and sit together to discuss these issues and after getting any answer to this solution then we will come back to you. Without doubts where there is a will there is a way. Then Saqr and Antar bid farewell to Queen Farna Bash and retuned to their homeland in the Empty quarters desert. Now my dear readers let us leave Saqr and Antar for the time being and go and find out where is Zarza Aarish at this time. Zarza was with her lover Prince Nuwr alaa Nuwr sitting somewhere in their regular place of meeting and were talking, they were discussing many things regarding this evil Jinni Khurkhush Majangar, Prince Nuwr then said "My dear God, give us strength, wisdom and means so we can conquer this evil jinni, this enemy of yours and your creations, you know him well of his strength, but Oh! God, there is no one among us all your creation who have the power to compete with your power, we request you, we beg you Oh! God, give us means of defeating this evil Jinni so we can save those who are still suffering in his jail, God please, answer our prayers as you are the only God who can answer prayers, you give to whom you want and deny to whom you want, please give us and do not deny us to give, let us win our war with this evil" and then Zarza answered "Amin yaa Rabbi-l-alamin, but please allow me to excuse myself for the time being, as I have to leave you now, and all because I have received a message that I am needed by other party on a matter of a very important, I believe that there must be good news have come from somewhere, till I see you again some other time, so long" and Zarza disappear in a split second decision.

If we go back to Saqr and Antar on their return journey from Queen Farna Bash Kingdom, they reached to their village and Saqr quickly went inside his home to inform the elders of what has been said and what is needed to be done, he explained in details all about the meeting between the Kings and the Queen. And outside in the stable Antar did send that urgent call to Zarza to come, and Zarza was there in a split of a second, and she came in same form as a bird as she came in her first visit, Antar when he saw that beautiful bird he knew that was Zarza she have arrived, he went to where Zarza was and explained to him of all what Queen Farna Bash has told them. Zarza after hearing what conclusion those Kings and a Queen have reached, in her mind then came an idea, she quickly then decided to go inside the house and meet the elders just to find out from them of what they have decided regarding this information from those Kings meeting, She knocked the door and was welcomed inside the house by Saqr, and those who were in the house were pleased to see Zarza have come back again to them, everyone there stood just to give Zarza a respect, and Zarza did return her respect to all of them by bowing her head down and bent down a little as a respect to the elders and her hand on her chest, Zarza then greeted "Peace be upon you all" and they answered back "Peace be upon you too Zarza Aarish, please have a sit and share with us in what good news we have received right now, "and Zarza answered "Thank you so much for your hospitality, and your good treatment to me, Yes I know about the news which Saqr has brought back from Queen Farna Bash, therefore there is no need to explain it to me, Now time has come to stop meetings and talking, now the time have matured for action only, and those action should be very hard and strong as well as very effective, and also here is where sacrificing is needed and all because where we will go there will be a great war to fight, as this war will be of do or die. My dear elders and my younger ones, I take this opportunity to tell you all openly of my intention in this war, that I have decided, Me Zarza Aarish to fight this war all by myself without including any of you except one, I do not want anyone among you to die as I know Khurkhush Majangar better than any one of you, and before I put myself in danger, I have to tell you that without Saqr and those two horses outside, than this mission will be impossible, nothing can be done or achieved. Secondly, tomorrow I have to go and meet King Kismat so I can ask him to call King Rawaanaz so I can explain to them of all my intentions and what else I want to do and how much I need their help and support, if they will

agree to help me and give me all the support I need, then you better know that
there will be no more time to waste as Zarza Aarish will throw herself in danger
to stop this cruelty once and for all, and finish off Khurkhush Majangar forever
and wipe out his name in the lips of our future generation children. Mr. Fairuz,
I know that your mind has been upset since I mentioned the name of Saqr in
joining hand with me to fight this evil cruel Jinni. I am not forcing him but I
have my own reason of why Saqr in particular, but unfortunately I cannot
reveal my reason here to you all, but I would like those reasons to remain secret
for the time being, but allow me to remind you, in the past years and before
Saqr was born, you Mr. Fairuz have been informed that the time will come
and this brave and courageous young boy will be a member of your family and
he will grow up to be tough and brave and fearless young lad, and he will be
among the saver, now Mr.Fairuz that time has come and this is that time for
your son to prove his braveness among you all. Saqr is not alone among those
who will join me but there is another young man like Saqr and he is not among
you here but among the people of King Kismat of where I am going to meet
the King and request his young man to join me in this war of fighting to the
end. Now I want to know among you two as the parents of Saqr, are you willing
to sacrifice your son in helping and saving the family of your brother here Abu
Mintasir or are you afraid for the death of your son where all of us are going
to die, as it has been written in books of Allah that every soul will taste death.
I now stop to speak for a short time as I am waiting an answer from you Mr.
Fairuz and your family regarding your son Saqr. I do not aquier much time for
waiting, so I ask you please hurry up yourselves in your answers." And after
Zarza finished speaks, none among all those who were in the house did speak
anything, everybody was like a dumb, and all because the issue is very essential
and heavy to carry as a burden, and then Maalim Mikdad broke the silence
and said "It is true Zarza, time is most valued thing, and no doubts we must
give you a quick answer, but I have some question I would like to ask you if
you will allow please, As I understood you, You said here a few moments ago
that you have prepare yourself to go ahead and fight this war by yourself, but
then you have requested that you want Saqr to be part of you with those two
horses outside in the stable, you mean Antar and Saharzena, and you did not
want any else among us to join you, now my question to you, what power do
you two posses that you have all the confidence that by that power you two
can win this war against Khrkhush Majangar?" and Zarza replied "No! Maalim
Mikdad, we are not just two but as I have mentioned before that where my
journey will take me this evening, and talking bout the power, yes, that power

of which I am seeking is there where I will go, I will find that power of how
to fight this war, because I know what kind of tactics I am going to use with
my colleagues of whom I have selected them, Yes it is true, I do not posses that
kind of power which you have image in your mind, but we Jinnis, have that
kind of power of which you human being do not posses it at all, as same as
that power you human being posses it and we Jinnis do not posses. I know
Khurkhush Majangar very well, and none among you have any kind of
information or any tactics. I know how he lived and where he lived, and also
do not forget that this is Zarza Aarish who is one among his subject. There
was a time that I too used to live like a Royal family; unfortunately that time
has passed away as it was a time of which I lost my dear husband as he has died
and all because of this evil Khurkhush Majangar, for me now is the right time
to get my revenge on him, as I took with me these young lads who I hope will
be willing to sacrifice their lives against Khurkhush Majangar, none of us here
today knows that are we going to come back or are we going to allow our dead
body remain there in his Kingdom. I only want to remind you all here you
good people, that I have none anyone of my blood in khurkhush jail to save,
but it is you people that you wanted this war to happened as it is your war
against this evil Jinni who captured your loved ones and keep them in his jail.
I did this all because I felt for you human beings, because I too believed in
your faith and convert myself to Islam, and this would never happened to me
if it is not that direction of knowing better your faith and not from you human
beings but from my friend who is just an animal, and he is a camel. Now I
need that answer of which I have waited for it for a long time." After a long
explanation, Mr. Fairuz then release his breathe and said "Oh! Zarza, a Jinni
girl and a trust friend, we understood you. Without any doubts what you have
said about fighting this evil Jinni is like fighting a Jihad (religious war) against
us human being, without any doubts that is exactly our intentions of wiping
him once and for all and no one else should take his place, but as a father of
only one child Saqr, this will be a very hard and bitter to swallow, but the
question here is, what about Abu Muntasir who has lost two instead of one, he
is here with us but all his thoughts are with his wife and son, though he always
trying not to show in front of us but within his inner he is suffering with agony
and tortures, then why not me and my family also join in hand and experience
the same but for hope of trying to win and not of lost all of our loved ones.
Yes! I said yes!, Saqr is allowed to join you in this very impossible mission of
less hope but let's hope, and all our prayers and blessing are with you, and may
Allah be with you and protect you all, until this earth remain safe and peaceful

place to live without any fear any more. Yes you may Go and our all trust are in God and he will be with you Insha'Allah" and Zarza then said "I thank you Mr. Fairuz for that courage and sacrifice soul you have, this is reminding of Prophet Abraham when he has sacrificed his son Prophet Ashmail to obey his Allah in fulfill his dream. But also there is another person permission, and that is my sister Saqr's mother, we should not just decide ourselves and forget those mothers who took all their pain and the patience waiting of what was in their bellies to come out and live, I request now Saqr mother if she have any objection for his son to sacrifice for this mission, then now is the right time to speak, without her permission then there will be no joining me of Saqr to this Jihad, please my dear sister Saqr mother, speak out and say it all and openly of your feelings about permitting Saqr in our mission, should he come with me or not, no one can dare to force you here, this is Zarza's promise" then Madame Ramziya, shyly and with a little smile she said "It is in our culture and heritage that when the elders speaks the young remain silent's, and on my side that was what I have learned and except, it was not right for me to say anything in front our elders, I did just follow our tradition and what we have been taught. To speak the truth this is not my ground to open my mouth, though my younger sister Zarza has fairly decided that I too has the right to speak as a mother of this young man, that should I allow and permit Saqr to go and sacrifice his life in this mission or not, to go in this journey of no one knows that will they come back alive or not, and like what Zarza has before said that this is that mission of either do or die, and I said this not a good bye journey but it is a farewell journey, as it is either to be back or not to, but here is also there a question to be asked, if I will not permit Saqr to go with Zarza in this do or die mission? Then what will happen to those still suffering in this evil Jinni prison? What next will happen if this Jinni still exsits? Will peace and security remain on this land? Will our children live in peace and enjoy their freedom? And who knows that until this moment those who are suffering in Khurkhush Majangar prison are they still alive or dead? No one knows anything about those mountains, until the news or information does come from those sources in the mountains, and who is there to bring us that information? From this land there is no one but from those mountains and those who knew well Khurkhush Majangar there is one, and none other than Zarza Aarish, This is not that session of discussing of what to do or who to send but to decide should we go and save our people or not, the matter has no more time to waste but to take action and now. On my side, I thank you so much Zarza Aarish, on your decision to sacrifice your life for us human beings, this braveness and dangerous mission you have decide to help us by saving our people, there is no place for it to avoided it but to give all the support it need to give, and on my side I fully support with all my clean heart and clear mind that Saqr should be allowed to join you in this mission. Go Saqr, and join hand with Zarza Aarish and my blessings are with you, And I will not stop always to raise my hands up in the sky begging and pray to Allah for your safe return, and I will not stop my lips to pray and asking Allah to prevent you with any evil there, and victory will be yours Insha'Allah, and tomorrow we will wake up with a bright shining day an no more darkness as darkness will dissolve and go away. I have no further saying more than what I have said in my long speech which came not from my lips but deep from my heart, though I have said before that when elders speaks younger must remain silent, and I forgot myself that I was among the elders here but keep on speaking without stop, I know that I have jump over boundaries of my display limit, may I be pardon and be forgiven please for that mistake." And after Madame Ramziya had stop speak and allow the permission of his son Saqr to join force with Zarza Aarish, then everybody there raises their hand and pray for this group of Zarza and her selected partners. Zarza then said "Tomorrow God willing I will go to pay a visit to King Kismat and his friend King Rawaanaz through our friend Queen Farna Bash, there will be no going to those mountains before I send to you all the information of what I have gain or discuss with those two Kings, and Saqr will be the one to inform you of the exact time which we will be going to leave this land heading to that Kingdom of Khurkhush Majangar. In this night I will request Maalim Mikdad to arrange a dua praying for all of us, may Allah protect and guide us, that will be awise thing to do this night for us all and for those who are going to join me in this Jihad against this evil Jinni Khurkhush Majangar.

CHAPTER TWENTY-ONE

(Zarza decided to fight by herself war to an end)

ZARZA THEN EXCUSE HERSELF AND went outside, outside she went to the animal stable, where Antar and Saharzena were and talk with Antar in his ear and then Antar nodded as he understood of what he has been told, Antar then went out of the stable and run away to that particular place of where he always secretly bring out his hidden wings, he then opened his wings and fly away high up in the sky until he became invisible, he then land down on the mountain of Kingdom of butterfly people at the same place where that big tree is, and there he saw a messenger of Queen Farna Bash waiting for him, he then told the messenger to inform the Queen that Antar is here with an important message from the village, the little butterfly man then disappeared and Antar was there waiting, within a short while there came a great wind and hit on the that big tree branches and here came the great Queen of butterfly people Kingdom who was a huge peacock and landed on her special made stand under that huge tree, Antar then bow her head down as a respect to the Queen, and greeted the Queen "Peace be upon you Oh! Queen Fana Bash" and the Queen replied "Peace be upon you too Sahib Antar, I am sure what that has brought you now must be of important matter" and Antar replied "Yes my dear Queen, I have come with a heavy strong message which also have some changing in it regarding your attacking of the Khurkhush Majangar army, I have been sent by Zarza Aarish on this special mission to you, she told to tell you that tomorrow she want you to accompany her with that visit to King Kismat together with King Rawaanaz there in the palace of King Kismat, because there are some changing regarding the attack which they have decided recently by all members of our group there in our village, if you agree with this message then please give me your answer so I can go back and deliver it to Zarza, so she can come tomorrow here to meet you before your visit to King Kismat" and Queen Farna Bash when she heard the name of Zarza Aarish, she asked but with surprise tone "Zarza Aarish? Saahib Antar, is this woman not among the followers of Khurkush Majangar? How come then Zarza be

264

on our side against her Master?" and Antar replied "Oh! You kind Queen and my friend, did you forgot that even I was one of tortured follower and close friend of Khurkhush Majangar? But when the situation was unbearable did I not leave all of my family and run away? And just waiting to that day that I can go back there and save every and each one of them, did you forget that?" and then Queen Farna Bash answered "Yes, it is true of what you have said, but when I heard this name of Zarza Aarish I was so much surprised, but now when I got your assurance you have cleared my doubts about her, so this mean that Zarza also join our group?" and Antar replied "Yes Queen Farna Bash, Zarza Aarish is among us, have no doubt for now but there are many surprise you might hear about her in this night, but just give me your answer so I can go and deliver it to her" and Queen Farna Bash said "Please Saahib Antar just give a moment and I will give you my answer as I have to send a messenger to King Kismat, and whatever the answer I will get from King Kismat then I will give you my answer" and Antar said "That is a wise decision, send your messenger and I will remain here for the answer".

Saqr flying on the back of Anta

King Kismat is a very good poem writer, that night he was in his room all by himself and was writing a poem regarding how to praise patience and its bitterness, some of the verses of that poem is as follows:-

Truth is pain and gives one agony inner in the ones heart
Truth is bitter to swallow it need courage to do it
And the one who did it is really one with patience
And that of what I really mean is a strong heart that have that patience
The heart of a wise one which have plenty of know how
Those who have it have won and those who have not they are losers
There is much to gain if one learns how to be patience
As it bears profitable fruits with high values
Patience needs wisdom patience needs care.

After finishing his poem writing, King Kismat suddenly felt that someone pinched his right ear, he knew then that there is messenger came, he said then "Be welcomed Oh! You messenger of Queen Farna Bash, please show yourself up and give me that message which you have to deliver to me" and then in a split of second a small butterfly man appear before him, and said "Peace be upon you Oh! King Kismat" and King Kismat replied "Peace be upon you too Oh! Messenger of my good friend Queen Farna Bash, Tell me what kind of an important message have you brought this night for me" and the little butterfly man then deliver the message in words to King Kismat, he said "My queen told me to tell you that, this night there came a messenger from the Empty quarters desert village, from that group of you know it well, The message is like this, that she has received a message from the desert that Zarza Aarish, a Jinni woman who had join this group, that she want to pay a visit to you here and meet both of you, You King Kismat as well as King Rawaanaz on an urgent meeting to discuss of how she can go ahead to accomplish this mission of finishing off Khurkhush Majangar, and this moment the messenger is waiting for your answer Your Majesty, as this lady will be visiting you this night if you will permit her to come, May I have your answer your Majesty" but for King Kismat, this was a very surprise news to him, especially when it concerns a strange member who has join the group, and above all, this member is not a human but a Jinni, he then said "the message you had deliver, really surprise me, surprise to the extent of knowing not what answer to give you for the group, I am afraid to deny this meeting for some reasons and to except also for some reasons, but allow me please Oh! You good messenger, to leave you for a short while and I will come back very soon so I can give you your answer to take back". And then King Kismat leaves that place and keeps the messenger waiting, he then went to his special visitors diwan, there was that silver bowl with water, he then put his right hand finger in the bowl of water and called for his friend King Rawaanaz, within a second the water in the silver bowl begins to boil with bubbles, and then came a frog from that water and jump out from it, and the frog none other than King Rawaanaz, and he wearing his small crown on his head, King Kismat then direct King Rawaaanaz on his special made table whenever he made a visit to his friend King Kismat, he then greeted his friend King Kismat and said "Peace be upon you King Ksimat" and King Kismat answered and said "Peace be upon you too my dear friend King Rawaanaz, please be welcomed in my humble palace, before anything please allow me to ask and beg for your forgiveness in this late hour call, but there is a messenger came in a short while and still is here, and this messenger came from our friend Queen Farna Bash" and then King Kismat explain in details of all what the messenger has come here for and what he has said to King Kismat, and he asked his friend King Rawaanaz what answer should he give to the messenger to take it back to his Queen, and King Rawaanaz answered King Kismat and said "Oh! King Kismat, please be calm and allow yourself to remain cool, and all because that message which the messenger has brought is a very important message and need not be ignored, time is very short for what going to be done by the group, and this Jinni girl is not foe to us but a real friend who really wants to help, it only needs from us a good faith to believe in her mission, I personally have a great faith in her, and she wants to come here for a good reason which is for and not against us, I think we should give her that chance of seeing her and sit down together and listen to what she has to say to us, Go and tell the messenger that he should go back and tell her Queen that on our side we have no objection but are waiting for the visit of Zarza Aarish to be here. And that we are waiting for her with all the pleasure, but she must come secretly that no one should know that she has come here, and if she will arrive here then she must signal us that she is already here and asking for permission to enter inside the palace" and here is where King Kismat rushed back of where the queen messenger was there waiting, and gave him that answer to send it back to his Queen. And the little butterfly man then disappeared to send back the answer he was given flor his Queen, and Queen Farna Bash when she got the answer from King Kismat, she then told Antar "Oh! My friend Saahib Antar, the answer has come and this what it says in details:-- Tell Zarza that the two Kings are so pleased within her visit to them any time tonight and they are waiting for her arrival to the palace any moment from now, but also that there is condition of which they give, and that she should not go there all by herself, she must be accompanied with me, this means that she must first come here to me and we can go there together as the Kings demands, Go Saahib Antar and inform Zarza of the answers from the Kings, if she agree with the conditions then she may come here and I will be waiting for her so we can go together to meet those Kings, and if she did not agree with those conditions then please Saahib Antar let me know by your call and I will send the message to those Kings that Zarza did not agree with conditions and she will not be there to meet them" and here is where Antar then leave the Kingdom of Queen Farna Bash and return to the village.

Zarza after she has received the answer from those two Kings, she then pass the information to those who were in the house of Mr.Fairuz, she said "My dear elders and the young ones, the time has come for action, I have no other choice but for the time being I have to leave this place and travel very far to where I am going to meet those who will guide me and show me the way of reaching to my mission, and I have to leave with my partners Saqr and Antar and Saharzena, heading to the Kingdom of Queen Farna Bash, because she too will accompany us to that journey far away to the Kingdom of King Kismat ibn Shahzara, I have nothing else to add but please have faith and pray for us that where we are going is that place where all the assistance and the information we need we will get there, and without their help then there is no any possibility of winning this war, we have to bid you goodbye for now and please all the time pray for us for our success and a return safely here. So long and not farewell till we meet again here.

Then Saqr mother requested to speak to his son in private and she was allowed to do so, she took his son into her room and there she said to him "Saqr my dear son, today is that day that befall upon you to prove yourself that you are a son of a brave family, for the first time in your life you are going to face things and situation you had not before experience or face it, you have no choice but to be courageous and brave and thaw all the fear in your mind and your heart, it is true that Allah provide you with a healthy strong and muscular body, but it is not the strongest of your body which will make you to win your war, but the best of your wisdom and knowledge that will help you to win this mission, a little mouse can kill a big huge elephant just by using his tactics and wisdom. I ask you my son, please be obey full to those who are with you and who tell you of what to do, do it with all the brave heart and no fear at all and Allah will guide you and those who will be with you. Secretly Zarza told me that you are going to meet with King Kismat, King Kismat is that King who transformed his children into the swans of which you saw them on the mountain of lake and have found their two rings which they have forgot to take, now I ask you Saqr my dear son, please take with you those two rings, maybe by the will of Allah you may come to meet them and return their rings to them, this is my wish to you, built good relation with them and so they too can built good and better relation with you, that is how you will live with peace in this earth, but also know that not every and each of us are good people, I believe and have all the faith that you will return back to us and with successes, and all the world happiness will be ours." And then they huge and Saqr kissed his mother forehead and her hands and tears were on both in their eyes, and then Saqr said to his mother "Yes Mother, I heard and understood every word you tolled me, I will treasure your will in my heart till I come back again here to kiss your forehead again dear mother, have no fear on me and my partners but I promise you that I will return to this land of where you had bear me dear mother" and Saqr and his mother again hug and share their feelings with more tears and love and prayers. Saqr then went to his room and picks those two rings which he found them on the lake mountain. Saqr and his mother then return to the sitting place where everyone were there waiting for them, and then every and each one of them hug and kiss on the chicks just to bid goodbye, and then all of those in the house came outside and Zarza and Saqr climb on those two horses, Antar and Saharzena and went away out of their sights with their hands waving for goodbye.

Queen Farna Bash was waiting under that huge tree in her Kingdom, no sooner she heard sound of wings and heavy wind was blowing down and then there were two flying horses and two figure riding them coming down to land of where she was, and this was for the first time for Queen Farna Bash to meet Zarza Aarish the jinni girl face to face, then Antar gave his respect to Queen Farna Bash by saying "Salaam to you Queen Farna Bash" and she replied "Wa aleykum Salaam my dear friends, please be welcome to our little Kingdom" and then Antar said "Oh! you good Queen, allow me please to introduce to you our associate and a good friend to this group, Zarza Aarish the Jinni girl from that Kingdom of Khurkhush Majangar, it is her who requested this night to be sent to that Kingdom of King Kismat, so she can meet those two Kings together, King Kismat and King Rawaanaz, she agree to all conditions given to her, and here she is together with us three, came to you so you can guide us to that Kingdom as you also are part of this meeting" and then Antar turned to Zarza and said "Dear sister Zarza, this is Queen Farna Bash who is the Queen of this Kingdom of butterfly people as well as she is the best and close friend to me and to others, you always used to hear her name mentioned between us, today you are here in her Kingdom, please feel proud to meet her in person" here then is where Zarza Aarish climb down from the back of Saharzena and slowly she went of where Queen Farna Bash sat on her special made stand, she then kneeled down to her knees and bow her head down just to give her highest respect to the Queen, then she said "Assalaam aleykum Queen Farna Bash" and Queen Farna Bash replied "Wa aleykum salaam Oh! you good Jinni girl Zarza Aarish, I have heard much about you joining our group and your intentions of fighting this war against Khurkhush Majangar your own King, and save those who still suffering in his jail. I welcome you here in my Kingdom and to this group with a clean heart, It will please me more to know if you will please tell me yourself about your intentions in fighting this war, either you will tell me now or after when you will meet those two great Kings, I do not mind, as those two Kings are waiting for our arrival in the Kingdom of King Kismat Shahzara, for that visit you have requested to meet them" and then Zarza said "I take this opportunity to thank you my dear Queen Farna Bash, for all your assistances and cooperation with me and my partners, these are matters of very important an essential for us all if we join forces hand in hand to play the right role so to overcome the winning targets of our mission against that evil Khurkhush Majangar, I have to cut short my talking now so I can save this value time for other means, and most important is that journey to where our destination is" and Queen Farna Bash said, "it is true that time must be saved, so we must leave this now, but now as we are more than what we said to be there, I have to send the message of requesting permission for others as well, so to be allowed all of us to be there in that urgent meeting" and Zarza said "That is quite a right decision and necessary to do it Queen Farna Bash, it is not the right manner to go to your host with an uninvited guests without seeking permission" and here is where Queen Farna Bash called of one of his personal servant, and it was an old man not more than one foot tall came there flying and floating on the air with his white long bearded, and bow to his Queen, and she called him to come more close to her mouth and she talked to him in his ear, and within a split second he disappear and with few seconds he appeared again in front of his Queen and went close to her ear and talked in low voice without anyone hear it, and then Queen Farna Bash announce and said The visit to the King palace has been permitted for all of us and without objection and with all the pleasure".

King Kismat then instruct one of the palace guard to go up on top of the palace building and watch there up in the sky, and if he see anyone flying in the sky then to direct them to land there where he is, the guard then went up the palace building keep his eyes watching up in the sky, then he heard sort of noise up in the sky and his eyes then begin to search and then he saw one big huge peacock flying in the sky accompany with two horses, first he was stunned as he never saw a flying horses all his life, he then direct them with his flame torch to land of where he has stand. Queen Farna Bash then saw the sign of the guard and tell her party to land there and they all land of where that guard has direct them. On top of the palace there was a big dome and enough place to land all of them, and they did, the guard then rushed down to the palace to inform His Majesty King Kismat about the arrival of the guests, King Kismat then took some of his guards and went up to meet his guests, when he reached up there on the dome of the palace, King Kismat saw there were two horses with two figures and Queen Farna Bash with them, here then Queen Farna Bash bow her head as well as Zarza and Saqr give their respect to the King who came with his guards to meet them, Queen Farna Bash then Greeted the King "Assalaam aleykum Your Majessty King Kismat" and King Kismat returned the greeting and said "Wa aleykum salaam my dear friend and my guests, please be welcomed in my humble palace" and then King Kismat direct his guests inside his palace escorted by those guards. Antar with Saharzena were left behind to remain there on top of the palace.

That palace inside was well decorated with many items of decoration, the floor decorations, and wall decorations and celling decorations, Saqr was just looking and admiring these pieces of decoration with his eyes in every step he was moving inside that palace, until they reached at the private diwan of King Kismat, that diwan of where King Kismat invites only his very important personal, in that diwan there was only one big frog wearing a crown on his head and sitting on his own kind of chair, and that frog was King Rawaanaz, King Kismet then introduce his guests to King Rawaanaz, but Queen Farna Bash as she is familiar guest to King Kismat, she then went to her particular place which was a small pillar where she always go and stand on its top, and left Zarza and Saqr all by themselves still standing in the center of that diwan surrounded by those great Kings in front of them, here then Queen Farna Bash took the opportunity of introducing Zarza and Saqr to those two Kings, she said "Your Majestys King Kismat Shahzara and King Rawaanaz, may I be allowed pleased, to introduce to you these two companion of mine, the lady in front of you is that Zarza Aarish of which you two have heard about her and which she is the main reason of this meeting tonight, she is that Jinni girl who has joining this group in fighting her own King just to save those who are suffering in his jail, before she left her Kingdom in those mountains of King Khurkhush Majangar, she has lost her husband who was one of the very close army commander of Khurkhush Majangar, but just for promoting him, Khurkhush Majangar has arrange a sword fighting between her husband and other commander, who will win that fight will take the higher position in his army, unfortunately Zarza's husband lost in that competition and was killed. And this young lad who's name is Saqr, son of Fairuz bin Haddad who is living in desert of Empty Quarters with his family, this is that family which those who have lost their beloved ones are staying with them, he is the chosen one by Zarza in this mission for he is a brave and a tough young lad, more details of this visits here tonight will be narrated by Zarza herself, as she has many to tell and explain to you. Please Zarza the gentlemen are waiting to hear from you of why you have asked for this urgent meeting to meet them" then King Kismat clap his hand for a call, and some palace servants hurriedly enter the diwan, he asked them to bring more chairs for the standing guests, and more chairs were brought for Zarza and Saqr to sit with. King Kismat then invited Zarza and Saqr to sit on those chairs, but before they sat, Zarza request permission to speak, and she was allowed to speak, she said "It is my duty now, to thank you Oh! You two great Kings, on my behalf and on the behalf of my companion this young lad Saqr, to thank you for many things, but first of all to thank you for your hospitality as well as excepting our request to be here with you in this emergency meeting of which I have asked" and then Zarza and Saqr put their right hands on their chests and bow as to give that respect to those two Kings as excepting the invitation of going to sit for the meeting, and King Kismat and King Rawaanaz also put their hands on the chests as giving back their respect to these two special guests on this night whom have came very far away for a special meeting in discussing the mission, then King Kismat said "We are pleased of your visits to this humble palace and to the main reason of your requested Zarza in discussion of our mission, we assured you that in every step you will take to finish of this evil Jinni Khurkhush Majangar, we will be with you, even if it will include ourselves to join this mission then know that we are ready to do that, please tell us of what you came for and what are your plans and we are willing to hear them"

Then Zarza started to give long story of her plans and how she will go there to that Kingdom for the attack of King Khurkhush Majangar, she said "My dear Your Majestys, first you must know that Khurkhush Majangar is not an easy target, he is a very clever one, he is one of the Jinni who is so powerful, it is not the power of our army that can destroy him, but it is the tactics and wisdom of know how to attack him, that can work better I hope so, none of any of you can be able to reach of where he is but I can, but if there is anyone who believe that he can reach Khurkhush then that person can only reach there with my help, I have long story and history of why I have left that Kingdom, Queen Farna Bash has explained to you just one among those many, but since I left my Kingdom I have never returned back yet, and I promise King Khurkhush Majangar the day I left there that I will never return until I will get of what I was looking for, and I got of what I was looking for but unfortunately I could never have it or maintain it as the rules of Allah did not allow me to have so, in the end I have to allow myself to except the fact and just remain as friends and never as a family. After so many months and days have passed by, I have to return to my homeland but I will never forgets you human beings for showing me many things of which I did not know before, I have learn a lot and except of what I did not had before, that is your faith, I have learned to believe in Allah as the creator and understood that I am nothing but just a creation of that Allah, and he is a Master while I am just his slave, a slave only to obey and not to challenge him, a slave just to follow and never to lead after him, a slave just to believe in his faith and never to live a life without any faith, and that is how I have changed a lot and became a faithful servant of my Master Allah and put all my trust in him and I am now a follower of his Prophet Muhammad. If it was not for my friend the camel, then for sure I would never know or understand of all of which I have learned from him and have perused me in believing that we are all Allah's creations and we have been created just to believe and have that strong faith that whatever he teaches us to do we must do it, and not for him but for ourselves, as in the end there is a day of judgment where we all Allah's creations going to be accounted for, for what we had done in this earth.

Now if we come to the agenda of our main topic, first of all I have to request you King Kismat to allow and permit your son-in-law Shuhur jaan to join us, for his is a well known bravery of being an expert archer, because I have a plan for him and this young lad here Saqr, this will be there essential plan during that time of attacking to destroy Khurkhush Majangar, and that plan will have to work before his army find out that there is a war going on. Khurkhush Majangar needs to be attacked secretly and with such tactics of fooling him, I know that place of where to perused him to believe in me and follow me there, somewhere in one of cave in his Kingdom, that of where I will take these two young lads and hide them without being seen, of how they will not be seen, this is the mission of that great King, and that King is none other than King Rawaanaz, and he is here and my next request from you King Rawaanaz that you must cover them with your power without been seen, you must make them invisible for all of this mission until we will accomplish our mission, but I only can communicate with them with our voices but unseen.

The plan of attacking Khurkhush Majangar will be by only three of us and no other, each one of us will have his duty to do of how and when to attack without failing, and the attack will take place at the same time from all three of us, so this attack should be very effective that will never give any chance this evil Jinni to stand again. Your Majesties, you better know that to destroy Khurkhush Majangar is to destroy the whole of his army, if they will know that Khurkhush Majangar has been killed and destroyed then for sure all of them they will surrender. These are my secret plan of which I came here to seek your help in joining hand with me so we can accomplish this mission secretly. I also want to point out to you your Highnesses that all the wars have two, to live or to die, and this you know it well. Secondly this our answers to you when you have asked before from your messengers of what is our plans of actions, so this is our plan and action of attacking that evil King who had destroyed our Kingdom and our people, the time has come for him now to be wipe out completely. I have come here for two, first to give the answer of our plan and request you to give us the help we need, and secondly to let you know of how we are going to attack Khurkhush Majangar and without even mentioned this plan to others in our group, they know nothing of this plan but yet they have trusted me and even giving me their own child to join hand just by trusting me and having faith that our mission will work out and we will win this war, and we have their blessings and their prayers, and we great faith that if we will get your blessings and your prayers as well as your helping hands, then we will have such a great protection and no one will be able to destroy us Insha'Allah. Your Majestys, I have talked for a long time now, I have talked for what I have come here for to talk, I have talked of our mission which also concerned others like these two young lads and there are two horses above this building who are Jinnis horses, who also are able to fly in the sky. If on your side you have any question which you need answer, please do not hesitate to ask me now, and all because this is the right time as there will be no more better time then this, when we leave this place this night it will be that night of no return until we accomplish our mission."

The two Kings and the Queen, all that time were remained in silence, just listen to Zarza Aarish of what her plans are in fighting this war with Khurkhush Majangar, no one said anything, as they do not know of what to add or of what to reduce in that long explanation of Zarza in her master plan of attacking Khurkhush Majangar, because that was the main issue here which for such a long time were disturbing the minds of many others as well as of these three Royals, how and who will be able to go there in those mountains of where there are strong army of jinnis, and that was a question of King Rawaanaz before, that who will be able to go there in the mountains of Kingdom of Jinnis, and here is where King Rawaanaz break the silence and said "My lady Zarza, we thank you for all the details of which you have come here to share with us in your master plan of attacking this evil Jinni Khurkhush Majangar, what I see in my mind is that yours is a very firm plan and has big hope in it, to win or to lose is a secret only Allah knows, yet we pray and ask Allah to help us and make this mission to be a success one, and Allah said to us through his Prophets and his books, that REQUEST FROM ME AND I WILL PROVIDE OF WHAT YOU HAVE ASKED, we all will join hands with those others who are far away in praying and begging Allah to protect and make you conquer your mission. The idea of wanting Shuhur jaan to join you in this mission, is the best idea and I support it, and all because I have seen this in a long time ago that this young lad is the bravest among all and he is very important figure in this mission, and that I have mentioned previously to my friend here King Kismat, Shuhur jaan is the right choice for this mission, this is the right time for Shuhur jaanto be called here and be informed of this mission and its importance, and what is his role in this mission will be and who he is going to fight in this mission, and that this mission is a mission of coming back or no return, the mission of do or die. I will allow that all which concern Shuhur jaan to my dear friend here King Kismat as he is closer related to Shuhur jaan, and he is the only person who can make his parents understand as well as Shuhur jaan's wife who is his daughter, that it is how important for Shuhur jaan to join this mission for his bravery and the best archer in the whole of this region" and then King Kismat said "Yes, I also agree with this master plan of which Zarza has brought before us, because as my dear friend here mentioned before that there is no in any human army which will be able to penetrate through the strong army of those Jinnis, but now my heart has full of hope and confidance on this master you have brought to us Zarza, though the situation is full of danger but a human being was created always to face any danger in this world, no matter who will live to succeed or will die and fail. Fortunately for Shuhur jaan is still here with me in my palace with his wife as well as his parents, yet they did not return to their home town in that palace of where I allow them to live in, please allow and excuse me for just a little while so I can go and inform Shuhur jaan and his wife regarding this mission and try to persuade him to join this mission without any obligation, and regarding his parents I will allow him to go to them and explain to them in his own way and make them understand the importance of this mission and allow him to join this mission with their blessings, as there is no more time to lose now, please excuse me." And King Kismat left his diwan and his guests, and went out to meet his family for that discussion.

When King Kismat left the diwan, Zarza told those who were with her there in the diwan "regarding of how I will go back to my Kingdom, first I will go back myself only, and I will see King Khurkhush Majangar and try to pursued him that I have come back to my Kingdom and that I have failed to get of what I was looking for, it will be my responsibility to try and find the right place of where I can hide my two partners, somewhere in the cave without being seen, what I request from you King Rawaanaz is that you must hide these two young lads to be invisible by using your power, as I know that you have it. When we will leave here we will go back to Queen Farna Bash Kingdom, there I will leave the lads and the horses and I will go alone first, and they will wait for my signal which I will send to them if the situation allowed and the hidden place is safe for them. I hope that each of you have understood me well, if you have any question to ask then ask it now, as there will be no any other opportunity for questions and answers" not Queen Farna Bash and neither King Rawaanaz has any question to ask but then the door of the diwan was opened and King Kismat enter inside the diwan with two young lads, a young man and a young lady, and immediately when they enter those two young lads bow and give their respect to those two Royals who were in the diwan as well as Saqr, then King Kismat said "Your Highnesses, allow me please to introduce to you my daughter Nazniyna and her husband Shuhur jaan, I haveexplained to them and gave them all the information of our mission and it plans, and they are willing to join this group, specially for Shuhur jaan who said that this is a rare opportunity and for him is chance of life and do not want to avoid it but to be part of it, My daughter on her behalf has permit her husband to join this group and also to take part of this mission though it is a risk but she said it is worth to this risk in saving others and stop this cruelty once and for all then live in fear and allow others to suffer" then King Kismat turn his head and face Shuhur jaan and said "Shuhur jaan, please allow me to introduce to you this young lad here, his name is Saqr bin Fairuz bin Haddad, he will be among your partner in this mission of which you will be together all the time, and this here is Zarza Aarish a Jinni girl, who will lead this mission, now we are complete group here, and there will be no turn back but to go ahead only, to do it or to die for it."

King Rawaanaz then called those two young boys Saqr and Shuhur jaan in front of him, he then told them to put their right hand second finger in his mouth together, and they did obey that instruction and within a few seconds and in front of all those who are there, those two young boys begin slowly to be invisible until they have all disappeared in front of everyone eyes, King Rawaanaz then asked "are you two still here in this diwan?" and there was a voice answered "Yes, we are here" then King Rawaanaz said "from now on you will see but not to be seen, this is the condition you will be and nobody will be able to see you, though your human being body odor smell will be noticed by those Jinnis but they will never see you, and this is the tactic which will be our main weapon to use it in this mission, all the instruction and command of how and where will be under the command of Zarza Aarish, for you two you have nothing to question but to obey only, when you will be at the battle ground which will be a secret place, each one of you will be instructed to perform his duty the way it needed. You Shuhur jaan will be using your bow and arrows to hit your target and that target will be the heart of Khurkhush Majangar, and you Saqr, when Zarza will signal you then immediately put your right hand finger in your mouth and suck it, and this act will transform you into that kind of animal who use poison as his weapon to attack, if your poison will penetrate in this evil enemy then for sure he will not survive at all, for now I will not tell you what kind of animal you will be, let us give time a chance to tell that for itself, you just prepare yourself of whatever you will be you will be, just known this that after your transformation you will gain more strength in your body, you must act exactly as that animal do in his natural way of life when he attacks, do you understood Saqr?" and Saqr answered "Yes Your Majesty, I did understand very well and I am ready for any command I will be instructed to do and without fear" and Shuhur jaan also replied, "And me too", and they all stood and went up to where the horses are, and they hug to each other and bid farewell, Shuhurjaan then climb on the back of Saharzena and Saqr on the back of Antar, and Queen Farna Bash and Zarza they have the ability to fly by themselves, then they all flown up in the sky and disappear in the darkness of the night.

There night journey took them up to the Kingdom of Queen Farna Bash together with her, when they have reached there, Zarza then asked Queen Farna Bash to be host to Shuhur jaan and Saqr as well as those two horses. She said "My dear Bash, I have to leave my partners with you here in your Kingdom, as our mission is on the other side of your Kingdom, it will take me just few time to reach there, please wait for my signal of which I will send it through Saahib Antar, to come of where I have found the right place for them to hide and the right time to enter in the Kingdom without been seen, though the young lads are invisible but the horses are not, I am afraid that, till I know how the situation is there then they have to be here for a while" Zarza is courageous girl who fear for nothing, if she decide to do something then nothing can stop her not to do it, and that is exactly what she has decide this night, that this night will be the night of ending Khurkhush Majangar. She knows that she put herself as well those others in the danger, but there is no other way back for cancellation of this mission. Enough should be enough and that day should be today, these evil doing must be stopped once and for all. Zarza then said to the group "I have to go and find where is Khurkhush Majnangar and try to pursued him to trust me, if I will get a help from any friend there, then that will help a lot, yet I do not lose hope also to search for someone whom can give me some information of Khurkhush and I know search a person who will do it either voluntary or by force.

CHAPTER TWENTY-TWO

(The tough fight of Khurkhush Majangar ends)

KHURKHUSH MAJANGAR WAS IN HIS hiding cave with his close advisers including his personal security guards commander, but also beneath that cave is where all the human prisons are jailed. Shamekhashar enter in that cave place of where Khurkhush Majangar all the time stay, when he was near him, he requests permission to come closer, he was permitted and then came closer, very close up to the near of Khurkhush ear, he then whisper into Khurkhush ear, and Khurkhush open his eyes and was stunned and surprised and asked "is this solid news?" and Shameshakhar answered "Yes you Majesty, it is true information and without doubts" Khurkhush Majangar then stood of where he was sited and started to pace in the room while screeching his bear, suddenly he stopped pacing and request Shameshakhar to come of where he was standing, he then whisper something in Shameshakhar and ear and then with his eyes signal ask him to leave the place, and Shame shakhar obeyed the order and left the place. Khurkhush Majangar then returned to where he was sitting and loudly announce so everyone in that place could hear clearly, he said "All of you who are here, hear this, one of my close subject who left this Kingdom for quite a while now and with my permission to go and find of what she was looking for, has returned back to our Kingdom, what has brought her back I do not know but the right to return back here is her right, let us wait for the time to tell us what has brought her back here, and what she have brought from where she had gone, I Khurkhush Majangar am here and waiting to meet my loyal subject with all pleasure.

Zarza Aarish in her searching that night he came to place of where she found a cave which she believe that is very suitable to for her operation, and said to herself "This wll be the right place to bring my partners and hide them here waiting for the right moment to attack, as well as the place for meeting Khurkhush Majangar here, I hope my plan will work well. Now is the time to signal my partners to come here immediately" and then Zarza send her telepath message to Antar, asking them to come to that cave which she has found and which will be the better battle ground of their creating war against Khurkhush Majangar. Immediately when Antar got the telepath message from Zarza, he informed his partners of the situation, and that they must leave Queen Farna Bash Kingdom right now and go to that place of where Zarza has found, that place is a quite a huge cave and Zarza believe that will be a perfect place to be as the battle ground to destroy Khurkhush Majangar. Antar as he is from that Kingdom took the lead, and they all fly together between Antar, Saqr, Shuhur jaan and Saharzena, and Antar was on the lead with invisible Saqr on his back, while Shuhur jaan was riding Saharzena on her back, they fly in the dark of night until they have reached that particular place of where Zarza have told them to land, then they lend on that mountain of where there was a big and huge cave in front of them, the cave entrance was so large that the whole of elephant can pass through without touching any side of the cave walls, Zarza was outside that cave waiting for them and after they have lend she said to them "Saqr and Shuhur jaan must follow me inside the cave but you Antar and Saharzena should not remain here, you must right now fly back to the Kingdom of Queen Farna bash and wait for my telepath message for any further information. Antar and Saharzena nodded and then fly away at the same moment, and Zarza spoke to those invisible young lads, she said "please follow me inside the cave and be very close with me, but whenever I give you instruction or to talk to you then you must reply me in voices, as I cannot not see you but only imagine that you are here with me, then know that your voices are the only communication which assuring me that you are here. I have to leave you two here all by yourselves and go to look for Khurkhush Majangar, be on alert, though you are invisible and useen but your human smell is all around this place, and this will raise suspicious and doubts to any Jinni who will come here, what remain ahead of us will be a team work, we have to fight and strike together and at the same time. Also remember that Khurkhush Majangar is not an easy target to destroy, as he is too very clever more than us, but it is our hope and the faith of our parents and others in their group prayers and blessing that we will win this war, have you understood me?" and then the voices answered "Yes Zarza, we did understood you" "My young brothers remember now that we have already arrived at that battle ground of death, no one knows who will die or who will survive here,

But this night should be that night that death must come here no matter to who, either us or Khurkhush Majangar. No matter what, but please do not leave this place, or take any action against my instruction, and if anything will happen to me there where I go, then know that for sure you will be informed by any means, and if for any reason that I will be in danger or have been caught, then you will get my message by feeling your body temperature to rise high, and I will send a telepath to Antar and Saharzena to come immediately and take you away from this place, but if you will feel nothing, then know that I am alright and in safe. Do we understood one another my brothers?" and the voices answered "Yes Zarza, we do understand very well, we wish you good luck and safe return" and she said:" Thank you my younger brothers" and then she left the place and disappear.

Zarza Aarish facing Shamekhashar with swords fighting

Zarza then fly above high in the sky, very high in the sky and for a good reason, she wants to know are there any Khurkhush Majangar spies above in the sky?, and also she wants to know did Khurkhush got the information from his spies that Zarza is already in the Kingdom? Because if the spies have the information of her arrival then for sure there will be tight security high in the sky and they will be looking for her, but also Zarza is that kind of Jinni girl who is very clever and bright minded, within a few seconds high there, she felt of little sparks of fire are coming on her direction, and they were coming at full speed, she immediately understood that those sparks are the army of Khurkhush and are there to welcome her, suddenly she felt someone held her hands, she asked "I ask you who have hold me, do you hold to welcome me or to arrest me?" no answer she have received but suddenly she felt that she was pulled down in a very high speed, and when she was very near to the earth she felt those holding hands have released her, and then before she touch the land she saw a hand without anybody appeared before her in front of her face, the hand then signaled her to go to the right, Zarza before following instruction she looked at the right direction to see what is there, she found there was a small open on the mountain, something like a cave door and there was a figure standing there, it was a little dark there and the face of that figure was unrecognizable, but behind that figure and inside that cave was very bright, Zarza then touched herself down on earth and begin to walk, she went to the direction of where that figure was standing, she then reached where that figure was, and the figure surprisingly bowed to Zarza to give her a respect, and then that figure signal to Zarza to follow him inside the cave, Zarza did not urge but obeyed the instruction and went inside the cave following behind that figure, then that cave inside it turned out to be a well decorated living house with many ornaments everywhere, and after a long walking then they have reached at one of the biggest well decorated door with beautiful patens, then the figure signed Zarza to remain and wait there in front of that door and he then disappeared and enter through that door without being open but pass through it, but not everyone can pass through that door but only who are entitled and who are invited to pass through, then that figure came back through the same door by just penetrating through and asked Zarza to follow him the same way, beyond that door Zarza found no one but only it was a very huge big room well decorated, but surprisingly that figure was not in the room, it was only Zarza who was inside that room though they enter together. Zarza then just stand in the center of that room all by herself and wait, Zarza was very darefull and full of brave heart and has no fear at all. But then she heard a voice called her name "Zarza, what has brought you back in this Kingdom and in this time of the night after you had left and disappeared for a long time" and Zarza answered "Pardon me, Oh! you invisible speaker, but I will not answer to any of your question blindly without yourself being present here, show yourself up and ask me face to face and I will give you the answers to all your questions" then the voice said "That is not compulsory for you to know me or to appear before you, you just answer the asking questions only" and then Zarza said "That will impossible on my side for me to speak to someone who is invisible, if you don't show yourself up, then I will account you as a weak person and afraid to face me, now you better decide, either show yourself up to me or allow me to complete my journey" Then suddenly Zarza felt a hand touched her shoulder from her back, she then turned her head to look back and see who is that touching her shoulder, she was surprised and anger raised in her mind, as that hand was the hand of her enemy, that enemy who had coursed the death of her husband in a duel fight to compete for the higher position of becoming more close to Khurkhush Majangar, and that person was none other than Shamekhashar. Zarza never forgot the face from that day of a duel between him and her husband. Anger raised more in her mind every now and then, she wished she could just jump on him and kill him or be killed by him, but then she remembered that responsibility of which was the reason of come here and those two young lads who are in a very dangerous hide out, she then remain to be patience but push off that hand on her shoulder, and she said "Shamekhashar! Are you the one who wants to know of why Zarza is back of where she belongs? On this land of where Zarza was born and got married and lost her husband from that man likes you? If you have other question regarding other issues then you can ask me, but this is not your concern and you do not have that right to question me on my birth place. For your information, know that I am not a refugee here and not either a criminal, this is my country and anyone who returned to his country is not a criminal but his or her right" and Shamekhashar said then "Zarza, for the position I am holding as head of the security intelligence for the security of the our King Khurkhush Majangar and all the Jinni living here in this Kingdom, I have their right to ask anyone who enter in this Kingdom without informing, and this is my first priority to do that, though it is true that you are not a stranger in our Kingdom neither a stranger to me, but it is your absent for a long period from our Kingdom and no one knows where you were that is the reason of our doubts on you, we do not know with whom you were associated, with whom you were living with, what are your intentions of returning back, what secrets are within you which brought you back, all these doubts on you are raising suspicion, therefore you must answer my questions, and this is an order and not a request from you" and Zarza said "the journey which I took to bring me back was a long one and I am so tired and I need a rest, so I Zarza have no more time to answer you, if, as you have said that you gave me an order and you are not requesting me, then let me tell you that I refuse to obey your order, you can have your responsibility and I also have mine, and one of my responsible is not to deal with you and take any instruction and any order from you killer of my husband, now choice is your either you leave me alone or either you face me with sword fighting and see for yourself that who will take order from who, you may chose your weapon and you will find me ready to face you anytime you are ready, and maybe it will be the best of a night for you, because if you will win this fight with me tonight then for sure tonight will be that night to surrender my hand to you in marriage as you had ask me before and I refuse it, and if I win, then know that your life will be in my hands and I will not give me a moment more to live, now give me your answer of what will be" then Shamekhashar said "Zarza you seem to be very rude and manner less, you do not even show me a respect as you know that I am too powerful figure in this Kingdom, where are your manners? Ok! If that is so, then let it be, I except your term of swords fighting with you, let us enter in this battleground of which you have suggested, winner should take of what you have suggested, and I have excepted willingly, we will fight with swords" and then Shamekhashar went to the wall and took his weapon which was hanging there and invite Zarza to pick hers, Zarza did the same she took her weapon of a sword and the face one another and the fight begin furiously, they fought with speed and each one of them tried very hard just to get that chance of penetrating his sword to the other but could not, Shamekhashar was very surprised of how Zarza fights with her sword and with great energy, as he was already feeling the pleasure of those strong swords strikes on his sword and that made him to use more strength. Shamekhashar then stopped a little and said "Now I believe myself of my doubts over you Zarza, you did not came back here in our Kingdom for nothing, you must have intentions, and you intentions are dangerous one, if that day of which I face your husband and killed him and you were there watching, and you could fight the same way I face you today, I am sure you would jump from your seat and defend your husband, but you did not take any action, that it means that all these days of your upsent here and wherever you was, you went to learn more of how to fight better so you can revenge the death of your husband, is this not true Zarza?" and Zarza said to him "Reduce asking many question and protect yourself from death, as this night will be the last night for you Shamekhashar to live on this land, fight and prove to me that you are a better fighter than me and try to win this fight" and here then the sword fighting was so in speed and each one of them tried to overtake with sword her opponent, yet the force of using power strength has started to show its weakness to Shamekhashar, he was breathing heavily by now and breath was coming from his mouth, Zarza noticed that, and took advantage of his weakness and put more heavy strikes of her sword on him though he was defending himself with his sword in all direction of which Zarza strikes, Shamekhashar by this time all his energy of using his strength has drained away, he has no more power of strength to fight much longer, Zarza when she saw that Shamekhashar was powerless, she said to him "You have no more strength in you to fight me Shamekhashar, surrender and obey all my orders or continue and allow me to finish you off" Shamekhshar then announce

"I surrender, and will no longer fight you Zarza, truly you are a better fighter then your husband, in whole my life I never saw or met any female Jinni who can fight furiously like you did Zarza, you fight with technique and well, and know how to strike your sword to your opponent, please Zarza give me back my life, allow me to live and I promise to obey all your orders" then Zarza said "Do you have that heart to obey all my orders Shamekhashar? Do you know how hard my orders are to obey? Are you willing to sacrifice everything and obey me and of what I will ask you to do Shamekhashar?" then he said "No matter how hard your orders will be, I will sacrifice my life for them, rather than die now with your sword Zarza, I promise to be your sincere servant, but please do not finish me now but give me another chance to live and help you in all your command" and Zarza said "Shamekhashar, if you did not know me well, then today I gave you just one of my lesson, know me well Shamekhashar, as this is Zarza Aarish, not that Zarza Aarish whom you saw when you killed her husband but this Zarza Aarish who came to wipe out all the oppressors who are destroying all others happiness, now stand up and sit in front me" while the point of Zarza sword was on his throught" listen careful to what I will tell and command you to do, yet I warn you Shamekhashar, know that you cannot at all escape or betray me, because you better bear in your mind that wherever you will be I will be there too, I ask you now, please, for your own good sake, behave and be faithful to me, mind yourself very much by taking precaution that you should not try at all to go against me, remember this promise you gave just now, that I should allow you to live and that you will obey my all commands. From now onward, enough should be enough, no more cruelty and oppressing on this land of ours, it is true that we are Jinni's but there is no any reason of why we should not live together with other Gods creations, with peace and harmony and friendship with them, why should always be us who create misunderstanding and hate against others?, why we are the one always to tortures others like human beings, are they not Gods creation like us? Are we really pleasing ourselves in doing that or we just please particular one? You Shamekhashar, I am asking you, are you really pleased and happy in what is going on here by taking prisoners human beings who passing in these mountains peaceful but capturing and tortures them? You just act as foolish person by obeying your master Khurkhush Majangar to whatever he commands you to do and you do it even though it is against God will or against nature, for all creation must live equal, till when this oppressing will continue without stopping? Can you please Shamekhashar give me answers to all these questions?" truly these questions of Zarza started to effects Shamekhashar's mind, as he was silent for a short time and then spoke "Oh! you good Zarza, believe me if I tell you that even me not pleased of what Khurkhush Majangar is doing, but I have no power to deny him as I am his loyal servant, I must obey him if I want to remain with him or to remain alive, as the human says, a messenger should not be killed, but after what you have explain in your long speech just now, you have open my mind, and I believe that what Khurkhush Majangar is doing is not right, Yes, the time has come that enough should be enough, I agree with you Zarza, and I am ready now to join hand with you for anything against this evil doing but to bring peace in this Kingdom for all us Gods creation to share this land and live in peace" Then Zarza said "Well done! Shamekhashar, this is the saying of a man, who stands for justice. Now listen to this of what I am going to tell and instruct you to do, there is no time to lose from now, we must work in hurry before the sun rise, I want you to go to Khurkhush Majangar and do all you can do to perused him to have trust in you and bring him in that cave of the south of the Kingdom as I will be there waiting for you, I know that he has the information the I am back here in his Kingdom and he wants very much to see me, and proof to that is you, you would never follow me if you do not have information about me coming back to this mountains, tell him that Zraza has came back with a very hot information about the human beings and their plans of attacking this Kingdom, but she wants to tell it to you only and no one else. This information may put interest in him to come and see me there. I promise you Shamekhashar, if we will win against Khurkhush Majangar, then you will never be forgotten of any blessings each of us will get, and every citizen of this Kingdom will never forget you, this is Zarza promise to you and Zarza promise never fell down. Shamekhashar then answered "I agree to do that as you have ordered me Zarza, I will put all my efforts to pursued Khurkhush Majangar to believe in what I will tell him and come with me to that south cave, then Zarza said "Ok Shamekhashar, do it now and in hurry before the sun rise, waste no time as time is on our side for now".

Khurkhush Majangar was in his cave all by himself sitting and enjoying the shouting of the tortures of which those human being are being tortures in his cave prisons, but the way he seems he was not in a good mood since he got that information about Zarza Aarish is back in his Kingdom, but he has no further information, every now and then he was asking "where is Shamekhashar, can anyone tell me where is he?" within a few second a message came that Shamekhashar is asking permission to enter in the King's court, and Khurkhush said "Permission is granted" and Shamekhashar enter the King's court, and Khurkhush asked him "since you left this place here what has delayed you not come back and bring me more of this Zarza news?" and Shamekhashar replied "My Master! Let it not bother you much of Zarza news, the fact about her is that she is here and I went to see her and she came with very important news regarding the human being plan to attack our Kingdom and save those of their relatives who are in our prisons, I ask her to feed me with more information regarding the attack which human beings are planning to do, she refuse completely to tell me anything else but she said that she must see you in private and alone so to give you this information and no one else, she has asked me to deliver the message to you personally so if you are interested to get more information from her then you have to go of where she is and meet her there, and at the time being she is at that south cave all by herself. But my Master, I think it is not advisable for you to go there alone and all by yourself, because we do not know what Zarza intentions are, I ask you please let me come with you just as matter of precaution and security if you have decided to go to her. Also Zarza insists that your visit to her should be tonight before sunrise as she also is afraid that those with her among the human being should not doubt her of being your spy, otherwise if they will found out that she has come here all by herself without the knowledge of others, they may change their entire plan and would not go ahead with their attack, and this is what Zarza has told me to tell you Oh! Master." Shamekhashar here did use the best of his diplomacy of not lying to Khurlkhush Majangar, as Khurkhush is not an easy Jinni to fool him, though he twisted his words to try in making Khurkhush of what he was telling is true, though he told him the true part yet

Khurkhush could have his doubt about Shamekhashar story, Shame khashar wants only Khurkhush to be pursued and agree to go there in the south cave and meet Zarza, so what remain will be the master plan of Zarza to finish off this evil Jinni. Khurkhush Majangar felt that Shamekhashar did not tell him all the truth, and here is where Khukhush stood up with high anger and smoke begin to come out from his mouth and his ears and the he started to change color and became all red figure and the turned into a big ball of fire, and then that ball of fire fly above and quickly came down on Shamekhashar and burn him, Shamekhashar felt the burning of the fire on his body and started to cry loudly with that fire pain and said "My Master! My Master! Please save me! Save me!" then from that fire the voice of Khurkhush talk and said "It seem you Shamekhashar do not want to live longer, so it is better that I will help you now to take your life away, you are trying to fool me and lying to me and hide the truth?" though Shamekhashar did not hide the truth, what he said was really the truth, he then beg more to Khurkhush and said "Oh! Master, please trust my words and have faith in me, what I have told is completely true, Zarza is really there in the south cave and the information I gave you is what I have learn from Zarza, human being have the plan of attacking your Kingdom and release those who are in your prisons, Please Oh! Master believe me and waste no more time but go to where Zarza is and you will learn more about the attack, please go Master as time is very short for you". Here I have to explain more about the ball of fire, that fire is not like as any other fire which is very hot and burn but this fire is just a cool fire and does not burn but only produce high grade heat which gives a mild pain. Here then that fire slowly started to deem away until the figure of Khurkhush Majangar appear again as himself, and said "You Shamekhashar, if you were telling me the truth about what Zarza has told and that there is really attack on my Kingdom, and Zarza has the complete information, then I will go to the south cave and meet her, but Shamekhashar, you know me well, as from now on you will be a half dead and half alive figure, and you will remain here in my court and never try to move or leave this place, but if this is your and Zarza plan to destroy me, then know that you both will be destroyed before me, and I forbid you to leave this place until I will return from meeting Zarza in that south cave" and then Khukhush Majangar point his hand to Shamekhashar and here appeared a big chain and that chain then started to bind the whole body of Shamekhashar tightly and pull him to where there was a pillar and bind him there on that pillar, and then disappear in the thin air.

In the south cave of where Zarza is waiting for Khurkhush to come, suddenly some fear came into her mind, she said to herself [Khurkhush is a very clever Jinni and I am all alone here to meet him, and my partners are far away from here, what will happen to me if this Jinni will over power me and cannot fight him all by myself?] Zarza then decided in a split second decision to go quickly and bring his partners here before Khurkhush Majangar has arrive and she disappear within a second and came back with Saqr and Shuhur jaan still invisible and put each one of them to his position and gave them their last instruction, Zarza felt now she has support of her partners, she felt comfortable. Her partners were also not comfortable because it only remain about two hours and the sun will rise, but Zarza had hope within her that Shamekhashar will not betray her but will stand to his words as he has promised, but the truth was that Shamekhashar did betrayed Zarza to Khurkhush, as he gave Khurkhush all the information of the attack by these human beings, but his betrayal was not in an evil faith but was in a good faith that he did to win the confidence of Khurkhush to believe in him in that information he gave him so he will believe and be persuaded to go and meet Zarza and that works well, though Shamekhashar was suffering from the punishment he got from Khurkhush Majangar. Inside that south cave of where Zarza and his invisible partners were waiting for the arrival of Khurkhush, suddenly they felt cold was coming inside the cave, and then there was a strong wind entering inside the cave, then that cold begin to increase more and more to a frozen point, and then all the wall inside that cave begin to change color and became white, the whiteness of the ice, and then the whole of the cave became like a cold chamber with full of ice, Zarza then said to her partners "My brothers, please try your best to resist this cold, as this is the tactic and the sign that Khurkhush is on his way to be here, he did this purposely to scare other, so they should leave here if there is anyone more than me here, this it means that Shamekhashar did his duty as he has promised me, there is no much time here now, I want you both to prepare yourselves and be ready for the attack, just wait for my signal only, and you Saqr, now is that time of which King Rawaanaz told you to suck your thumb, do it now" and Saqr did that, he put his right hand thumb in his mouth and suck it, and he felt some liquid came out of his thumb and was testing like honey and very sweat, he swallow that liquid, he then start to feel hot temperature in his body, and then he felt his body begins to change and something came out from his body, he then saw that those were legs with spike which came out from his body, and he was all transformed into a huge Tarantula, a most deadly spider, but all this transformation none other saw it but only himself, as he was invisible, he than saw after the transformation that he have now eight legs and two black fangs in front of him and he can also have the power to produce silk and create a web. Zarza then instructed the (Saqr) spider to climb on the wall and remain there on the center of the ceiling waiting, and she told him "when you will get your good chance climb down using your silk thread and strike him with your fangs and put all your poison in his body. And you Shuhur jaan, whenever you get a good opportunity to send your arrows on your target of hitting Khurkhush Majangar, then hit him and let your arrow penetrate in his chest and reach to his heart" Zarza then prepare herself for anything that will happen here this day, the important thing she did, was to take that sword from Shamekhashar room, the same sword which she fought with Shamekhashar, then she did find a right place somewhere behind the rock and hide that sword, a place very close to her. Then suddenly a high speed wind enter in the cave with plenty of dust, the wind was so cold that make everyone there to shiver, but Zarza stand in the center of that cave just waiting of whatever will happen she can face it, then that wind begin to circle with speed and change itself like a tornado or a huge pillar, and Zarza seem to be a very small figure in front that huge pillar of wind of which still circling, then slowly that wind begin to reduce it circling speed and slowly coming down while begin to transform into a human shape, and became a huge male figure with white hair and beards, on his head there were two horns, this figure was really scaring to look at, his eyes were wild and shining. After he became complete in human shape but huge and tall, he said to Zarza "Zarza, you have become very intelligent to this standard? Instead of you coming to see me, you are asking me to come and see you? you have been absent in our Kingdom for a long time now, today you came back with the information which you said that there people who are planning to attack me here, let me ask you, is there anyone, any living figure can dare to attack me? Who are those human beings who want to do their attack here in my Kingdom? Who is that person who can be so brave and can just try to attack me Khurkhush Majangar without fearing of his life? Who is he? Tell me Zarza" and here is where Zarza never showed her anger to Khurkhush but use her wisdom, because she was just waiting for the right chance and at the right moment to strike with her partners, Zarza then said "Oh you Good King of this mountains Kingdom,

Allow me please to greet you after so many days of my absent here and of course with your permission, secondly, regarding those human beings who are planning to come and attack here, this is true information and without doubts, because this planning I have heard it myself, there is a group of people whom their relatives are here in your prisons, this group is the one which is going to do the attacking and if they get any chance to kill you then they will do it as well" then Khurkhush said "Listen Zarza, I do not care, I do not fear those human beings, he who thinks that he can come here and save those who in my prisons then I welcome him or them,

I give them the chance, let them try to be here in my Kingdom and see what will be their fate. If you have other information more this one of human beings then gives it to me, tell me of what you have learn then and what you have seen from these human being of which I have not seen, this is what I want to hear and know, please tell me" and Zarza then said "Oh! Khurkhush, what new I have brought with me is just advice, I have come to advise you to release those who are in your prisons, give them their freedom which they have earn it and you have denying it for them, many of their relatives are suffering with agony and torments because they do not know what kind of conditions are their relatives are, are they alive or are they dead, parents are crying day night for their children and children are suffering a lot because their parents are not with them, you just like this just like a game to entertain yourself and make others to suffer for your pleasure, your pleasure is others suffering, and this is not good attitude for a leader to behave, a leader like you King Khurkhush. Please my King, with politeness I ask you to take my advice and release those human beings as well as others in your prisons" and Khurkhush then said

"And if not, what will happen Zarza?" and Zarza said "Oh! King Khurkhush, do not be stubborn, for the last time please listens to my advice and releases those human beings. Just look at yourself, you have already begins to show your age, you have became old and much of your strength have drained away in you, what if I tell you that those who are planning the attack are not only human beings but with Jinnis and others as well, and some of them are here in your Kingdom, then what will you say about it?" Khurkhush with anger then asked Zarza "Do you mean to tell me that there are Jinnis in my own Kingdom who can dare go against me?" then Zarza said "Khurkhush, now you have became so cruel and lack of kindness within you, and if you had kindness then you would be kind and show respect to your own parents whom you have over thrown them and took power of ruling by force and put them in jail, even your own friends who were very close to you, you have let them suffer by transforming them into animals, a friend like Saahib whom you have transformed him and all his relatives into horses, this is proof enough that you are lack of kindness and you are a cruel Jinni" then suddenly he shouted and said "Enough! Do not add any more words of attacking me Zarza; are you not afraid of my anger and to lose your life Zarza? You know me well Zarza that I do not like anyone to interfere in my personal matters, I think the time has come for you Zarza to stop your talking and leave this land for good and never to return here at all again, I forbid you to be my subject any more again. I found now those human beings have brainwashed you very well, that you love them more than love us your own kind" and Zarza then said "That will not be possible on my side Khurkhush, though I have come here to warn and advice you, but also I have come here with intentions as well as one important mission, and that is to release every and each of those who in your jail. Like it or not but you have no other choice, otherwise you better know Khurkhush, this night and in this same place will be your last night and here will be your grave and the end of you as a King, Khurkhush Majangar, time is very important for me and I value every single passing moment, now I ask you for the last time, are you going to release those who are in your jails or are you not?, and if not, then I Zarza Aarish will release them myself and witout your permission, give me your answer now and quickly" here the Khurkhush was more angry and he started to make noise and change slowly into an animal, suddenly he became a lion, one great huge furious lion, that lion then roared loudly, that loud that everyone was scare in there. When Zarza saw that Khurkhush changed and became a lion and was so furious, that was exactly what Zarza want him to be, and all because she knew that if Khurkhush will lose his temper and became angry, he will lose his wisdom and do of what he did not intend to do, and that is a chance Zarza she was looking for. The lion then was starring direct into Zarza eyes. All the power of his eyes were looking into Zarza eyes, he then slowly started to move forward step by step toward where Zarza was. Zarza new that the time to strike is now, she then looked up and with her eyes gave sign to her partners to be standby. Zarza then made herself also to be angry, she also opened her mouth and produce such a noise, not a human noise but very scary hush noise, when Khurkhush saw that Zarza produce that noise, he then stopped to move forward but wait and see of what will going to happen next.

Zarza then begin to change and on whole of her body there were marks of patens existing, patens like those of the snakes and pythons, Khurkhush was just looking at the transformation which took place in front of his own eyes, and saw that Zarza now changed into one big hell of a python, the python was so angry then started to raise her head and half of her body and bent her head ready to strike. The lion when he saw that python was ready to strike, he quickly strike first by jumping on that python and the python also at the same time strikes in whole of her strength to attack that lion, the lion used all of his claws on the body of that python, but the skin of that python was slippery and no claws or teeth could hold her, here then the python raised half of her body in circle ring and put it over the neck of that lion, again and again she did that until the whole body of the lion was surrounded by the python heavy body until that lion could not move even a little and became breathless and started to cry of pain of which the python was pulling to tighten her body and give him pain, and when the chance came on her side the python open her mouth and strikes on the throught of that lion and bite him with her long teeth. Shuhur jaan then aimed well and allow his arrow to fly direct on the chest of that lion, and the lion when he felt the pain of the arrow he cried more and loudly, and here was the chance of that Tarantula who was up in the celling, he quickly came down on his web and aimed at the head of that lion and landed exactly on his target and without hesitation, and with full strength bite that lion on his nose and allow the poison to come out of his fangs and pass through to that lion nose, the pain of the poison that lion felt was unbearable as the lion felt the bite but do not know what has bite on his nose, the lion used all his strength in trying to get out of that python body ringlets but could not, because that python was more stronger than the weaked poisoned lion, the lion was breathing heavily with his mouth wide open, Shuhur jaan then aimed another arrow and send it inside the mouth of the lion, The lion then was so powerless and poison did affect him well, he then slowly begin to change and be again that Jinni Khurkhush Majangar but breathing and has no more strength in his body, two arrows and poison plus the squeezing of that python body was too much for him, he has loosed too much blood from those arrows wounds, and the python then transform herself back to Zarza Aarish, but she also was breathless as she was using her all strength to strangle that lion to his death. Zarza then stood up and went to where she has hide the sword she brought with her, Zarza came back and stand in front of Khurkhush who was laying down on the floor of the cave still breathing, she said "Oh! you Khurkhushs Majangar, I did gave you my advice to help and save you from this death but you did ignored me and thought that you are so powerful to the extent, I told you to release those who are in your jails to allow them to go back to their families, still you ignored me, and all because you was a very stubborn Jinni, this is now the results of your being stubbornness, I came to you with clean and clear intentions to pass to you the true information of the attack, you did not believe me and you said you are not afraid of those human beings, you thought you will be able with your power to win every war, but in life that is not how things goes, and that is not how God plan is, one can have his plan but also God can have his, everything God has created has an end but only God himself has no end. Khurkhush, in these last minutes of your life, I ask you again, are you willing now to surrender and obey of what you will be asked to do? Or are you still going to be ejective and die unfaithful to your God? Give me your answer now" but he was really in very bad condition, even to speak for him was difficult, the pain which was in his body was unbearable, those two arrows did hurt him deep inside but the poison of that Tarantula did gave him more pain, and that poison is working very well in his body right now, there is no much time to live for, he is finished. He then opened his eyes slowly and tried to speak, he said though not perfectly "Zarza! To me... to...day... you ...are ...showing ... me... miracle..., from... where... did... you... got.... This... all... Knowledge ...and experience..., and... Such ...courage... to come... and attack...me? then Zarza replied him and said "First of all, it pain me to see you suffer to your death, and all these would never happen if you have listen and take my advices, you thought that how in the world a young girl like me could give advice to a powerful King like you, many have suffered because of you Khurkhush, people who done nothing at all to harm you or even interfere in your personal affairs, yet you have captured them and put them in your jail and torture them just for your pleasure and entertainments, yes Khurkhush I saw how their relatives suffer by just crying day and night hoping that there will come a day they will unite again, just by hope. I saw how their eyes shed tears nonstop, I did not felt their inner agony and pain but I imagine it, as the same pain I suffer that day you have allowed my husband to be killed, and till this day I did not wipe my pain but let it to remain in there for the whole of my life, if those relative cry for their loved one then what about those who are in your jails how much they suffer how much they cry. Now listen to me and listen to me well, I came here after joining force with human beings and other Jinni's but not like you, as well as other creation that have the power more than you. I repeat my words again to tell that you have no much time to live Khurkhush, very soon you will die, and after you death we will not allow any more Jinni like you to be our King, we will make our Kingdom a safe place for anyone to pass through or pay a visit here, this Kingdom will be a land of peace and harmony for all of us to live, either we Jinni's or Human beings or any other creation of God" hearing this, Khurkhush tried to gain power so he could stand and attack Zarza, but Zarza saw him and new of what he wanted to do, she just swing her sword and reached on the neck of Khurkhush and cut off his head away from his body, and that was the end of Khurkhush Majangar, all that time of conversation between Zarza and Khurkhush, Shuhur jaan and Saqr were just kept themselves silent and remain just watching what was going on and how it will be the end of this cruel Jinni, but Saqr after Khurkhush head was cut off apart from his body, he felt his body is returning to its original shape of a human being, and within a few minutes he was again Saqr and no longer that Tarantula the spider, and when Khurkhush was completely dead, Shuhur jaan and Saqr became visible and they can see each other in their really shape, then they came out of their hiding place and climb down to where Zarza and the dead Khurkhush body is, Zarza when she saw his two partners in their human shape and are visible, she throw down her sword and stood up waiting for them to reach of where she were, and she could not believe herself that just three of them manage to kill so powerful Jinni in the whole mountains Kingdoms, and they all look at each other's in their eyes and within a minute their eyes were filled with tears and then they rushed to one another and hug, and then Zarza said "La ilaha illa llah" and those two replied back by saying ": Muhammad Rasulullah" it means [There is no God other than Allah and Muhammad is his messenger], and all three then sobbed in lower voice for the happiness and not the sorrow for what they have achieved in winning their war against the oppressor.

Zarza Aarish cutting off Khurkhush Majangar's head

Now let us go back to where we have left Shamekhashar bind with chain on the pillar, though Shamekhashar is also a Jinni, but he could not untight himself those chains because they have been cursed by Khurkhush Majangar, he has that feeling that today is his last day to live, because if Khurkhush will return back here then there will be no peace but death here, but after some time, while still he is chained at that pillar, he fall to a sleep and went to a deep sleep, but while in his sleep he felt those chains are unlocking by themselves and drop down, this was a big surprise to him, then he remembered Zarza and said "this would never happen but for sure Zarza has worn her war against Khurkhush" then he decided to leave that place and go to that south cave and make sure himself about the real fact of that war between Zarza and Khurkhush Majangar. Shamekhashar when he arrived at the south cave he went inside and saw Zarza with two young human beings, but before he could speak he got a surprise of his life, he was shocked for what he saw and he could not believe his own eyes, because all his eyes were focusing at the dead body without head of Khurkhush Majangar laying down on the cave floor, surprisingly he asked "Zarza! This is the really body of Khurkhush?" and Zarza answered and said "Yes Shamekhashar, this is the really body of Khurkhush and his head is there on top of that rock" Shamekhashar then gave a look at the head and said "Why then he changed his color, why he became more black then his original color?" Zarza answered him and said "The poison in his body has changed his color, and this poison is one of the weapon used to destroy him by one of my two partners who are here" and Skamekhashar then asked "Your partners? Who are your partners? Where are they? I see no one here else more then you" and Zarza said "Yes you cannot see them because they have been covered to be invisible not to be seen, and that purposely is tactic which we used to fool him, that he should not see who are going to attack him, and my partners are not Jinni's like us but they are human beings, who have join me for this mission" then Shamekhashar asked "Is it possible to see them please? so I can personally thank them for coming here joining hand with you and destroy the great Jinni of our time and saved our Kingdom and our people who are living here from his cruel ruling" and Zarza replied and said "Yes, Shamekhashar you can see them, and all because if it was not for your help and your assistance this war would never be able for us to win it, we won this war because part of it is your joining hand with me, though not voluntary but by forcing you with a sword, also you deserve to be thanks, and on behalf of all those who suffered I thank you Shamekhashar" then Zarza asked and request her partners to appear before Shamekhashar, then Saqr and Shuhur jaan removed their rings which they have been given by King Rawaanaz to make them invisible, and Shamekhashar when he saw that true there are two young human beings here in this cave, he then said "Well done young courageous and brave men, it is my duty now that I should kneel before you to give more respects which you deserve in joining this mission with Zarza to come here in our kingdom and complete of what many could not even dare, but you three have done it, I am proud of you young men, I promise you with my true tongue, as one of the son of this land and one of the close officer who had been with Khurkhush for a long time, that I will release all those who are in the jails of Khurkhush, our people and your people as well as our previous leader who was our King and he was also Khurkhush's father with many of elders who opposed him and then took power by force and put his own parents and others in jail" and then Shamekhashar went down to his knees and bent his head before those two young men and gave them that respects of which they deserved, then he stood up and said to Zarza "Oh! You Zarza, an expert of all experts, I believe today that you are really a brave woman, and dareful without any fear, you have beaten me with a fight of where your brave husband could not, and also for destroying Khurkhush Majangar, of where all the living Jinni's could not dare, as they use to feared him, Yes Zarza you are the right one to lead this Kingdom as our leader, and no one alse is worth then you to lead us and this land. And now please allow me to leave you and go to tell everyone of your victory and of the end of Khurkhush Majangar, how happy will our people be, and also to make sure that each and every prisoner is free and those who are living not in this land should be sent to their homeland so to make their loved one happy. And you Zarza and these two young men I request you please be at my humble house so to find and chose who will be our next King to lead us. Till we meet again, farewell" And Shamekhashar then disappear from that cave.

Zarza then said to those young lads "as long as the sun has already rise, I have to send telepath message to Saahib and Saharzena and call them to come here so also to meet their parents who are also in the jail and will be released" and Saqr said "That will be a very wise decision" and then Zarza close here eyes and send the telepath message to Saahib (Antar), it did not take much time and Antar and Saharzena were outside the entrance of the south cave, they made their voices by horses crying, and Zarza and Saqr and Shuhur jaan were there waiting for them. Antar greeted the heroes with happiness and smile, Antar asked about their health, and Zarza replied "Health wise we are all right Saahib, as I have mentioned in my message to you, the King is dead and his body is still inside the cave, do go inside and see for yourself his body, so to believe of what we have said" Antar and Saharzena then went inside the cave, while Zarza and her partners were outside waiting, suddenly they heard a loud horses cry inside the cave, the cry did stunned Shuhur jaan and Saqr and did put fear in them but Zarza then calm them down an she said "those were the celebration and happiness cry, do not bother" then the cry noises were heard coming outside from inside the cave, and Antar and Saharzena then came outside rushing and stood with their hind legs and make more noises, and then both horse stopped crying and came in front of Zarza and bent their front legs and kneel with their heads facing down to the earth, Saqr and Shuhur jaan was just watching all their dramas, yet they did understood of why they did that, that was their sign of saying THANK YOU and showing their appreciation for the achievement of their victory, then they came to where Saqr and Shuhur jaan were sited and then they stood with their hind legs and more noises, and then walked slowly to where Saqr and Shuhur jaan were standing and go so close and each of them kiss the forehead of those young lads, then Saqr notice in the eyes of Antar there were tears nearly to fall down, Saqr asked "Oh Antar! Why these tears while just awhile ago we saw you two cheers?" Antar the spoke and said "Oh! My young master, even my tears are part of my cheer, and part of our happiness, such a great happiness in our hearts and all because in this moment I really feel that I am a free Jinni, I have gained my freedom after I witness with my own eyes the dead body of Khurkhush Majangar, his distraction is a freedom for us all who for many years now we are living in not our natural way of life, I feel today Antar that this will be my end of living as an animal life, I feel that sooner or later I will return to my original life as a normal Jinni, together with the whole members of my family" and Zarza then said "Yes Saahib, it is true of what you have said, I hope and pray to God that by his will Insha'Allah he will return all of you into your original creation, that the evil power of which has transformed you all, should vanish as Khurkhush have vanished in our life now, that you all who suffered in evil transformation of Khurkhush should be free and return to you normal original creation. Oh! Allah, I am not one among your Prophets but I am one among your believer, I believe in you Allah, I have faith in you Allah I always pray to obey your command Allah, you know all of my inside and all of my outside that I am your servant who put all her faith in trusting you and be always under your teaching and you command, I ask you my God, please wipe out all that evil spell of which Khurkhush has used to transform your creations into differences transformation, please allow them to return into their original of which you created them, none other can do this more than you God" then Zarza stood up and pick that sword of which has cut off Khurkhush Majangar head from his body, and raise that sword high and said "In the name of Allah, may the evil spell of Khurkhsh Majangar be wipe out this moment" and send that sword with all her force in the huge stone which was there outside that south cave, and that sword did penetrate easily through that stone, and it was a miracle to everyone who were there witnessing Zarza of what she was saying and what she was doing. This is really Allah miracle, and when that sword was penetrating in that stone, everyone there felt a little earth quake, within s few minutes then another miracle happened, Antar and Saharzena felt high temperature heat in their bodies, and then the hair on their bodies started to fall down, and they felt that they are losing their weight and slowly start to change from horses to human shape forms, and then they were completely transformed into two young lads, a very handsome young man and a very beautiful young girl standing there before Zarza and Saqr and Shuhur jaan, every one of them was surprised by this reaction and no one know what made that to happen, but it was another miracle, here is where Zarza slowly stood up and raise her hands high up in the sky with her face looking up and slowly said in Arabic "Allahumma laka shukur" it means [Many thanks to you Allah], and all remaining there, raise their hands up in the sky and answered "Alhamdulillah" it means [Thank you Allah]. None among those two Antar an Saharzena thoughts or believe that there will be a day coming and they will returned to their natural forms, and that day is today, they were so happy that they could not stop shed tears from their eyes, then they embrace themselves and then to all who were there, Zarza Saqr and Shuhur jaan, then Zarza said "we have to be now at Shamekhashar house, he is waiting for us, please Saahib and Saharzena hold the hands of Shuhr jaan and Saqr and fly with them. When they reached near Shamekhashar cave house, yet still up in the air, they look down and saw so many people and Jinnis were there, they were shouting and laughing with joy and full of happiness and suddenly there were voices shounting "Zarza! Zarza! Here come Zarza and her brave human friends" some of these were those who were put in prison by Khurkhush Majangar. Many and many of the jinnis in those mountains were so happy for the news death of Khurkhush Majangar, they felt now their Kingdom has gain its reputation of being the Kingdom of peace and the land of freedom. Now the time has ended for all oppressing and cruelty, now they can live without fear and tensions. Zarza and his partners then landed somewhere on the mountains and walk down their way toward Shamekhashar house, everyone were cheering them for their victory, because the news spread everywhere to what they have done in achieving this victory, so to all those who are living in the Kingdom felt proud and to them these five were their heroes.

Shamekhashar did a very good job of spreading the news of Khurkhush Majangar death, when Zarza and her partners reached the cave house of Shamekhashar there were so many of jinnis population there, these were those jinni's who came to give their thanks to those heroes who have freed their relatives who were in Khrkhush Majangar jail, all of them were welcomed in that case, and then Zarza her partners were welcomed inside the house, there inside there were many human beings but these human beings were so weak and were so thin, Shamekhashar then invite Zarza and her partners to sit on the cushions and he stood and said a speech, he said

"Our dear brothers Oh! You Human beings, it is my duty now to introduce to you these five young lads who have arrived just now, these are those heroes who brought back the freedom of this land, who brought back the love between us the Human and the Jinnis, and these are those heroes who made you free from that cruel jails of Khurkhush Majangar, two of these young men are Human beings like you and three of these are Jinnis like me, the united they have create to fight this dangerous war against Khukhush was such a great step of a cooperation and sacrifice of their lives, but also it so not only them who join hands in fighting this war, there are others who in one way or another have share their abilities and their advices in their group, though those others are not here with us but are here from the beginning of creating this war with us, and we the Jinnis of this Kingdom let us together bow and kneel to give them our thanks and respect for sharing their thoughts and abilities with our young lads until making our Kingdom a free land again. On behalf of all those who are living in our Kingdom and those who have suffered in this Kingdom, either Jinnis or Human beings, allow us to thank you to all who have created this war and won it's victory to bow and kneel before you as to thank you all for what you have done for us" and All who were inside the room and those who were outside in the cave house, bow and kneel to give their thanks to those five young lads who were sitting on the cushions there, Zarza immediately stood and other follows to except the thank giving from all those people and Jinnis who were there, and in return all five of them bow their heads down and keep their right hand on their chests, then Zarza request permission from Shamekhashar to speak, and she said "Oh! You, my fellow creations, Oh! You, Good creation of God, Nothing could have happen today if not Allah allow it, I speak to you first my brothers and sisters all Jinnis, who are living in this

Kingdom, that it was our parents decision to except the Islamic faith willingly, and follow and believe our Prophet Muhammad of what he has brought before us of what he has been command by Allah to do so, for us all, and Allah said in his Holly book the Qur'an [AND I DID NOT CREATE JINNIS AND HUMAN BEINGS BUT TO WORSHIP ME. (SURAT AL DHARIYAT = VERSE 56.] (it means to have a faith and believe in me, and follow my command) and not to be like illiteracy and without any faith but be educated, and to believe that there is power beyond, that has created all these and all of us, even this air and the sea and the water which falls from the sky, and all these beautiful animals and birds and even small insects, all of these are the work of that power beyond, and that power is none other than God himself. It is not possible that all of these I have mentioned could have been created by it selves and there is no power attached to it, no! that I do not believe, and all because I have learn a lot from these human beings and have faith in God that he exists, and that power beyond is God. God has sent to us his books through his messengers that we human and Jinni's as well as Angels and other creations should learn, that in these books there is wisdom and knowledge and history of the past and all about God and how he became that power beyond, God has created this universe for us to live with, he created earth which stood still and without moving and sky that hang there up and without falling, these all are the proof that his so powerful, and he is that power beyond our knowledge, but to those who had no any chance of learning or been taught by those who had knowledge and have learned, I thank my God that from him I had chance to learn from these human beings, so many things of which I did not know them before, but have learned and they keep on teaching to all their generation to come so the knowledge and the wisdom of Allah should remain forever and never to be forgotten. What God is asking from us that we should have faith that we all his creation are his servants and he is the Master, the only Master who have the power to create all these. Oh! My brothers and sisters, Allow me now just for few moments to tell you a true story of my life. I was married to a wonderful person, the person I loved most, I had a very good position after my marriage as I was a wife of personal commander so security force of Khurkhush Majangar, for some reason there came I a day I lost all of that, I lost that position, I lost the power and the pride and because I lost my husband against the higher position Khurkhush has offered for just one person, but he had two of the most powerful and sincere commanders, my husband and this man here Shamekhashar. Unfortunately to earn that position, Khurkhush arrange a duel fight, he who will win will take the position and the loser should die, my husband lost the fight and he was killed by the sword of Shamekhashar, for many years I stayed a widow until one night with the permission of Khurkhush I leaved these mountain Kingdom to go down to earth and look for what I wanted, I promise Khurkhush that I will not come back here if I will not get what I was looking for,, but what I was looking for? Maybe many of you will ask that question, I went there to look for a sincere friend, an honest person, and a loving man who can give me happiness and security, I found of what I was looking for, but also I found of what I was not intend to look for, and that is the right path of faith of which I had no idea about it before, but there are among these human being I have learn a lot from them until I saw the difference of our way of living and these human beings of how they live, and it is completely difference between us, they lived to believe and worship God, and we lived not to believe in God but only few among us here, and in the end all of them who have faith in God among us ended in jail because of their faith. It begins when I met with this animal, the camel, he open my mind and in just one night, taught me a lot about these human and their faiths to God, in the end that same night I surrender my soul to God and became a follower on Muhammad, and in the same night I did found of what I came to look for, a friend, that friend who has all those quality I mentioned them before, but unfortunately the will of Allah did not allow us to create a family life and all because I was Jinni created with fire and he was a human being created with clay, the law of Allah never before us allowed any of these two creations to join hands in matrimonial ceremony, so I found of what I was looking for but could never own it as mine, yet it was this young man who became my loyal friend till this moment, taught of how to learn the Book of Allah the Qur'an, and from that book I learned so much and feed my mind which was empty and have nothing at, with full of knowledge and wisdom and obedient to Allah and his Prophets and the compulsory of worshiping and allow myself to lean on those five pillars of Islam and perform my duty to follow them, though I did not up to now follow all of them, but with the will Allah Insha'a,mlla I will. In short, this is the story of my life. But here is a question, why should I tell you a story of my life? What good is to you? The answers to these two questions are, many among you, Jinni's and Human beings, have lived the life of ignorance and careless, you did not allow even for a short term to learn of how others live and why they chose that way to live, and if you have done that, than for sure you will would have gain a lot like I gained and would learn of that power beyond which exists and which had said in his book as a message to us that, and that message is [I have only created

Jinn's and human beings, that they may worship me] So my brothers and sisters, the message of Allah is clear, that we have been all created by Allah {The mighty power beyond} just to worship him, and if we do not obey this, then we are walking on that stray path which will let us be lost, while Allah has already shown us a straight path with a perfect destination. So my dear brothers and sisters, God does exists and deserved to be worshiped by having a faith, a true faith and not any others faiths and that faith is a faith which of Prophet Muhammad{pbuh}was his mission to deliver to us the message of Allah. That was the main reason for me to have faith in God and convert into worshiping Allah and join the Islamic faith, and if it was not for me that night of which I was allowed to come in that world of these human being live and saw experience of how they live then I think I would remain the same as I was, but yet I have to thank my friend the camel, who opened my eyes and cultivate that seed of faith in my mind and that was the reason of all the changes of which what I am today. Thank you God for everything you gave me, thank you for showing that straight path of which now I working on it till I will reach to the doors of heaven and waiting for my turn to be called and enter inside it. Please I ask all of you who are here; let us raise our hands up to beg Allah that we also should be among those who will be in the heaven. And here is where I end to speak and be allowed to sit, thank you all". And here where all those who were there stood and applaud loudly to Zarza foe her long speech which have a very good fundamental reason of wisdom and good teaching for others to learn and do so to follow on her path.

There were disturbing noises in the outside hall near the room of where all human beings were there and where Zarza and her partners were sited, and then the footsteps of the soldiers were heard coming to the room, eight Jinni's soldiers enter the room forming in two lines and in their centers were two very old figure but wearing very good clothes, an old man and an old woman, every Jinni who was there outside and inside the room when they saw those two figures, stood up and bow their heads down, including Shamekhashar and Zarza Aarish and all said "Your Majesteis" and those human beings prisoners including Saqar and Shuhur jaan follow the others, they all stood and bow their heads to give their respects to these two figures who were entering in that big room. The figures were lad to where there were two big seats and sat there and all the guards went to stand behind them. These two figures were none others than the parents of Khurkhush Majangar, who were prisoner by their own son Khurkhush, for a long time they remained in jail after Khurkhush seized power and put them in jail, after Khurkhush they were freed by

Shamekhashar with all who were in jails, the King then said "Zarza and Shamekhashar, please raise your heads and stand" and Shamekhashar and Zarza obey the order, then King Majangar said "I was outside this room for quite a time now, I was listening to what Zarza was speaking to others, I was very interested in her life story, but the really fact of our visit here to Shamekhashar, is to come and gives our thanks to all those who join hands in getting our freedom, not us two only but to all those who were in jails, we also came here to try and find out the real facts of why sudden change?, why suddenly there is bright light on these mountains and on this Kingdom?, why there are cheers on every corner of this land?, why all these Jinnis are happy and why our freedom from jails? We were just waiting for our death in those jails But suddenly that dream has changed and we saw the bright light again and we in hell a pure clean air again, but what I would like to know who behind all these and where is Khurkhush and what has happen to him? Please anyone tell me who is behind all these?" and then King Majangar stood and went where Zarza was and asked her "Tell me my dear, what is your name?" and Zarza replied "My dear Your Majesty, I am called Zarza bint Aarish, I am that young girl who is responsible for the death of your son Khurkhush, I am responsible of cutting off the head of your son and destroyed him completely, I am with here my partners who are some of them not Jinnis but are human beings, took the all the blame and responsibilities of wipe out all the oppressing caused by your son, we are also responsible of bringing back that brightness you had just mentioned on this our land, we also are the responsible of giving back all of you here your freedom, and we are also responsible of returning back your ruling as our King and our Queen again. If for any reason you have found that we guilty for doing all of these I have mentioned, then we are all under your command your Majesty and whatever judgment you think we deserve than we will without any doubts will except it. King Majangar then said "No! Zarza, all of you are no guilty, but speaking the truth, I even feel shame to be called the father of that cruel Jinni, but by destroying him and bring back all these happiness and joy in our people hearts, is itself is a blessing, and if it was not for you all, maybe we would not have much time to live and enjoy with your today the freedom of this Kingdom and the happiness of those others who have missed their loved one for such a long time now. Thank you Zarza and all your partners in saving us all here and saved our Kingdom from the hands of that evil one. Let us not hate those who were in his command, they just were performing their duties and obeying command from that evil one, even them they were just defending and safeguarding their own lives.

Zarza Aarish, I am now an old man, and my future l.ife is limited I do not have much time left to rule this Kingdom, even my strengths of mind and body has drained away, the time has come now that I should hand over the reins of leadership of our Kingdom to a more younger leaders. Zarza believe me that the time has come for changing the leadership of this Kingdom to a very young brave and suitable young one to be your leader, Zarza you are that young one to me of whom I think will be a perfect leader to lead this Kingdom, as you are a brave and a courageous young one, and also a religious minded one, I think you should take the reins of the leadership to lead our people and our Kingdom, I ask you, I request you and I beg you please except my request and say "Yes" to the leadership." And then suddenly there were shouting and cheers in the whole place "Zarza Aarish! Zarza Aarish!" But to Zarza that was not possible at all, she said "Your Majesty, our beloved King Majangar, allow me to remain under your feet but give me a chance also to give my opinion" and King Makjangar then said "Please Zarza, speak of what you want to say" and Zarza then said "Your Majesty, our loving King! It is not that I refuse to accept this great offer of yours and of our people, but I have other great idea than yours, and I request you that idea to give more consideration and accept it. At the present time there is no better Jinni who loves more his country and his people other than Shamekhashar. Yet! It was true that in the past ruling Shamekhashar was a very close assistance and a secret keeper of Khurkhush, but like you have said, he also was doing that for fear of his life, and if he was as cruel as Khurkhush, than Your Majesty believe me that he would not agree to join hand with me and go against his own King Khurkhush, yet he did participate though in a very tough way which was to fight me to death, either me or either Khurkhush, and in the end with a point of my sword he agrees to chose me. It was Shamekhashar who has sacrifice and put his life in danger and went and to pursued Khurkhush to trust his words that I came back here with great news of human beings are preparing a war against him and wants to save their people. He betrayed his King just because he also did not like of how Khurkhush was torturing others just for his pleasure. If it was not for Shamekhashar participation in betraying his master, I and my partners would never be able today to finish off the King of tortures and all his cruelty. The main part of this mission was ours but the great part of this mission was Shamekhashar one. Your Majesty, This is the same Shamekhashar who has killed my husband, but it was not his intentions but it was planned by Khurkhush to wipe off one of them, either Shamekhashar or my husband will take the position of the higher personal security commander of Khurkhush.

In that duel fight, my husband lose the fight and was killed by Shamekhashar, yet I do not love him up to this day, I hate him more than anything but I do not hold any grudges against him when I weight the fact reason of my husband death, and then I remembered the saying of those who have passed away, that hate does not build but destroy, hate is not constructive but destructive of all happiness within us. I put all my faith to God by not showing him of how much I hate him, because I had faith that maybe it will come anyway in our life Shamekhashar will be useful to me. Here is a proof that Shamekhashar has been a very useful to all of here, including you my dear Your Majesty. It is my opinion Your Majesty, that there is no other capable leader to lead this nation and this Kingdom other than Shamekhashar, Yet before anyone chosen to lead, I have one suggestion to give, that no one should be chosen to lead if he has no religious faith, and there is no excepted religion to Allah other than Islam. Here he will be able to rule with fairness and justices. If you will agree with me and allow Shamekhashar to take your place and ruled this Kingdom, then before he led this Kingdom he should clean his mind and his heart by converting himself into believing in the faith of God. My second request Your Majesty, among these prisoners there are human beings, they have their homes and their relatives in difference places down there in the earth, we have enjoyed our joys and happiness here in our Kingdom, but their relatives they are still in sorrows and sadness just waiting and hoping that someday somehow their loved ones will return to them, I will request a permission from you Your Majesty King Majangar, that you will allow me and two of my partners Saqr and Shuhur jaan to return to their homeland one young man by the name of Muntasir and his mother, as they are the main source of all this war against Khurkhush, and also you should permit Saahib and Saharzena to return Sheikh Shammaakh to his country side home. I have finished my talking Your Majesty; I seek your permission to sit down". King Majangar than said "I swear to God that yours is a clean heart Zarza, you are not at all a mean person, these are such an examples you are showing to us today, that you have refused such a position of being a Queen of a Kingdom, many out of many would die just to serve under such a leader, but not you, you got it yet you refuse it, and these blessings you prefer to be given to another one, that one whom till to this day you hate him, yet you prefer him more than yourself to lead our nation under his umbrella and not you, you are a surprise example in our nation Zarza, Thank you so much, but before I give my judgment of who will be leading this nation and be a leader of this Kingdom, I would like to ask all those who are present here, is anyone among you here that do not agree with Zarza suggestion?

Especially regarding the leadership, that Shamekhashar should your next King after me? Is anyone who has better opinion or suggestion than of Zarza? If there is anyone here among, than I ask him or her to come forward and tell us of what he has in his mind" but whole the place was quite, no one raise any hand as a sign he wants to speak, then Shamekhashar request permission to say something, he was permitted, he says "Your Majesty our beloved King, Shamekhashar stands here before and under your obedient. Zarza gave us her suggestion of who will be a better ruler after she refused to take that position, and she suggested that should be appointed as the ruling King of this Kingdom. Your Majesty, personally I did not object to her suggestion but I thank her so much for suggesting me to lead the Jinnis who are living here in this Kingdom, in peace and harmony between us Jinnis and other God's creations, and her second suggestion was that he who will be the leader must be religion faith minded one, must be he perform and have faith in God, this too I did not reject it, and all because the time of evil ruling has passed away, and the time of loving one another and have faith in believing in God has arrived, and Zarza also quote to us a verse from a Holly book that God create us Jinnis and Human beings to worship him, and this To I have objection with, but from this moment I announce myself that I believe in God and his Prophets and his Book, I am from now a believer of God and will follow his teaching from his Book. Your Majesty, in the past, I request a hand of Zarza in marriage but of what has happened between me and her husband, she refused me, still today I request again her hand in marriage and in front of you all" and Shamekhashar turned to Zarza and said "Let us forget the past and build the future Zarza, I again request your hand in marriage, will you please marry me?" if you will agree your marriage with me, you will be my personal adviser, we can lead and rule our Kingdom together" all that time was remain quiet and was looking down, and when she raised her head there was a big change in her look, she was angry and her face was red, tears were filled her both eyes. Shamekhashar when he noticed that changing he knew that Zarza now is in high temperature of anger, he then said "I think I have made a mistake, I think this was not the right time to bring this issue, please Zarza forgive me, I had no intention of making you angry this time, but I thought maybe I could bring you back your happiness which you have lost it long time now" and then Shamekhashar retuned his face to the other side and was trying to move at that place near Zarza and go to other place, but after just two steps he heard Zarza shouted at him "Stop of where you are and do not move" commanded Zarza with loud voice, she then continued with lower voice "It is true that I had within me much anger, especially when I see your face, but just when you asked my hand for marriage, then I asked myself, is this what God wants that we always should keep anger and revenge in our mind and our hearts? My heart refuses that and commands my mind to bring better thoughts, the answer I got from my mind was this, that hate rage is not the right pillar to lean on, hate rage only bring more misunderstanding and create the unfortunates, in the end I came to this conclusion Shamnekhashar, you have asked my hand for marriage in front of our King and Queen and to all those who are present here between Jinnis and Human bangs, my answer to you is that I need more time to think and consider with my soul, mind and my heart, I do not know what kind answer if I will get, but the situation here is not in good looking that the killer of my husband should be my next husband. Give me more time and I will give you your answer" Shamekhashar was pleased with Zarza replied, and toes who would like to see them to be gather as man and wife, were also happy with Zarza answer. Then there were missions of returning those human beings primroses to their homeland, here is where Saar asked permission to speak, and King Manager allowed him to do so "Your Majesty, the King of this Kingdom, before all, allow me to give thanks on my behalf and on the behalf of all us human beings who are here now, truly your Majesty you are a very kind King, and also your subjects are good Jinnis who loved us human beings, when I said this, it does not mean I speak about all of your Jinnis subjects are good, many of us living creatures are living but with two purpose, purpose and intentions, even us who had this opportunity to be here and meet with you all we had our plan and our intentions, another example is of my sister here Zarza, when she was permitted to leave here that first night by the permission of her King Khurkhush, she had her purpose and her intention, even Saahib and Saharzena they came to our land also with purpose and intentions of living in a safe place, even the death of your evil Khurkhush had its purpose and its intentions, your Majesty if any of God creation among us human beings and maybe you Jinnis too, are living our lives with purpose and intentions, is it not also that God created us all for purpose and intentions? and God's purpose was that he want us to believe that we have been created and that he is the creator, in other words that his our master and we all are his slaves, slaves just to believe in him and to worship him by obeying of what he has taught us through his books and his Prophets, and that is exactly what we Gods creation are doing from generation after generations. When we left our desert land that night for this mission, our parents knew that this was a mission to do it or to die for it, they all prayed for our safe return, all five of us, though by time the two of us were still in the shape of animal as horses who are able to fly up in the sky. In our parents minds. They think that it was Zarza and me who have left out on the back of the horses to come here and save our beloved one, as Shuhur jaan came on the other side of our land, he came from the land of Persia and join us. My question here is what we will tell our parents if they asked us where are Antar and Saharzena? What has happened to them? the house will be full of happiness and joy for the return of Muntasir and his mother, but just for a short while, as my father will miss his two best friends whom always are there to give our family a protection, for this reason Your majesty, can you please allow Saahib and Sharzena to come with us to our homeland and let all of those knew Antas and Saharzena the horses are now no longer horses but they have returned in their natural forms of Jinnis? so by understanding the real facts maybe this will cool down the heart and the mind of my father if he will see them by himself, and maybe that will be a very good reason for all five us to be there together with Muntasir and his mother, I think that will big happiness and such a wonderful joy to everyone at my homeland. This is all of which I want to say and request Your Majesty" here then the King of the mountain Jinnis Kingdom replied and said "What this young lad has said is very logical point of view, it is true that everyone of us have those things in our minds, mostly a purpose and an intentions before doing anything, Intentions are the main reason to follow the purposes idea, and next step is that person to complete its plan, either you success or you fail, that is not in our hands but it is God's will.

Regarding Saahib and Saharzena, yes I agree with Saar, how he can explain if asked by his father, where are the horses whom you ride to leave this place, where is Antar and Saharzena? Yes I agree with Saqr that Saahib and Saharzena in their real shape now and no longer should horses return together with Saqr as well as Shuhur jaan and with them so those people there should rejoice more if the whole force of these brave lads be seen together by those families in the deserts of Empty quarters where Mr. Fairuz and his family and his friends are waiting for the result of that war which they have won. The morning turns into a bright day and the journey to return those who are saved and freed should begin, Zarza then prepared herself with her partners and the two freed prisoners and of course with the permission of her King. Let us now close this page here and open new pages of what will happen after here.

In the desert home of Mr. Faired, the news of Khurkhush death have already reached there, it was Anta who had sent the news to Queen Farina Bash after Anta saw the dead body in the south cave, as Queen Farna Bash also was waiting for any news which Anta will send, and as she got the happy news immediately he asked one of her servant to Wright a letter addressing Mr. Fairuz and send it there. The messengers took that letter to Mr. Fairuz house and clips it on the door and then knock the door and disappear, Mr. Fairuz was sleeping but he heard the knock of the door and went to door and asked "who is there knocking?" he got no answer but then open the door and no one was there outside that door, he came out and look to the right and then to the left with just few steps but no one, he then decided to go back to the house, when he reached his house door he saw the letter hanging there on the door, he pick and opened it, and start to read the letter, and here what was written on that letter:-

Bismillahi arrahmani arrahiym,

To Mr. Fairuz bin Haddad, Abu Saqaar,

> *With great pleasure I am sending this letter to you which carries very important news which inform of what has happen this morning in the Kingdom of the Jinnis,*
> *Khurkhush Majangar is finish, he has been destroy by that force of our young people, he was stroked with just one heavy blow of a sword and cut off his head from his body, all of our young lads are safe and very soon they will be back. I send to you all my hand of congratulation on this victory. God willing, all those who were in his prisoners will be realized soon and return home to their loved ones.*

I have nothing else to add but I beg to remain,

Your humble servant Abu Saqr
Queen Farna Bash.

After reading that letter, Mr. Fairuz could not hold himself and resists shouting, but he just shouts loudly "God is great! God is great! My brother's wake up all of you, a great news have arrived" everyone there inside woke up by the shouting of Mr. Fairuz, he then enter the house and show those in the house the letter he have received a few moment and read it to them all, this was after morning prayers but let us now come to has happened during noon prayers, this was the arrival time of Zarza with prisoners released and all his partners

It was a celebration day at that residence of Mr. Fairuz from the moment they received Queen Farna Bash letter until now after noon prayers, as Mr. Fairuz ordered slaughtering of some animals for the great feast for celebration of their force victory, though they do not know when the released relatives will come back home, but the news gave them hope and know now that their children will come back safely. While they were in celebration and enjoying their feast of many cooked local food, there was a far away voice heard in the house coming outside, that voice was calling "Yubba! (Father) Yumma! (Mother)" and voice was keep calling while its coming near and dear to the house, suddenly Mr. fairuz stood up and said "That voice is Saqr calling, that is my son calling" and immediately he went and open the outside door, when he look outside he far away there was a group of men and women coming to the house direction, Mr. Fairuz concentrate more on the group and he saw among them one was rushing speedily while opened his hand wide, Mr. Fairuz that figure that it was his son Saqr, Mr., Fairuz when he was sure that that was Saar, he could not resist himself but called loudly and start also to rush with speed towards that coming figure "Saqr! Saqr! My son Saqr" Oh! Piece of my heart Saqr" both of them then rushed to each other and in the middle of that desert land, hug forcedly to one another while kissing each other, on their forehead, on their hands, on their chicks, and then Mr. Fairuz could not hold himself but cried loudly "Oh! My God! Oh! My God! You are great God Oh! Yes you are, Thank you God! Thank you God!" That loudly voice of Mr. Fairuza when he called the name of Saqr, everyone inside heard it and stood to follow outside, and when they were outside the house door they saw Mr. Fairuz was rushing after someone who was also rushing towards him, and behind that figure there were others, though they were far away and walking on the desert sands, and here is Abu Muntasir did recognize his son Muntasir and his wife, he too then rushed quickly towards that coming caroming yelling and calling loudly "Oh! My loving one! Oh! Muntasir's mother! Oh! my son Muntasir!" and he also opened his arms and running faster while also Muntasir was running towards him until to one another and hug to each other and cry was heard loudly in the whole area of the neighborhood, The women hug and kissing each other and the men hugging to each other, and they all walked on that golden desert sand of their homeland feeling proud to be home again and join with their families until they reach their home and enter inside. The happiness and the joys mixing with laugh and tears were more than celebration, and after sat down all together and arrival guests were feasting with many kind of foods and fruits. Mr. Fairuz asked his son Saqr "My son Saqr, where did you leave

Antar and Saharzena? Why they did not came back with you? Is there any evil happened to them?" before Saar could answer his father, Zarza requested Saqr for her to answer those questions, and she said "Mr. Fairuz, we all knew that if you will not see Anta and Saharzena, you will not be happy and maybe that will worry you, But did you forgot that in those mountain of the Kingdom of Khurkhush is where they have come, that they just runaway from the evil? It is there where all their relatives are living, and just after our victory do you think then that they will their relatives and closed ones and came back with us? Just at this house now, it was always full of sadness and sorrows and today is full of happiness and laughing, and Anta and Saharzena also at this moment they are doing the same with their families, and they ask us to deliver their regards and asked for their forgiveness for not coming back here as your horses, and they said to tell if for any reasons they are going to came back, then they will not come back as horses again but they will come back here in their natural shape and forms as Jinnis just like myself" Mr.Fairuz then was so disappointed and look down in silence, and then the whole place was silence joining Fairuz as his was completely with sorrow and sadness for missing Antar and Saharzena, but then Mr., Fairuz raise his head and said "Yes Zarza, I can understand their situation of how it is, our ancestors said to us [one should be proud of where he belongs and not where he will be] as they reasons of them leaving their homeland does not exists anymore, and as long as there is happiness and joy there of where they belong then why they should be here of where they do not belong. Yes Zarza, what action Antar and Saharzena took, is the right action and decision, and it is a lesson for me to accept the how fact is and should remain, though to me is a very hard task and very bitter to swallow, and my heart is beating faster all because I miss them, I will remember them and never will I forgot those beautiful creatures who are our friends and our protectors" and ten Mr. Fairuz wipe his tears which were coming out of his eyes, and that make all others to shed tears as well.

Saqr then looks at Zarza and then slowly stood and walks to where his fathers was, and sat in front of him and look into his eyes and he saw that how much his father was effected for by the absent of those two loving friends Antar and Saharzena, and he saw how hard was to swallow the truth and the facts, though this was not true and neither fact but just a little drama, Saar then wipe those tear in his father's eyes, and Zarza also stood and to where Mr. fairuz and Saqr were and kneel down in front of him and took his hand and kiss it and then said "Oh! You beautiful human being, Oh! you father of all us young ones here, Your daughter Zarza was just enjoying the fun with you, do forgive me, I throw myself under your feet for being disobedient and enjoying the fun, I spoke to you of no truth but just words of not to believe, as Anta and Saharzena will leave you and forgets you of you love and of your kindness and how you have kept them as your own children, only permit me to call them here in front of you and they will be here in front of you but as horses but as their real natural forms as Jinnis" and Mr. Fairuz stood and said "Please Zarza where are they, please call them, I want see my children again" and then Zarza turn around and called "Please Saahib and Saharzena, do come forward and meet your adopting father" and then Saahib and Saharzena stood as those two young lads and walked towards where Zarza was, everyone was surprised and look stunned, and those two lads did wear the best of orient dresses and each of them then took Mr. Fairuz right hand and kiss it and said "Peace be upon you Oh! Master" Mr. Fairuz completely surprise for what his eyes are seeing, is true that these two young lads are those horses whom I use to feed them wheat and grass?, how good looking these two young lads are, he was asking himself, but knew what was Mr. Fairuz thoughts were, she jump to conclusion and said "Yes my dear Sir, I know that you will be stunned and surprise for what you will see and will never your eyes, not just you but all of you who are here. Speaking the truth my dear Sir, these two are those two horses Antar and Saharzena, just remember when you met with Anta for the first he did tell you all about where he came from and why he left his homeland and came here, when we have destroyed Khurkhush majangar then all those were transformed formed their originate and into other animal forms by his spell, were released at the moment he died, and so Antar (Saahib) and Saharzena returned to their original natural forms and shape, it was impossible for them to remain with their relatives without retuning here and revealing their story and for you and others to see them of how their originality are, and this will not be the last of your relations between you and them but they will continue to pay a visit every now and then, as to them now you are their parents also" and Mr. Fairuz add "I swear to Allah Zarza, that one needs to in a very strong patience if one believes in God, this day has brought joy and happiness more and over again and again, this my family has expanded more than of what I was before, and these all are gifts from God to me his servant for the patience I took, Zarza and Saahib and Saharzena are parts of our family, from this day on they are not just friend and servants to us here but they are our children though they are Jinnis. I have one more request to ask you, that you should not leave this place today as we have a big celebration tonight to do, by thanking Allah for his blessings and sitting and chatting of all your adventures and of how did you manage to kill Khurkhush Majangar, so your story should remain in our today and forever and the coming generations can hear it from our own lips or from the lips of these younger ones here, after the celebration you can return to your Kingdom with all our blessings and all our prayers will be with you." Then he notice one extra young man whom he never saw before came with them and he asked "Why no one tell me about that young man there who came with you, who is he?" Saqr then called Shuhur jaan to come forwad and took him to his father, and said "Father! This is Shuhur jaan, this that young man whom we have heard all about his love affairs with Princess Nazniyna, this is the husband of Nazniyna and the son-in-law of King Kismat Shahzara, to me he is like a brother, I ask you father that you also regard him as your own son, he deserve all the love from all of you here, and all because it him and me and our sister Zarza who have completed that mission of destroying Khurkhush Majangar to his death, when he was order to join this force after expelled it to him, he did not refuse but join us with open heart" Then Saqr nodded to Shuhur jaan, and Shuhur jaan took the hand of Mr. Fairuz and kiss it and then he kissed his forehead. All who were there stood and applaud to Shuhur jaan for his bravery with his partners for the victory they have brought to make this land a peaceful place to live. Then Saar took Shuhur jaan to his mother and his grandmother and told him "Brother Shuhur jaan, I think the time have matured for me to return to you of what it belongs to you or I have save it for quite a long time now" then Saqr open his pocket and produce two rings and gave them to Shuhur jaan, and said "Shuhur jaan it was my mother's advice that when I will get a chance to meet you, then I should hand over these two rings which your properties, we have met there in the mission but there were no proper chance to do this, but now here and in front of all these people I return to you of what I have found and belongs to you" Shuhur jaan opened his hand and Saqr put those two rings in his hand, and Shuhur jaan was quite surprise of what he has seen, he smiled and look at Saqr, and Saqr said to him" Do not be surprise my brother, the time will come and we will sit together and I will tell you full story of how I got these two rings" and Shuhur jaan then hug Saqr as to say thank you.

And this is where I have come to the end of my story writing for you my dear readers who are enjoying such classical fictions stories, I did follow the footsteps of those before me who wrote many classical stories like A thousand and one night and like those. I did put all my efforts and my energy in days and nights to create such an entertaining story which will please my readers who are interested in reading sumac a classical stories and imaginations of the past. Before I close this last page, let me tell you that Shuhur jaan were flown back in the air by those three Jinnis, Zarza Aarish together with Saahib and Shaharzena to his homeland in the Persian Kingdom.

I hope that you have enjoyed reading this books of classical tales, and if for any reason you have find this book is boring, than I deserve to accept your criticism and if this book has entertained you, than I deserve to be praised and be encourage and Wright more stories of these kind just for you my dear reader.

I finished translating this book from Swahili version into English, today Friday the 19th February 2016. At exactly 2010hrs.

Jawad Ibrahim Al Bahrani

Printed in the United States
By Bookmasters